WAR STORIES AND POEMS

RUDYARD KIPLING (1865–1936) was born in Bombay in December 1865. He returned to India from England in the autumn of 1882, shortly before his seventeenth birthday, to work as a journalist first on the *Civil and Military Gazette* in Lahore, then on the *Pioneer* at Allahabad. The poems and stories he wrote over the next seven years laid the foundation of his literary reputation, and soon after his return to London in 1889 he found himself world-famous. Throughout his life his works enjoyed great acclaim and popularity, but he came to seem increasingly controversial because of his political opinions, and it has been difficult to reach literary judgements unclouded by partisan feeling. This series, published half a century after Kipling's death, provides the opportunity for reconsidering his remarkable achievement.

ANDREW RUTHERFORD is Vice-Chancellor Elect, University of London, and former Warden of Goldsmith's College. He is the editor of *Kipling's Early Verse 1879–1889*, *Kipling's Mind and Art*, and *Plain Tales from the Hills* (World's Classics Series).

THE WORLD'S CLASSICS

RUDYARD KIPLING
War Stories
and Poems

Edited with an Introduction by
ANDREW RUTHERFORD

Oxford   New York
OXFORD UNIVERSITY PRESS

Oxford University Press, Walton Street, Oxford OX2 6DP

Oxford New York
Athens Auckland Bangkok Bombay
Calcutta Cape Town Dar es Salaam Delhi
Florence Hong Kong Istanbul Karachi
Kuala Lumpur Madras Madrid Melbourne
Mexico City Nairobi Paris Singapore
Taipei Tokyo Toronto

and associated companies in
Berlin Ibadan

Oxford is a trade mark of Oxford University Press

General Preface, Select Bibliography, Chronology
© Andrew Rutherford 1987
Introduction, Note on the Text, Explanatory Notes
© Andrew Rutherford 1990

First published by Oxford University Press as a World's Classics paperback 1990

British Library Cataloguing in Publication Data
Data available

Library of Congress Cataloging in Publication Data
Kipling, Rudyard, 1865–1936.
War stories and poems / Rudyard Kipling: edited with an
introduction by Andrew Rutherford.
p. cm.—(The World's classics)
Includes bibliographical references.
1. War—Literary collections. 2. South African War, 1899–1902
—Literary collections. 3. World War, 1914–1918—Literary
collections. 4. War stories, English. 5. War poetry, English.
I. Rutherford, Andrew. II. Title. III. Series.
PR4852.R87 1990 828'.809—dc20 90–6847
ISBN 0–19–282656–5

3 5 7 9 10 8 6 4

Printed in Great Britain by
BPC Paperbacks Ltd
Aylesbury, Bucks

CONTENTS

GENERAL PREFACE

RUDYARD KIPLING (1865–1936) was for the last decade of the nineteenth century and at least the first two decades of the twentieth the most popular writer in English, in both verse and prose, throughout the English-speaking world. Widely regarded as the greatest living English poet and story-teller, winner of the Nobel Prize for Literature, recipient of honorary degrees from the Universities of Oxford, Cambridge, Edinburgh, Durham, McGill, Strasbourg, and the Sorbonne, he also enjoyed popular acclaim that extended far beyond academic and literary circles.

He stood, it can be argued, in a special relation to the age in which he lived. He was primarily an artist, with his individual vision and techniques, but his was also a profoundly representative consciousness. He seems to give expression to a whole phase of national experience, symbolizing in appropriate forms (as Lascelles Abercrombie said the epic poet must do) the 'sense of the significance of life he [felt] acting as the unconscious metaphysic of the time'.[1] He is in important ways a spokesman for his age, with its sense of imperial destiny, its fascinated contemplation of the unfamiliar world of soldiering, its confidence in engineering and technology, its respect for craftsmanship, and its dedication to Carlyle's gospel of work. That age is one about which many Britons—and to a lesser extent Americans and West Europeans—now feel an exaggerated sense of guilt; and insofar as Kipling was its spokesman, he has become our scapegoat. Hence, in part at least, the tendency in recent decades to dismiss him so contemptuously, so unthinkingly, and so mistakenly. Whereas if we approach him more historically, less hysterically, we shall find in this very relation to his age a cultural phenomenon of absorbing interest.

Here, after all, we have the last English author to appeal to readers of all social classes and all cultural groups, from low-

[1] Cited in E. M. W. Tillyard, *The Epic Strain in the English Novel*, London, 1958, p. 15.

brow to highbrow; and the last poet to command a mass audience. He was an author who could speak directly to the man in the street, or for that matter in the barrack-room or factory, more effectively than any left-wing writer of the thirties or the present day, but who spoke just as directly and effectively to literary men like Edmund Gosse and Andrew Lang; to academics like David Masson, George Saintsbury, and Charles Eliot Norton; to the professional and service classes (officers and other ranks alike) who took him to their hearts; and to creative writers of the stature of Henry James, who had some important reservations to record, but who declared in 1892 that 'Kipling strikes me personally as the most complete man of genius (as distinct from fine intelligence) that I have ever known', and who wrote an enthusiastic introduction to *Mine Own People* in which he stressed Kipling's remarkable appeal to the sophisticated critic as well as to the common reader.[2]

An innovator and a virtuoso in the art of the short story, Kipling does more than any of his predecessors to establish it as a major genre. But within it he moves confidently between the poles of sophisticated simplicity (in his earliest tales) and the complex, closely organized, elliptical and symbolic mode of his later works which reveal him as an unexpected contributor to modernism.

He is a writer who extends the range of English literature in both subject-matter and technique. He plunges readers into new realms of imaginative experience which then become part of our shared inheritance. His anthropological but warmly human interest in mankind in all its varieties produces, for example, sensitive, sympathetic vignettes of Indian life and character which culminate in *Kim*. His sociolinguistic experiments with proletarian speech as an artistic medium in *Barrack-Room Ballads* and his rendering of the life of private soldiers in all their unregenerate humanity gave a new dimension to war literature. His portrayal of Anglo-Indian life ranges from cynical triviality in some of the *Plain Tales from the Hills*

---

[2] See *Kipling: The Critical Heritage*, ed. Roger Lancelyn Green, London, 1971, pp. 159–60. *Mine Own People*, published in New York in 1891, was a collection of stories nearly all of which were to be subsumed in *Life's Handicap* later that year.

to the stoical nobility of the best things in *Life's Handicap* and *The Day's Work*. Indeed Mrs Hauksbee's Simla, Mulvaney's barrack-rooms, Dravot and Carnehan's search for a kingdom in Kafiristan, Holden's illicit, star-crossed love, Stalky's apprenticeship, Kim's Grand Trunk Road, 'William' 's famine relief expedition, and the Maltese Cat's game at Umballa, establish the vanished world of Empire for us (as they established the unknown world of Empire for an earlier generation), in all its pettiness and grandeur, its variety and energy, its miseries, its hardships, and its heroism.

In a completely different vein Kipling's genius for the animal fable as a means of inculcating human truths opens up a whole new world of joyous imagining in the two *Jungle Books*. In another vein again are the stories in which he records his delighted discovery of the English countryside, its people and traditions, after he had settled at Bateman's in Sussex: England, he told Rider Haggard in 1902, 'is the most wonderful foreign land I have ever been in'[3]; and he made it peculiarly his own. Its past gripped his imagination as strongly as its present, and the two books of Puck stories show what Eliot describes as 'the development of the imperial . . . into the historical imagination.'[4] In another vein again he figures as the bard of engineering and technology. From the standpoint of world history, two of Britain's most important areas of activity in the nineteenth century were those of industrialism and imperialism, both of which had been neglected by literature prior to Kipling's advent. There is a substantial body of work on the Condition of England Question and the socio-economic effects of the Industrial Revolution; but there is comparatively little imaginative response in literature (as opposed to painting) to the extraordinary inventive energy, the dynamic creative power, which manifests itself in (say) the work of engineers like Telford, Rennie, Brunel, and the brothers Stephenson—men who revolutionized communications within Britain by their road, rail and harbour systems, producing in the process masterpieces of industrial art, and who went on to revolutionize ocean travel as well. Such achievements are acknowledged

---

[3] *Rudyard Kipling to Rider Haggard*, ed. Morton Cohen, London, 1965, p. 51.
[4] T. S. Eliot, *On Poetry and Poets*, London, 1957, p. 247.

on a sub-literary level by Samuel Smiles in his best-selling *Lives of the Engineers* (1861–2). They are acknowledged also by Carlyle, who celebrates the positive as well as denouncing the malign aspects of the transition from the feudal to the industrial world, insisting as he does that the true modern epic must be technological, not military: 'For we are to bethink us that the Epic verily is not *Arms and the Man*, but *Tools and the Man*,—an infinitely wider kind of Epic.'[5] That epic has never been written in its entirety, but Kipling came nearest to achieving its aims in verses like 'McAndrew's Hymn' (*The Seven Seas*) and stories like 'The Ship that Found Herself' and 'Bread upon the Waters' (*The Day's Work*) in which he shows imaginative sympathy with the machines themselves as well as sympathy with the men who serve them. He comes nearer, indeed, than any other author to fulfilling Wordsworth's prophecy that

If the labours of men of Science should ever create any material revolution, direct or indirect, in our condition, and in the impressions which we habitually receive, the Poet will sleep then no more than at present, but he will be ready to follow the steps of the Man of Science, not only in those general indirect effects, but he will be at his side, carrying sensation into the midst of the objects of the Science itself.[6]

This is one aspect of Kipling's commitment to the world of work, which, as C. S. Lewis observes, 'imaginative literature in the eighteenth and nineteenth centuries had [with a few exceptions] quietly omitted, or at least thrust into the background', though it occupies most of the waking hours of most men:

And this did not merely mean that certain technical aspects of life were unrepresented. A whole range of strong sentiments and emotions—for many men, the strongest of all—went with them. . . . It was Kipling who first reclaimed for literature this enormous territory.[7]

He repudiates the unspoken assumption of most novelists that the really interesting part of life takes place outside working hours: men at work or talking about their work are among his favourite subjects. The qualities men show in their work, and

[5] *Past and Present* (1843), Book iv, ch. 1. Cf. ibid., Book iii, ch. 5.
[6] *Lyrical Ballads*, ed. R. L. Brett and A. R. Jones, London, 1963, pp. 253–4.
[7] 'Kipling's World', *Literature and Life: Addresses to the English Association*, London, 1948, pp. 59–60.

the achievements that result from it (bridges built, ships salvaged, pictures painted, famines relieved) are the very stuff of much of Kipling's fiction. Yet there also runs through his *œuvre*, like a figure in the carpet, a darker, more pessimistic vision of the impermanence, the transience—but not the worthlessness—of all achievement. This underlies his delighted engagement with contemporary reality and gives a deeper resonance to his finest work, in which human endeavour is celebrated none the less because it must ultimately yield to death and mutability.

ANDREW RUTHERFORD

INTRODUCTION

I

FOR at least a quarter of a century Kipling was the most widely read and influential writer on war in the English-speaking world, and this volume contains a selection of his stories and poems on the subject.

They fall into three groups which differ radically in mood and subject-matter, deriving as they do from three distinct phases of national experience.

The stories and poems of the first group, published in the period 1886–97, deal with wars fought on the imperial frontiers —in Afghanistan, Burma, the Sudan, and tribal territories on the North-West Frontier. They draw on the knowledge of soldiers and soldiering which Kipling had acquired in India by mixing with officers and Other Ranks alike; they celebrate the zest, the toughness, the wry stoicism and high morale which he had found amongst them; and although he readily acknowledges failures as well as triumphs—like the panic-stricken flight of the English regiment he calls the 'Fore and Aft'—the basic mood is one of confidence in an expanding Empire and the men who do her work.

The stories and poems of the second group, published between 1900 and 1903, deal with the Boer War, which he observed at first hand and which provided him with his first experience of being under fire, when he attended as a spectator at the Battle of Kari Siding. He never questioned the necessity or justice of this war, but he was dismayed by the inefficiency displayed at so many levels throughout the Army; his stories of this period are cautionary tales; and his denunciation of incompetence in high and low places foreshadows some of the protest literature of the First World War.

The third group of stories and poems, consisting of works published between 1915 and 1932, deals with the Great War itself—the Armageddon which he had long foretold, but which proved to be even more terrible than he had prophesied. At an early stage in the long agony his only son was killed on his first day in action; and Kipling's writings on the War, shot through with anger at the Germans for their assault on the values of European civilization, are from this point on pervaded also by suppressed grief at his own loss and the losses suffered by so many hundred thousands more.

The epic, the satiric, and the elegiac, therefore, mark important stages in his Patriot's Progress.

II

Kipling's adolescence and young-manhood were passed in an era of minor but savagely fought wars on the frontiers of Empire, and these bulked large in his youthful awareness. The United Services College at Westward Ho!, where he spent four formative years from 1878 to 1882, was 'in the nature of a company promoted by poor officers and the like for the education of their sons . . . It was largely a caste-school [he tells us]— some seventy-five per cent of us had been born outside England and hoped to follow their fathers in the Army.'[1] He himself did not altogether subscribe to its orthodoxies: as a schoolboy, his own interests were more literary than military or political; love, not war, was his preferred theme; and his poetry was more introspective, passionate, and confessional than his verse of later years. None the less, in one experimental poem, *'Ave Imperatrix!'*,[2] he did offer a public statement on the ethos of the College and its function as a training-ground for Empire. Written on the occasion of an attempt to assassinate Queen Victoria in March 1882, it conveys to her from the school

> Such greetings as should come from those
>> Whose fathers faced the Sepoy hordes,
> Or served you in the Russian snows,
>> And, dying, left their sons their swords.
>
> And some of us have fought for you
>> Already in the Afghan pass—

---

[1] *Something of Myself*, London, 1937, p. 22.
[2] *Ave Imperatrix!* ('Hail to the Empress!') was the title of an earlier poem by Oscar Wilde.

> Or where the scarce-seen smoke-puffs flew
> From Boer marksmen in the grass . . . [3]

The Indian Mutiny and Crimean War, referred to in the first of
these stanzas, formed part of the experience of an older gener-
ation; but the Abyssinian campaign of 1869, the Red River
Expedition of 1870, and the Ashanti War of 1874 were much
more recent conflicts; while the Zulu War of 1879, the Second
Afghan War of 1878–80, and the First Boer War of 1880–1 all
fell within his period at College. The Egyptian campaign of
1882 culminated in the Battle of Tel-el-Kebir, fought in the
month Kipling sailed (via the Suez Canal) for India; and in his
years there, from 1882 to 1889, wars and rumours of wars
continued to abound—and were, of course, fully reported in
the newspapers he worked for. The early campaigns in the
Sudan and the expedition to relieve Gordon in Khartoum made
headline news between 1883 and 1885. The Third Burmese
War of 1885 resulted in the annexation of Upper Burma in
January 1886, but this was followed by a long period of anti-
guerrilla campaigning, extensively covered by the *Civil and
Military Gazette*. Although the North-West Frontier was
quiescent during Kipling's years in India, a friendly Amir hav-
ing been established in Afghanistan, it was constantly in the
news. There were recurrent fears about Russia's intentions,
occasional minor campaigns like the Black Mountain Expedi-
tion of 1888, and frequent disturbances caused by freebooters
like Kamal—an historical figure whom Kipling celebrated in
'The Ballad of East and West'. In the late 1890s, moreover,
widespread risings in the Malakand, Tirah, Tochi, Buner, and
Chitral areas re-emphasized the prevalence of war as a common
feature of life on the imperial frontiers.

This catalogue may recall *1066 and All That*'s 'Wave of Justi-
fiable Wars' ('*War against Zulus.* Cause: the Zulus. Zulus
exterminated. Peace with Zulus.').[4] Yet it seemed self-evident
to many of Kipling's contemporaries that such frontiers had to
be policed and defended, and that from time to time they might
need to be extended, either for strategic reasons as with the

---

[3] *Definitive Edition of Rudyard Kipling's Verse* (henceforth cited as *Verse*), London,
1940, p. 169.
[4] W. C. Sellar and R. J. Yeatman, *1066 And All That*, London, 1930, p. 106.

'Forward' policy in Afghanistan (see p. 340), or for the wider diffusion of good government, as in Upper Burma. Kipling himself, however, was not really very interested in the causes of the wars which he portrays in these early poems and stories: what interests him is how they are conducted and how men behave in them in the face of hardships and extremities of danger. Such campaigns, in spite of modern views to the contrary, were very far from being walk-overs: quite apart from climate and disease which always took their toll, the enemies involved were often formidable. The annihilation of a British column by the Zulus at Isandhlwana in 1879, the destruction of a British and Indian brigade by the Afghan army and irregulars at Maiwand in 1880, the massacre of Egyptian forces under British officers by the Sudanese in 1883–4, the killing of Gordon himself in Khartoum in January 1885, and the humiliating defeats inflicted by the Boers on British troops in 1880–1, were all reminders that if war might be regarded as a Great Game, it was a game in which the stakes were very high.

Kipling conveys the nature of that game and of the men who played it in stories which are a blend of documentary, moral fable, and adventure story, firmly rooted, however, in historical reality; and in poems based on songs he had heard sung in canteens, around camp-fires on manœuvres, and in London music-halls, in which the proletarian idiom and outlook of soldiers themselves are used to give a remarkably frank and inclusive account of their experiences in peace and war. Kipling became indeed in a very real sense the chronicler and laureate of the old regular Army of the later nineteenth century—that élite professional force, admirably fitted for the tasks it was currently being asked to undertake, but unprepared as yet for the problems it would face in a more modern type of warfare.

III

The confidence which underlies these early stories and poems verges on hubris by the later 1890s, with Kipling's embarrassingly hyperbolic praise of Stalky (see pp. 105–22 below), his suggestion that far from being unique Stalky is by way of being *the* archetypal British officer, and his relish at the prospect of such officers' involvement in a major European war:

'I see,' said Dick Four, nodding. '. . . There's nobody like Stalky.'

'That's just where you make the mistake,' I said. 'India's full of Stalkies—Cheltenham and Haileybury and Marlborough chaps—that we don't know anything about, and the surprises will begin when there is really a big row on.'

'Who will be surprised?' said Dick Four.

'The other side. The gentlemen who go to the front in first-class carriages. Just imagine Stalky let loose on the the south side of Europe with a sufficiency of Sikhs and a reasonable prospect of loot. Consider it quietly.'[5]

Nemesis followed quickly with the outbreak in 1899 of the Boer War, a big enough row by the standards of the day: it is indeed described by a recent historian as 'the longest (two and three-quarter years), the costliest (over £200 million), the bloodiest (at least twenty-two thousand British, twenty-five thousand Boer and twelve thousand African lives) and the most humiliating war for Britain between 1815 and 1914'.[6]

The *casus belli* was the Boer treatment of foreigners, including British immigrants, in the Transvaal (see p. 346 below), but the basic issue was the independence of the Boer Republics —the Transvaal and Orange Free State—versus British hegemony in Southern Africa. Kipling's hostility to the Boer cause was intensified by his contempt for their agricultural and technological backwardness and his distaste for their ill-treatment of the Africans: in his old age he reflected sardonically that the hard-won victories of the Boer War had been thrown away by a Liberal government which simply left the Afrikaners 'in a position to uphold and expand their primitive lust for racial domination'.[7] But he had anything but contempt for their military skills, and it was a matter of some chagrin to him that so much of the 'stalkiness' in this war was shown by Boer rather than by British soldiers.

It was the first war British troops had fought against 'European' enemies since the Crimea, apart from their brief

[5] See below, p. 122.
[6] Thomas Pakenham, *The Boer War*, London, 1979, p. xv.
[7] *Something of Myself*, p. 166.

conflict with the Boers themselves in 1880–1; and while the tactics of an earlier era had proved thoroughly effective in what the Army used to call 'savage warfare', rapid developments in weaponry had rendered them obsolete for battle between equally armed forces. Accurate rifle-fire at long ranges had been possible for a considerable time, but the single-shot Sniders and Martini-Henrys of the 1880s had now been super-seded by magazine rifles which made possible a much higher rate of fire. The adoption of cordite as a 'smokeless powder' enabled riflemen to fire from concealed positions without giv-ing these away: together with Boer fieldcraft and tactical ingenuity this made traditional military formations suicidal. Boer mobility gave them advantages over predominantly infantry forces; the British cavalry was slow to adapt to the new style of war; it took time for Mounted Infantry to learn their trade; and guerrilla warfare, as the twentieth century has shown, admits of no easy solutions. But the biggest single problem for the British was rigidity of mind on the part of their commanders, and many reputations made in other campaigns were deservedly lost in South Africa.

Kipling had something of a ringside seat. He had holidayed in Cape Town in 1898, and he returned in January 1900, soon after the first Boer incursions into Cape Colony and Natal, their investment of Ladysmith, Mafeking, and Kimberley, and their defeat of British counter-attacks in the 'Black Week' of Decem-ber 1899 which saw the battles of Stormberg, Magersfontein, and Colenso, following another débâcle at the Modder River in November. A further defeat was sustained at Spion Kop on 24 January 1900; but in February Lord Roberts, the new Com-mander-in-Chief, began a great flank march, taking the Boers by surprise, turning some of their main positions, relieving Kimberley, defeating their army in the field at Paardeberg, and occupying Bloemfontein, the capital of the Orange Free State, on 13 March, while General Buller in Natal moved at the same time to the relief of Ladysmith.

Kipling had been able to discuss events in Cape Town with Lord Roberts himself, with Cecil Rhodes on his release from Kimberley, and with Sir Alfred Milner, the High Commis-sioner for South Africa. But he also went to see things for himself, travelling up to the Modder River in an ambulance-train, and returning in late February with a trainload of casualties. ('They were wonderful', he wrote years afterwards, 'even in the hour of death—these men and boys—lodge-keepers and ex-butlers of the Reserve and raw town-lads of twenty.'[8]) He was also invited by Roberts to visit Bloemfontein soon after its capture, to co-operate with a group of war correspondents on an army newspaper to which he contributed among other items satirical 'Kopje-Book Maxims' and 'Fables for the Staff'. He observed the Battle of Kari Siding on 28 March, and heard first-hand accounts of Christiaan De Wet's ambush of a British column at Sanna's Post, near Bloemfontein, just three days afterwards. He saw much to concern him in administrative and hospital arrangements:

First and last there were, I think, eight thousand cases of typhoid in Bloemfontein. ... Our own utter carelessness, officialdom and ignorance were responsible for much of the death-rate. I have seen a Horse Battery, 'dead to the wide', come in at midnight in raging rain and be assigned, by some idiot saving himself trouble, the site of an evacuated fever-hospital. Result—thirty cases after a month. I have seen men drinking raw Modder-river a few yards below where the mules were staling; and the organisation and siting of latrines seemed to be considered 'nigger-work'. .... To typhoid was added dysentery, the smell of which is even more depressing than the stench of human carrion. One could wind the dysentery tents a mile off ...[9]

Kipling returned to England in April but was back in Cape Town by Christmas 1900, and for several years thereafter he and his family spent their winters in a house on Rhodes's estate there. He kept closely in touch with the course of events in South Africa as Roberts's advance continued, supported by Buller's in Natal, and Pretoria, the capital of the Transvaal, was captured in June 1900. Boer armies could no longer take the field, but a guerrilla war continued to be waged with some ferocity on both sides, and the Boers did not admit final defeat till 31 May 1902.

Some of Kipling's Boer War stories, including 'The Way That He Took', 'The Outsider', and 'A Sahibs' War', were

---

[8] *Something of Myself*, p. 156.
[9] Ibid., pp. 154–5.

published while the war was still in progress; others—'The Comprehension of Private Copper' and 'The Captive'—very soon after its conclusion. They are contemporary comments, extremely topical, highly polemical, on the blunders and failings revealed by events as they unfolded, and on the lessons to be learned from them. The same is true of many of the 'Service Songs'—Barrack-Room Ballads of the Boer War—which appeared in *The Five Nations* in 1903; and the overwhelming impression is of the steepness of the learning-curve for all those capable of learning:

I wish myself could talk to myself as I left 'im a year ago;
I could tell 'im a lot that would save 'im a lot on the things that 'e
  ought to know!
When I think o' that ignorant barrack-bird, it almost makes me cry.
  I used to belong in an Army once
  (Gawd! what a rum little Army once,
  Red little, dead little Army once),
    But now I am M.I.[10]

Yet as so often with Kipling, there are unexpected dimensions to his work, like the surprising range of his imaginative sympathy—for Boer prisoners of war in the 'Half-Ballade of Waterval', for British deserters in 'Wilful-Missing', above all, perhaps, for the returned irregular of 'Chant-Pagan' who cannot readjust to the class-ridden hierarchy of English society—and his anti-Establishment intensity in 'Rimmon', with its fear that the Army's Old Guard would even now resist essential reforms.

IV

From now on Kipling's thoughts turned more and more to problems of national defence. The hostility of major European powers, particularly Germany, had been openly expressed in the course of the Boer War, and Britain's unpreparedness was all too evident. In bitter polemical verses like 'The Islanders' and 'The Dykes' (both 1902), in impassioned pamphleteering like 'The Army of a Dream' (1904) and 'The Parable of Boy

[10] 'M.I.' [Mounted Infantry], *Verse*, p. 465.

Jones' (1910), he warned Britain of the need to prepare for Armageddon, to introduce some form of universal military training, to make ready to defend herself against dangers of invasion and defeat which she had not had to face since the overthrow of Napoleon. His nightmare vision was of an undefended island and a generation in danger of being sacrificed by its unthinking and uncaring elders:

> Now we can only wait till the day, wait and apportion our shame.
> These are the dykes our fathers left, but we would not look to the same.
> Time and again we were warned of the dykes, time and again we delayed:
> Now, it may be, we have slain our sons as our fathers we have betrayed.[11]

Both the Navy and the Army were in fact subjected to radical reform between 1902 and 1914, the former under pressure from Admiral Sir John Fisher as First Sea Lord, the latter mainly under the policies of R. B. Haldane as Secretary of State for War. But although the Regular Army of 1914 was a far more effective instrument for modern warfare than that of 1899, and although the Territorial Army had been effectively organized as a second line of defence, the scale of preparations for a continental war fell far short of what would actually be required. And when the conflict which he had foretold did come in 1914, Kipling met it not with confidence or exultation, but with grim fortitude and a bleak awareness of its likely hazards:

> Comfort, content, delight,
> The ages' slow-bought gain,
> They shrivelled in a night.
> Only ourselves remain
> To face the naked days
> In silent fortitude,
> Through perils and dismays
> Renewed and re-renewed.[12]

His writings on the War itself are curiously fragmentary.

[11] 'The Dykes', *Verse*, p. 307.
[12] 'For All We have and Are', *Verse*, p. 330.

Large though they are in number, they seem none the less to avoid imaginative engagement with the actual experience of battle. This is attributable partly to his own humility—to his realization that he simply did not have the right to present imitations of actions of which he himself had no experience— but partly also to the traumatic effect of his son's death in September 1915. Prior to that he had produced a number of stories which related more or less directly to contemporary events: ' "Swept and Garnished" ' mediates his horror at German atrocities in Belgium in 1914 (see p. 358 below); 'Sea Constables' was provoked by the German declaration of a naval blockade of Britain in February 1915, and her policy of unrestricted submarine warfare; 'Mary Postgate' is at one level a response to German air raids on civilian targets, though it also involves a profound exploration of the moral ambiguity of war and of the wish for vengeance. But this sequence was broken in the autumn of 1915.

John Kipling, aged just seventeen, had volunteered soon after the outbreak of war, but had been turned down because of his poor eyesight. Kipling then prevailed on Lord Roberts to secure him a commission in the Irish Guards, and this was effected in September 1914. He was kept at the depôt till he had reached the age of eighteen, but went out to France with the 2nd Battalion in August 1915. They went into action for the first time at Loos on 27 September; John Kipling was reported wounded and missing, and for a time the Kiplings desperately hoped he was a prisoner; but that hope was vain. Reports gradually reached them of how well he had behaved in the attack and how he had been wounded, but his body was never found—it must have been destroyed or buried by shell-fire— and by 12 November Kipling was writing with tight-lipped reticence to Brigadier L. C. Dunsterville ('Stalky'):

It was a short life. I'm sorry that all the years' work ended in that one afternoon but—lots of people are in our position—and it's something to have bred a man. The wife is standing it wonderfully tho' she, of course, clings to the bare hope of his being a prisoner. I've seen what shells can do, and I don't.[13]

[13] Quoted in Charles Carrington, *Rudyard Kipling: His Life and Work*, London, 1955, p. 438.

Tight-lipped reticence was indeed to be Kipling's policy
from now on. Only on two or three occasions—in 'A Recan-
tation', for example—does he allow himself a direct expression
of grief, yet the intensity of his emotion seems to have numbed
his creative urge as far as fiction was concerned. (He published
no more new stories for the duration of the War, though a
collection of those already in existence appeared as *A Diversity
of Creatures* in 1917.) He continued with war journalism like
France at War, *The Fringes of the Fleet*, *Tales of 'The Trade'*,
Destroyers at Jutland, *The War in the Mountains*, and *The Eyes of
Asia*. He continued to publish poems on public events—like
his bitter indictment in 'Mesopotamia' of those who, as
revealed by a Parliamentary Commission of enquiry, were
responsible for the callous neglect of the wounded and sick
entrusted to their care in that campaign. He also wrote poems
like 'Gethsemane' and 'Epitaphs of the War' which avoided the
confessional or autobiographical but gave a more impersonal,
generalized response to death and bereavement. From 1917
onwards he was also engaged in the vast commemorative task
of compiling from records and personal reminiscences his
history of *The Irish Guards in the Great War* (1923). The chis-
elled, lapidary Introduction is included in this collection as his
most sustained, systematic, and carefully pondered account of
what was involved in active service on the Western Front; but
it is as if the meticulous narrative which followed exhausted his
capacity or desire to write directly about battle experience.
When he does return to fiction, while still working on the
History, his treatment of the subject is more indirect, oblique,
elliptical. He is concerned now less with men in action than
with men reflecting on that action in tranquillity—or at least in
retrospect. He is preoccupied by the psychological rather than
the physical casualties of war. Non-combatants, including the
bereaved, remain a major focus of attention. He still believes in
justice and retribution (see 'A Friend of the Family'), but he is
also interested now in possibilities of healing, mercy, and forgive-
ness, as in 'The Gardener'. The War is almost omnipresent in his
later fiction, as a theme, a point of reference, a source of shared
allusion, a cause of heartbreak and bereavement, an experience of
ultimates in horror and endurance, a self-sacrificial ordeal like the

crucifixion—an analogy explicit in 'Gethsemane'. But it is never seen as futile, since however great the loss and suffering, they are attributable partly indeed to Britain's culpable unpreparedness and partly to the operations of blind chance— 'a shell-splinter dropping out of a wet dawn'—but partly also to the inevitable cost, as evidenced by history, of struggles— necessary struggles as he saw them—against evil or aggression.

V

War as a recurrent theme in Kipling's work needs no apology, since it is, however regrettably, a recurrent element in human experience. 'War is waged by men; not by beasts or by gods', writes Frederick Manning: 'It is a peculiarly human activity.'[14] An activity, moreover, the significance of which can be denied only by a kind of intellectual prudery or wilful blindness, such as have often characterized what Lionel Trilling called 'the liberal imagination'.

The importance of war and military institutions [as Correlli Barnett writes] has been generally neglected in British historical writing, whose tone has been set by the Whig and liberal emphasis on peaceful constitutional progress. In this . . . view war appears as an aberration, an interruption of a 'natural' condition of peace: almost as a form of delinquency unworthy of intellectual attention. The liberal, pacifistic view of history can only be maintained by resolute aversion of the gaze from the facts. For conflict between tribal or social groups and nations constitutes the essential human condition in the absence of a world-state with a monopoly of force . . . Peace and war in history flow continually in and out of each other, alternative aspects of the single phenomenon of the struggle for power . . . The liberal optimism and pacifism of the nineteenth century themselves were made possible by victory over Napoleon, a victory consummated by a British general and partly by British troops at Waterloo; liberalism was guarded by the largest navy in the world and by a mercenary army more continually in action than any of the armies of the militaristic nations of Europe.[15]

To this tradition of tough-minded realism Kipling too

[14] *Her Privates We*, London, 1930, p. v.
[15] *Britain and Her Army: A Military, Political and Social Survey*, London, 1970, pp. xvii–xviii.

belonged. Throughout his life he despised what he saw as liberal-pacifist illusions, including failure to face the facts of power, of conflict, and of human evil. The futility and self-deception of sheltered intellectuals are caricatured in the complaint of the Progressive in 'Natural Theology' (1919):

> Money spent on an Army or Fleet
> Is homicidal lunacy ...
> My son has been killed in the Mons retreat.
> Why is the Lord afflicting me?
> Why are murder, pillage and arson
> And rape allowed by the Deity?
> I will write to the *Times*, deriding our parson,
> Because my God has afflicted me.[16]

Not only intellectuals, however, but society at large seemed to Kipling to have fallen into habits of wishful thinking and to have forgotten the age-old, unfashionable wisdom enunciated by the Gods of the Copybook Headings ('With the Hopes that our World is built on they were utterly out of touch, / They denied that the Moon was Stilton; they denied she was even Dutch. / They denied that Wishes were Horses; they denied that a Pig had Wings. / So we followed the Gods of the Market Who promised these beautiful things').[17] *His* Gods are the Gods of Things as They Are; the verities they assert are rooted in experience; his fictions are based firmly on reality as he observed it; and part of that reality was the fact of war, and the recurrent necessity of using force in self-defence, or as a restraint on evil, violence, and anarchy.

Nor had that necessity been ended by the defeat of Germany in what Correlli Barnett calls 'the British army's hardest fought and greatest victory',[18] because by the early 1930s German militarism was again resurgent. In his old age Kipling viewed the rise of Nazism with horror—when Hitler came to power he instructed his publishers to remove the Hindu swastika sign from all his works;[19] less than a year before his death he

[16] *Verse*, pp. 344–5.
[17] Ibid., p. 793.
[18] *Britain and Her Army*, p. 409.
[19] Macmillan Archive, British Library Additional MS 54902 (letter from Kipling's agents to Harold Macmillan, dated 29 May 1933).

warned, in his address 'An Undefended Island', of the renewed threat from Germany;[20] and one of his last poems, 'The Storm Cone', is a grim prediction of the conflict still to come:

This is the midnight—let no star
Delude us—dawn is very far.
This is the tempest long foretold—
Slow to make head but sure to hold.

Stand by! The lull 'twixt blast and blast
Signals the storm is near, not past;
And worse than present jeopardy
May our forlorn to-morrow be.

If we have cleared the expectant reef,
Let no man look for his relief.
Only the darkness hides the shape
Of further peril to escape.

It is decreed that we abide
The weight of gale against the tide
And those huge waves the outer main
Sends in to set us back again.

They fall and whelm. We strain to hear
The pulses of her labouring gear,
Till the deep throb beneath us proves,
After each shudder and check, she moves!

She moves, with all save purpose lost,
To make her offing from the coast;
But, till she fetches open sea,
Let no man deem that he is free![21]

---

[20] Address to Royal Society of St George, 6 May 1935 (*The Nineteenth Century and After*, Vol. cxvii, no. 700, June 1935).

[21] *Verse*, p. 824.

NOTE ON THE TEXT[1]

THE text of Kipling's works has never been subjected to scholarly analysis; a major scholarly task has yet to be undertaken in this field; and a full investigation of the textual history of the stories and poems in this collection would go far beyond the scope of this edition.

For the stories, Macmillan's Uniform Edition, which was for decades the most widely read edition of Kipling's works, has been used as copy-text, except for 'The Way That He Took', which was first collected in *Land and Sea Tales for Scouts and Guides* (1923), and 'The Outsider', which was first collected in *Uncollected Prose: Part II* of the Sussex Edition (Vol. XXX, 1938): I have used these as the copy-text for the two stories in question. The text of all the stories has, however, been amended in minor respects to take account of Kipling's own amendments in his autograph proof corrections to the Sussex Edition, which have been preserved in the Macmillan Archive in the British Library.

These involve a very large number of adjustments to the punctuation and typography, nearly all of which I have incorporated, though I have at times resisted Kipling's later addiction to excessive capitalization. There is also in his corrections a regularizing of the spelling of words variously rendered in earlier editions: 'bazar' for 'bazaar', 'Rajah' for 'Raja', 'Pushtu' for 'Pushto', 'Rissaldar' for 'Ressaldar', 'Maharajah' for 'Maharaja', 'Gurkhas' for 'Goorkhas', 'wallahs' for 'wallas', 'Khyber' for 'Khaibar', 'Naik' for 'Naick', 'Patiala' for 'Puttiala', 'mehters' for 'mehtars', 'Sudan' for 'Soudan', 'Assiut' for 'Assioot', 'Cleever' for 'Cleaver', 'Cape Town' for 'Capetown', etc. Then there are corrections of words wrongly or idiosyncratically spelt in earlier editions: 'hara-kiri' for 'hari-kari', 'tremor' for 'tremour', 'vrouws' for 'vrows', 'Bloemfontein' for 'Blomfontein', 'blur' for 'blurr', 'whizzbang' for 'whizbang', 'puttees' for 'putties', 'morale' for 'moral', 'teeter-

---

[1] All page-references are to the present edition.

ing' for 'teturing', and several words in the Afrikaans song in
'The Way That He Took'. There are also minor changes
designed to achieve a more precise phonetic rendering of
dialect or accent: 'dyin'' for 'dying', 'good-lookin'' for 'good-
looking', 'actin'' for 'acting', 't'other' for 'th'other', ''and' for
'hand', 'slicin'' for 'slicing', 'somethin'' for 'something', ''urt'
for 'hurt', and 'comin'' for 'coming' in 'The Drums of the Fore
and Aft'; 'wud' for 'would' and 'bekaze' for 'becase' ('because')
in 'The Mutiny of the Mavericks'; 'desuetood' for 'desuetude'
and 'presoom' for 'presume' in 'The Captive', ''E's' and ''E'd'
for 'He's' and 'He'd' in 'The Comprehension of Private Cop-
per'; ''old' for 'hold', ''ad' for 'had', ''and' for 'hand', and ''ere
or 'ereafter' (among others) in 'A Madonna of the Trenches',
are examples to which others could be added.

Some changes are more substantial, and I shall take 'The
Drums of the Fore and Aft' as an example. Over and above
changes in punctuation, typography, spelling, and the render-
ing of dialect, we have such amendments as the following.
'Auspach' in the title of the Fore and Aft becomes 'Anspach'.
The regiment is referred to throughout by its accepted nick-
name of 'the Fore and Fit' instead of the derisive 'Fore and Aft'
which resulted from events recounted in the story. 'Freshet'
(p. 7) had been corrupted to 'freshest' in many editions, but
this had already been rectified and needed no correction by the
author. On p. 11 'they' is inserted before 'amassed' and ''is'
before 'pocket'; on p. 20 'now' is inserted before 'allowed'; on
p. 22 'their study' becomes 'that study'; and on p. 24 'own' is
inserted before 'comrades'. On p. 24 also 'they don't quite
understand it'—the original reading—replaces the garbled ver-
sion 'they quite don't understand it', which had appeared in
successive editions. On p. 25 'that' is cut after 'notion'; on
p. 28 'That battalion' replaces 'That regiment'; and 'the leap-
ing Martini' becomes 'the jolting Martini'; on p. 30 'rear rank'
in line 1 becomes 'rear ranks', and 'there below was the enemy'
becomes 'there below were the enemy'; on p. 31 'was quiver-
ing with pain' becomes 'were quivering with pain', and
'go anywhere' becomes 'get anywhere'; on p. 33 'by the
wounded' becomes 'with the wounded'; on p. 37 'disgraced
yourself' becomes 'disgraced yourselves', 'It's not a matter'

becomes 'It isn't a matter', and 'half-a-dozen' becomes 'any amount of'. Similar changes occur throughout the volume, though the incidence varies considerably from story to story; and my policy has been to adopt the changes unless there is good reason to the contrary. I have rejected, for example, the change of 'hanty-room' to 'ante-room' in 'The Drums of the Fore and Aft', since it makes against Kipling's own intensified attempt to establish the uneducated speech of the two drummer boys; and I also reject his proposed change (on p. 34) of 'those' to 'these' in the phrase 'those vicious Gurkha knives', since it is grammatically inappropriate. Similarly I reject a number of other proposed variants throughout the volume, including, for example, 'Simon's Town' for 'Simonstown' (by false analogy with Cape Town); 'starts' for 'starts *bukhing*' on p. 108, since it detracts from the authenticity of the Anglo-Indian jargon; 'sorry for it' instead of 'sorry for this' on p. 54, because of the weakening of emphasis; 'had betrayed' for 'betrayed' on p. 131 since the betrayal had not previously taken place; 'commandoes' for 'commanders' on p. 202, since the sense is better and the British force in any case could hardly be termed a 'commando'; the suggested comma after 'Now' in 'Now a woman's business (p. 249), since it suggests that the comment refers only to immediate circumstances, whereas the reflection relates to Mary Postgate's whole adult life; and 'Palanseum' for 'Palemseum' (p. 252) since the former is a less felicitous and less interpretable portmanteau coinage.

As well as exercising editorial judgement in such matters, I have corrected a few manifest errors which appear in all editions I have used, including the Sussex. The most obvious are the reference (p. 29) to the neighing of the Highland pipes coming from 'the left', when the whole narrative makes clear this should have been 'the right'; and the misspelling of 'Merawi and Huella' as 'Herawi and Muella' (p. 63)—a mistake established in the first publication of *The Light that Failed* in *Lippincott's Monthly Magazine*, and never eliminated.

The variant readings between the Uniform and Sussex Editions are important for the establishment of the present text; but they are much less spectacular than the variation between the texts of the stories as originally published and as they appear in their collected form. Here again the extent of variance differs greatly: in an early story like 'The Drums of the Fore and Aft' or a late one like 'The Gardener', the first collected version is almost identical with that originally published, the variants being few in number and minor in character, whereas at the other end of the spectrum stories like 'The Way That He Took' or 'Sea Constables' have a very large number, including substantial passages of dialogue, narrative, or commentary which figure in the original but not in the collected versions.

In 'The Way That He Took', for example, as it first appeared in the *Daily Express*, in addition to the verse-heading which is cited in the Explanatory Notes, in addition too to single-word, single-phrase, or single-line variations (of which there are a great number—over 120—far from insignificant in their implications, as in the many references to the Afrikaner Bond), there are extended passages like the following:

(i) On the breakdown of the ambulance train: ' "It's worn out—overworked and worn out—like the rest of us," said the engineer. "If we 'ad 'arf a loyal government be'ind us, damn 'em, instead o' a gang o' Dutch rebels they would 'ave got us decent rolling stock for the war instead o' spending their time railin' ammunition to their Boer friends. Me 'ush?"—to the guard. "I won't! I ain't in Cape Town now, I'm among white people. It'll take an hour to botch this tube up—an' the 'ole of the timetables thrown out between 'ere and De Aar! I told 'em at Triangle what she was like—" He kicked the furnace door savagely and went to work.'

(ii) On the commando-leader's threats to the farmers of Cape Colony who had not risen in their support: 'Among his own kind the Boer is phenomenally incontinent of tongue, and it is to just this kind of threat, many times repeated by hasty commandants, that we owe much of the largely advertised Dutch loyalty. As Van der Hooven of Cradock put it, after Bloemfontein, when he attended the annexation meeting, "Our friends fought too soon and talked much too soon." '

(iii) On the winking night-lamp (p. 135): 'Time was when a Boer helio worked by a German print-seller from Johannesburg would have joined in the talk with derision and obscenities, but the German had foolishly got himself shot.'

(iv) On the possibility of the British fixing bayonets (p. 137): ' "Um! We must not let them get as near as that," said a Vryheid man, who had assisted at a white-flag play on the Belmont side, and remembered the outcome. "Don't you be afraid. We shall keep behind the stones . ..." '

(v) On the inadequacies of the Mounted Infantry training (p. 138). '. . . hours they had been in the saddle. They learned to loathe the business of horse-holding, at best a dreary job; to make a fool of the third man, which, too, is easily learned; and they learned to rejoice . . .'

(vi) Comment by private on the Captain's simulated interest in the vulture (p. 141): ' "Gawd! Ain't 'e seen enough stinkin' aasvogels in this country to leave 'em alone? Blowed if 'e ain't unstrappin' 'is binos to squint at it. 'E's got a touch o' fever 'e 'as!" '; and on the detour (p. 142), ' "Swelp me, I'll 'ave to draw on my emergency rations." '

To complicate things still further, the version of the story reprinted in *The Cosmopolitan* in November 1900 has additional passages interpolated, including the following:

(i) Opening sentence: ' "What a country to fight for!" said the major of artillery, for the twentieth time.'

(ii) On the difference between Sister Margaret and other Sisters he had known: 'He had met many—at Cape Town—and later at Matjesfontein when he was sick with dysentery and Sister Galbraith of Guy's had dissolved him in homesickness by talking about London and the horrors of old and unimprovable Africa.'

(iii) On subjects of discussion in the Major's tent: 'the scanty news, and—for reinforcements had not arrived—the standing miracle of De Aar with her million pounds' worth of stores then guarded by some four hundred men.'

The elimination of all these passages and the extensive minor revisions Kipling also made undoubtedly strengthen the story by making it less discursive and more economical in its effect. There is, however, one possible exception where the change obscures the logic of the passage. On the scouts' return to camp a 'dripping private' exclaims, "Ere's a rummy picnic. We left camp, as it were, by the front door. 'E *as* given us a giddy-go-round, an' no mistake.' In the original the phrase 'front door' was followed by 'an' now we're comin' in by the back door': this completes the sense very satisfactorily, and I have with some temerity incorporated it in the present text.

These passages, together with an indication of the number of variants in this one story—too great to be listed individually here—suggest the magnitude of the task which would be involved in the production of a scholarly edition of Kipling's work, but also the potential value of a proper *apparatus criticus*.

For the poems included in this volume I have used the 'Definitive Edition' as copy-text, not because it is truly definitive, but because it incorporates revisions Kipling had made to various Inclusive Editions of his Verse, whereas he did not live to revise the poetry volumes of the Sussex Edition.[2] On the other hand he did revise the text of poems which figure in the volumes of prose fiction in that edition, and these must therefore be recognized as having more authority; but in fact the changes from the texts as they had appeared in *Barrack-Room Ballads, The Seven Seas, The Five Nations, The Years Between*, etc., are minimal in number and significance. In one or two cases I have amended what appears to be defective punctuation. In 'Ford o' Kabul River' I have given preference to the original *Barrack-Room Ballads* reading 'Blow the bugle . . .' rather than the later version 'Blow the trumpet . . .', introduced, presumably, for the sake of accuracy, since cavalry regiments did use trumpets. One regrets the loss of the potent alliteration of the original but there is better cause than that for re-instating it: the word 'bugles' is retained in the verse-heading to Chapter 2 of *The Light that Failed*, which Kipling *did* revise for the Sussex Edition ('Then we brought the lances down, then the bugles blew'); and it is presumably in accordance with this that the Sussex Edition itself reverts to

[2] See *Early Verse by Rudyard Kipling 1879–1889*, London, 1986, pp. 34–7.

'bugles' in its text of 'Ford o' Kabul River'. More controversially, perhaps, I have cut the appended 'Me!' at the end of the last stanza of 'Chant-Pagan', although it figures in the 'Inclusive' and 'Definitive' Editions, because it is superfluous and has the air of having been introduced, whether or not with Kipling's authority, simply to accord with the pattern of preceding stanzas, whereas neither the sense nor the rhetoric of the poem requires its presence here (nor did it figure in the original publication in *The Five Nations*).

I have not sought to embark here on the sometimes complicated textual history of the poems prior to their first being collected.

SELECT BIBLIOGRAPHY

THE standard bibliography is J. McG. Stewart's *Rudyard Kipling: A Bibliographical Catalogue*, ed. A. W. Yeats (1959). Reference may also be made to two earlier works: Flora V. Livingston's *Bibliography of the Works of Rudyard Kipling* (1927) with its *Supplement* (1938), and Lloyd H. Chandler's *Summary of the Work of Rudyard Kipling, Including Items ascribed to Him* (1930). We still await a bibliography which will take account of the findings of modern scholarship over the last quarter-century.

The official biography, authorized by Kipling's daughter Elsie, is Charles Carrington's *Rudyard Kipling: His Life and Work* (1955; 3rd edn., revised, 1978). Other full-scale biographies are Lord Birkenhead's *Rudyard Kipling* (1978) and Angus Wilson's *The Strange Ride of Rudyard Kipling* (1977). Briefer, copiously illustrated surveys are provided by Martin Fido's *Rudyard Kipling* (1974) and Kingsley Amis's *Rudyard Kipling and his World* (1975), which combine biography and criticism, as do the contributions to *Rudyard Kipling: the man, his work and his world* (also illustrated), ed. John Gross (1972). Information on particular periods of his life is also to be found in such works as A. W. Baldwin, *The Macdonald Sisters* (1960); Alice Macdonald Fleming (*née* Kipling), 'Some Childhood Memories of Rudyard Kipling' and 'More Childhood Memories of Rudyard Kipling', *Chambers Journal*, 8th series, vol. 8 (1939); L. C. Dunsterville, *Stalky's Reminiscences* (1928); G. C. Beresford, *Schooldays with Kipling* (1936); E. Kay Robinson, 'Kipling in India', *McClure's Magazine*, Vol. 7 (1896); Edmonia Hill, 'The Young Kipling', *Atlantic Monthly*, vol. 157 (1936); *Kipling's Japan*, ed. Hugh Cortazzi and George Webb (1988); H. C. Rice, *Rudyard Kipling in New England* (1936); Frederic Van de Water, *Rudyard Kipling's Vermont Feud* (1937); Julian Ralph, *War's Brighter Side* (1901); Angela Thirkell, *Three Houses* (1931); *Rudyard Kipling to Rider Haggard: The Record of a Friendship*, ed. Morton Cohen (1965); and *'O Beloved Kids': Rudyard Kipling's Letters to his Children*, ed. Elliot L. Gilbert (1983). Useful background on the India he knew is provided by 'Philip Woodruff' (Philip Mason) in *The Men Who Ruled India* (1954), and by Pat Barr and Ray Desmond in their illustrated *Simla: A Hill Station in British India* (1978). Kipling's own autobiography, *Something of Myself* (1937), is idiosyncratic but indispensable.

The early reception of Kipling's work is usefully documented in *Kipling: The Critical Heritage*, ed. Roger Lancelyn Green (1971).

Richard Le Gallienne's *Rudyard Kipling: A Criticism* (1900), Cyril Falls's *Rudyard Kipling: A Critical Study* (1915), André Chevrillon's *Three Studies in English Literature* (1923) and *Rudyard Kipling* (1936), Edward Shanks's *Rudyard Kipling: A Study in Literature and Political Ideas* (1940), and Hilton Brown's *Rudyard Kipling: A New Appreciation* (1945) were all serious attempts at reassessment; while Ann M. Weygandt's study of *Kipling's Reading and Its Influence on His Poetry* (1939), and (in more old-fashioned vein) Ralph Durand's *Handbook to the Poetry of Rudyard Kipling* (1914) remain useful pieces of scholarship.

T. S. Eliot's introduction to *A Choice of Kipling's Verse* (1941; see *On Poetry and Poets*, 1957) began a period of more sophisticated reappraisal. There are influential essays by Edmund Wilson (1941; see *The Wound and the Bow*), George Orwell (1942; see his *Critical Essays*, 1946), Lionel Trilling (1943; see *The Liberal Imagination*, 1951), W. H. Auden (1943; see *New Republic*, vol. 109), and C. S. Lewis (1948; see *They Asked for a Paper*, 1962). These were followed by a series of important book-length studies which include J. M. S. Tompkins, *The Art of Rudyard Kipling* (1959); C. A. Bodelsen, *Aspects of Kipling's Art* (1964); Roger Lancelyn Green, *Kipling and the Children* (1965); Louis L. Cornell, *Kipling in India* (1966); and Bonamy Dobrée, *Rudyard Kipling: Realist and Fabulist* (1967), which follows on from his earlier studies in *The Lamp and the Lute* (1929) and *Rudyard Kipling* (1951). There were also two major collections of critical essays: *Kipling's Mind and Art*, ed. Andrew Rutherford (1964); and *Kipling and the Critics*, ed. Elliot L. Gilbert (1965). Nirad C. Chaudhuri's essay on *Kim* as 'The Finest Story about India—in English' (1957) is reprinted in John Gross's collection (see above). *The Reader's Guide to Rudyard Kipling's Work*, ed. R. E. Harbord (8 vols., privately printed, 1961–72) is an eccentric compilation, packed with useful information but by no means infallible.

Other studies devoted in whole or in part to Kipling include Richard Faber, *The Vision and the Need: Late Victorian Imperialist Aims* (1966); T. R. Henn, *Kipling* (1967); Alan Sandison, *The Wheel of Empire* (1967); Herbert L. Sussman, *Victorians and the Machine: The Literary Response to Technology* (1968); P. J. Keating, *The Working Classes in Victorian Fiction* (1971); Elliot L. Gilbert, *The Good Kipling: Studies in the Short Story* (1972); Jeffrey Meyers, *Fiction and the Colonial Experience* (1972); Shamsul Islam, *Kipling's 'Law'* (1975); J. S. (1966); T. R. Henn, *Kipling* (1967); Alan Sandison, *The Wheel of Empire* (1967); Herbert L. Sussman, *Victorians and the Machine: The Literary Response to Technology* (1968); P. J. Keating, *The Working Classes in Victorian Fiction* (1971); Elliot L. Gilbert, *The Good Kipling: Studies in the Short Story* (1972); Jeffrey Meyers, *Fiction and the Col-*

onial Experience (1972); Shamsul Islam, *Kipling's 'Law'* (1975); J. S. Bratton, *The Victorian Popular Ballad* (1975); Philip Mason, *Kipling: The Glass, The Shadow and The Fire* (1975); John Bayley, *The Uses of Division* (1976); M. Van Wyk Smith, *Drummer Hodge: The Poetry of the Anglo-Boer War 1899–1902* (1978); Stephen Prickett, *Victorian Fantasy* (1979); Martin Green, *Dreams of Adventure, Deeds of Empire* (1980); J. A. McClure, *Kipling and Conrad* (1981); R. F. Moss, *Rudyard Kipling and the Fiction of Adolescence* (1982); S. S. Azfar Husain, *The Indianness of Rudyard Kipling: A Study in Stylistics* (1983); Norman Page, *A Kipling Companion* (1984); B. J. Moore-Gilbert, *Kipling and 'Orientalism'* (1986); Sandra Kemp, *Kipling's Hidden Narratives* (1988); Norah Crook, *Kipling's Myths of Love and Death* (1989); and Ann Parry, *The Poetry of Rudyard Kipling* (1992); while further collections of essays include *Rudyard Kipling*, ed. Harold Bloom (1987); *Kipling Considered*, ed. Phillip Mallett (1989); and *Critical Essays on Rudyard Kipling*, ed. Harold Orel (1989). Among the most important recent studies are Edward Said, *Culture and Imperialism* (1991); Sara Suleri, *The Rhetoric of English India* (1992); Zohrah T. Sullivan, *Narratives of Empire: The Fictions of Rudyard Kipling* (1993); and Peter Keating, *Kipling the Poet* (1994).

Two important additions to the available corpus of Kipling's writings are *Kipling's India: Uncollected Sketches*, ed. Thomas Pinney (1986); and *Early Verse by Rudyard Kipling 1879–89: Unpublished, Uncollected and Rarely Collected Poems*, ed. Andrew Rutherford (1986). Indispensable is Pinney's edition of *The Letters of Rudyard Kipling*, of which Vols. I and II appeared in 1990, while Vol. III is eagerly awaited, and Vol. IV is in preparation.

A CHRONOLOGY OF KIPLING'S
LIFE AND WORKS

THE dates given here for Kipling's works are those of first authorized publication in volume form, whether this was in India, America, or England. (The dates of subsequent editions are not listed.) It should be noted that individual poems and stories collected in these volumes had in many cases appeared in newspapers or magazines of earlier dates. For full details see James McG. Stewart, *Rudyard Kipling: A Bibliographical Catalogue*, ed. A. W. Yeats, Toronto, 1959; but see also the editors' notes in this World's Classics series.

1865   Rudyard Kipling born at Bombay on 30 December, son of John Lockwood Kipling and Alice Kipling (*née* Macdonald).

1871   In December Rudyard and his sister Alice Macdonald Kipling ('Trix'), who was born in 1868, are left in the charge of Captain and Mrs Holloway at Lorne Lodge, Southsea ('The House of Desolation'), while their parents return to India.

1877   Alice Kipling returns from India in March/April and removes the children from Lorne Lodge, though Trix returns there subsequently.

1878   Kipling is admitted in January to the United Services College at Westward Ho! in Devon. First visit to France with his father that summer. (Many visits later in his life.)

1880   Meets and falls in love with Florence Garrard, a fellow-boarder of Trix's at Southsea and prototype of Maisie in *The Light that Failed*.

1881   Appointed editor of the *United Services College Chronicle*. *Schoolboy Lyrics* privately printed by his parents in Lahore, for limited circulation.

1882   Leaves school at end of summer term. Sails for India on 20 September; arrives Bombay on 18 October. Takes up post as assistant-editor of the *Civil and Military Gazette* in Lahore in the Punjab, where his father is now Principal of the Mayo College of Art and Curator of the Lahore Museum. Annual leaves from 1883 to 1888 are spent at Simla, except in 1884 when the family goes to Dalhousie.

1884   *Echoes* (by Rudyard and Trix, who has now rejoined the family in Lahore).

1885   *Quartette* (a Christmas Annual by Rudyard, Trix, and their parents).

1886   *Departmental Ditties.*

1887   Transferred in the autumn to the staff of the *Pioneer*, the *Civil and Military Gazette*'s sister-paper, in Allahabad in the North-West Provinces. As special correspondent in Rajputana he writes the articles later collected as 'Letters of Marque' in *From Sea to Sea*. Becomes friendly with Professor and Mrs Hill, and shares their bungalow.

1888   *Plain Tales from the Hills.* Takes on the additional responsibility of writing for the *Week's News*, a new publication sponsored by the *Pioneer*.

1888–9 *Soldiers Three; The Story of the Gadsbys; In Black and White; Under the Deodars; The Phantom Rickshaw; Wee Willie Winkie.*

1889   Leaves India on 9 March; travels to San Francisco with Professor and Mrs Hill via Rangoon, Singapore, Hong Kong, and Japan. Crosses the United States on his own, writing the articles later collected in *From Sea to Sea*. Falls in love with Mrs Hill's sister Caroline Taylor. Reaches Liverpool in October, and makes his début in the London literary world.

1890   Enjoys literary success, but suffers breakdown. Visits Italy. *The Light that Failed.*

1891   Visits South Africa, Australia, New Zealand, and (for the last time) India. Returns to England on hearing of the death of his American friend Wolcott Balestier. *Life's Handicap.*

1892   Marries Wolcott's sister Caroline Starr Balestier ('Carrie') in January. (The bride is given away by Henry James.) Their world tour is cut short by the loss of his savings in the collapse of the Oriental Banking Company. They establish their home at Brattleboro in Vermont, on the Balestier family estate. Daughter Josephine born in December. *The Naulahka* (written in collaboration with Wolcott Balestier). *Barrack-Room Ballads.*

1893   *Many Inventions.*

1894   *The Jungle Book.*

1895   *The Second Jungle Book.*

1896   Second daughter Elsie born in February. Quarrel with
        brother-in-law Beatty Balestier and subsequent court case
        end their stay in Brattleboro. Return to England (Torquay).
        The Seven Seas.

1897   Settles at Rottingdean in Sussex. Son John born in August.
        Captains Courageous.

1898   The first of many winters at Cape Town. Meets Sir Alfred
        Milner and Cecil Rhodes who becomes a close friend. Visits
        Rhodesia. *The Day's Work.*

1899   Disastrous visit to the United States. Nearly dies of
        pneumonia in New York. Death of Josephine. Never
        returns to USA. *Stalky and Co.*; *From Sea to Sea.*

1900   Helps for a time with army newspaper *The Friend* in South
        Africa during Boer War. Observes minor action at Kari
        Siding.

1901   *Kim.*

1902   Settles at 'Bateman's' at Burwash in Sussex. *Just So Stories.*

1903   *The Five Nations.*

1904   *Traffics and Discoveries.*

1906   *Puck of Pook's Hill.*

1907   Nobel Prize for Literature. Visit to Canada. *Collected Verse.*

1909   *Actions and Reactions*; *Abaft the Funnel.*

1910   *Rewards and Fairies.* Death of Kipling's mother.

1911   Death of Kipling's father.

1913   Visit to Egypt. *Songs from Books.*

1914–18 Visits to the Front and to the Fleet. *The New Army in
        Training*, *France at War*, *Sea Warfare*, and other war
        pamphlets.

1915   John Kipling reported missing on his first day in action with
        the Irish Guards in the Battle of Loos on 27 September. His
        body was never found.

1917   *A Diversity of Creatures.* Kipling becomes a member of the
        Imperial War Graves Commission.

1919   *The Years Between*; *Rudyard Kipling's Verse: Inclusive
        Edition.*

1920   *Letters of Travel.*

1923   *The Irish Guards in the Great War*; *Land and Sea Tales for
        Scouts and Guides.*

1924   Daughter Elsie marries Captain George Bambridge, MC.

1926   *Debits and Credits*.

1927   Voyage to Brazil.

1928   *A Book of Words*.

1930   *Thy Servant a Dog*. Visit to the West Indies.

1932   *Limits and Renewals*.

1933   *Souvenirs of France*.

1936   Kipling's death, 18 January.

1937   *Something of Myself For My Friends Known and Unknown*.

1937–9   *The Complete Works of Rudyard Kipling*, Sussex Edition. Prepared by Kipling in the last years of his life, this edition contains some previously uncollected items; but in spite of its title it does not include all his works.

1939   Death of Mrs Kipling.

1940   *The Definitive Edition of Rudyard Kipling's Verse*. This is the last of the series of 'Inclusive Editions' of his verse published in 1919, 1921, 1927, and 1933. In spite of its title the edition is far from definitive in terms of its inclusiveness or textual authority.

1948   Death of Kipling's sister Trix (Mrs John Fleming).

1976   Death of Kipling's daughter Elsie (Mrs George Bambridge).

WAR STORIES AND POEMS

PART ONE

The Imperial Frontiers

The Widow's Party*

'WHERE have you been this while away,
        Johnnie, Johnnie?'
Out with the rest on a picnic lay,
        Johnnie, my Johnnie, aha!
They called us out of the barrack-yard
To Gawd knows where from Gosport Hard,
And you can't refuse when you get the card,
        And the Widow gives the party.
            (*Bugle*: Ta—rara—ra-ra-rara!)

'What did you get to eat and drink,
        Johnnie, Johnnie?'
Standing water as thick as ink,
        Johnnie, my Johnnie, aha!
A bit o' beef that were three year stored,
A bit o' mutton as tough as a board,
And a fowl we killed with a sergeant's sword,
        When the Widow give the party.

'What did you do for knives and forks,
        Johnnie, Johnnie?'
We carries 'em with us wherever we walks,
        Johnnie, my Johnnie, aha!
And some was sliced and some was halved,
And some was crimped and some was carved,
And some was gutted and some was starved,
        When the Widow give the party.

'What ha' you done with half your mess,
        Johnnie, Johnnie?'
They couldn't do more and they wouldn't do less,
        Johnnie, my Johnnie, aha!
They ate their whack and they drank their fill,
And I think the rations has made them ill,
For half my comp'ny's lying still
        Where the Widow give the party.

'How did you get away—away,
   Johnnie, Johnnie?'
On the broad o' my back at the end o' the day,
   Johnnie, my Johnnie, aha!
I comed away like a bleedin' toff,
For I got four niggers to carry me off,
As I lay in the bight of a canvas trough,
    When the Widow give the party.

'What was the end of all the show,
   Johnnie, Johnnie?'
Ask my Colonel, for I don't know,
   Johnnie, my Johnnie, aha!
We broke a King and we built a road—
A court-house stands where the Reg'ment goed.
And the river's clean where the raw blood flowed
    When the Widow give the party.
     (*Bugle*: Ta—rara—ra-ra-rara!)

The Drums of the Fore and Aft*

IN the Army List they still stand as 'The Fore and Fit Princess Hohenzollern-Sigmaringen-Anspach's Merthyr-Tydfilshire Own Royal Loyal Light Infantry, Regimental District 329A', but the Army through all its barracks and canteens knows them now as the 'Fore and Aft'. They may in time do something that shall make their new title honourable, but at present they are bitterly ashamed, and the man who calls them 'Fore and Aft' does so at the risk of the head which is on his shoulders.

Two words* breathed into the stables of a certain Cavalry Regiment will bring the men out into the streets with belts and mops and bad language; but a whisper of 'Fore and Aft' will bring out this regiment with rifles.

Their one excuse is that they came again and did their best to finish the job in style. But for a time all their world knows that they were openly beaten, whipped, dumb-cowed, shaking, and afraid. The men know it; their officers know it; the Horse Guards* know it, and when the next war comes the enemy will know it also. There are two or three regiments of the Line that have a black mark against their names which they will then wipe out; and it will be excessively inconvenient for the troops upon whom they do their wiping.

The courage of the British soldier is officially supposed to be above proof, and, as a general rule, it is so. The exceptions are decently shovelled out of sight, only to be referred to in the freshet of unguarded talk that occasionally swamps a Mess-table at midnight. Then one hears strange and horrible stories of men not following their officers, of orders being given by those who had no right to give them, and of disgrace that, but for the standing luck of the British Army, might have ended in brilliant disaster. These are unpleasant stories to listen to, and the Messes tell them under their breath, sitting by the big wood fires, and the young officer bows his head and thinks to himself, please God, his men shall never behave unhandily.

The British soldier is not altogether to be blamed for occasional lapses; but this verdict he should not know. A moderately intelligent General will waste six months of mastering the craft of the particular war that he may be waging; a Colonel may utterly misunderstand the capacity of his regiment for three months after it has taken the field; and even a Company Commander may err and be deceived as to the temper and temperament of his own handful: wherefore the soldier, and the soldier of to-day more particularly, should not be blamed for falling back. He should be shot or hanged afterwards—to encourage the others; but he should not be vilified in newspapers, for that is want of tact and waste of space.

He has, let us say, been in the service of the Empress* for, perhaps, four years. He will leave in another two years.* He has no inherited morals, and four years are not sufficient to drive toughness into his fibre, or to teach him how holy a thing is his Regiment. He wants to drink, he wants to enjoy himself —in India he wants to save money—and he does not in the least like getting hurt. He has received just sufficient education to make him understand half the purport of the orders he receives, and to speculate on the nature of clean, incised, and shattering wounds. Thus, if he is told to deploy under fire preparatory to an attack, he knows that he runs a very great risk of being killed while he is deploying, and suspects that he is being thrown away to gain ten minutes' time. He may either deploy with desperate swiftness, or he may shuffle, or bunch, or break, according to the discipline under which he has lain for four years.

Armed with imperfect knowledge, cursed with the rudiments of an imagination, hampered by the intense selfishness of the lower classes, and unsupported by any regimental associations, this young man is suddenly introduced to an enemy who in Eastern lands is always ugly, generally tall and hairy, and frequently noisy. If he looks to the right and the left and sees old soldiers—men of twelve years' service, who, he knows, know what they are about—taking a charge, rush, or demonstration without embarrassment, he is consoled and applies his shoulder to the butt of his rifle with a stout heart. His peace is the greater if he hears a senior, who has taught him his soldiering and broken his head on occasion, whispering:

'They'll shout and carry on like this for five minutes. Then they'll rush in, and then we've got 'em by the short hairs!'

But, on the other hand, if he sees only men of his own term of service turning white and playing with their triggers, and saying: 'What the Hell's up now?' while the Company Commanders are sweating into their sword-hilts and shouting: 'Front-rank, fix bayonets! Steady there—steady! Sight for three hundred—no, for five! Lie down, all! Steady! Front-rank kneel!' and so forth, he becomes unhappy; and grows acutely miserable when he hears a comrade turn over with the rattle of fire-irons falling into the fender, and the grunt of a pole-axed ox. If he can be moved about a little and allowed to watch the effect of his own fire on the enemy he feels merrier, and may be then worked up to the blind passion of fighting, which is, contrary to general belief, controlled by a chilly Devil and shakes men like ague. If he is not moved about, and begins to feel cold at the pit of the stomach, and in that crisis is badly mauled, and hears orders that were never given, he will break, and he will break badly; and of all things under the light of the sun there is nothing more terrible than a broken British regiment. When the worst comes to the worst and the panic is really epidemic, the men must be e'en let go, and the Company Commanders had better escape to the enemy and stay there for safety's sake. If they can be made to come again they are not pleasant men to meet; because they will not break twice.

About thirty years from this date, when we have succeeded in half-educating everything that wears trousers, our Army will be a beautifully unreliable machine. It will know too much and it will do too little. Later still, when all men are at the mental level of the officer of to-day, it will sweep the earth. Speaking roughly, you must employ either blackguards or gentlemen, or, best of all, blackguards commanded by gentlemen, to do butcher's work with efficiency and despatch. The ideal soldier should, of course, think for himself—the *Pocket-book** says so. Unfortunately, to attain this virtue he has to pass through the phase of thinking *of* himself, and that is misdirected genius. A blackguard may be slow to think for himself, but he is genuinely anxious to kill, and a little punishment teaches him how to guard his own skin and perforate another's. A powerfully prayerful Highland Regiment, officered by rank Presbyterians, is, perhaps, one degree more terrible in action than a hard-bitten thousand of irresponsible Irish ruffians led by most improper young unbelievers. But these things prove the rule—which is that the midway men are not to be trusted alone. They have ideas about the value of life and an upbringing that has not taught them to go on and take the chances. They are carefully unprovided with a backing of comrades who have been shot over, and until that backing is re-introduced,* as a great many Regimental Commanders intend it shall be, they are more liable to disgrace themselves than the size of the Empire or the dignity of the Army allows. Their officers are as good as good can be, because their training begins early, and God has arranged that a clean-run youth of the British middle classes shall, in the matter of backbone, brains, and bowels, surpass all other youths. For this reason a child of eighteen will stand up, doing nothing, with a tin sword in his hand and joy in his heart until he is dropped. If he dies, he dies like a gentleman. If he lives, he writes Home that he has been 'potted', 'sniped', 'chipped', or 'cut over', and sits down to besiege Government for a wound-gratuity until the next little war breaks out, when he perjures himself before a Medical Board, blarneys his Colonel, burns incense round his Adjutant, and is allowed to go to the Front once more.

Which homily brings me directly to a brace of the most finished little fiends that ever banged drum or tootled fife in the Band of a British regiment. They ended their sinful career by open and flagrant mutiny and were shot for it. Their names were Jakin and Lew—Piggy Lew—and they were bold, bad drummer-boys, both of them frequently birched by the Drum-Major of the Fore and Fit.

Jakin was a stunted child of fourteen, and Lew was about the same age. When not looked after, they smoked and drank. They swore habitually after the manner of the Barrack-room, which is cold swearing and comes from between clinched teeth; and they fought religiously once a week. Jakin had sprung from some London gutter and may or may not have passed through Dr Barnardo's hands* ere he arrived at the dignity of drummer-boy. Lew could remember nothing except the regiment and the delight of listening to the Band from his earliest years. He hid somewhere in his grimy little soul a genuine love for music, and was most mistakenly furnished with the head of a cherub: insomuch that beautiful ladies who watched the Regiment in church were wont to speak of him as a 'darling'. They never heard his vitriolic comments on their manners and morals, as he walked back to barracks with the Band and matured fresh causes of offence against Jakin.

The other drummer-boys hated both lads on account of their illogical conduct. Jakin might be pounding Lew, or Lew might be rubbing Jakin's head in the dirt, but any attempt at aggression on the part of an outsider was met by the combined forces of Lew and Jakin; and the consequences were painful. The boys were the Ishmaels* of the corps, but wealthy Ishmaels, for they sold battles in alternate weeks for the sport of the barracks when they were not pitted against other boys; and thus they amassed money.

On this particular day there was dissension in the camp. They had just been convicted afresh of smoking, which is bad for little boys who use plug tobacco, and Lew's contention was that Jakin had 'stunk so 'orrid bad from keepin' the pipe in 'is pocket,' that he and he alone was responsible for the birching they were both tingling under.

'I tell you I 'id the pipe back o' barracks,' said Jakin pacifically.

'You're a bloomin' liar,' said Lew without heat.

'You're a bloomin' little barstard,' said Jakin, strong in the knowledge that his own ancestry was unknown.

Now there is one word in the extended vocabulary of barrack-room abuse that cannot pass without comment. You may call a man a thief and risk nothing. You may even call him a coward without finding more than a boot whiz past your ear, but you must not call a man a bastard unless you are prepared to prove it on his front teeth.

'You might ha' kep' that till I wasn't so sore,' said Lew sorrowfully, dodging round Jakin's guard.

'I'll make you sorer,' said Jakin genially, and got home on Lew's alabaster forehead. All would have gone well and this story, as the books say, would never have been written, had not his evil fate prompted the Bazar-Sergeant's* son, a long, employless man of five-and-twenty, to put in an appearance after the first round. He was eternally in need of money, and knew that the boys had silver.

'Fighting again,' said he. 'I'll report you to my father, and he'll report you to the Colour-Sergeant.'

'What's that to you?' said Jakin with an unpleasant dilation of the nostrils.

'Oh! nothing to *me*. You'll get into trouble, and you've been up too often to afford that.'

'What the Hell do you know about what we've done?' asked Lew the Seraph. '*You* aren't in the Army, you lousy, cadging civilian.'

He closed in on the man's left flank.

'Jes' 'cause you find two gentlemen settlin' their diff'rences with their fists you stick in your ugly nose where you aren't wanted. Run 'ome to your 'arf-caste slut of a Ma—or we'll give you what-for,' said Jakin.

The man attempted reprisals by knocking the boys' heads together. The scheme would have succeeded had not Jakin punched him vehemently in the stomach, or had Lew refrained from kicking his shins. They fought together, bleeding and breathless, for half an hour, and, after heavy punishment, triumphantly pulled down their opponent as terriers pull down a jackal.

'Now,' gasped Jakin, 'I'll give you what-for.' He proceeded to pound the man's features while Lew stamped on the outlying portions of his anatomy. Chivalry is not a strong point in the composition of the average drummer-boy. He fights, as do his betters, to make his mark.

Ghastly was the ruin that escaped, and awful was the wrath of the Bazar-Sergeant. Awful, too, was the scene in Orderly-Room when the two reprobates appeared to answer the charge of half-murdering a 'civilian'. The Bazar-Sergeant thirsted for a criminal action, and his son lied. The boys stood to attention while the black clouds of evidence accumulated.

'You little devils are more trouble than the rest of the Regiment put together,' said the Colonel angrily. 'One might as well admonish thistledown, and I can't well put you in cells or under stoppages. You must be birched again.'

'Beg y' pardon, Sir. Can't we say nothin' in our own defence, Sir?' shrilled Jakin.

'Hey! What? Are you going to argue with *me*?' said the Colonel.

'No, Sir,' said Lew. 'But if a man come to you, Sir, and said he was going to report you, Sir, for 'aving a bit of a turn-up with a friend, Sir, an' wanted to get money out o' *you*, Sir——'

The Orderly-Room exploded in a roar of laughter. 'Well?' said the Colonel.

'That was what that measly *jarnwar** there did, Sir, and 'e'd 'a' *done* it, Sir, if we 'adn't prevented 'im. We didn't 'it 'im much, Sir. 'E 'adn't no manner o' right to interfere with us, Sir. I don't mind bein' birched by the Drum-Major, Sir, nor yet reported by *any* Corp'ral, but I'm—but I don't think it's fair, Sir, for a civilian to come an' talk over a man in the Army.'

A second shout of laughter shook the Orderly-Room, but the Colonel was grave.

'What sort of characters have these boys?' he asked of the Regimental Sergeant-Major.

'Accordin' to the Bandmaster, Sir,' returned that revered official—the only soul in the Regiment whom the boys feared—'they do everything *but* lie, Sir.'

'Is it like we'd go for that man for fun, Sir?' said Lew, pointing to the plaintiff.

'Oh, admonished—admonished!' said the Colonel testily, and when the boys had gone he read the Bazar-Sergeant's son a lecture on the sin of unprofitable meddling, and gave orders that the Bandmaster should keep the Drums in better discipline.

'If either of you comes to practice again with so much as a scratch on your two ugly little faces,' thundered the Bandmaster, 'I'll tell the Drum-Major to take the skin off your backs. Understand that, you young devils.'

Then he repented of his speech for just the length of time that Lew, looking like a seraph in red worsted embellishments, took the place of one of the trumpets—in hospital—and rendered the echo of a battle-piece. Lew certainly was a musician, and had often in his more exalted moments expressed a yearning to master every instrument of the Band.

'There's nothing to prevent your becoming a Bandmaster, Lew,' said the Bandmaster, who had composed waltzes of his own, and worked day and night in the interests of the Band.

'What did he say?' demanded Jakin after practice.

'Said I might be a bloomin' Bandmaster, an' be asked in to 'ave a glass o' sherry-wine on Mess-nights.'

'Ho! Said you might be a bloomin' non-combatant, did 'e! That's just about wot 'e would say. When I've put in my boy's service—it's a bloomin' shame that doesn't count for pension—I'll take on as a privit. Then I'll be a Lance in a year—knowin' what I know about the ins an' outs o' things. In three years I'll be a bloomin' Sergeant. I won't marry then, not me! I'll 'old on and learn the orf'cers' ways an' apply for exchange into a reg'ment that doesn't know all about me. Then I'll be a bloomin' orf'cer. Then I'll ask you to 'ave a glass o' sherry-wine, *Mister* Lew, an' you'll bloomin' well 'ave to stay in the hanty-room* while the Mess-Sergeant brings it to your dirty 'ands.'

"S'pose I'm going to be a Bandmaster? Not I, quite. I'll be a orf'cer too. There's nothin' like taking to a thing an' stickin' to it, the Schoolmaster says. The Reg'ment don't go 'ome for another seven years. I'll be a Lance then or near to.'

Thus the boys discussed their futures, and conducted themselves piously for a week. That is to say, Lew started a flirtation with the Colour-Sergeant's daughter, aged thirteen—'not,' as he explained to Jakin, 'with any intention o' matrimony, but by way o' keepin' my 'and in.' And the black-haired Cris Delighan enjoyed that flirtation more than previous ones, and the other drummer-boys raged furiously together, and Jakin preached sermons on the dangers of 'bein' tangled along o' petticoats'.

But neither love nor virtue would have held Lew long in the paths of propriety had not the rumour gone abroad that the Regiment was to be sent on active service, to take part in a war which, for the sake of brevity, we will call 'The War of the Lost Tribes'.

The barracks had the rumour almost before the Mess-room,

and of all the nine hundred men in barracks not ten had seen a shot fired in anger. The Colonel had, twenty years ago, assisted at a Frontier expedition; one of the Majors had seen service at the Cape; a confirmed deserter in E Company had helped to clear streets in Ireland; but that was all. The Regiment had been put by for many years. The overwhelming mass of its rank and file had from three to four years' service; the non-commissioned officers were under thirty years old; and men and sergeants alike had forgotten to speak of the stories written in brief upon the Colours*—the New Colours that had been formally blessed by an Archbishop in England ere the Regiment came away.

They wanted to go to the Front—they were enthusiastically anxious to go—but they had no knowledge of what war meant, and there was none to tell them. They were an educated regiment, the percentage of school-certificates in their ranks was high, and most of the men could do more than read and write. They had been recruited in loyal observance of the territorial idea;* but they themselves had no notion of that idea. They were made up of drafts from an over-populated manufacturing district. The system had put flesh and muscle upon their small bones, but it could not put heart into the sons of those who for generations had done over-much work for over-scanty pay, had sweated in drying-rooms, stooped over looms, coughed among white-lead, and shivered on lime-barges. The men had found food and rest in the Army, and now they were going to fight 'niggers'—people who ran away if you shook a stick at them. Wherefore they cheered lustily when the rumour ran, and the shrewd, clerkly non-commissioned officers speculated on the chances of batta* and of saving their pay. At Headquarters men said: 'The Fore and Fit have never been under fire within the last generation. Let us, therefore, break them in easily by setting them to guard lines of communication.' And this would have been done but for the fact that British Regiments were wanted—badly wanted—at the Front, and there were doubtful Native Regiments that could fill the minor duties. 'Brigade 'em with two strong Regiments,' said Headquarters. 'They may be knocked about a bit, but they'll learn their business before they come through. Nothing like a night-alarm and a little cutting-up of stragglers to make a Regiment smart in the field. Wait till they've had half-a-dozen sentries' throats cut.'

The Colonel wrote with delight that the temper of his men was excellent, that the Regiment was all that could be wished, and as sound as a bell. The Majors smiled with a sober joy, and the subalterns waltzed in pairs down the Mess-room after dinner, and nearly shot themselves at revolver-practice. But there was consternation in the hearts of Jakin and Lew. What was to be done with the Drums? Would the Band go to the Front? How many of the Drums would accompany the Regiment?

They took counsel together, sitting in a tree and smoking.

'It's more than a bloomin' toss-up they'll leave us be'ind at the Depôt with the women. You'll like that,' said Jakin sarcastically.

''Cause o' Cris, y' mean? Wot's a woman, or a 'ole bloomin' depôt o' women, 'longside o' the chanst o' field-service? You know I'm as keen on goin' as you,' said Lew.

'Wish I was a bloomin' bugler,' said Jakin sadly. 'They'll take Tom Kidd along, that I can plaster a wall with, an' like as not they won't take us.'

'Then let's go an' make Tom Kidd so bloomin' sick 'e can't bugle no more. You 'old 'is 'ands an' I'll kick him,' said Lew, wriggling on the branch.

'That ain't no good neither. We ain't the sort o' characters to presoom on our rep'tations—they're bad. If they leave the Band at the Depôt we don't go, and no error *there*. If they take the Band we may get cast for medical unfitness. Are you medical fit, Piggy?' said Jakin, digging Lew in the ribs with force.

'Yus,' said Lew with an oath. 'The Doctor says your 'eart's weak through smokin' on an empty stummick. Throw a chest an' I'll try yer.'

Jakin threw out his chest, which Lew smote with all his might. Jakin turned very pale, gasped, crowed, screwed up his eyes, and said—'That's all right.'

'You'll do,' said Lew. 'I've 'eard o' men dyin' when you 'it 'em fair on the breastbone.'

'Don't bring us no nearer goin', though,' said Jakin. 'Do you know where we're ordered?'

'Gawd knows, an' 'E won't split on a pal.* Somewheres up to the Front to kill Paythans*—hairy big beggars that turn you inside out if they get 'old o' you. They say their women are good-lookin', too.'

'Any loot?' asked the abandoned Jakin.

'Not a bloomin' anna,* they say, unless you dig up the ground an' see what the niggers 'ave 'id. They're a poor lot.' Jakin stood upright on the branch and gazed across the plain.

'Lew,' said he, 'there's the Colonel coming. 'Colonel's a good old beggar. Let's go an' talk to 'im.'

Lew nearly fell out of the tree at the audacity of the suggestion. Like Jakin he feared not God, neither regarded he Man, but there are limits even to the audacity of drummer-boy, and to speak to a Colonel was——

But Jakin had slid down the trunk and doubled in the direction of the Colonel. That officer was walking wrapped in thought and visions of a C.B.—yes, even a K.C.B.,* for had he not at command one of the best Regiments of the Line—the Fore and Fit? And he was aware of two small boys charging down upon him. Once before it had been solemnly reported to him that 'the Drums were in a state of mutiny', Jakin and Lew being the ringleaders. This looked like an organized conspiracy.

The boys halted at twenty yards, walked to the regulation four paces, and saluted together, each as well-set-up as a ramrod and little taller.

The Colonel was in a genial mood; the boys appeared very forlorn and unprotected on the desolate plain, and one of them was handsome.

'Well?' said the Colonel, recognizing them. 'Are you going to pull me down in the open? I'm sure I never interfere with you, even though'—he sniffed suspiciously—'you have been smoking.'

It was time to strike while the iron was hot. Their hearts beat tumultuously.

'Beg y' pardon, Sir,' began Jakin. 'The Reg'ment's ordered on active service, Sir?'

'So I believe,' said the Colonel courteously.

'Is the Band goin', Sir?' said both together. Then, without pause, 'We're goin', Sir, ain't we?'

'You!' said the Colonel, stepping back the more fully to take in the two small figures. 'You! You'd die in the first march.'

'No, we wouldn't, Sir. We can march with the Reg'ment anywheres—p'rade an' anywhere else,' said Jakin.

'If Tom Kidd goes 'e'll shut up like a clasp-knife,' said Lew. 'Tom 'as very-close veins in both 'is legs, Sir.'

'Very how much?'

'Very-close veins, Sir. That's why they swells after long p'rade, Sir. If 'e can go, we can go, Sir.'

Again the Colonel looked at them long and intently.

'Yes, the Band is going,' he said as gravely as though he had been addressing a brother officer. 'Have you any parents, either of you two?'

'No, Sir,' rejoicingly from Lew and Jakin. 'We're both orphans, Sir. There's no one to be considered of on our account, Sir.'

'You poor little sprats, and you want to go up to the Front with the Regiment, do you? Why?'

'I've wore the Queen's Uniform for two years,' said Jakin. 'It's very 'ard, Sir, that a man don't get no recompense for doin' of 'is dooty, Sir.'

'An'——an' if I don't go, Sir,' interrupted Lew, 'the Bandmaster 'e says 'e'll catch an' make a bloo— a blessed musician o' me, Sir. Before I've seen any service, Sir.'

The Colonel made no answer for a long time. Then he said quietly: 'If you're passed by the Doctor I daresay you can go. I shouldn't smoke if I were you.'

The boys saluted and disappeared. The Colonel walked home and told the story to his wife, who nearly cried over it. The Colonel was well pleased. If that was the temper of the children, what would not the men do?

Jakin and Lew entered the boys' barrack-room with great stateliness, and refused to hold any conversation with their comrades for at least ten minutes. Then, bursting with pride, Jakin drawled: 'I've bin intervooin' the Colonel. Good old beggar is the Colonel. Says I to 'im, "Colonel," says I, "let me go to the Front, along o' the Reg'ment."—"To the Front you shall go," says 'e, "an' I only wish there was more like you among the dirty little devils that bang the bloomin' drums." Kidd, if you throw your 'courtrements at me for tellin' you the truth to your own advantage, your legs'll swell.'

None the less there was a battle-royal in the barrack-room, for the boys were consumed with envy and hate, and neither Jakin nor Lew behaved in conciliatory wise.

'I'm goin' out to say adoo to my girl,' said Lew, to cap the climax. 'Don't none o' you touch my kit because it's wanted for active service; me bein' specially invited to go by the Colonel.'

He strolled forth and whistled in the clump of trees at the back of the Married Quarters till Cris came to him, and, the preliminary kisses being given and taken, Lew began to explain the situation.

'I'm goin' to the Front with the Reg'ment,' he said valiantly.

'Piggy, you're a little liar,' said Cris, but her heart misgave her, for Lew was not in the habit of lying.

'Liar yourself, Cris,' said Lew, slipping an arm round her. 'I'm goin'. When the Reg'ment marches out you'll see me with 'em, all galliant and gay. Give us another kiss, Cris, on the strength of it.'

'If you'd on'y 'a' stayed at the Depôt—where you *ought* to ha' bin—you could get as many of 'em as—as you dam please,' whimpered Cris, putting up her mouth.

'It's 'ard, Cris. I grant you it's 'ard. But what's a man to do? If I'd 'a' stayed at the Depôt, you wouldn't think anything of me.'

'Like as not, but I'd 'ave you with me, Piggy. An' all the thinkin' in the world isn't like kissin'.'

'An' all the kissin' in the world isn't like 'avin' a medal to wear on the front o' your coat.'

'*You* won't get no medal.'

'Oh yus, I shall though. Me an' Jakin are the only actin'-drummers that'll be took along. All the rest is full men, an' we'll get our medals with them.'

'They might ha' taken anybody but you, Piggy. You'll get killed—you're so venturesome. Stay with me, Piggy darlin', down at the Depôt, an' I'll love you true, for ever.'

'Ain't you goin' to do that *now*, Cris? You said you was.'

'O' course I am, but t' other's more comfortable. Wait till you've growed a bit, Piggy. You aren't no taller than me now.'

'I've bin in the Army for two years an' I'm not goin' to get out of a chanst o' seein' service, an' don't you try to make me do so. I'll come back, Cris, an' when I take on as a man I'll marry you—marry you when I'm a Lance.'

'Promise, Piggy?'

Lew reflected on the future as arranged by Jakin a short time previously, but Cris's mouth was very near to his own.

'I promise, s'elp me Gawd!' said he.

Cris slid an arm round his neck.

'I won't 'old you back no more, Piggy. Go away an' get your medal, an' I'll make you a new button-bag as nice as I know how,' she whispered.

'Put some o' your 'air into it, Cris, an' I'll keep it in my pocket so long's I'm alive.'

Then Cris wept anew, and the interview ended. Public feeling among the drummer-boys rose to fever pitch and the lives of Jakin and Lew became unenviable. Not only had they been permitted to enlist two years before the regulation boy's age— fourteen—but, by virtue, it seemed, of their extreme youth, they were now allowed to go to the Front—which thing had not happened to acting-drummers within the knowledge of boy. The Band which was to accompany the Regiment had been cut down to the regulation twenty men, the surplus returning to the ranks. Jakin and Lew were attached to the Band as supernumeraries, though they would much have preferred being Company buglers.

'Don't matter much,' said Jakin, after the medical inspection. 'Be thankful that we're 'lowed to go at all. The Doctor 'e said that if we could stand what we took from the Bazar-Sergeant's son we'd stand pretty nigh anything.'

'Which we will,' said Lew, looking tenderly at the ragged and ill-made housewife* that Cris had given him, with a lock of her hair worked into a sprawling 'L' upon the cover.

'It was the best I could,' she sobbed. 'I wouldn't let mother nor the Sergeants' tailor 'elp me. Keep it always, Piggy, an' remember I love you true.'

They marched to the railway station, nine hundred and sixty

strong, and every soul in cantonments turned out to see them go. The drummers gnashed their teeth at Jakin and Lew marching with the Band, the married women wept upon the platform, and the Regiment cheered its noble self black in the face.

'A nice level lot,' said the Colonel to the Second-in-Command as they watched the first four companies entraining.

'Fit to do anything,' said the Second-in-Command enthusiastically. 'But it seems to me they're a thought too young and tender for the work in hand. It's bitter cold up at the Front now.'

'They're sound enough,' said the Colonel. 'We must take our chance of sick casualties.'

So they went northward, ever northward, past droves and droves of camels, armies of camp followers, and legions of laden mules, the throng thickening day by day, till with a shriek the train pulled up at a hopelessly congested junction where six lines of temporary track accommodated six forty-waggon trains; where whistles blew, Babus* sweated, and Commissariat officers swore from dawn till far into the night amid the wind-driven chaff of the fodder-bales and the lowing of a thousand steers.

'Hurry up—you're badly wanted at the Front,' was the message that greeted the Fore and Fit, and the occupants of the Red Cross carriages told the same tale.

'"Tisn't so much the bloomin' fightin',' gasped a headbound trooper of Hussars to a knot of admiring Fore and Fits. ''Tisn't so much the bloomin' fightin', though there's enough o' that. It's the bloomin' food an' the bloomin' climate. Frost all night 'cept when it hails, an' biling sun all day, an' the water stinks fit to knock you down. I got my 'ead chipped like a egg; I've got pneumonia too, an' my guts is all out o' order. 'Tain't no bloomin' picnic in those parts, I can tell you.'

'Wot are the niggers like?' demanded a private.

'There's some prisoners in that train yonder. Go an' look at 'em. They're the aristocracy o' the country. The common folk are a dashed sight uglier. If you want to know what they fight with, reach under my seat an' pull out the long knife that's there.'

They dragged out and beheld for the first time the grim, bone-handled, triangular Afghan knife. It was almost as long as Lew.

'That's the thing to jint ye,' said the trooper feebly. 'It can take off a man's arm at the shoulder as easy as slicin' butter. I halved the beggar that used that ''un, but there's more of his likes up above. They don't understand thrustin', but they're devils to slice.'

The men strolled across the tracks to inspect the Afghan prisoners. They were unlike any 'niggers' that the Fore and Fit had ever met—these huge, black-haired, scowling sons of the Beni-Israel.* As the men stared the Afghans spat freely and muttered one to another with lowered eyes.

'My eyes! Wot awful swine!' said Jakin, who was in the rear of the procession. 'Say, old man, how you got puckrowed,* eh? Kiswasti* you wasn't hanged for your ugly face, hey?'

The tallest of the company turned, his leg-irons clanking at the movement, and stared at the boy. 'See!' he cried to his fellows in Pushtu.* 'They send children against us. What a people, and what fools!'

'Hya*!' said Jakin, nodding his head cheerily. 'You go down-country. Khana get, peenikapanee* get—live like a bloomin' Rajah ke marfik.* That's a better bundobust* than baynit get it in your innards. Good-bye, ole man. Take care o' your beautiful figure-'ed, an' try to look kushy.'*

The men laughed and fell in for their first march, when they began to realize that a soldier's life was not all beer and skittles. They were much impressed with the size and bestial ferocity of the niggers whom they had now learned to call 'Paythans', and more with the exceeding discomfort of their own surroundings. Twenty old soldiers in the corps would have taught them how to make themselves moderately snug at night, but they had no old soldiers, and, as the troops on the line of march said, 'they lived like pigs'. They learned the heart-breaking cussedness of camp-kitchens and camels and the depravity of an E. P.* tent and a wither-wrung mule. They studied animalculæ in water, and developed a few cases of dysentery in that study.

At the end of their third march they were disagreeably surprised by the arrival in their camp of a hammered iron slug which, fired from a steady rest at seven hundred yards, flicked out the brains of a private seated by the fire. This robbed them of their peace for a night, and was the beginning of a long-range fire carefully calculated to that end. In the daytime they saw nothing except an unpleasant puff of smoke from a crag above the line of march. At night there were distant spurts of flame and occasional casualties, which set the whole camp blazing into the gloom and, occasionally, into opposite tents. Then they swore vehemently, and vowed that this was magnificent but not war.

Indeed it was not. The Regiment could not halt for reprisals against the sharpshooters of the countryside. Its duty was to go forward and make connection with the Scotch and Gurkha troops* with which it was brigaded. The Afghans knew this, and knew too, after their first tentative shots, that they were dealing with a raw regiment. Thereafter they devoted themselves to the task of keeping the Fore and Fit on the strain. Not for anything would they have taken equal liberties with a seasoned corps—with the wicked little Gurkhas, whose delight it was to lie out in the open on a dark night and stalk their stalkers—with the terrible, big men dressed in women's clothes, who could be heard praying to their God in the night-watches, and whose peace of mind no amount of sniping could shake—or with those vile Sikhs, who marched so ostentatiously unprepared, and who dealt out such grim reward to those who tried to profit by that unpreparedness. This white regiment was different—quite different. It slept like a hog, and, like a hog, charged in every direction when it was roused. Its sentries walked with a footfall that could be heard for a quarter of a mile; would fire at anything that moved—even a driven donkey—and when they had once fired, could be scientifically 'rushed' and laid out a horror and an offence against the morning sun. Then there were camp-followers who straggled and could be cut up without fear. Their shrieks would disturb the white boys, and the loss of their services would inconvenience them sorely.

Thus, at every march, the hidden enemy became bolder and the regiment writhed and twisted under attacks it could not avenge. The crowning triumph was a sudden night-rush ending in the cutting of many tent-ropes, the collapse of the sodden canvas, and a glorious knifing of the men who struggled and kicked below. It was a great deed, neatly carried out, and it shook the already shaken nerves of the Fore and Fit. All the courage that they had been required to exercise up to this point was the 'two o'clock in the morning courage'; and, so far, they had only succeeded in shooting their own comrades and losing their sleep.

Sullen, discontented, cold, savage, sick, with their uniforms dulled and unclean, the Fore and Fit joined their Brigade.

'I hear you had a tough time of it coming up,' said the Brigadier. But when he saw the hospital-sheets his face fell.

'This is bad,' said he to himself. 'They're as rotten as sheep.' And aloud to the Colonel—'I'm afraid we can't spare you just yet. We want all we have, else I should have given you ten days to recover in.'

The Colonel winced. 'On my honour, Sir,' he returned, 'there is not the least necessity to think of sparing us. My men have been rather mauled and upset without a fair return. They only want to go in somewhere where they can see what's before them.'

'Can't say I think much of the Fore and Fit,' said the Brigadier in confidence to his Brigade-Major. 'They've lost all their soldiering, and, by the trim of them, might have marched through the country* from the other side. A more fagged-out set of men I never put eyes on.'

'Oh, they'll improve as the work goes on. The parade gloss has been rubbed off a little, but they'll put on field polish before long,' said the Brigade-Major. 'They've been mauled, and they don't quite understand it.'

They did not. All the hitting was on one side, and it was cruelly hard hitting with accessories that made them sick. There was also the real sickness that laid hold of a strong man and dragged him howling to the grave. Worst of all, their officers knew just as little of the country as the men themselves, and looked as if they did. The Fore and Fit were in a thoroughly unsatisfactory condition, but they believed that all would be well if they could once get a fair go-in at the enemy. Pot-shots up and down the valleys were unsatisfactory, and the bayonet never seemed to get a chance. Perhaps it was as well, for a long-limbed Afghan with a knife had a reach of eight feet, and could carry away lead that would disable three Englishmen.

The Fore and Fit would like some rifle-practice at the enemy—all seven hundred rifles blazing together. That wish showed the mood of the men.

The Gurkhas walked into their camp, and in broken, bar-rack-room English strove to fraternise with them; offered them pipes of tobacco and stood them treat at the canteen. But the Fore and Fit, not knowing much of the nature of the Gurkhas, treated them as they would treat any other 'niggers', and the little men in green trotted back to their firm friends the High-landers, and with many grins confided to them: 'That dam white regiment no dam use. Sulky—ugh! Dirty—ugh! *Hya*, any tot for Johnny?' Whereat the Highlanders smote the Gurkhas as to the head, and told them not to vilify a British Regiment, and the Gurkhas grinned cavernously, for the High-landers were their elder brothers and entitled to the privileges of kinship. The common soldier who touches a Gurkha is more likely to have his head sliced open.

Three days later the Brigadier arranged a battle according to the rules of war and the peculiarity of the Afghan tempera-ment. The enemy were massing in inconvenient strength among the hills, and the moving of many green standards warned him that the tribes were 'up' in aid of the Afghan regular troops. A squadron and a half of Bengal Lancers represented the available Cavalry, and two screw-guns* bor-rowed from a column thirty miles away, the Artillery at the General's disposal.

'If they stand, as I've a very strong notion they will, I fancy we shall see an infantry fight that will be worth watching,' said the Brigadier. 'We'll do it in style. Each regiment shall be played into action by its Band, and we'll hold the Cavalry in reserve.'

'For *all* the reserve?' somebody asked.

'For all the reserve; because we're going to crumple them up,' said the Brigadier, who was an extraordinary Brigadier, and did not believe in the value of a reserve when dealing with

Asiatics. Indeed, when you come to think of it, had the British Army consistently waited for reserves in all its little affairs, the boundaries of Our Empire would have stopped at Brighton beach.

That battle was to be a glorious battle.

The three regiments debouching from three separate gorges, after duly crowning the heights above,* were to converge from the centre, left, and right upon what we will call the Afghan army, then stationed towards the lower extremity of a flat-bottomed valley. Thus it will be seen that three sides of the valley practically belonged to the English, while the fourth was strictly Afghan property. In the event of defeat the Afghans had the rocky hills to fly to, where the fire from the guerrilla tribes in aid would cover their retreat. In the event of victory these same tribes would rush down and lend their weight to the rout of the British.

The screw-guns were to shell the head of each Afghan rush that was made in close formation, and the Cavalry, held in reserve in the right valley, were to gently stimulate the break-up which would follow on the combined attack. The Brigadier, sitting upon a rock overlooking the valley, would watch the battle unrolled at his feet. The Fore and Fit would debouch from the central gorge, the Gurkhas from the left, and the Highlanders from the right, for the reason that the left flank of the enemy seemed as though it required the most hammering. It was not every day that an Afghan force would take ground in the open, and the Brigadier was resolved to make the most of it.

'If we only had a few more men,' he said plaintively, 'we could surround the creatures and crumple 'em up thoroughly. As it is, I'm afraid we can only cut them up as they run. It's a great pity.'

The Fore and Fit had enjoyed unbroken peace for five days, and were beginning, in spite of dysentery, to recover their nerve. But they were not happy, for they did not know the work in hand, and had they known, would not have known how to do it. Throughout those five days in which old soldiers might have taught them the craft of the game, they discussed together their misadventures in the past—how such an one was alive at dawn and dead ere the dusk, and with what shrieks and struggles such another had given up his soul under the Afghan knife. Death was a new and horrible thing to the sons of mechanics who were used to die decently of zymotic* disease; and their careful conservation in barracks had done nothing to make them look upon it with less dread.

Very early in the dawn the bugles began to blow, and the Fore and Fit, filled with a misguided enthusiasm, turned out without waiting for a cup of coffee and a biscuit; and were rewarded by being kept under arms in the cold while the other regiments leisurely prepared for the fray. All the world knows that it is ill taking the breeks off a Highlander. It is much iller to try to make him stir unless he is convinced of the necessity for haste.

The Fore and Fit waited, leaning upon their rifles and listening to the protests of their empty stomachs. The Colonel did his best to remedy the default of lining as soon as it was borne in upon him that the affair would not begin at once, and so well did he succeed that the coffee was just ready when—the men moved off, their Band leading. Even then there had been a mistake in time, and the Fore and Fit came out into the valley ten minutes before the proper hour. Their Band wheeled to the right after reaching the open, and retired behind a little rocky knoll still playing while the regiment went past.

It was not a pleasant sight that opened on the uninstructed view, for the lower end of the valley appeared to be filled by an army in position—real and actual regiments attired in red coats, and—of this there was no doubt—firing Martini–Henry bullets* which cut up the ground a hundred yards in front of the leading company. Over that pock-marked ground the regiment had to pass, and it opened the ball with a general and profound courtesy to the piping pickets;* ducking in perfect time, as though it had been brazed on a rod. Being half capable of thinking for itself, it fired a volley by the simple process of pitching its rifle into its shoulder and pulling the trigger. The bullets may have accounted for some of the watchers on the hillside, but they certainly did not affect the mass of enemy in front, while the noise of the rifles drowned any orders that might have been given.

'Good God!' said the Brigadier, sitting on the rock high above all. 'That battalion has spoilt the whole show. Hurry up the others, and let the screw-guns get off.'

But the screw-guns, in working round the heights, had stumbled upon a wasps' nest of a small mud fort which they incontinently shelled at eight hundred yards, to the huge discomfort of the occupants, who were unaccustomed to weapons of such devilish precision.

The Fore and Fit continued to go forward, but with shortened stride. Where were the other regiments, and why did these niggers use Martinis? They took open order instinctively, lying down and firing at random, rushing a few paces forward and lying down again, according to the regulations. Once in this formation, each man felt himself desperately alone, and edged in towards his fellow for comfort's sake.

Then the crack of his neighbour's rifle at his ear led him to fire as rapidly as he could—again for the sake of the comfort of the noise. The reward was not long delayed. Five volleys plunged the files in banked smoke impenetrable to the eye,* and the bullets began to take ground twenty or thirty yards in front of the firers, as the weight of the bayonet dragged down and to the right arms wearied with holding the kick of the jolting Martini. The Company Commanders peered helplessly through the smoke, the more nervous mechanically trying to fan it away with their helmets.

'High and to the left!' bawled a Captain till he was hoarse. 'No good! Cease firing, and let it drift away a bit.'

Three and four times the bugles shrieked the order, and when it was obeyed the Fore and Fit looked that their foe should be lying before them in mown swaths of men. A light wind drove the smoke to leeward, and showed the enemy still in position and apparently unaffected. A quarter of a ton of lead had been buried a furlong in front of them, as the ragged earth attested.

That was not demoralizing to the Afghans, who have not European nerves. They were waiting for the mad riot to die down, and were firing quietly into the heart of the smoke. A private of the Fore and Fit spun up his company shrieking with agony, another was kicking the earth and gasping, and a third, ripped through the lower intestines by a jagged bullet, was calling aloud on his comrades to put him out of his pain. These were the casualties, and they were not soothing to hear or see. The smoke cleared to a dull haze.

Then the foe began to shout with a great shouting, and a mass—a black mass—detached itself from the main body, and rolled over the ground at horrid speed. It was composed of, perhaps, three hundred men, who would shout and fire and slash if the rush of their fifty comrades who were determined to die carried home. The fifty were Ghazis,* half maddened with drugs and wholly mad with religious fanaticism. When they rushed the British fire ceased, and in the lull the order was given to close ranks and meet them with the bayonet.

Any one who knew the business could have told the Fore and Fit that the only way of dealing with a Ghazi rush is by volleys at long ranges; because a man who means to die, who desires to die, who will gain heaven by dying, must, in nine cases out of ten, kill a man who has a lingering prejudice in favour of life. Where they should have closed and gone forward, the Fore and Fit opened out and skirmished, and where they should have opened out and fired, they closed and waited.

A man dragged from his blankets half awake and unfed is never in a pleasant frame of mind. Nor does his happiness increase when he watches the whites of the eyes of three hundred six-foot fiends upon whose beards the foam is lying, upon whose tongues is a roar of wrath, and in whose hands are yard-long knives.

The Fore and Fit heard the Gurkha bugles bringing that regiment forward at the double, while the neighing of the Highland pipes came from the right.* They strove to stay where they were, though the bayonets wavered down the line like the oars of a ragged boat. Then they felt body to body the amazing physical strength of their foes; a shriek of pain ended the rush, and the knives fell amid scenes not to be told. The men clubbed together and smote blindly—as often as not at their own fellows. Their front crumpled like paper, and the fifty Ghazis passed on; their backers, now drunk with success, fighting as madly as they.

Then the rear ranks were bidden to close up, and the

subalterns dashed into the stew—alone. For the rear ranks had heard the clamour in front, the yells and the howls of pain, and had seen the dark stale blood that makes afraid. They were not going to stay. It was the rushing of the camps over again. Let their officers go to Hell, if they chose; they would get away from the knives.

'Come on!' shrieked the subalterns, and their men, cursing them, drew back, each closing into his neighbour and wheeling round.

Charteris and Devlin, subalterns of the last company, faced their death alone in the belief that their men would follow.

'You've killed me, you cowards,' sobbed Devlin and dropped, cut from the shoulder-strap to the centre of the chest, and a fresh detachment of his men retreating, always retreating, trampled him under foot as they made for the pass whence they had emerged. . .

> 'I kissed her in the kitchen and I kissed her in the hall.
>   Child'un, child'un, follow me!
> "Oh Golly", said the cook, "is he gwine to kiss us all?"
>   Halla—Halla—Halla—Hallelujah!'*

The Gurkhas were pouring through the left gorge and over the heights at the double to the invitation of their Regimental Quick-step. The black rocks were crowned with dark green spiders as the bugles gave tongue jubilantly:—

> 'In the morning! In the morning by the bright light!
> When Gabriel blows his trumpet in the morning!'*

The Gurkha rear companies tripped and blundered over loose stones. The front-files halted for a moment to take stock of the valley and to settle stray boot-laces. Then a happy little sigh of contentment soughed down the ranks, and it was as though the land smiled, for behold there below were the enemy, and it was to meet them that the Gurkhas had doubled so hastily. There was much enemy. There would be amusement. The little men hitched their *kukris** well to hand, and gaped expectantly at their officers as terriers grin ere the stone is cast for them to fetch. The Gurkhas' ground sloped downward to the valley, and they enjoyed a fair view of the proceedings. They sat upon the boulders to watch, for their officers

were not going to waste their wind in assisting to repulse a
Ghazi rush more than half a mile away. Let the white men look
to their own front.

'Hi! yi!' said the Subadar-Major,* who was sweating pro-
fusely. 'Dam fools yonder, stand close-order! This is no time
for close order, it is the time for volleys. Ugh!'

Horrified, amused, and indignant, the Gurkhas beheld the
retirement of the Fore and Fit with a running chorus of oaths
and commentaries.

'They run! The white men run! Colonel Sahib, may *we* also
do a little running?' murmured Runbir Thappa, the Senior
Jemadar.*

But the Colonel would have none of it. 'Let the beggars be
cut up a little,' said he wrathfully. 'Serves 'em right. They'll be
prodded into facing round in a minute.' He looked through his
field-glasses, and caught the glint of an officer's sword.

'Beating 'em with the flat—damned conscripts! How the
Ghazis are walking into them!' said he.

The Fore and Fit, heading back, bore with them their offi-
cers. The narrowness of the pass forced the mob into solid
formation, and the rear-rank delivered some sort of a wavering
volley. The Ghazis drew off, for they did not know what
reserves the gorge might hide. Moreover, it was never wise to
chase white men too far. They returned as wolves return to
cover, satisfied with the slaughter that they had done, and only
stopping to slash at the wounded on the ground. A quarter of a
mile had the Fore and Fit retreated, and now, jammed in the
pass, were quivering with pain, shaken and demoralized with
fear, while the officers, maddened beyond control, smote the
men with the hilts and the flats of their swords.

'Get back! Get back, you cowards—you women! Right about
face—column of companies, form—you hounds!' shouted the
Colonel, and the subalterns swore aloud. But the Regiment
wanted to go—to get anywhere out of the range of those merci-
less knives. It swayed to and fro irresolutely with shouts and
outcries, while from the right the Gurkhas dropped volley after
volley of cripple-stopper Snider bullets* at long range into the
mob of the Ghazis returning to their own troops.

The Fore and Fit Band, though protected from direct fire by

the rocky knoll under which it had sat down, fled at the first rush. Jakin and Lew would have fled also, but their short legs left them fifty yards in the rear, and by the time the Band had mixed with the regiment, they were painfully aware that they would have to close in alone and unsupported.

'Get back to that rock,' gasped Jakin. 'They won't see us there.'

And they returned to the scattered instruments of the Band, their hearts nearly bursting their ribs.

'Here's a nice show for *us*,' said Jakin, throwing himself full length on the ground. 'A bloomin' fine show for British Infantry! Oh, the devils! They've gone an' left us alone here! Wot'll we do?'

Lew took possession of a cast-off water bottle, which naturally was full of canteen rum, and drank till he coughed again.

'Drink,' said he shortly. 'They'll come back in a minute or two—you see.'

Jakin drank, but there was no sign of the regiment's return. They could hear a dull clamour from the head of the valley of retreat, and saw the Ghazis slink back, quickening their pace as the Gurkhas fired at them.

'We're all that's left of the Band, an' we'll be cut up as sure as death,' said Jakin.

'I'll die game, then,' said Lew thickly, fumbling with his tiny drummer's sword. The drink was working on his brain as it was on Jakin's.

''Old on! I know somethin' better than fightin',' said Jakin, 'stung by the splendour of a sudden thought'* due chiefly to rum. 'Tip our bloomin' cowards yonder the word to come back. The Paythan beggars are well away. Come on, Lew! We won't get 'urt. Take the fife an' give me the drum. The Old Step for all your bloomin' guts are worth! There's a few of our men comin' back now. Stand up, ye drunken little defaulter. By your right—quick march!'

He slipped the drum-sling over his shoulder, thrust the fife into Lew's hand, and the two boys marched out of the cover of the rock into the open, making a hideous hash of the first bars of the 'British Grenadiers'.

As Lew had said, a few of the Fore and Fit were coming back sullenly and shamefacedly under the stimulus of blows and abuse. Their red coats shone at the head of the valley, and behind them were wavering bayonets. But between this shattered line and the enemy, who with Afghan suspicion feared that the hasty retreat meant an ambush, and had not moved therefore, lay half a mile of level ground dotted only with the wounded.

The tune settled into full swing and the boys kept shoulder to shoulder, Jakin banging the drum as one possessed. The one fife made a thin and pitiful squeaking, but the tune carried far, even to the Gurkhas.

'Come on, you dogs!' muttered Jakin to himself. 'Are we to play forhever?' Lew was staring straight in front of him and marching more stiffly than ever he had done on parade.

And in bitter mockery of the distant mob, the old tune of the Old Line* shrilled and rattled:—

> 'Some talk of Alexander,
>   And some of Hercules;
> Of Hector and Lysander,
>   And such great names as these!'

There was a far-off clapping of hands from the Gurkhas, and a roar from the Highlanders in the distance, but never a shot was fired by British or Afghan. The two little red dots moved forward in the open parallel to the enemy's front.

> 'But of all the world's great heroes
>   There's none that can compare,
> With a tow-row-row-row-row-row,
>   To the British Grenadier!'

The men of the Fore and Fit were gathering thick at the entrance to the plain. The Brigadier on the heights far above was speechless with rage. Still no movement from the enemy. The day stayed to watch the children.

Jakin halted and beat the long roll of the Assembly, while the fife squealed despairingly.

'Right about face! Hold up, Lew, you're drunk,' said Jakin. They wheeled and marched back:—

'Those heroes of antiquity
      Ne'er saw a cannon-ball,
Nor knew the force o' powder'

'Here they come!' said Jakin. 'Go on, Lew':—

'To scare their foes withal!'

The Fore and Fit were pouring out of the valley. What officers had said to men in that time of shame and humiliation will never be known; for neither officers nor men speak of it now.

'They are coming anew!' shouted a priest among the Afghans. 'Do not kill the boys! Take them alive, and they shall be of our faith.'

But the first volley had been fired, and Lew dropped on his face. Jakin stood for a minute, spun round and collapsed, as the Fore and Fit came forward, the curses of their officers in their ears, and in their hearts the shame of open shame.

Half the men had seen the drummers die, and they made no sign. They did not even shout. They doubled out straight across the plain in open order, and they did not fire.

'This,' said the Colonel of Gurkhas softly, 'is the real attack, as it should have been delivered. Come on, my children.'

'Ulu-lu-lu-lu!' squealed the Gurkhas, and came down with a joyful clicking of *kukris*—those vicious Gurkha knives.

On the right there was no rush. The Highlanders, cannily commending their souls to God (for it matters as much to a dead man whether he has been shot in a Border scuffle or at Waterloo), opened out and fired according to their custom, that is to say, without heat and without intervals, while the screw-guns, having disposed of the impertinent mud fort afore-mentioned, dropped shell after shell into the clusters round the flickering green standards on the heights.

'Charrging is an unfortunate necessity,' murmured the Colour-Sergeant of the right company of the Highlanders. 'It makes the men sweer so—but I am thinkin' that it will come to a charrge if these black devils stand much longer. Stewarrt, man, you're firing into the eye of the sun, and he'll not take any harm for Government ammuneetion. A foot lower and a great deal slower! What are the English doing? They're very quiet there in the centre. Running again?'

The English were not running. They were hacking and hewing and stabbing, for though one white man is seldom physically a match for an Afghan in a sheepskin or wadded coat, yet, through the pressure of many white men behind, and a certain thirst for revenge in his heart, he becomes capable of doing much with both ends of his rifle. The Fore and Fit held their fire till one bullet could drive through five or six men, and the front of the Afghan force gave on the volley. They then selected their men, and slew them with deep gasps and short hacking coughs, and groanings of leather belts against strained bodies, and realized for the first time that an Afghan attacked is far less formidable than an Afghan attacking: which fact old soldiers might have told them.

But they had no old soldiers in their ranks.

The Gurkhas' stall at the bazar was the noisiest, for the men were engaged—to a nasty noise as of beef being cut on the block—with the *kukri*, which they preferred to the bayonet; well knowing how the Afghan hates the half-moon blade.

As the Afghans wavered, the green standards on the mountain moved down to assist them in a last rally. This was unwise. The Lancers chafing in the right gorge had thrice despatched their only subaltern as galloper to report on the progress of affairs. On the third occasion he returned, with a bullet-graze on his knee, swearing strange oaths in Hindustani, and saying that all things were ready. So that squadron swung round the right of the Highlanders with a wicked whistling of wind in the pennons of its lances, and fell upon the remnant just when, according to all the rules of war, it should have waited for the foe to show more signs of wavering.

But it was a dainty charge, deftly delivered, and it ended by the Cavalry finding itself at the head of the pass by which the Afghans intended to retreat; and down the track that the lances had made streamed two companies of the Highlanders, which was never intended by the Brigadier. The new development was successful. It detached the enemy from his base as a sponge is torn from a rock, and left him ringed about with fire in that pitiless plain. And as a sponge is chased round the bath-tub by the hand of the bather, so were the Afghans chased till they broke into little detachments much more difficult to dispose of than large masses.

'See!' quoth the Brigadier. 'Everything has come as I arranged. We've cut their base, and now we'll bucket 'em to pieces.'

A direct hammering was all that the Brigadier had dared to hope for, considering the size of the force at his disposal; but men who stand or fall by the errors of their opponents may be forgiven for turning Chance into Design. The bucketing went forward merrily. The Afghan forces were upon the run—the run of wearied wolves who snarl and bite over their shoulders. The red lances dipped by twos and threes, and, with a shriek, up rose the lance-butt, like a spar on a stormy sea, as the trooper cantering forward cleared his point. The Lancers kept between their prey and the steep hills, for all who could were trying to escape from the valley of death. The Highlanders gave the fugitives two hundred yards' law, and then brought them down, gasping and choking, ere they could reach the protection of the boulders above. The Gurkhas followed suit; but the Fore and Fit were killing on their own account, for they had penned a mass of men between their bayonets and a wall of rock, and the flash of the rifles was lighting the wadded coats.

'We cannot hold them, Captain Sahib!' panted a Rissaldar* of Lancers. 'Let us try the carbine. The lance is good, but it wastes time.'

They tried the carbine, and still the enemy melted away— fled up the hills by hundreds when there were only twenty bullets to stop them. On the heights the screw-guns ceased firing—they had run out of ammunition—and the Brigadier groaned, for the musketry fire could not sufficiently smash the retreat. Long before the last volleys were fired the doolies* were out in force looking for the wounded. The battle was over, and, but for want of fresh troops, the Afghans would have been wiped off the earth. As it was they counted their dead by hundreds, and nowhere were the dead thicker than in the track of the Fore and Fit.

But the Regiment did not cheer with the Highlanders, nor did they dance uncouth dances with the Gurkhas among the dead. They looked under their brows at the Colonel as they leaned upon their rifles and panted.

'Get back to camp, you. Haven't you disgraced yourselves enough for one day? Go and look to the wounded. It's all you're fit for,' said the Colonel. Yet for the past hour the Fore and Fit had been doing all that mortal commander could expect. They had lost heavily because they did not know how to set about their business with proper skill, but they had borne themselves gallantly, and this was their reward.

A young and sprightly Colour-Sergeant, who had begun to imagine himself a hero, offered his water-bottle to a High-lander, whose tongue was black with thirst. 'I drink with no cowards,' answered the youngster huskily, and, turning to a Gurkha, said, '*Hya*, Johnny! Drink water got it?' The Gurkha grinned and passed his bottle. The Fore and Fit said no word.

They went back to camp when the field of strife had been a little mopped up and made presentable, and the Brigadier, who saw himself a Knight in three months, was the only soul who was complimentary to them. The Colonel was heart-broken, and the officers were savage and sullen.

'Well,' said the Brigadier, 'they are young troops of course, and it was not unnatural that they should retire in disorder for a bit.'

'Oh, my only Aunt Maria!' murmured a junior Staff Officer. 'Retire in disorder! It was a bally run!'

'But they came again, as we all know,' cooed the Brigadier, the Colonel's ashy-white face before him, 'and they behaved as well as could possibly be expected. Behaved beautifully, indeed. I was watching them. It isn't a matter to take to heart, Colonel. As some German General said of his men, they wanted to be shooted over a little, that was all.' To himself he said— 'Now they're blooded I can give 'em responsible work. It's as well that they got what they did. Teach 'em more than any amount of rifle flirtations, that will—later—run alone and bite. Poor old Colonel, though!'

All that afternoon the heliograph* winked and flickered on the hills, striving to tell the good news to a mountain forty miles away. And in the evening there arrived, dusty, sweating, and sore, a misguided Correspondent who had gone out to assist at a trumpery village-burning, and who had read off the message from afar, cursing his luck the while.

'Let's have the details somehow—as full as ever you can, please. It's the first time I've ever been left this campaign,' said the Correspondent to the Brigadier, and the Brigadier, nothing loth, told him how an Army of Communication had been crumpled up, destroyed, and all but annihilated by the craft, strategy, wisdom, and foresight of the Brigadier.

But some say, and among these be the Gurkhas who watched on the hillside, that that battle was won by Jakin and Lew, whose little bodies were borne up just in time to fit two gaps at the head of the big ditch-grave for the dead under the heights of Jagai.

That Day*

IT GOT beyond all orders an' it got beyond all 'ope;
   It got to shammin' wounded an' retirin' from the 'alt.
'Ole companies was lookin' for the nearest road to slope;
   It were just a bloomin' knock-out—an' our fault!

     Now there ain't no chorus 'ere to give,
       Nor there ain't no band to play;
     An' I wish I was dead 'fore I done what I did,
       Or seen what I seed that day!

We was sick o' bein' punished, an' we let 'em know it, too;
   An' a company-commander up an' 'it us with a sword,
An' some one shouted ''Ook it!' an' it come to *sove-ki-poo*,*
   An' we chucked our rifles from us—O my Gawd!

There was thirty dead an' wounded on the ground we
     wouldn't keep—
   No, there wasn't more than twenty when the front begun
     to go—
But, Christ! along the line o' flight they cut us up like sheep,
   An' that was all we gained by doin' so!

I 'eard the knives be'ind me, but I dursn't face my man,
   Nor I don't know where I went to, 'cause I didn't 'alt to see,
Till I 'eard a beggar squealin' out for quarter as 'e ran,
   An' I thought I knew the voice an'—it was me!

We was 'idin' under bedsteads more than 'arf a march away:
   We was lyin' up like rabbits all about the country-side;
An' the Major cursed 'is Maker 'cause 'e'd lived to see that
     day,
   An' the Colonel broke 'is sword acrost, an' cried.

We was rotten 'fore we started—we was never disci*plined*;
   We made it out a favour if an order was obeyed.
Yes, every little drummer 'ad 'is rights an' wrongs to mind,
   So we had to pay for teachin'—an' we paid!

The papers 'id it 'andsome, but you know the Army knows;
  We was put to groomin' camels till the regiments
    withdrew.
An' they gave us each a medal for subduin' England's foes,
  An' I 'ope you like my song—because it's true!

> *An' there ain't no chorus 'ere to give,*
> *Nor there ain't no band to play;*
> *But I wish I was dead 'fore I done what I did,*
> *Or seen what I seed that day!*

A Conference of the Powers*

Life liveth but in life, and doth not roam
To other lands if all be well at home:
'Solid as ocean foam,' quoth ocean foam.*

THE room was blue with the smoke of three pipes and a cigar. The leave-season had opened in India, and the firstfruits on this side of the water were 'Tick' Boileau, of the 45th Bengal Cavalry, who called on me, after three years' absence, to discuss old things which had happened. Fate, who always does her work handsomely, sent up the same staircase within the same hour The Infant,* fresh from Upper Burma, and he and Boileau looking out of my window saw walking in the street one Nevin, late in a Gurkha regiment which had been through the Black Mountain Expedition.* They yelled to him to come up, and the whole street was aware that they desired him to come up, and he came up, and there followed Pandemonium in my room because we had foregathered from the ends of the earth, and three of us were on a holiday, and none of us were twenty-five, and all the delights of all London lay waiting our pleasure.

Boileau took the only other chair, The Infant, by right of his bulk, the sofa; and Nevin, being a little man, sat cross-legged on the top of the revolving bookcase, and we all said, 'Who'd ha' thought it!' and 'What are you doing here?' till speculation was exhausted and the talk went over to inevitable 'shop'. Boileau was full of a great scheme for winning a military attaché-ship at St Petersburg; Nevin had hopes of the Staff College, and The Infant had been moving heaven and earth and the Horse Guards* for a commission in the Egyptian army.

'What's the use o' that?' said Nevin, twirling round on the bookcase.

'Oh, heaps! 'Course, if you get stuck with a Fellaheen* regiment, you're sold; but if you are appointed to a Sudanese lot, you're in clover. They are first-class fighting-men—and just think of the eligible central position of Egypt in the next row.'

This was putting the match to a magazine. We all began to explain the Central Asian question off-hand, flinging army corps from the Helmund to Kashmir with more than Russian recklessness. Each of the boys made for himself a war to his own liking, and when we had settled all the details of Armageddon,* killed all our senior officers, handled a division apiece, and nearly torn the Atlas in two in attempts to explain our theories, Boileau needs must lift up his voice above the clamour, and cry, 'Anyhow it'll be the hell of a row!' in tones that carried conviction far down the staircase.

Entered, unperceived in the smoke, William the Silent. 'Gen'leman to see you sir,' said he, and disappeared, leaving in his stead none other than Mr Eustace Cleever. William would have introduced the Dragon of Wantley* with equal disregard of present company.

'I—I beg your pardon. I didn't know that there was anybody—with you. I——'

But it was not seemly to allow Mr Cleever to depart: for he was a great man. The boys remained where they were, since any movement would have choked up the little room. Only when they saw his grey hairs they stood on their feet, and when The Infant caught the name, he said:

'Are you—did you write that book called *As it was in the Beginning*?'

Mr Cleever admitted that he had written the book.

'Then—then I don't know how to thank you, sir,' said The Infant, flushing pink. 'I was brought up in the country you wrote about—all my people live there; and I read the book in camp on the Hlinedatalone, and I knew every stick and stone, and the dialect too; and, by Jove! it was just like being at home and hearing the country-people talk. Nevin, you know *As it was in the Beginning*. So does Ti—Boileau.'

Mr Cleever has tasted as much praise, public and private, as one man may safely swallow; but it seemed to me that the outspoken admiration in The Infant's eyes and the little stir in the little company came home to him very nearly indeed.

'Won't you take the sofa?' said The Infant. 'I'll sit on

Boileau's chair, and——' Here he looked at me to spur me to my duties as a host; but I was watching the novelist's face. Cleever had not the least intention of going away, but settled himself on the sofa.

Following the first great law of the Army, which says 'all property is common except money, and you've only got to ask the next man for that', The Infant offered tobacco and drink. It was the least he could do; but not the most lavish praise in the world held half as much appreciation and reverence as The Infant's simple 'Say when, sir,' above the long glass.

Cleever said 'when', and more thereto, for he was a golden talker, and he sat in the midst of hero-worship devoid of all taint of self-interest. The boys asked him of the birth of his book and whether it was hard to write, and how his notions came to him; and he answered with the same absolute simplicity as he was questioned. His big eyes twinkled, he dug his long thin hands into his grey beard and tugged it as he grew animated. He dropped little by little from the peculiar pinching of the broader vowels—the indefinable 'Euh', that runs through the speech of the pundit caste*—and the elaborate choice of words, to freely-mouthed 'ows' and 'ois', and, for him at least, unfettered colloquialisms. He could not altogether understand the boys who hung upon his words so reverently. The line of the chin-strap, that still showed white and untanned on cheek-bone and jaw, the steadfast young eyes puckered at the corners of the lids with much staring through red-hot sunshine, the slow, untroubled breathing, and the curious, crisp, curt speech seemed to puzzle him equally. He could create men and women, and send them to the uttermost ends of the earth, to help delight and comfort; he knew every mood of the fields, and could interpret them to the cities, and he knew the hearts of many in cities and the country, but he had hardly, in forty years, come into contact with the thing which is called a Subaltern of the Line. He told the boys this in his own way.

'Well, how should you?' said The Infant. 'You—you're quite different, y' see, sir.'

The Infant expressed his ideas in his tone rather than his words, but Cleever understood the compliment.

'We're only Subs,' said Nevin, 'and we aren't exactly the sort of men you'd meet much in your life, I s'pose.'

'That's true,' said Cleever. 'I live chiefly among men who write, and paint, and sculp, and so forth. We have our own talk and our own interests, and the outer world doesn't trouble us much.'

'That must be awfully jolly,' said Boileau, at a venture. 'We have our own "shop", too, but 'tisn't half as interesting as yours, of course. You know all the men who've ever done anything; and we only knock about from place to place, and we do nothing.'

'The Army's a very lazy profession if you choose to make it so,' said Nevin. 'When there's nothing going on, there is nothing going on, and you lie up.'

'Or try to get a billet somewhere, to be ready for the next show,' said The Infant with a chuckle.

'To me,' said Cleever softly, 'the whole idea of warfare seems so foreign and unnatural, so essentially vulgar, if I may say so, that I can hardly appreciate your sensations. Of course, though, any change from life in garrison towns must be a godsend to you.'

Like many home-staying Englishmen, Cleever believed that the newspaper phrase he quoted covered the whole duty of the Army whose toils enabled him to enjoy his many-sided life in peace. The remark was not a happy one, for Boileau had just come off the Frontier, The Infant had been on the warpath for nearly eighteen months, and the little red man Nevin two months before had been sleeping under the stars at the peril of his life. But none of them tried to explain, till I ventured to point out that they had all seen service and were not used to idling. Cleever took in the idea slowly.

'Seen service?' said he. Then, as a child might ask, 'Tell me. Tell me everything about everything.'

'How do you mean?' said The Infant, delighted at being directly appealed to by the great man.

'Good Heavens! How am I to make you understand if you can't see? In the first place, what is your age?'

'Twenty-three next July,' said The Infant promptly.

Cleever questioned the others with his eyes.

'I'm twenty-four,' said Nevin.

'And I'm twenty-two,' said Boileau.

'And you've all seen service?'

'We've all knocked about a little bit, sir, but The Infant's the war-worn veteran. He's had two years' work in Upper Burma,' said Nevin.

'When you say work, what do you mean, you extraordinary creatures?'

'Explain it, Infant,' said Nevin.

'Oh, keeping things in order generally, and running about after little *dakus*—that's dacoits*—and so on. There's nothing to explain.'

'Make that young Leviathan speak,' said Cleever impatiently, above his glass.

'How can he speak?' said I. 'He's done the work. The two don't go together. But, Infant, you're ordered to *bukh*.'*

'What about? I'll try.'

'*Bukh* about a *daur*.* You've been on heaps of 'em,' said Nevin.

'What in the world does that mean? Has the Army a language of its own?'

The Infant turned very red. He was afraid he was being laughed at, and he detested talking before outsiders; but it was the author of *As it was in the Beginning* who waited.

'It's all so new to me,' pleaded Cleever; 'and—and you said you liked my book.'

This was a direct appeal that The Infant could understand, and he began rather flurriedly, with much slang bred of nervousness—

'Pull me up, sir, if I say anything you don't follow. About six months before I took my leave out of Burma, I was on the Hlinedatalone, up near the Shan States, with sixty Tommies—private soldiers, that is—and another subaltern, a year senior to me. The Burmese business was a subalterns' war, and our forces were split up into little detachments, all running about the country and trying to keep the dacoits quiet. The dacoits were having a first-class time, y' know—filling women up with kerosine and setting 'em alight, and burning villages, and crucifying people.'

The wonder in Eustace Cleever's eyes deepened. He could not quite realize that the Cross still existed in any form.

'Have you ever seen a crucifixion?' said he.

'Of course not. Shouldn't have allowed it if I had; but I've seen the corpses. The dacoits had a trick of sending a crucified corpse down the river on a raft, just to show they were keeping their tails up and enjoying themselves. Well, that was the kind of people I had to deal with.'

'Alone?' said Cleever. Solitude of the soul he could understand—none better—but he had never in the body moved five miles from his fellows.

'I had my men, but the rest of it was pretty much alone. The nearest post that could give me orders was fifteen miles away, and we used to heliograph to them, and they used to give us orders same way—too many orders.'

'Who was your C.O.?' said Boileau.

'Bounderby—Major. *Pukka** Bounderby; more Bounder than *pukka*. He went out up Bhamo way. Shot, or cut down, last year,' said The Infant.

'What are these interludes in a strange tongue?' said Cleever to me.

'Professional information—like the Mississippi pilots' talk,' said I. 'He did not approve of his major, who died a violent death. Go on, Infant.'

'Far too many orders. You couldn't take the Tommies out for a two days' *daur*—that's expedition—without being blown up for not asking leave. And the whole country was humming with dacoits. I used to send out spies, and act on their information. As soon as a man came in and told me of a gang in hiding, I'd take thirty men with some grub, and go out and look for them, while the other subaltern lay doggo in camp.'

'Lay! Pardon me, but *how* did he lie?' said Cleever.

'Lay doggo—lay quiet, with the other thirty men. When I came back, he'd take out his half of the men, and have a good time of his own.'

'Who was he?' said Boileau.

'Carter-Deecey, of the Aurungabadis. Good chap, but too *zubberdusty*, and went *bokhar* four days out of seven. He's gone out, too. Don't interrupt a man.'

Cleever looked helplessly at me.

'The other subaltern,' I translated swiftly, 'came from a native regiment, and was overbearing in his demeanour. He suffered much from the fever of the country, and is now dead. Go on, Infant.'

'After a bit we got into trouble for using the men on frivolous occasions, and so I used to put my signaller under arrest to prevent him reading the helio-orders. Then I'd go out and leave a message to be sent an hour after I got clear of the camp, something like this: "Received important information; start in an hour unless countermanded." If I was ordered back, it didn't much matter. I swore the C. O.'s watch was wrong, or something, when I came back. The Tommies enjoyed the fun, and—Oh, yes, there was one Tommy who was the bard of the detachment. He used to make up verses on everything that happened.'

'What sort of verses?' said Cleever.

'Lovely verses; and the Tommies used to sing 'em. There was one song with a chorus, and it went something like this.' The Infant dropped into the true barrack-room twang:

'Theebaw,* the Burma king, did a very foolish thing,
   When 'e mustered 'ostile forces in ar-rai,
'E little thought that *we*, from far across the sea,
   Would send our armies up to Mandalai!'

'O gorgeous!' said Cleever. 'And how magnificently direct! The notion of a regimental bard is new to me, but of course it must be so.'

'He was awf'ly popular with the men,' said The Infant. 'He had them all down in rhyme as soon as ever they had done anything. He was a great bard. He was always ready with an elegy when we picked up a Boh—that's a leader of dacoits.'

'How did you pick him up?' said Cleever.

'Oh! shot him if he wouldn't surrender.'

'You! Have you shot a man?'

There was a subdued chuckle from all three boys, and it dawned on the questioner that one experience in life which was denied to himself, and he weighed the souls of men in a balance, had been shared by three very young gentlemen of engaging appearance. He turned round on Nevin, who had climbed to the top of the bookcase, and was sitting cross-legged as before.

'And have you, too?'

'Think so,' said Nevin sweetly. 'In the Black Mountain. He was rolling cliffs on to my half-company, and spoiling our formation. I took a rifle from a man, and brought him down at the second shot.'

'Good Heavens! And how did you feel afterwards?'

'Thirsty. I wanted a smoke, too.'

Cleever looked at Boileau—the youngest. Surely his hands were guiltless of blood.

Boileau shook his head and laughed. 'Go on, Infant,' said he.

'And you too?' said Cleever.

'Fancy so. It was a case of cut, cut or be cut, with me; so I cut—One. I couldn't do any more, sir.'

Cleever looked as though he would like to ask many questions, but The Infant swept on, in the full tide of his tale.

'Well, we were called insubordinate young whelps at last, and strictly forbidden to take the Tommies out any more without orders. I wasn't sorry, because Tommy is such an exacting sort of creature. He wants to live as though he were in barracks all the time. I was grubbing on fowls and boiled corn, but my Tommies wanted their pound of fresh meat, and their half ounce of this, and their two ounces of t'other thing, and they used to come to me and badger me for plug-tobacco when we were four days in jungle. I said: "I can get you Burma tobacco, but I don't keep a canteen up my sleeve." They couldn't see it. They wanted all the luxuries of the season, confound 'em.'

'You were alone when you were dealing with these men?' said Cleever, watching The Infant's face under the palm of his hand. He was getting new ideas, and they seemed to trouble him.

'Of course, unless you count the mosquitoes. They were nearly as big as the men. After I had to lie doggo I began to look for something to do; and I was great pals with a man called Hicksey in the Police, the best man that ever stepped on earth; a first-class man.'

Cleever nodded applause. He knew how to appreciate enthusiasm.

'Hicksey and I were as thick as thieves. He had some Burma mounted police—rummy chaps, armed with sword and snider carbine. They rode punchy* Burma ponies with string stirrups, red cloth saddles, and red bell-rope head-stalls. Hicksey used to lend me six or eight of them when I asked him—nippy little devils, keen as mustard. But they told their wives too much, and all my plans got known, till I learned to give false marching orders over-night, and take the men to quite a different village in the morning. Then we used to catch the simple *daku* before breakfast, and made him very sick. It's a ghastly country on the Hlinedatalone; all bamboo jungle, with paths about four feet wide winding through it. The *dakus* knew all the paths, and potted at us as we came round a corner; but the mounted police knew the paths as well as the *dakus*, and we used to go stalking 'em in and out. Once we flushed 'em, the men on the ponies had the advantage of the men on foot. We held all the country absolutely quiet, for ten miles round, in about a month. Then we took Boh Na-ghee, Hicksey and I and the Civil officer. That was a lark!'

'I think I am beginning to understand a little,' said Cleever. 'It was a pleasure to you to administer and fight?'

'Rather! There's nothing nicer than a satisfactory little expedition, when you find your plans fit together, and your conformation's *teek*—correct, you know, and the whole *sub-chiz**—I mean, when everything works out like formulæ on a blackboard. Hicksey had all the information about the Boh. He had been burning villages and murdering people right and left, and cutting up Government convoys and all that. He was lying doggo in a village about fifteen miles off, waiting to get a fresh gang together. So we arranged to take thirty mounted police, and turn him out before he could plunder into our newly-settled villages. At the last minute, the Civil officer in our part of the world thought he'd assist at the performance.'

'Who was he?' said Nevin.

'His name was Dennis,' said The Infant slowly. 'And we'll let it stay so. He's a better man now than he was then.'

'But how old was the Civil power?' said Cleever. 'The situation is developing itself.'

'He was about six-and-twenty, and he was awf'ly clever. He knew a lot of things, but I don't think he was quite steady enough for dacoit-hunting. We started overnight for Boh Naghee's village, and we got there just before morning, without raising an alarm. Dennis had turned out armed to his teeth —two revolvers, a carbine, and all sorts of things. I was talking to Hicksey about posting the men, and Dennis edged his pony in between us, and said, "What shall I do? What shall I do? Tell me what to do, you fellows." We didn't take much notice till his pony tried to bite me in the leg, and I said, "Pull out a bit, old man, till we've settled the attack." He kept edging in, and fiddling with his reins and his revolvers, and saying, "Dear me! Dear me! Oh, dear me! What do you think I'd better do?" The man was in a deadly funk, and his teeth were chattering.'

'I sympathize with the Civil power,' said Cleever. 'Continue, young Clive.'*

'The fun of it was, that he was supposed to be our superior officer. Hicksey took a good look at him, and told him to attach himself to my party. Beastly mean of Hicksey, that. The chap kept on edging in and bothering, instead of asking for some men and taking up his own position, till I got angry, and the carbines began popping on the other side of the village. Then I said, "For God's sake be quiet, and sit down where you are! If you see anybody come out of the village, shoot at him." I knew he couldn't hit a hayrick at a yard. Then I took my men over the garden wall—over the palisades, y'know—somehow or other, and the fun began. Hicksey had found the Boh in bed under a mosquito-curtain, and he had taken a flying jump on to him.'

'A flying jump!' said Cleever. 'Is *that* also war?'

'Yes,' said The Infant, now thoroughly warmed. 'Don't you know how you take a flying jump on to a fellow's head at school, when he snores in the dormitory? The Boh was sleeping in a bedful of swords and pistols, and Hicksey came down like Zazel* through the netting, and the net got mixed up with the pistols and the Boh and Hicksey, and they all rolled on the floor together. I laughed till I couldn't stand, and Hicksey was cursing me for not helping him. So I left him to sort it out and went into the village. Our men were slashing about and firing, and so were the dacoits, and in the thick of the mess some ass set fire to a house, and we all had to clear out. I froze on to the nearest *daku* and ran to the palisade, shoving him in front of me. He wriggled loose, and bounded over the other side. I came after him; but when I had one leg one side and one leg the other of the palisade, I saw that the *daku* had fallen flat on Dennis's head. That man had never moved from where I left him. They rolled on the ground together, and Dennis's carbine went off and nearly shot me. The *daku* picked himself up and ran, and Dennis buzzed his carbine after him, and it caught him on the back of his head, and knocked him silly. You never saw anything so funny in your life. I doubled up on the top of the palisade and hung there, yelling with laughter. But Dennis began to weep like anything. "Oh, I've killed a man," he said. "I've killed a man, and I shall never know another peaceful hour in my life! Is he dead? Oh, *is* he dead? Good Lord, I've killed a man!" I came down and said, "Don't be a fool;" but he kept on shouting, "Is he dead?" till I could have kicked him. The *daku* was only knocked out of time with the carbine. He came to after a bit, and I said, "Are you hurt much?" He groaned and said "No." His chest was all cut with scrambling over the palisade. "The white man's gun didn't do that," he said "I did that, and *I* knocked the white man over." Just like a Burman, wasn't it? But Dennis wouldn't be happy at any price. He said, "Tie up his wounds. He'll bleed to death. Oh, he'll bleed to death!" "Tie 'em up yourself," I said, "if you're so anxious." "I can't touch him," said Dennis, "but here's my shirt." He took off his shirt, and fixed the braces again over his bare shoulders. I ripped the shirt up, and bandaged the dacoit quite professionally. He was grinning at Dennis all the time; and Dennis's haversack was lying on the ground, bursting full of sandwiches. Greedy hog! I took some, and offered some to Dennis. "How can I eat?" he said. "How can you ask me to eat? His very blood is on your hands now, and you're eating *my* sandwiches!" "All right," I said; "I'll give 'em to the *daku*." So I did, and the little chap was quite pleased, and wolfed 'em down like one o'clock.'

Cleever brought his hand down on the table with a thump that made the empty glasses dance. 'That's Art!' he said. 'Flat, flagrant mechanism! Don't tell me that happened on the spot!'

The pupils of the Infant's eyes contracted to two pin-points. 'I beg your pardon,' he said, slowly and stiffly, 'but I am telling this thing *as* it happened.'

Cleever looked at him a moment. 'My fault entirely,' said he; 'I should have known. Please go on.'

'Hicksey came out of what was left of the village with his prisoners and captives, all neatly tied up. Boh Na-ghee was first, and one of the villagers, as soon as he found the old ruffian helpless, began kicking him quietly. The Boh stood it as long as he could, and then groaned, and we saw what was going on. Hicksey tied the villager up, and gave him a half-a-dozen, good, with a bamboo, to remind him to leave a prisoner alone. You should have seen the old Boh grin. Oh! but Hicksey was in a furious rage with everybody. He'd got a wipe over the elbow that had tickled up his funny-bone, and he was rabid with me for not having helped him with the Boh and the mosquito-net. I had to explain that I couldn't do anything. If you'd seen 'em both tangled up together on the floor in one kicking cocoon, you'd have laughed for a week. Hicksey swore that the only decent man of his acquaintance was the Boh, and all the way to camp Hicksey was talking to the Boh, and the Boh was complaining about the soreness of his bones. When we got back, and had had a bath, the Boh wanted to know when he was going to be hanged. Hicksey said he couldn't oblige him on the spot, but had to send him to Rangoon. The Boh went down on his knees, and reeled off a catalogue of his crimes—he ought to have been hanged seventeen times over, by his own confession —and implored Hicksey to settle the business out of hand. "If I'm sent to Rangoon," said he, "they'll keep me in jail all my life, and that is a death every time the sun gets up or the wind blows." But we had to send him to Rangoon, and, of course, he was let off down there, and given penal servitude for life. When I came to Rangoon I went over the jail—I had helped to fill it, y' know—and the old Boh was there, and he spotted me at once. He begged for some opium first, and I tried to get him some, but that was against the rules. Then he asked me to have his sentence changed to death, because he was afraid of being sent to the Andamans.* I couldn't do that either, but I tried to cheer him, and told him how things were going up-country, and the last thing he said was—"Give my compliments to the fat white man who jumped on me. If I'd been awake I'd have killed him." I wrote that to Hicksey next mail, and—and that's all. I'm 'fraid I've been gassing awf'ly, sir.'

Cleever said nothing for a long time. The Infant looked uncomfortable. He feared that, misled by enthusiasm, he had filled up the novelist's time with unprofitable recital of trivial anecdotes.

Then said Cleever, 'I can't understand. Why should you have seen and done all these things before you have cut your wisdom-teeth?'

'Don't know,' said The Infant apologetically. 'I haven't seen much—only Burmese jungle.'

'And dead men, and war, and power, and responsibility,' said Cleever, under his breath. 'You won't have any sensations left at thirty, if you go on as you have done. But I want to hear more tales—more tales!' He seemed to forget that even subalterns might have engagements of their own.

'We're thinking of dining out somewhere—the lot of us—and going on to the Empire* afterwards,' said Nevin, with hesitation. He did not like to ask Cleever to come too. The invitation might be regarded as perilously near to 'cheek'. And Cleever, anxious not to wag a grey beard unbidden among boys at large, said nothing on his side.

Boileau solved the little difficulty by blurting out: 'Won't you come too, sir?'

Cleever almost shouted 'Yes,' and while he was being helped into his coat, continued to murmur 'Good Heavens!' at intervals in a way that the boys could not understand.

'I don't think I've been to the Empire in my life,' said he; 'but—what *is* my life after all? Let us go.'

They went out with Eustace Cleever, and I sulked at home because they had come to see me but had gone over to the better man; which was humiliating. They packed him into a cab with utmost reverence, for was he not the author of *As it was in the Beginning*, and a person in whose company it was an honour to go abroad? From all I gathered later, he had taken less interest in the performance before him than in their conversations, and they protested with emphasis that he was 'as good a man as they make. Knew what a man was driving at almost before he said it; and yet he's so damned simple about things that any man knows.' That was one of many comments.

At midnight they returned, announcing that they were 'highly respectable gondoliers',* and that oysters and stout were what they chiefly needed. The eminent novelist was still with them, and I think he was calling them by their shorter names. I am certain that he said he had been moving in worlds not realized, and that they had shown him the Empire in a new light.

Still sore at recent neglect, I answered shortly, 'Thank heaven we have within the land ten thousand as good as they,'* and when he departed, asked him what he thought of things generally.

He replied with another quotation, to the effect that though singing was a remarkably fine performance, I was to be quite sure that few lips would be moved to song if they could find a sufficiency of kissing.*

Whereby I understood that Eustace Cleever, decorator and colourman in words, was blaspheming his own Art, and would be sorry for this in the morning.

The Young British Soldier*

WHEN the 'arf-made recruity goes out to the East
  'E acts like a babe an' 'e drinks like a beast,
An' 'e wonders because 'e is frequent deceased
    Ere 'e's fit for to serve as a soldier.
      Serve, serve, serve as a soldier,
      Serve, serve, serve as a soldier,
      Serve, serve, serve as a soldier,
        So-oldier *of* the Queen!

Now all you recruities what's drafted to-day,
You shut up your rag-box* an' 'ark to my lay,
An' I'll sing you a soldier as far as I may:
    A soldier what's fit for a soldier.
      Fit, fit, fit for a soldier . . .

First mind you steer clear o' the grog-sellers' huts,
For they sell you Fixed Bay'nets that rots out your guts—
Ay, drink that 'ud eat the live steel from your butts—
    An' it's bad for the young British soldier.
      Bad, bad, bad for the soldier . . .

When the cholera comes—as it will past a doubt—
Keep out of the wet and don't go on the shout,*
For the sickness gets in as the liquor dies out,
    An' it crumples the young British soldier.
      Crum-, crum-, crumples the soldier . . .

But the worst o' your foes is the sun over'ead:
You *must* wear your 'elmet for all that is said:
If 'e finds you uncovered 'e'll knock you down dead,
    An' you'll die like a fool of a soldier.
      Fool, fool, fool of a soldier . . .

If you're cast for fatigue by a sergeant unkind,
Don't grouse like a woman nor crack on nor blind;*
Be handy and civil, and then you will find
    That it's beer for the young British soldier.
      Beer, beer, beer for the soldier . . .

Now, if you must marry, take care she is old—
A troop-sergeant's widow's the nicest, I'm told,
For beauty won't help if your rations is cold,
    Nor love ain't enough for a soldier.
        'Nough, 'nough, 'nough for a soldier . . .

If the wife should go wrong with a comrade, be loth
To shoot when you catch 'em—you'll swing on my oath!—
Make 'im take 'er and keep 'er: that's Hell for them both,
    An' you're shut o' the curse of a soldier.
        Curse, curse, curse of a soldier . . .

When first under fire an' you're wishful to duck
Don't look nor take 'eed at the man that is struck.
Be thankful you're livin', and trust to your luck
    And march to your front like a soldier.
        Front, front, front like a soldier . . .

When 'arf of your bullets fly wide in the ditch,
Don't call your Martini* a cross-eyed old bitch;
She's human as you are—you treat her as sich,
    An' she'll fight for the young British soldier.
        Fight, fight, fight for the soldier . . .

When shakin' their bustles like ladies so fine,
The guns o' the enemy wheel into line,
Shoot low at the limbers* an' don't mind the shine,
    For noise never startles the soldier.
        Start-, start-, startles the soldier . . .

If your officer's dead and the sergeants look white,
Remember it's ruin to run from a fight:
So take open order, lie down, and sit tight,
    And wait for supports like a soldier.
        Wait, wait, wait like a soldier . . .

When you're wounded and left on Afghanistan's plains,
And the women come out to cut up what remains,
Jest roll up your rifle and blow out your brains
    An' go to your Gawd like a soldier.
        Go, go, go like a soldier,

Go, go, go like a soldier,
Go, go, go like a soldier,
So-oldier *of* the Queen!

The Light that Failed*

CHAPTER 2

Then we brought the lances down, then the bugles blew,
When we went to Kandahar, ridin' two an' two,
   Ridin', ridin', ridin', two an' two,
     Ta-ra-ra-ra-ra-ra-ra,
All the way to Kandahar,* ridin' two an' two.
                Barrack-Room Ballad

'I'M not angry with the British public, but I wish we had a few thousand of them scattered among these rocks. They wouldn't be in such a hurry to get at their morning papers then. Can't you imagine the regulation householder—Lover of Justice, Constant Reader, Paterfamilias, and all that lot—frizzling on hot gravel?'

'With a blue veil over his head, and his clothes in strips. Has any man here a needle? I've got a bit of sugar-sack.'

'I'll lend you a packing-needle for six square inches of it then. Both my knees are worn through.'

'Why not six square acres, while you're about it? But lend me the needle, and I'll see what I can do with the selvage. I don't think there's enough to protect my royal body from the cold blast as it is. What are you doing with that everlasting sketch-book of yours, Dick?'

'Study of our Special Correspondent repairing his wardrobe,' said Dick gravely, as the other man kicked off a pair of sorely worn riding-breeches and began to fit a square of coarse canvas over the most obvious open space. He grunted disconsolately as the vastness of the void developed itself.

'Sugar-bags, indeed! Hi! you pilot-man there! Lend me all the sails of that whale-boat.'*

A fez-crowned head bobbed up in the stern-sheets, divided itself into exact halves with one flashing grin, and bobbed down again. The man of the tattered breeches, clad only in a Norfolk jacket and a grey flannel shirt, went on with his clumsy sewing, while Dick chuckled over the sketch.

Some twenty whale-boats were nuzzling a sand-bank which was dotted with English soldiery of half a dozen corps, bathing or washing their clothes. A heap of boat-rollers, commissariat-boxes, sugar-bags, and flour- and small-arm-ammunition-cases showed where one of the whale-boats had been compelled to unload hastily; and a regimental carpenter was swearing aloud as he tried, on a wholly insufficient allowance of white lead, to plaster up the sun-parched gaping seams of the boat herself.

'First the bloomin' rudder snaps,' said he to the world in general; 'then the mast goes; an' then, s' 'elp me, when she can't do nothin' else, she opens 'erself out like a cock-eyed Chinese lotus.'

'Exactly the case with my breeches, whoever you are,' said the tailor, without looking up. 'Dick, I wonder when I shall see a decent shop again.'

There was no answer, save the incessant angry murmur of the Nile as it raced round a basalt-walled bend and foamed across a rock-ridge half a mile upstream. It was as though the brown weight of the river would drive the white men back to their own country. The indescribable scent of Nile mud in the air told that the stream was falling and that the next few miles would be no light thing for the whale-boats to overpass. The desert ran down almost to the banks, where, among grey, red, and black hillocks, a camel-corps* was encamped. No man dared even for a day lose touch of the slow-moving boats; there had been no fighting for weeks past, and throughout all that time the Nile had never spared them. Rapid had followed rapid, rock rock, and island-group island-group, till the rank and file had long since lost all count of direction and very nearly of time. They were moving somewhere, they did not know why, to do something, they did not know what. Before them lay the Nile, and at the other end of it was one Gordon, fighting for the dear life, in a town called Khartoum. There were columns of British troops in the desert, or in one of the many deserts; there were columns on the river; there were yet more columns waiting to embark on the river; there were fresh drafts waiting at Assiut and Assuan;* there were lies and rumours running over the face of the hopeless land from Suakin to the Sixth Cataract,* and men supposed generally that there must be some one in authority to direct the general scheme of the many movements. The duty of that particular river-column was to keep the whale-boats afloat in the water, to avoid trampling on the villagers' crops when the gangs 'tracked' the boats with lines thrown from midstream, to get as much sleep and food as was possible, and, above all, to press on without delay in the teeth of the churning Nile.

With the soldiers sweated and toiled the correspondents of the newspapers, and they were almost as ignorant as their companions. But it was above all things necessary that England at breakfast should be amused and thrilled and interested, whether Gordon lived or died, or half the British army went to pieces in the sands. The Sudan campaign was a picturesque one, and lent itself to vivid word-painting. Now and again a 'Special' managed to get slain,—which was not altogether a disadvantage to the paper that employed him,—and more often the hand-to-hand nature of the fighting allowed of miraculous escapes which were worth telegraphing home at eighteenpence the word. There were many correspondents with many corps and columns,—from the veterans who had followed on the heels of the cavalry that occupied Cairo in '82, what time Arabi Pasha* called himself king, who had seen the first miserable work round Suakin* when the sentries were cut up nightly and the scrub swarmed with spears, to youngsters jerked into the business at the end of a telegraph-wire to take the place of their betters killed or invalided.

Among the seniors—those who knew every shift and change in the perplexing postal arrangements, the value of the seediest, weediest Egyptian garron offered for sale in Cairo or Alexandria, who could talk a telegraph clerk into amiability and soothe the ruffled vanity of a newly appointed Staff-officer when press regulations became burdensome—was the man in the flannel shirt, the black-browed Torpenhow. He represented the Central Southern Syndicate in the campaign, as he had represented it in the Egyptian war, and elsewhere. The syndicate did not concern itself greatly with criticisms of attack and the like. It supplied the masses, and all it demanded was picturesqueness and abundance of detail; for there is more joy in England over a soldier who insubordinately steps out of square to rescue a comrade than over twenty generals slaving even to baldness at the gross details of transport and commissariat.

He had met at Suakin a young man, sitting on the edge of a recently abandoned redoubt about the size of a hat-box, sketching a clump of shell-torn bodies on the gravel plain.

'What are you for?' said Torpenhow. The greeting of the correspondent is that of the commercial traveller on the road.

'My own hand,' said the young man, without looking up. 'Have you any tobacco?'

Torpenhow waited till the sketch was finished, and when he had looked at it said, 'What's your business here?'

'Nothing. There was a row, so I came. I'm supposed to be doing something down at the painting-slips among the boats, or else I'm in charge of the condenser on one of the water-ships. I've forgotten which.'

'You've cheek enough to build a redoubt with,' said Torpenhow, and took stock of the new acquaintance. 'Do you always draw like that?'

The young man produced more sketches. 'Row on a Chinese pig-boat,' said he sententiously, showing them one after another. — 'Chief mate dirked by a comprador. — Junk ashore off Hakodate.* — Somali muleteer being flogged. — Star-shell bursting over camp at Berbera.* — Slave-dhow being chased round Tajurrah Bay.* — Soldier lying dead in the moonlight outside Suakin, — throat cut by Fuzzies.'*

'H'm!' said Torpenhow, 'can't say I care for Verestchagin*-and-water myself, but there's no accounting for tastes. Doing anything now, are you?'

'No. I'm amusing myself here.'

Torpenhow looked at the aching desolation of the place. ''Faith, you've queer notions of amusement. Got any money?'

'Enough to go on with. Look here: do you want me to do war-work?'

'*I* don't. My syndicate may, though. You can draw more than a little, and I don't suppose you care much what you get, do you?'

'Not this time. I want my chance first.'

Torpenhow looked at the sketches again, and nodded. 'Yes, you're right to take your first chance when you can get it.'

He rode away swiftly through the Gate of the Two War-Ships,* rattled across the causeway into the town, and wired to his syndicate, 'Got man here, picture-work. Good and cheap. Shall I arrange? Can do letterpress with sketches.'

The man on the redoubt sat swinging his legs and murmuring, 'I knew the chance would come, sooner or later. By Gad, they'll have to sweat for it if I come through this business alive!'

In the evening Torpenhow was able to announce to his friend that the Central Southern Agency was willing to take him on trial, paying expenses for three months. 'And, by the way, what's your name?' said Torpenhow.

'Heldar. Do they give me a free hand?'

'They've taken you on chance. You must justify the choice. You'd better stick to me. I'm going up-country with a column, and I'll do what I can for you. Give me some of your sketches taken here, and I'll send 'em along.' To himself he said, 'That's the best bargain the Central Southern has ever made; and they got *me* cheaply enough.'

So it came to pass that, after some purchase of horse-flesh and arrangements financial and political, Dick was made free of the New and Honourable Fraternity of war-correspondents, who all possess the inalienable right of doing as much work as they can and getting as much for it as Providence and their owners shall please. To these things are added in time, if the brother be worthy, the power of glib speech that neither man nor woman can resist when a meal or a bed is in question, the eye of a horse-coper, the skill of a cook, the constitution of a bullock, the digestion of an ostrich, and an infinite adaptability to all circumstances. But many die before they attain to this degree, and the past-masters in the craft appear for the most part in dress-clothes when they are in England, and thus their glory is hidden from the multitude.

Dick followed Torpenhow wherever the latter's fancy chose to lead him, and between the two they managed to accomplish some work that almost satisfied themselves. It was not an easy life in any way, and under its influence the two were drawn very closely together, for they ate from the same dish, they shared the same water-bottle, and, most binding tie of all, their mails went off together. It was Dick who managed to make gloriously drunk a telegraph-clerk in a palm hut far beyond the Second Cataract, and, while the man lay in bliss on the floor, possessed himself of some laboriously acquired exclusive information, forwarded by a confiding correspondent of an opposition syndicate, made a careful duplicate of the matter, and brought the result to Torpenhow, who said that all was fair in love or war-correspondence, and built an excellent descriptive article from his rival's riotous waste of words. It was Torpenhow who—but the tale of their adventures, together and apart, from Philae to the waste wilderness of Merawi and Huella,* would fill many books. They had been penned into a square side by side, in deadly fear of being shot by over-excited soldiers; they had fought with baggage-camels in the chill dawn; they had jogged along in silence under blinding sun on indefatigable little Egyptian horses; and they had floundered on the shallows of the Nile when the whale-boat in which they had found a berth chose to hit a hidden rock and rip out half her bottom-planks.

Now they were sitting on the sand-bank, and the whale-boats were bringing up the remainder of the column.

'Yes,' said Torpenhow, as he put the last rude stitches into his over-long-neglected gear, 'it has been a beautiful business.'

'The patch or the campaign?' said Dick. 'Don't think much of either, myself.'

'You want the Euryalus* brought up above the Third Cataract, don't you? and eighty-one-ton guns at Jakdul? Now, *I*'m quite satisfied with my breeches.' He turned round gravely to exhibit himself, after the manner of a clown.

'It's very pretty. Specially the lettering on the sack. G.B.T. —Government Bullock Train. That's a sack from India.'

'It's my initials,—Gilbert Belling Torpenhow. I stole the cloth on purpose. What the mischief are the camel-corps doing yonder?' Torpenhow shaded his eyes and looked across the scrub-strewn gravel.

A bugle blew furiously, and the men on the bank hurried to their arms and accoutrements.

' "Pisan soldiery surprised while bathing," '* remarked Dick calmly. 'D'you remember the picture? It's by Michael Angelo. All beginners copy it. That scrub's alive with enemy.'

The camel-corps on the bank yelled to the infantry to come to them, and a hoarse shouting down the river showed that the remainder of the column had wind of the trouble and was hastening to take share in it. As swiftly as a reach of still water is crisped by the wind, the rock-strewn ridges and scrub-topped hills were troubled and alive with armed men. Mercifully, it occurred to these to stand far off for a time, to shout and gesticulate joyously. One man even delivered himself of a long story. The camel-corps did not fire. They were only too glad of a little breathing-space, until some sort of square could be formed. The men on the sand-bank ran to their side; and the whale-boats, as they toiled up within shouting distance, were thrust into the nearest bank and emptied of all save the sick and a few men to guard them. The Arab orator ceased his outcries, and his friends howled.

'They look like the Mahdi's men,' said Torpenhow, elbowing himself into the crush of the square. 'But what thousands of 'em there are! The tribes hereabout aren't against us, I know.'

'Then the Mahdi's taken another town,' said Dick, 'and set all these yelping devils free to chaw us up. Lend us your glass.'

'Our scouts should have told us of this. We've been trapped,' said a subaltern. 'Aren't the camel-guns ever going to begin? Hurry up, you men!'

There was no need for any order. The men flung themselves panting against the sides of the square, for they had good reason to know that whoso was left outside when the fighting began would very probably die in an extremely unpleasant fashion. The little hundred-and-fifty-pound camel-guns posted at one corner of the square opened the ball as the square moved forward by its right to get possession of a knoll of rising ground. All had fought in this manner many times before, and there was no novelty in the entertainment: always the same hot and stifling formation, the smell of dust and leather, the same boltlike rush of the enemy, the same pressure on the weakest side of the square, the few minutes of desperate hand-to-hand scuffle, and then silence of the desert, broken only by the yells of those whom the handful of cavalry attempted to pursue. They had grown careless. The camel-guns spoke at intervals, and the square slouched forward amid the protests of the camels. Then came the attack of three thousand men who had not learned from books that it is impossible for troops in close order to attack against breech-loading fire. A few dropping shots heralded their approach, and a few horsemen led, but the bulk of the force was naked humanity, mad with rage, and armed with the spear and the sword. The instinct of the desert, where there is always much war, told them that the right flank of the square was the weakest, for they swung clear of the front. The camel-guns shelled them as they passed, and opened for an instant lanes through their midst, most like those quick-closing vistas in a Kentish hop-garden seen when the train races by at full speed; and the infantry fire, held till the opportune moment, dropped them in close-packed hundreds. No civilized troops in the world could have endured the hell through which they came, the living leaping high to avoid the dying who clutched at their heels, the wounded cursing and staggering forward, till they fell—a torrent black as the sliding water above a mill-dam—full on the right flank of the square. Then the line of the dusty troops and the faint blue desert sky overhead went out in rolling smoke, and the little stones on the heated ground and the tinder-dry clumps of scrub became matters of surpassing interest, for men measured their agonized retreat and recovery by these things, counting mechanically and hewing their way back to chosen pebble and branch. There was no semblance of any concerted fighting. For aught the men knew, the enemy might be attempting all four sides of the square at once. Their business was to destroy what lay in front of them, to bayonet in the back those who passed over them, and, dying, to drag down the slayer till he could be knocked on the head by some avenging gun-butt. Dick waited quietly with Torpenhow and a young doctor till the stress became unendurable. There was no hope of attending to the wounded till the attack was repulsed, so the three moved forward gingerly towards the weakest side. There was a rush from without, the short *hough-hough* of the stabbing spears, and a man on a horse, followed by thirty or forty others, dashed through, yelling and hacking. The right flank of the square sucked in after them, and the other sides sent help. The wounded, who knew that they had but a few hours more to live, caught at the enemy's feet and brought them down, or, staggering to a discarded rifle, fired blindly into the scuffle that raged in the centre of the square. Dick was conscious that somebody had cut him violently across his helmet, that he had fired his revolver into a black, foam-flecked face which forthwith ceased to bear any resemblance to a face, and that Torpenhow had gone down under an Arab whom he had tried to 'collar low', and was turning over and over with his captive, feeling for the man's eyes. The doctor was jabbing at a venture with a bayonet, and a helmetless soldier was firing over Dick's shoulder: the flying grains of powder stung his cheek. It was to Torpenhow that Dick turned by instinct. The representative of the Central Southern Syndicate had shaken himself clear of his enemy, and rose, wiping his thumb on his trousers. The Arab, both hands to his forehead, screamed aloud, then snatched up his spear and rushed at Torpenhow, who was panting under shelter of Dick's revolver. Dick fired twice, and the man dropped limply. His upturned face lacked one eye. The musketry-fire redoubled, but cheers mingled with it. The rush had failed, and the enemy were flying. If the heart of the square were a shambles, the ground beyond was a butcher's shop. Dick thrust his way forward between the maddened men. The remnant of the enemy were retiring, as the few—the very few—English cavalry rode down the laggards.

Beyond the lines of the dead, a broad blood-stained Arab spear cast aside in the retreat lay across a stump of scrub, and beyond this again the illimitable dark levels of the desert. The sun caught the steel and turned it into a savage red disc. Some one behind him was saying, 'Ah, get away, you brute!' Dick raised his revolver and pointed towards the desert. His eye was held by the red splash in the distance, and the clamour about him seemed to die down to a very far-away whisper, like the whisper of a level sea. There was the revolver and the red light, . . . and the voice of some one scaring something away, exactly as had fallen somewhere before,—probably in a past life. Dick waited for what should happen afterwards. Something seemed to crack inside his head, and for an instant he stood in the dark,—a darkness that stung. He fired at random, and the bullet went out across the desert as he muttered, 'Spoilt my aim. There aren't any more cartridges. We shall have to run home.' He put his hand to his head and brought it away covered with blood.

'Old man, you're cut rather badly,' said Torpenhow. 'I owe you something for this business. Thanks. Stand up! I say, you can't be sick here.'

Dick had fallen stiffly on Torpenhow's shoulder, and was muttering something about aiming low and to the left.* Then he sank to the ground and was silent. Torpenhow dragged him off to a doctor and sat down to work out an account of what he was pleased to call 'a sanguinary battle, in which our arms had acquitted themselves,' etc.

All that night, when the troops were encamped by the whale-boats, a black figure danced in the strong moonlight on the sand-bar and shouted that Gordon the accursed one was dead, —was dead,—was dead,*—that two steamers were rock-staked on the Nile outside the city,* and that of all their crews there remained not one; and Gordon was dead,—was dead,—was dead!

But Torpenhow took no heed. He was watching Dick, who was calling aloud to the restless Nile for Maisie,—and again Maisie!

'Behold a phenomenon,' said Torpenhow, rearranging the blanket. 'Here is a man, presumably human, who mentions the name of one woman only. And I've seen a good deal of delirium, too.—Dick, here's some fizzy drink.'

'Thank you, Maisie,' said Dick.

'Fuzzy-Wuzzy'*

(*Sudan Expeditionary Force. Early Campaigns*)

We've fought with many men acrost the seas,
    An' some of 'em was brave an' some was not:
The Paythan an' the Zulu an' Burmese;
    But the Fuzzy was the finest o' the lot.
We never got a ha'porth's change of 'im:
    'E squatted in the scrub an' 'ocked our 'orses,
'E cut our sentries up at Suakim,*
    An' 'e played the cat an' banjo with our forces.

    So 'ere's *to* you, Fuzzy-Wuzzy, at your 'ome in the
        Soudan;
        You're a pore benighted 'eathen but a first-class fightin'
        man;
        We gives you your certificate, an' if you want it signed
        We'll come an' 'ave a romp with you whenever you're
        inclined.

We took our chanst among the Khyber 'ills,
    The Boers knocked us silly at a mile,
The Burman give us Irriwaddy chills,
    An' a Zulu *impi* dished us up in style:*
But all we ever got from such as they
    Was pop to what the Fuzzy made us swaller;
We 'eld our bloomin' own, the papers say,
    But man for man the Fuzzy knocked us 'oller.

        Then 'ere's *to* you, Fuzzy-Wuzzy, an' the missis and the
            kid;
        Our orders was to break you, an' of course we went an'
            did.
        We sloshed you with Martinis,* an' it wasn't 'ardly
            fair;
        But for all the odds agin' you, Fuzzy-Wuz, you broke
            the square.*

'E 'asn't got no papers of 'is own,
 'E 'asn't got no medals nor rewards,
So *we* must certify the skill 'e's shown
 In usin' of 'is long two-'anded swords:
When 'e's 'oppin' in an' out among the bush
 With 'is coffin-'eaded shield an' shovel-spear,
An 'appy day with Fuzzy on the rush
 Will last an 'ealthy Tommy for a year.
  So 'ere's *to* you, Fuzzy-Wuzzy, an' your friends which
   are no more,
  If we 'adn't lost some messmates we would 'elp you to
   deplore.
  But give an' take's the gospel, an' we'll call the bargain
   fair,
  For if you 'ave lost more than us, you crumpled up the
   square!

'E rushes at the smoke when we let drive,
 An', before we know, 'e's 'ackin' at our 'ead;
'E's all 'ot sand an' ginger when alive,
 An' 'e's generally shammin' when 'e's dead.
'E's a daisy, 'e's a ducky, 'e's a lamb!
 'E's a injia-rubber idiot on the spree,
'E's the on'y thing that doesn't give a damn
 For a Regiment o' British Infantree!
  So 'ere's *to* you, Fuzzy-Wuzzy, at your 'ome in the
   Soudan;
  You're a pore benighted 'eathen but a first-class fightin'
   man;
  An' 'ere's *to* you, Fuzzy-Wuzzy, with your 'ayrick 'ead
   of 'air—
  You big black boundin' beggar—for you broke a British
   square!

The Mutiny of the Mavericks*

	Causing			
Sec. 7. (1)	Conspiring with other persons to cause	a mutiny sedition	in forces belonging to Her Majesty's	Regular forces, Reserve forces, Auxiliary forces, Navy.*

WHEN three obscure gentlemen in San Francisco argued on insufficient premises they condemned a fellow-creature to a most unpleasant death in a far country, which had nothing whatever to do with the United States. They foregathered at the top of a tenement-house in Tehama Street, an unsavoury quarter of the city, and, there calling for certain drinks, they conspired because they were conspirators by trade, officially known as the Third Three of the I.A.A.*—an institution for the propagation of pure light, not to be confounded with any others, though it is affiliated to many. The Second Three live in Montreal, and work among the poor there; the First Three have their home in New York, not far from Castle Garden,* and write regularly once a week to a small house near one of the big hotels at Boulogne. What happens after that, a particular section of Scotland Yard* knows too well, and laughs at. A conspirator detests ridicule. More men have been stabbed with Lucrezia Borgia* daggers and dropped into the Thames for laughing at Head Centres and Triangles than for betraying secrets; for this is human nature.

The Third Three conspired over whisky cocktails and a clean sheet of notepaper against the British Empire and all that lay therein. This work is very like what men without discernment call politics before a general election. You pick out and discuss, in the company of congenial friends, all the weak points in your opponents' organization, and unconsciously dwell upon and exaggerate all their mishaps, till it seems to you a miracle that the hated party holds together for an hour.

'Our principle is not so much active demonstration—that we leave to others—as passive embarrassment, to weaken and unnerve,' said the first man. 'Wherever an organization is crippled, wherever a confusion is thrown into any branch of any department, we gain a step for those who take on the work; we are but the forerunners.' He was a German enthusiast, and editor of a newspaper, from whose leading articles he quoted frequently.

'That cursed Empire makes so many blunders of her own that unless we doubled the year's average I guess it wouldn't strike her anything special had occurred,' said the second man. 'Are you prepared to say that all our resources are equal to blowing off the muzzle of a hundred-ton gun or spiking a ten-thousand-ton ship on a plain rock in clear daylight?* They can beat us at our own game. Better join hands with the practical branches; we're in funds now. Try a direct scare in a crowded street. They value their greasy hides.' He was the drag upon the wheel, and an Americanized Irishman of the second generation, despising his own race and hating the other. He had learned caution.

The third man drank his cocktail and spoke no word. He was the strategist, but unfortunately his knowledge of life was limited. He picked a letter from his breast-pocket and threw it across the table. That epistle to the heathen contained some very concise directions from the First Three in New York. It said—

'*The boom in black iron has already affected the eastern markets, where our agents have been forcing down the English-held stock among the smaller buyers who watch the turn of shares. Any immediate operations, such as western bears,* would increase their willingness to unload. This, however, cannot be expected till they see clearly that foreign iron-masters are willing to co-operate. Mulcahy should be dispatched to feel the pulse of the market, and act accordingly. Mavericks are at present the best for our purpose. —P.D.Q.'**

As a message referring to an iron crisis in Pennsylvania, it was interesting, if not lucid. As a new departure in organized attack on an outlying English dependency, it was more than interesting.

The second man read it through and murmured—

'Already? Surely they are in too great a hurry. All that

Dhulip Singh* could do in India he has done, down to the distribution of his photographs among the peasantry. Ho! Ho! The Paris firm arranged that, and he has no substantial money backing from the Other Power.* Even our agents in India know he hasn't. What is the use of our organization wasting men on work that is already done? Of course the Irish regiments in India are half mutinous as they stand.'

This shows how near a lie may come to the truth. An Irish regiment, for just so long as it stands still, is generally a hard handful to control, being reckless and rough. When, however, it is moved in the direction of musketry-firing, it becomes strangely and unpatriotically content with its lot. It has even been heard to cheer the Queen with enthusiasm on these occasions.

But the notion of tampering with the Army was, from the point of view of Tehama Street, an altogether sound one. There is no shadow of stability in the policy of an English Government, and the most sacred oaths of England would, even if engrossed on vellum, find very few buyers among the colonies and dependencies that have suffered from vain beliefs. But there remains to England always her Army. That cannot change except in the matter of uniform and equipment. The officers may write to the papers demanding the heads of the Horse Guards* in default of cleaner redress for grievances; the men may break loose across a country town and seriously startle the publicans; but neither officers nor men have it in their composition to mutiny after the Continental manner. The English people, when they trouble to think about the Army at all, are, and with justice, absolutely assured that it is absolutely trustworthy. Imagine for a moment their emotions on realizing that such and such a regiment was in open revolt from causes directly due to England's management of Ireland. They would probably send the regiment to the polls forthwith and examine their own consciences as to their duty to Erin; but they would never be easy any more. And it was this vague, unhappy mistrust that the I.A.A. were labouring to produce.

'Sheer waste of breath,' said the second man after a pause in the council, 'I don't see the use of tampering with their fool-Army, but it has been tried before and we must try it again. It looks well in the reports. If we send one man from here you may bet your life that other men are going too. Order up Mulcahy.'

They ordered him up—a slim, slight, dark-haired young man, devoured with that blind rancorous hatred of England that only reaches its full growth across the Atlantic. He had sucked it from his mother's breast in the little cabin at the back of the northern avenues of New York; he had been taught his rights and his wrongs, in German and Irish, on the canal fronts of Chicago; and San Francisco held men who told him strange and awful things of the great blind Power over the seas. Once, when business took him across the Atlantic, he had served in an English regiment, and being insubordinate had suffered extremely. He drew all his ideas of England that were not bred by the cheaper patriotic prints from one iron-fisted colonel and an unbending adjutant. He would go to the mines if need be to teach his gospel. And he went as his instructions advised *p.d.q.*—which means 'with speed'—to introduce embarrassment into an Irish regiment, 'already half-mutinous, quartered among Sikh peasantry, all wearing miniatures of His Highness Dhulip Singh, Maharajah of the Punjab, next their hearts, and all eagerly expecting his arrival.' Other information equally valuable was given him by his masters. He was to be cautious, but never to grudge expense in winning the hearts of the men in the regiment. His mother in New York would supply funds, and he was to write to her once a month. Life is pleasant for a man who has a mother in New York to send him two hundred pounds a year over and above his regimental pay.

In process of time, thanks to his intimate knowledge of drill and musketry exercise, the excellent Mulcahy, wearing the corporal's stripe, went out in a troopship and joined Her Majesty's Royal Loyal Musketeers, commonly known as the 'Mavericks', because they were masterless and unbranded cattle—sons of small farmers in County Clare, shoeless vagabonds of Kerry, herders of Ballyvegan, much wanted 'moonlighters'* from the bare rainy headlands of the south coast, officered by O'Mores, Bradys, Hills, Kilreas, and the like. Never to outward seeming was there more promising material to work on. The First Three had chosen their regiment well. It feared nothing

that moved or talked save the Colonel and the regimental
Roman Catholic Chaplain, the fat Father Dennis, who held the
keys of Heaven and Hell, and blared like an angry bull when he
desired to be convincing. Him also it loved because on occa-
sions of stress he was used to tuck up his cassock and charge
with the rest into the merriest of the fray, where he always
found, good man, that the saints sent him a revolver when
there was a fallen private to be protected, or—but this came as
an afterthought—his own grey head to be guarded.

Cautiously as he had been instructed, tenderly and with
much beer, Mulcahy opened his projects to such as he deemed
fittest to listen. And these were, one and all, of that quaint,
crooked, sweet, profoundly irresponsible and profoundly lov-
able race that fight like fiends, argue like children, reason like
women, obey like men, and jest like their own goblins of the
rath* through rebellion, loyalty, want, woe, or war. The
underground work of a conspiracy is always dull and very
much the same the world over. At the end of six months—the
seed always falling on good ground—Mulcahy spoke almost
explicitly, hinting darkly in the approved fashion at dread
powers behind him, and advising nothing more nor less than
mutiny. Were they not dogs, evilly treated? had they not all
their own and their national revenges to satisfy? Who in these
days would do aught to nine hundred men in rebellion? Who,
again, could stay them if they broke for the sea, licking up on
their way other regiments only too anxious to join? And after-
wards . . . here followed windy promises of gold and prefer-
ment, office, and honour, ever dear to a certain type of
Irishman.

As he finished his speech, in the dusk of a twilight, to his
chosen associates, there was a sound of a rapidly unslung belt
behind him. The arm of one Dan Grady flew out in the gloom
and arrested something. Then said Dan—

'Mulcahy, you're a great man, an' you do credit to whoever
sent you. Walk about a bit while we think of it.' Mulcahy
departed elate. He knew his words would sink deep.

'Why the triple-dashed asterisks did ye not let me belt him?'
grunted a voice.

'Because I'm not a fat-headed fool. Boys, 'tis what he's been driving at these six months—our superior corp'ril with his education and his copies of the Irish papers and his everlasting beer. He's been sent for the purpose and that's where the money comes from. Can ye not see? That man's a gold-mine, which Horse Egan here wud have destroyed with a belt-buckle. It would be throwing away the gifts of Providence not to fall in with his little plans. Of coorse we'll mut'ny till all's dry. Shoot the Colonel on the parade-ground, massacree the company officers, ransack the arsenal, and then—Boys, did he tell you what next? He told *me* the other night when he was beginning to talk wild. Then we're to join with the niggers, and look for help from Dhulip Singh and the Russians!'

'And spoil the best campaign that ever was this side of Hell! Danny, I'd have lost the beer to ha' given him the belting he requires.'

'Oh, let him go this awhile, man! He's got no—no constructiveness, but that's the egg-meat of his plan, and you must understand that I'm in with it, an' so are you. We'll want oceans of beer to convince us—firmaments full. We'll give him talk for his money, and one by one all the boys'll come in and he'll have a nest of nine hundred mutineers to squat in an' give drink to.'

'What makes me killing-mad is his wanting us to do what the niggers did thirty years gone.* That an' his pig's cheek in saying that other regiments would come along,' said a Kerry man.

'That's not so bad as hintin' we should loose off on the Colonel.'

'Colonel be sugared!* I'd as soon as not put a shot through his helmet to see him jump and clutch his old horse's head. But Mulcahy talks o' shootin' our comp'ny orf'cers accidental.'

'He said that, did he?' said Horse Egan.

'Somethin' like that, anyways. Can't ye fancy ould Barber Brady wid a bullet in his lungs, coughin' like a sick monkey, an' sayin', "Bhoys, I do not mind your gettin' dhrunk, but you must hould your liquor like men. The man that shot me is dhrunk. I'll suspend investigations for six hours, while I get this bullet cut out, an' then—"'

'An' then,' continued Horse Egan, for the peppery Major's

peculiarities of speech and manner were as well known as his tanned face; ' "an' then, ye dissolute, half-baked, putty-faced scum o' Connemara, if I find a man so much as lookin' confused, begad, I'll coort-martial the whole company. A man that can't get over his liquor in six hours is not fit to belong to the Mavericks!" '

A shout of laughter bore witness to the truth of the sketch.

'It's pretty to think of,' said the Kerry man slowly. 'Mulcahy would have us do all the devilmint, and get clear himself, someways. He wudn't be takin' all this fool's throuble in shpoilin' the reputation of the Regiment——'

'Reputation of your grandmother's pig!' said Dan.

'Well, an' *he* had a good reputation tu; so it's all right. Mulcahy must see his way to clear out behind him, or he'd not ha' come so far, talkin' powers of darkness.'

'Did you hear anything of a regimental court-martial among the Black Boneens,* these days? Half a company of 'em took one of the new draft an' hanged him by his arms with a tent-rope from a third-storey verandah. They gave no reason for so doin', but he was half dead. I'm thinking that the Boneens are short-sighted. It was a friend of Mulcahy's, or a man in the same trade. They'd a deal better ha' taken his beer,' returned Dan reflectively.

'Better still ha' handed him up to the Colonel,' said Horse Egan, 'onless—but sure the news wud be all over the counthry an' give the Reg'ment a bad name.'

'An' there'd be no reward for that man—he but went about talkin',' said the Kerry man artlessly.

'You speak by your breed,' said Dan with a laugh. 'There was never a Kerry man yet that wudn't sell his brother for a pipe o' tobacco an' a pat on the back from a p'liceman.'

'Praise God I'm not a bloomin' Orangeman,' was the answer.

'No, nor never will be,' said Dan. 'They breed *men* in Ulster. Wud you like to thry the taste of one?'

The Kerry man looked and longed, but forebore. The odds of battle were too great.

'Then you'll not even give Mulcahy a—a strike for his money,' said the voice of Horse Egan, who regarded what he called 'trouble' of any kind as the pinnacle of felicity.

Dan answered not at all, but crept on tip-toe, with large strides, to the mess-room, the men following. The room was empty. In a corner cased like the King of Dahomey's state umbrella, stood the regimental colours. Dan lifted them tenderly and unrolled in the light of the candles the record of the Mavericks—tattered, worn, and hacked. The white satin was darkened everywhere with big brown stains, the gold threads on the crowned harp were frayed and discoloured, and the Red Bull, the totem of the Mavericks, was coffee-hued. The stiff, embroidered folds, whose price is human life, rustled down slowly. The Mavericks keep their colours long and guard them very sacredly.

'Vittoria, Salamanca, Toulouse, Waterloo, Moodkee, Feroz-shah, an' Sobraon—that was fought close next door here, against the very beggars he wants us to join. Inkerman, The Alma, Sebastopol!* What are those little businesses compared to the campaigns of General Mulcahy? The Mut'ny, think o' that; the Mut'ny an' some dirty little matters in Afghanistan; an' for that an' these an' those'—Dan pointed to the names of glorious battles—'that Yankee man with the partin' in his hair comes an' says as easy as "Have a drink." .... Holy Moses, there's the Captain!'

But it was the Mess-Sergeant who came in just as the men clattered out, and found the colours uncased.

From that day dated the mutiny of the Mavericks, to the joy of Mulcahy and the pride of his mother in New York—the good lady who sent the money for the beer. Never, so far as words went, was such a mutiny. The conspirators, led by Dan Grady and Horse Egan, poured in daily. They were sound men, men to be trusted, and they all wanted blood; but first they must have beer. They cursed the Queen, they mourned over Ireland, they suggested hideous plunder of the Indian country-side, and then, alas!—some of the younger men would go forth and wallow on the ground in spasms of wicked laughter. The genius of the Irish for conspiracies is remarkable. None the less they would swear no oaths but those of their own making, which were rare and curious, and they were always at pains to impress Mulcahy with the risks they ran. Naturally the flood of beer wrought demoralization. But

Mulcahy confused the causes of things, and when a very muzzy
Maverick smote a sergeant on the nose or called his Command-
ing Officer a bald-headed old lard-bladder, and even worse
names, he fancied that rebellion and not liquor was at the
bottom of the outbreak. Other gentlemen who have concerned
themselves in larger conspiracies have made the same error.

The hot season, in which they protested no man could rebel,
came to an end, and Mulcahy suggested a visible return for his
teachings. As to the actual upshot of the mutiny he cared
nothing. It would be enough if the English, infatuatedly trust-
ing to the integrity of their Army, should be startled with news
of an Irish regiment revolting from political considerations. His
persistent demands would have ended, at Dan's instigation, in
a regimental belting which in all probability would have killed
him and cut off the supply of beer, had not he been sent on
special duty some fifty miles away from the cantonment to cool
his heels in a mud fort and dismount obsolete artillery. Then
the Colonel of the Mavericks, reading his newspaper diligently,
and scenting Frontier trouble from afar, posted to the Army
headquarters and pled with the Commander-in-Chief for
certain privileges, to be granted under certain contingencies;
which contingencies came about only a week later, when the
annual little war on the Border developed itself, and the
Colonel returned to carry the good news to the Mavericks. He
held the promise of the Chief for active service, and the men
must get ready.

On the evening of the same day, Mulcahy, an unconsidered
corporal—yet great in conspiracy—returned to cantonments,
and heard sounds of strife and howlings from afar off. The
mutiny had broken out and the barracks of the Mavericks were
one white-washed pandemonium. A private tearing through
the barrack-square gasped in his ear, 'Service! Active service.
It's a burnin' shame.' Oh joy, the Mavericks had risen on the
eve of battle! They would not—noble and loyal sons of Ireland
—serve the Queen longer. The news would flash through the
country-side and over to England, and he—Mulcahy—the
trusted of the Third Three, had brought about the crash. The
private stood in the middle of the square and cursed colonel,
regiment, officers, and doctor, particularly the doctor, by his

gods. An orderly of the native cavalry regiment clattered through the mob of soldiers. He was half lifted, half dragged from his horse, beaten on the back with mighty hand-claps till his eyes watered, and called all manner of endearing names. Yes, the Mavericks had fraternized with the native troops. Who then was the agent among the latter that had blindly wrought with Mulcahy so well?

An officer slunk, almost ran, from the Mess to a barrack. He was mobbed by the infuriated soldiery, who closed round but did not kill him, for he fought his way to shelter, flying for the life. Mulcahy could have wept with pure joy and thankfulness. The very prisoners in the guard-room were shaking the bars of their cells and howling like wild beasts, and from every barrack poured the booming as of a big war-drum.

Mulcahy hastened to his own barrack. He could hardly hear himself speak. Eighty men were pounding with fist and heel the tables and trestles—eighty men, flushed with mutiny, stripped to their shirt sleeves, their knapsacks half-packed for the march to the sea, made the two-inch boards thunder again as they chanted to a tune that Mulcahy knew well, the Sacred War Song of the Mavericks—

> 'Listen in the North, my boys, there's trouble on the wind;
> Tramp o' Cossack hooves in front, grey great-coats behind,
> Trouble on the Frontier of a most amazin' kind,
> Trouble on the waters o' the Oxus!'*

Then, as a table broke under the furious accompaniment—

> 'Hurrah! hurrah! it's north by west we go;
> Hurrah! hurrah! the chance we wanted so;
> Let 'em hear the chorus from Umballa to Mos*cow*,
> As we go marchin' to the Kremling.'

'Mother of all the saints in bliss and all the devils in cinders, where's my fine new sock widout the heel?' howled Horse Egan, ransacking everybody's valise but his own. He was engaged in making up deficiencies of kit preparatory to a campaign, and in that work he steals best who steals last. 'Ah, Mulcahy, you're in good time,' he shouted. 'We've got the route, and we're off on Thursday for a picnic wid the Lancers next door.'

An ambulance orderly appeared with a huge basket full of lint rolls, provided by the forethought of the Queen for such as might need them later on. Horse Egan unrolled his bandage, and flicked it under Mulcahy's nose, chanting—

'Sheepskin an' bees' wax, thunder, pitch, and plaster,
The more you try to pull it off, the more it sticks the faster.
As I was goin' to New Orleans—*

'You know the rest of it, my Irish-American-Jew-boy. By gad, ye have to fight for the Queen in the inside av a fortnight, my darlin'.'

A roar of laughter interrupted. Mulcahy looked vacantly down the room. Bid a boy defy his father when the pantomime-cab is at the door; or a girl develop a will of her own when her mother is putting the last touches to the first ball-dress; but do not ask an Irish regiment to embark upon mutiny on the eve of a campaign; when it has fraternized with the native regiment that accompanies it, and driven its officers into retirement with ten thousand clamorous questions, and the prisoners dance for joy, and the sick men stand in the open, calling down all known diseases on the head of the doctor, who has certified that they are 'medically unfit for active service'. At even the Mavericks might have been mistaken for mutineers by one so unversed in their natures as Mulcahy. At dawn a girls' school might have learned deportment from them. They knew that their Colonel's hand had closed, and that he who broke that iron discipline would not go to the front: nothing in the world will persuade one of our soldiers when he is ordered to the North on the smallest of affairs, that he is not immediately going gloriously to slay Cossacks and cook his kettles in the palace of the Czar. A few of the younger men mourned for Mulcahy's beer, because the campaign was to be conducted on strict temperance principles, but as Dan and Horse Egan said sternly, 'We've got the beer-man with us. He shall drink now on his own hook.'*

Mulcahy had not taken into account the possibility of being sent on active service. He had made up his mind that he would not go under any circumstances, but fortune was against him.

'Sick—you?' said the doctor, who had served an unholy

apprenticeship to his trade in Tralee poorhouses. 'You're only home-sick, and what you call varicose veins come from over-eating. A little gentle exercise will cure that.' And later, 'Mulcahy, my man, everybody is allowed to apply for a sick-certificate *once*. If he tries it twice we call him by an ugly name. Go back to your duty, and let's hear no more of your diseases.'

I am ashamed to say that Horse Egan enjoyed the study of Mulcahy's soul in those days, and Dan took an equal interest. Together they would communicate to their corporal all the dark lore of death which is the portion of those who have seen men die. Egan had the larger experience, but Dan the finer imagination. Mulcahy shivered when the former spoke of the knife as an intimate acquaintance, or the latter dwelt with loving particularity on the fate of those who, wounded and helpless, had been overlooked by the ambulances, and had fallen into the hands of the Afghan women-folk.

Mulcahy knew that the mutiny, for the present at least, was dead, knew, too, that a change had come over Dan's usually respectful attitude towards him, and Horse Egan's laughter and frequent allusions to abortive conspiracies emphasized all that the conspirator had guessed. The horrible fascination of the death-stories, however, made him seek the men's society. He learnt much more than he had bargained for; and in this manner. It was on the last night before the Regiment entrained to the front. The barracks were stripped of everything mov-able, and the men were too excited to sleep. The bare walls gave out a heavy hospital smell of chloride of lime.

'And what,' said Mulcahy in an awe-stricken whisper, after some conversation on the eternal subject, 'are you going to do to me, Dan?' This might have been the language of an able conspirator conciliating a weak spirit.

'You'll see,' said Dan grimly, turning over in his cot, 'or I rather shud say you'll not see.'

This was hardly the language of a weak spirit. Mulcahy shook under the bed-clothes.

'Be easy with him,' put in Egan from the next cot. 'He has got his chanst o' goin' clean. Listen Mulcahy, all we want is for the good sake of the Regiment that you take your death stand-ing up, as a man shud. There's be heaps an' heaps of enemy—plenshus heaps. Go there an' do all you can and die decent. You'll die with a good name *there*. 'Tis not a hard thing considerin'.'

Again Mulcahy shivered.

'An' how could a man wish to die better than fightin',' added Dan consolingly.

'And if I won't?' said the corporal in a dry whisper.

'There'll be a dale of smoke,' returned Dan, sitting up and ticking off the situation on his fingers, 'sure to be, an' the noise of the firin' 'll be tremenjus, an' we'll be running about up and down, the Regiment will. But *we*, Horse and I—we'll stay by you, Mulcahy, and never let you go. Maybe there'll be an accident.'

'It's playing it low on me. Let me go. For pity's sake let me go. I never did you harm, and—and I stood you as much beer as I could. Oh, don't be hard on me, Dan! You are—you were in it too. You won't kill me up there, will you?'

'I'm not thinkin' of the treason; though you shud be glad any honest boys drank with you. It's for the Regiment. We can't have the shame o' you bringin' shame on us. You went to the doctor quiet as a sick cat to get and stay behind an' live with the women at the depôt—you that wanted us to run to the sea in wolf-packs like the rebels none of your black blood dared to be! But *we* knew about your goin' to the doctor, for he told in Mess, and it's all over the Regiment. Bein', as we are, your best friends, we didn't allow any one to molest you *yet*. We will see to you ourselves. Fight which you will—us or the enemy—you'll never lie in that cot again, and there's more glory and maybe less kicks from fightin' the enemy. That's fair speakin'.'

'And he told us by word of mouth to go and join with the niggers—you've forgotten that, Dan,' said Horse Egan, to justify sentence.

'What's the use of plaguin' the man. One shot pays for all. Sleep ye sound, Mulcahy. But you onderstand, do ye not?'

Mulcahy for some weeks understood very little of anything at all save that ever at his elbow, in camp, or at parade, stood two big men with soft voices adjuring him to commit *hara-kiri**
lest a worse thing should happen—to die for the honour of the

Regiment in decency among the nearest knives. But Mulcahy dreaded death. He remembered certain things that priests had said in his infancy, and his mother—not the one at New York —starting from her sleep with shrieks to pray for a husband's soul in torment. It is well to be of a cultured intelligence, but in time of trouble the weak human mind returns to the creed it sucked in at the breast, and if that creed be not a pretty one trouble follows. Also, the death he would have to face would be physically painful. Most conspirators have large imaginations. Mulcahy could see himself, as he lay on the earth in the night, dying by various causes. They were all horrible; the mother in New York was very far away, and the Regiment, the engine that, once you fall in its grip, moves you forward whether you will or won't, was daily coming closer to the enemy!

*   *   *

They were brought to the field of Marzun-Katai, and with the Black Boneens to aid, they fought a fight that has never been set down in the newspapers. In response, many believe, to the fervent prayers of Father Dennis, the enemy not only elected to fight in the open, but made a beautiful fight, as many weeping Irish mothers knew later. They gathered behind walls or flickered across the open in shouting masses, and were pot-valiant* in artillery. It was expedient to hold a large reserve and wait for the psychological moment that was being prepared by the shrieking shrapnel. Therefore the Mavericks lay down in open order on the brow of a hill to watch the play till their call should come. Father Dennis, whose duty was in the rear, to smooth the trouble of the wounded, had naturally managed to make his way to the foremost of his boys, and lay like a black porpoise at length on the grass. To him crawled Mulcahy, ashen-grey, demanding absolution.

'Wait till you're shot,' said Father Dennis sweetly. 'There's a time for everything.'

Dan Grady chuckled as he blew for the fiftieth time into the breech of his speckless rifle. Mulcahy groaned and buried his head in his arms till a stray shot spoke like a snipe immediately above his head, and a general heave and tremor rippled the line. Other shots followed and a few took effect, as a shriek or a grunt attested. The officers, who had been lying down with the men, rose and began to walk steadily up and down the front of their companies.

This manœuvre, executed, not for publication, but as a guarantee of good faith, to soothe men, demands nerve. You must not hurry, you must not look nervous, though you know that you are a mark for every rifle within extreme range, and above all, if you are smitten you must make as little noise as possible and roll inwards through the files. It is at this hour, when the breeze brings the first salt whiff of the powder to noses rather cold at the tip, and the eye can quietly take in the appearance of each red casualty, that the strain on the nerves is strongest. Scotch regiments can endure for half a day and abate no whit of their zeal at the end; English regiments sometimes sulk under punishment, while the Irish, like the French, are apt to run forward by ones and twos, which is just as bad as running back. The truly wise commandant of highly-strung troops allows them, in seasons of waiting, to hear the sound of their own voices uplifted in song. There is a legend of an English regiment that lay by its arms under fire chanting 'Sam Hall',* to the horror of its newly appointed and pious colonel. The Black Boneens, who were suffering more than the Mavericks, on a hill half a mile away, began presently to explain to all who cared to listen—

'We'll sound the jubilee, from the centre to the sea.
And Ireland shall be free, says the Shan-van Vogh.'*

'Sing, boys,' said Father Dennis softly. 'It looks as if we cared for their Afghan peas.'

Dan Grady raised himself to his knees and opened his mouth in a song imparted to him, as to most of his comrades, in the strictest confidence by Mulcahy—that Mulcahy then lying limp and fainting on the grass, the chill fear of death upon him.

Company after company caught up the words which, the I.A.A. say, are to herald the general rising of Erin, and to breathe which, except to those duly appointed to hear, is death. Wherefore they are printed in this place.

'The Saxon in Heaven's just balance is weighed,
His doom like Belshazzar's* in death has been cast,

And the hand of the 'venger shall never be stayed
Till his race, faith, and speech are a dream of the past.'*

They were heart-filling lines and they ran with a swirl; the
I.A.A. are better served by their pens than their petards. Dan
clapped Mulcahy merrily on the back, asking him to sing up.
The officers lay down again. There was no need to walk any
more. Their men were soothing themselves thunderously,
thus—

'St Mary in Heaven has written the vow
That the land shall not rest till the heretic blood,
From the babe at the breast to the hand at the plough
Has rolled to the ocean like Shannon in flood!'

'I'll speak to you after all's over,' said Father Dennis
authoritatively in Dan's ear. 'What's the use of confessing to
me when you do this foolishness? Dan, you've been playing
with fire! I'll lay you more penance in a week than——'

'Come along to Purgatory with us, Father dear. The Boneens
are on the move; they'll let us go now!'

The Regiment rose to the blast of the bugle as one man; but
one man there was who rose more swiftly than all the others,
for half an inch of bayonet was in the fleshy part of his leg.

'You've got to do it,' said Dan grimly. 'Do it decent, any-
how'; and the roar of the rush drowned his words, for the rear
companies thrust forward the first, still singing as they swung
down the slope—

'From the child at the breast to the hand at the plough,
Shall roll to the ocean like Shannon in flood!'

They should have sung it in the face of England, not of the
Afghans, whom it impressed as much as did the wild Irish yell.

'They came down singing,' said the unofficial report of the
enemy, borne from village to village the next day. 'They con-
tinued to sing, and it was written that our men could not abide
when they came. It is believed that there was magic in the
aforesaid song.'

Dan and Horse Egan kept themselves in the neighbourhood
of Mulcahy. Twice the man would have bolted back in the

confusion. Twice he was heaved, kicked, and shouldered back again into the unpaintable inferno of a hotly contested charge.

At the end, the panic excess of his fear drove him into madness beyond all human courage. His eyes staring at nothing, his mouth open and frothing, and breathing as one in a cold bath, he went forward demented, while Dan toiled after him. The charge checked at a high mud wall. It was Mulcahy who scrambled up tooth and nail and hurled down among the bayonets the amazed Afghan who barred his way. It was Mulcahy, keeping to the straight line of the rabid dog, who led a collection of ardent souls at a newly unmasked battery, and flung himself on the muzzle of a gun as his companions danced among the gunners. It was Mulcahy who ran wildly on from that battery into the open plain, where the enemy were retiring in sullen groups. His hands were empty, he had lost helmet and belt, and he was bleeding from a wound in the neck. Dan and Horse Egan, panting and distressed, had thrown themselves down on the ground by the captured guns, when they noticed Mulcahy's charge.

'Mad,' said Horse Egan critically. 'Mad with fear! He's going straight to his death, an' shouting's no use.'

'Let him go. Watch now! If we fire we'll hit him maybe.'

The last of a hurrying crowd of Afghans turned at the noise of shod feet behind him, and shifted his knife ready to hand. This, he saw, was no time to take prisoners. Mulcahy tore on, sobbing; the straight-held blade went home through the defenceless breast, and the body pitched forward almost before a shot from Dan's rifle brought down the slayer and still further hurried the Afghan retreat. The two Irishmen went out to bring in their dead.

'He was given the point and that was an easy death,' said Horse Egan, viewing the corpse. 'But would you ha' shot him, Danny, if he had lived?'

'He didn't live, so there's no sayin'. But I doubt I wud have bekaze of the fun he gave us—let alone the beer. Hike up his legs, Horse, and we'll bring him in. Perhaps 'tis better this way.'

They bore the poor limp body to the mass of the Regiment, lolling open-mouthed on their rifles; and there was a general snigger when one of the younger subalterns said, 'That was a good man!'

'Phew,' said Horse Egan, when a burial-party had taken over the burden. 'I'm powerful dhry, and this reminds me there'll be no more beer at all.'

'Fwhy not?' said Dan, with a twinkle in his eye as he stretched himself for rest. 'Are we not conspirin' all we can, an' while we conspire are we not entitled to free dhrinks? Sure his ould mother in New York would not let her son's comrades perish of drouth—if she can be reached at the end of a letter.'

'You're a janius,' said Horse Egan. 'O' coorse she will not. I wish this crool war was over, an' we'd get back to canteen. Faith, the Commander-in-Chief* ought to be hanged in his own little sword-belt for makin' us work on wather.'*

The Mavericks were generally of Horse Egan's opinion. So they made haste to get their work done as soon as possible, and their industry was rewarded by unexpected peace. 'We can fight the sons of Adam,' said the tribesmen, 'but we cannot fight the sons of Eblis,* and this regiment never stays still in one place. Let us therefore come in.' They came in and 'this regiment' withdrew to conspire under the leadership of Dan Grady.

Excellent as a subordinate, Dan failed altogether as a chief-in-command—possibly because he was too much swayed by the advice of the only man in the Regiment who could manufacture more than one kind of handwriting. The same mail that bore to Mulcahy's mother in New York a letter from the Colonel, telling her how valiantly her son had fought for the Queen, and how assuredly he would have been recommended for the Victoria Cross had he survived, carried a communication signed, I grieve to say, by that same Colonel and all the officers of the Regiment, explaining their willingness to do 'anything which is contrary to the regulations and all kinds of revolutions' if only a little money could be forwarded to cover incidental expenses. Daniel Grady, Esquire, would receive funds, *vice* Mulcahy, who 'was unwell at this present time of writing'.

Both letters were forwarded from New York to Tehama Street, San Francisco, with marginal comments as brief as they were bitter. The Third Three read and looked at each other.

Then the Second Conspirator—he who believed in 'joining hands with the practical branches'—began to laugh, and on recovering his gravity said, 'Gentlemen, I consider this will be a lesson to us. We're left again. Those cursed Irish have let us down. I knew they would, but'—here he laughed afresh—'I'd give considerable to know what was at the back of it all.'

His curiosity would have been satisfied had he seen Dan Grady, discredited regimental conspirator, trying to explain to his thirsty comrades in India the non-arrival of funds from New York.

Ford O' Kabul River*

KABUL town's by Kabul river—
  Blow the bugle, draw the sword—
There I lef' my mate for ever,
  Wet an' drippin' by the ford.
    Ford, ford, ford o' Kabul river,
      Ford o' Kabul river in the dark!
    There's the river up and brimmin', an' there's 'arf a
      squadron swimmin'
      'Cross the ford o' Kabul river in the dark.

Kabul town's a blasted place—
  Blow the bugle, draw the sword—
'Strewth I shan't forget 'is face
  Wet an' drippin' by the ford!
    Ford, ford, ford o' Kabul river,
      Ford o' Kabul river in the dark!
    Keep the crossing-stakes beside you, an' they will
      surely guide you
      'Cross the ford o' Kabul river in the dark.

Kabul town is sun and dust—
  Blow the bugle, draw the sword—
I'd ha' sooner drownded fust
  'Stead of 'im beside the ford.
    Ford, ford, ford o' Kabul river,
      Ford o' Kabul river in the dark!
    You can 'ear the 'orses threshin'; you can 'ear the
      men a-splashin',
      'Cross the ford o' Kabul river in the dark.

Kabul town was ours to take—
  Blow the bugle, draw the sword—
I'd ha' left it for 'is sake—
  'Im that left me by the ford.
    Ford, ford, ford o' Kabul river,

Ford o' Kabul river in the dark!
It's none so bloomin' dry there; ain't you never
comin' nigh there,
'Cross the ford o' Kabul river in the dark?

Kabul town'll go to hell—
Blow the bugle, draw the sword—
'Fore I see him 'live an' well—
'Im the best beside the ford.
Ford, ford, ford o' Kabul river,
Ford o' Kabul river in the dark!
Gawd 'elp 'em if they blunder, for their boots'll pull
'em under,
By the ford o' Kabul river in the dark.

Turn your 'orse from Kabul town—
Blow the bugle, draw the sword—
'Im an' 'arf my troop is down,
Down an' drownded by the ford.
Ford, ford, ford o' Kabul river,
Ford o' Kabul river in the dark!
There's the river low an' fallin', but it ain't no use
a-callin'
'Cross the ford o' Kabul river in the dark!

The Lost Legion*

WHEN the Indian Mutiny broke out, and a little time before the siege of Delhi, a regiment of Native Irregular Horse was stationed at Peshawur on the frontier of India. That regiment caught what John Lawrence* called at the time 'the prevalent mania,' and would have thrown in its lot with the mutineers had it been allowed to do so. The chance never came, for, as the regiment swept off down south, it was headed up by a remnant of an English corps into the hills of Afghanistan, and there the newly-conquered tribesmen turned against it as wolves turn against buck. It was hunted for the sake of its arms and accoutrements from hill to hill, from ravine to ravine, up and down the dried beds of rivers and round the shoulders of bluffs, till it disappeared as water sinks in the sand—this officerless, rebel regiment. The only trace left of its existence to-day is a nominal roll drawn up in neat round hand and countersigned by an officer who called himself 'Adjutant, late——Irregular Cavalry'. The paper is yellow with years and dirt, but on the back of it you can still read a pencil note by John Lawrence, to this effect: 'See that the two native officers who remained loyal are not deprived of their estates.— J. L.' Of six hundred and fifty sabres only two stood strain, and John Lawrence in the midst of all the agony of the first months of the Mutiny found time to think about their merits.

That was more than thirty years ago, and the tribesmen across the Afghan border who helped to annihilate the regiment are now old men. Sometimes a greybeard speaks of his share in the massacre. 'They came,' he will say, 'across the border, very proud, calling upon us to rise and kill the English, and go down to the sack of Delhi. But we who had just been conquered by the same English knew that they were over-bold, and that the Government could account easily for those down-country dogs. This Hindustani regiment, therefore, we treated with fair words, and kept standing in one place till the redcoats came after them very hot and angry. Then this regiment ran

forward a little more into our hills to avoid the wrath of the
English, and we lay upon their flanks watching from the sides
of the hills till we were well assured that their path was lost
behind them. Then we came down, for we desired their
clothes, and their bridles, and their rifles, and their boots—
more especially their boots. That was a great killing—done
slowly.' Here the old man will rub his nose, and shake his long
snaky locks, and lick his bearded lips, and grin till the yellow
tooth-stumps show. 'Yes, we killed them because we needed
their gear, and we knew that their lives had been forfeited to
God on account of their sin—the sin of treachery to the salt
which they had eaten. They rode up and down the valleys,
stumbling and rocking in their saddles, and howling for mercy.
We drove them slowly like cattle till they were all assembled in
one place, the flat wide valley of Sheor Kôt. Many had died
from want of water, but there still were many left, and they
could not make any stand. We went among them, pulling them
down with our hands two at a time, and our boys killed them
who were new to the sword. My share of the plunder was such-
and-such—so many guns, and so many saddles. The guns were
good in those days. Now we steal the Government rifles, and
despise smooth barrels. Yes, beyond doubt we wiped that regi-
ment from off the face of the earth, and even the memory of the
deed is now dying. But men say——'

At this point the tale would stop abruptly, and it was imposs-
ible to find out what men said across the border. The Afghans
were always a secretive race, and vastly preferred doing some-
thing wicked to saying anything at all. They would be quiet
and well-behaved for months, till one night, without word or
warning, they would rush a police-post, cut the throats of a
constable or two, dash through a village, carry away three or
four women, and withdraw, in the red glare of burning thatch,
driving the cattle and goats before them to their own desolate
hills. The Indian Government would become almost tearful on
these occasions. First it would say, 'Please be good and we'll
forgive you.' The tribe concerned in the latest depredation
would collectively put its thumb to its nose and answer rudely.
Then the Government would say: 'Hadn't you better pay up a
little money for those few corpses you left behind you the other

night?' Here the tribe would temporize, and lie and bully, and some of the younger men, merely to show contempt of authority, would raid another police-post and fire into some frontier mud fort, and, if lucky, kill a real English officer. Then the Government would say: 'Observe! If you really persist in this line of conduct you will be hurt.' If the tribe knew exactly what was going on in India, it would apologize or be rude, according as it learned whether the Government was busy with other things, or able to devote its full attention to their performances. Some of the tribes knew to one corpse how far to go. Others became excited, lost their heads, and told the Government to come on. With sorrow and tears, and one eye on the British taxpayer at home, who insisted on regarding these exercises as brutal wars of annexation, the Government would prepare an expensive little field-brigade and some guns, and send all up into the hills to chase the wicked tribe out of the valleys where the corn grew, into the hill-tops where there was nothing to eat. The tribe would turn out in full strength and enjoy the campaign, for they knew that their women would never be touched, that their wounded would be nursed, not mutilated, and that as soon as each man's bag of corn was spent they would surrender and palaver with the English General just as though they had been a real enemy. Afterwards, years afterwards, they would pay the blood-money, driblet by driblet, to the Government and tell their children how they had slain the redcoats by thousands. The only drawback to this kind of picnic-war was the weakness of the redcoats for solemnly blowing up with powder their fortified towers and keeps. This the tribes always considered mean.

Chief among the leaders of the smaller tribes—the little clans who knew to a penny the expense of moving white troops against them—was a priest-bandit-chief whom we will call the Gulla Kutta Mullah.* His enthusiasm for border murder as an art was almost dignified. He would cut down a mail-runner from pure wantonness, or bombard a mud fort with rifle fire when he knew that our men needed to sleep. In his leisure moments he would go on circuit among his neighbours, and try to incite other tribes to devilry. Also, he kept a kind of hotel for fellow-outlaws in his own village, which lay in a valley called

Bersund. Any respectable murderer on that section of the Frontier was sure to lie up at Bersund, for it was reckoned an exceedingly safe place. The sole entry to it ran through a narrow gorge which could be converted into a death-trap in five minutes. It was surrounded by high hills, reckoned inaccessible to all save born mountaineers, and here the Gulla Kutta Mullah lived in great state, the head of a colony of mud and stone huts, and in each mud hut hung some portion of a red uniform and the plunder of dead men. The Government particularly wished for his capture, and once invited him formally to come out and be hanged on account of a few of the murders in which he had taken a direct part. He replied:—

'I am only twenty miles, as the crow flies, from your border. Come and fetch me.'

'Some day we will come,' said the Government, 'and hanged you will be.'

The Gulla Kutta Mullah let the matter from his mind. He knew that the patience of the Government was as long as a summer day; but he did not realize that its arm was as long as a winter night. Months afterwards, when there was peace on the border, and all India was quiet, the Indian Government turned in its sleep and remembered the Gulla Kutta Mullah at Bersund with his thirteen outlaws. The movement against him of one single regiment—which the telegrams would have translated as war—would have been highly impolitic. This was a time for silence and speed, and, above all, absence of bloodshed.

You must know that all along the North-West Frontier of India there is spread a force* of some thirty thousand foot and horse, whose duty it is quietly and unostentatiously to shepherd the tribes in front of them. They move up and down, and down and up, from one desolate little post to another; they are ready to take the field at ten minutes' notice; they are always half in and half out of a difficulty somewhere along the monotonous line; their lives are as hard as their own muscles, and the papers never say anything about them. It was from this force that the Government picked its men.

One night at a station where the mounted Night Patrol fire as they challenge, and the wheat rolls in great blue-green waves under our cold northern moon, the officers were playing billiards in the mud-walled club-house, when orders came to them that they were to go on parade at once for a night-drill. They grumbled, and went to turn out their men—a hundred English troops, let us say, two hundred Gurkhas, and about a hundred cavalry of the finest native cavalry in the world.*

When they were on the parade-ground, it was explained to them in whispers that they must set off at once across the hills to Bersund. The English troops were to post themselves round the hills at the side of the valley; the Gurkhas would command the gorge and the death-trap, and the cavalry would fetch a long march round and get to the back of the circle of hills, whence, if there were any difficulty, they could charge down on the Mullah's men. But orders were very strict that there should be no fighting and no noise. They were to return in the morning with every round of ammunition intact, and the Mullah and his thirteen outlaws bound in their midst. If they were successful, no one would know or care anything about their work; but failure meant probably a small border war, in which the Gulla Kutta Mullah would pose as a popular leader against a big bullying Power, instead of a common border murderer.

Then there was silence, broken only by the clicking of the compass-needles and snapping of watch-cases, as the heads of columns compared bearings and made appointments for the rendezvous. Five minutes later the parade-ground was empty; the green coats of the Gurkhas and the overcoats of the English troops had faded into the darkness, and the cavalry were cantering away in the face of a blinding drizzle.

What the Gurkhas and the English did will be seen later on. The heavy work lay with the horses, for they had to go far and pick their way clear of habitations. Many of the troopers were natives of that part of the world, ready and anxious to fight against their kin, and some of the officers had made private and unofficial excursions into those hills before. They crossed the border, found a dried river bed, cantered up that, walked through a stony gorge, risked crossing a low hill under cover of the darkness, skirted another hill, leaving their hoof-marks deep in some ploughed ground, felt their way along another watercourse, ran over the neck of a spur, praying that no one would hear their horses grunting, and so worked on in the rain and the darkness, till they had left Bersund and its crater of hills a little behind them, and to the left, and it was time to swing round. The ascent commanding the back of Bersund was steep, and they halted to draw breath in a broad level valley below the height. That is to say, the men reined up, but the horses, blown as they were, refused to halt. There was unchristian language, the worse for being delivered in a whisper, and you heard the saddles squeaking in the darkness as the horses plunged.

The subaltern at the rear of one troop turned in his saddle and said very softly:—

'Carter, what the blessed heavens are you doing at the rear? Bring your men up, man.'

There was no answer, till a trooper replied:—

'Carter Sahib is forward—not there. There is nothing behind us.'

'There is,' said the subaltern. 'The squadron's walking on its own tail.'

Then the Major in command moved down to the rear swearing softly and asking for the blood of Lieutenant Halley—the subaltern who had just spoken.

'Look after your rearguard,' said the Major. 'Some of your infernal thieves have got lost. They're at the head of the squadron, and you're a several kinds of idiot.'

'Shall I tell off my men, sir?' said the subaltern sulkily, for he was feeling wet and cold.

'Tell 'em off!' said the Major. '*Whip* 'em off, by Gad! You're squandering them all over the place. There's a troop behind you *now*!'

'So I was thinking,' said the subaltern calmly. 'I have all my men here, sir. Better speak to Carter.'

'Carter Sahib sends salaam and wants to know why the regiment is stopping,' said a trooper to Lieutenant Halley.

'Where under heaven *is* Carter?' said the Major.

'Forward with his troop,' was the answer.

'Are we walking in a ring , then, or are we the centre of a blessed brigade?' said the Major.

By this time there was silence all along the column. The

horses were still; but, through the drive of the fine rain, men could hear the feet of many horses moving over stony ground.

'We're being stalked,' said Lieutenant Halley.

'They've no horses here. Besides, they'd have fired before this,' said the Major. 'It's—it's villagers' ponies.'

'Then our horses would have neighed and spoilt the attack long ago. They must have been near us for half an hour,' said the subaltern.

'Queer that we can't smell the horses,' said the Major, damping his finger and rubbing it on his nose as he sniffed up wind.

'Well, it's a bad start,' said the subaltern, shaking the wet from his overcoat. 'What shall we do, sir?'

'Get on,' said the Major. 'We shall catch it to-night.'

The column moved forward very gingerly for a few paces. Then there was an oath, a shower of blue sparks as shod hooves crashed on small stones, and a man rolled over with a jangle of accoutrements that would have waked the dead.

'Now we've gone and done it,' said Lieutenant Halley. 'All the hillside awake, and all the hillside to climb in the face of musketry-fire. This comes of trying to do night-hawk work.'

The trembling trooper picked himself up, and tried to explain that his horse had fallen over one of the little cairns that are built of loose stones on the spot where a man has been murdered. There was no need for reasons. The Major's big Australian charger blundered next, and the column came to a halt in what seemed to be a very graveyard of little cairns all about two feet high. The manœuvres of the squadron are not reported. Men said that it felt like mounted quadrilles without training and without the music; but at last the horses, breaking rank and choosing their own way, walked clear of the cairns, till every man of the squadron re-formed and drew rein a few yards up the slope of the hill. Then, according to Lieutenant Halley, there was another scene very like the one which has been described. The Major and Carter insisted that all the men had not joined rank, and that there were more of them in the rear clicking and blundering among the dead men's cairns. Lieutenant Halley told off his own troopers once again and resigned himself to wait. Later on he told me:—

'I didn't much know, and I didn't much care what was going

on. The row of that trooper falling ought to have scared half the country, and I would take my oath that we were being stalked by a full regiment in the rear, and *they* were making row enough to rouse all Afghanistan. I sat tight, but nothing happened.'

The mysterious part of the night's work was the silence on the hillside. Everbody knew that the Gulla Kutta Mullah had his outpost huts on the reverse side of the hill, and everybody expected by the time that the Major had sworn himself into a state of quiet that the watchmen there would open fire. When nothing occurred, they said that the gusts of the rain had deadened the sound of the horses, and thanked Providence. At last the Major satisfied himself (*a*) that he had left no one behind among the cairns, and (*b*) that he was not being taken in the rear by a large and powerful body of cavalry. The men's tempers were thoroughly spoiled, the horses were lathered and unquiet, and one and all prayed for the daylight.

They set themselves to climb up the hill, each man leading his mount carefully. Before they had covered the lower slopes or the breastplates* had begun to tighten, a thunderstorm came up behind, rolling across the low hills and drowning any noise less than that of cannon. The first flash of the lightning showed the bare ribs of the ascent, the hill-crest standing steely blue against the black sky, the little falling lines of the rain, and, a few yards to their left flank, an Afghan watch-tower, two-storeyed, built of stone, and entered by a ladder from the upper storey. The ladder was up, and a man with a rifle was leaning from the window. The darkness and the thunder rolled down in an instant, and, when the lull followed, a voice from the watch-tower cried, 'Who goes there?'

The cavalry were very quiet, but each man gripped his carbine and stood beside his horse. Again the voice called, 'Who goes there?' and in a louder key, 'O, brothers, give the alarm!' Now, every man in the cavalry would have died in his long boots sooner than have asked for quarter; but it is a fact that the answer to the second call was a long wail of 'Marf karo! Marf karo!' which means, 'Have mercy! Have mercy!' It came from the climbing regiment.

The cavalry stood dumbfounded, till the big troopers had

time to whisper one to another: 'Mir Khan, was that thy voice? Abdullah, didst *thou* call?' Lieutenant Halley stood beside his charger and waited. So long as no firing was going on he was content. Another flash of lightning showed the horses with heaving flanks and nodding heads, the men, white eye-balled, glaring beside them, and the stone watch-tower to the left. This time there was no head at the window, and the rude iron-clamped shutter that could turn a rifle bullet was closed.

'Go on, men,' said the Major. 'Get up to the top at any rate.' The squadron toiled forward, the horses wagging their tails and the men pulling at the bridles, the stones rolling down the hillside and the sparks flying. Lieutenant Halley declares that he never heard a squadron make so much noise in his life. They scrambled up, he said, as though each horse had eight legs and a spare horse to follow him. Even then there was no sound from the watch-tower, and the men stopped exhausted on the ridge that overlooked the pit of darkness in which the village of Bersund lay. Girths were loosed, curb-chains shifted, and saddles adjusted, and the men dropped down among the stones. Whatever might happen now, they had the upper ground of any attack.

The thunder ceased, and with it the rain, and the soft thick darkness of a winter night before the dawn covered them all. Except for the sound of falling water among the ravines below, everything was still. They heard the shutter of the watch-tower below them thrown back with a clang, and the voice of the watcher calling: 'Oh, Hafiz Ullah!'

The echoes took up the call, 'La-la-la!' And an answer came from the watch-tower hidden round the curve of the hill, 'What is it, Shahbaz Khan?'

Shahbaz Khan replied in the high-pitched voice of the mountaineer: 'Hast thou seen?'

The answer came back: 'Yes. God deliver us from all evil spirits!'

There was a pause, and then: 'Hafiz Ullah, I am alone! Come to me!'

'Shahbaz Khan, I am alone also, but I dare not leave my post!'

'That is a lie; thou art afraid.'

A longer pause followed, and then: 'I am afraid. Be silent! They are below us still. Pray to God and sleep.'

The troopers listened and wondered, for they could not understand what save earth and stone could lie below the watch-towers.

Shahbaz Khan began to call again: 'They are below us. I can see them. For the pity of God come over to me, Hafiz Ullah! My father slew ten of them. Come over!'

Hafiz Ullah answered in a very loud voice: 'Mine was guilt-less. Hear, ye Men of the Night, neither my father nor my blood had any part in that sin. Bear thou thine own punish-ment, Shahbaz Khan.'

'Oh, some one ought to stop those two chaps crowing away like cocks there,' said Lieutenant Halley, shivering under his rock.

He had hardly turned round to expose a new side of him to the rain before a bearded, long-locked, evil-smelling Afghan rushed up the hill, and tumbled into his arms. Halley sat upon him, and thrust as much of a sword-hilt as could be spared down the man's gullet. 'If you cry out, I kill you,' he said cheerfully.

The man was beyond any expression of terror. He lay and quaked, grunting. When Halley took the sword-hilt from between his teeth, he was still inarticulate, but clung to Hal-ley's arm, feeling it from elbow to wrist.

'The Rissala!* The dead Rissala!' he gasped. 'It is down there!'

'No; the Rissala, the very much alive Rissala. It is up here,' said Halley, unshipping his watering-bridle, and fastening the man's hands. 'Why were you in the towers so foolish as to let us pass?'

'The valley is full of the dead,' said the Afghan. 'It is better to fall into the hands of the English than the hands of the dead. They march to and fro below there. I saw them in the lightning.'

He recovered his composure after a little, and whispering, because Halley's pistol was at his stomach, said: 'What is this? There is no war between us now, and the Mullah will kill me for not seeing you pass!'

'Rest easy,' said Halley; 'we are coming to kill the Mullah, if God please. His teeth have grown too long. No harm will come to thee unless the daylight shows thee as a face which is desired by the gallows for crime done. But what of the dead regiment?'

'I only kill within my own border,' said the man, immensely relieved. 'The Dead Regiment is below. The men must have passed through it on their journey—four hundred dead on horses, stumbling among their own graves, among the little heaps—dead men all, whom we slew.'

'Whew!' said Halley. 'That accounts for my cursing Carter and the Major cursing me. Four hundred sabres, eh? No wonder we thought there were a few extra men in the troop. Kurruk Shah,' he whispered to a grizzled native officer that lay within a few feet of him, 'hast thou heard anything of a dead Rissala in these hills?'

'Assuredly,' said Kurruk Shah with a grim chuckle. 'Otherwise, why did I, who have served the Queen for seven-and-twenty years, and killed many hill-dogs, shout aloud for quarter when the lightning revealed us to the watch-towers? When I was a young man I saw the killing in the valley of Sheor Kôt there at our feet, and I know the tale that grew up there-from. But how can the ghosts of unbelievers prevail against us who are of the Faith? Strap that dog's hands a little tighter, Sahib. An Afghan is like an eel.'

'But a dead Rissala,' said Halley, jerking his captive's wrist, —'that is foolish talk, Kurruk Shah. The dead are dead. Hold still, *sag*.'* The Afghan wriggled.

'The dead are dead, and for that reason they walk at night. What need to talk? We be men; we have our eyes and ears. Thou canst both see and hear them, down the hillside,' said Kurruk Shah composedly.

Halley stared and listened long and intently. The valley was full of stifled noises, as every valley must be at night; but whether he saw or heard more than was natural Halley alone knows, and he does not choose to speak on the subject.

At last, and just before the dawn, a green rocket shot up from the far side of the valley of Bersund, at the head of the gorge, to show that the Gurkhas were in position. A red light from the infantry at left and right answered it, and the cavalry burnt a white flare. Afghans in winter are late sleepers, and it was not till full day that the Gulla Kutta Mullah's men began to straggle from their huts, rubbing their eyes. They saw men in green, and red, and brown uniforms, leaning on their arms, neatly arranged all round the crater of the village of Bersund, in a cordon that not even a wolf could have broken. They rubbed their eyes the more when a pink-faced young man, who was not even in the Army, but represented the Political Department, tripped down the hillside with two orderlies, rapped at the door of the Gulla Kutta Mullah's house, and told him quietly to step out and be tied up for safe transport. That same young man passed on through the huts, tapping here one cateran* and there another lightly with his cane; and as each was pointed out, so he was tied up, staring hopelessly at the crowned heights around where the English soldiers looked down with incurious eyes. Only the Mullah tried to carry it off with curses and high words, till a soldier who was tying his hands said:—

'None o' your lip! Why didn't you come out when you was ordered, instead o' keepin' us awake all night? You're no better than my own barrack-sweeper, you white-'eaded old polyan-thus! Kim up!'

Half an hour later the troops had gone away with the Mullah and his thirteen friends. The dazed villagers were looking rue-fully at a pile of broken muskets and snapped swords, and wondering how in the world they had come so to miscalculate the forbearance of the Indian Government.

It was a very neat little affair, neatly carried out, and the men concerned were unofficially thanked for their services.

Yet it seems to me that much credit is also due to a regiment whose name did not appear in the Brigade Orders, and whose very existence is in danger of being forgotten.

Arithmetic on the Frontier*

A GREAT and glorious thing it is
   To learn, for seven years or so,
The Lord knows what of that and this,
   Ere reckoned fit to face the foe—
The flying bullet down the Pass,
That whistles clear: 'All flesh is grass.'*

Three hundred pounds per annum spent
   On making brain and body meeter
For all the murderous intent
   Comprised in 'villainous saltpetre'*
And after?—Ask the Yusufzaies*
What comes of all our 'ologies.

A scrimmage in a Border Station—
   A canter down some dark defile—
Two thousand pounds of education
   Drops to a ten-rupee jezail—*
The Crammer's boast,* the Squadron's pride,
Shot like a rabbit in a ride!

No proposition Euclid wrote,
   No formulæ the text-books know,
Will turn the bullet from your coat,
   Or ward the tulwar's* downward blow.
Strike hard who cares—shoot straight who can—
The odds are on the cheaper man.

One sword-knot stolen from the camp
   Will pay for all the school expenses
Of any Kurrum Valley scamp
   Who knows no word of moods and tenses,
But, being blessed with perfect sight,
Picks off our messmates left and right.

With home-bred hordes the hillsides teem.
   The troopships bring us one by one,

At vast expense of time and steam,
 To slay Afridis where they run.
The 'captives of our bow and spear'*
Are cheap, alas! as we are dear.

Slaves of the Lamp*

PART 2

That very Infant who told the story of the capture of Boh Na Ghee to Eustace Cleever, novelist,* inherited an estateful baronetcy, with vast revenues, resigned the Service, and became a landholder, while his mother stood guard over him to see that he married the right girl. But, new to his position, he presented the local Volunteers with a full-sized magazine-rifle range, two miles long, across the heart of his estate, and the surrounding families, who lived in savage seclusion among woods full of pheasants, regarded him as an erring maniac. The noise of the firing disturbed their poultry, and Infant was cast out from the society of J.P.'s and decent men till such time as a daughter of the county might lure him back to right thinking. He took his revenge by filling the house with choice selections of old schoolmates home on leave—affable detrimentals,* at whom the bicycle-riding maidens of the surrounding families were allowed to look from afar. I knew when a troopship was in port by The Infant's invitations. Sometimes he would produce old friends of equal seniority; at others, young and blushing giants whom I had left small fags far down in the Lower Second; and to these Infant and the elders expounded the whole duty of Man in the Army.

'I've had to cut the Service,' said The Infant; 'but that's no reason why my vast stores of experience should be lost to posterity.' He was just thirty, and in that same summer an imperious wire drew me to his baronial castle: 'Got good haul; ex *Tamar*.* Come along.'

It was an unusually good haul, arranged with a single eye to my benefit. There was a baldish, broken-down captain of Native Infantry, shivering with ague behind an indomitable red nose—and they called him Captain Dickson. There was another captain, also of Native Infantry, with a fair moustache; his face was like white glass, and his hands were fragile, but he

answered joyfully to the cry of Tertius. There was an enor-
mously big and well-kept man, who had evidently not
campaigned for years, clean-shaved, soft-voiced, and cat-like,
but still Abanazar* for all that he adorned the Indian Political
Service; and there was a lean Irishman,* his face tanned blue-
black with the suns of the Telegraph Department. Luckily the
baize doors of the bachelors' wing fitted tight, for we dressed
promiscuously in the corridor or in each other's rooms, talking,
calling, shouting, and anon waltzing by pairs to songs of Dick
Four's own devising.

There were sixty years of mixed work to be sifted out
between us, and since we had met one another from time to
time in the quick scene-shifting of India—a dinner, camp, or a
race-meeting here; a *dâk*-bungalow* or railway station up
country somewhere else—we had never quite lost touch. Infant
sat on the banisters, hungrily and enviously drinking it in. He
enjoyed his baronetcy, but his heart yearned for the old days.

It was a cheerful babel of matters personal, provincial,* and
imperial, pieces of old call-over lists, and new policies, cut
short by the roar of a Burmese gong, and we went down not
less than a quarter of a mile of stairs to meet Infant's mother,
who had known us all in our school-days and greeted us as if
those had ended a week ago. But it was fifteen years since, with
tears of laughter, she had lent me a grey princess-skirt for
amateur theatricals.

That was a dinner from the *Arabian Nights* served in an
eighty-foot hall full of ancestors and pots of flowering roses,
and (this was more impressive) heated by steam. When it was
ended and the little mother had gone away—('You boys want
to talk, so I shall say good-night now')—we gathered about an
apple-wood fire, in a gigantic polished steel grate, under a
mantelpiece ten feet high, and The Infant compassed us about
with curious liqueurs and that kind of cigarette which serves
best to introduce your own pipe.

'Oh, bliss!' grunted Dick Four from a sofa, where he had
been packed with a rug over him. 'First time I've been warm
since I came home.'

We were all nearly on top of the fire, except Infant, who had
been long enough at Home to take exercise when he felt chil-

led. This is a grisly diversion, but one much affected by the English of the Island.

'If you say a word about cold tubs and brisk walks,' drawled M'Turk, 'I'll kill you, Infant. I've got a liver, too. 'Member when we used to think it a treat to turn out of our beds on a Sunday morning—thermometer fifty-seven degrees if it was summer—and bathe off the Pebble Ridge? Ugh!'

'Thing I don't understand,' said Tertius, 'was the way we chaps used to go down into the lavatories, boil ourselves pink, and then come up with all our pores open into a young snow-storm or a black frost. Yet none of our chaps died, that I can remember.'

'Talkin' of baths,' said M'Turk, with a chuckle, ''member our bath in Number Five, Beetle, the night Rabbits-Eggs rocked King?* What wouldn't I give to see old Stalky* now! He is the only one of the two studies not here.'

'Stalky is the Great Man of his Century,' said Dick Four.

'How d'you know?' I asked.

'How do I know?' said Dick Four scornfully. 'If you've ever been in a tight place with Stalky you wouldn't ask.'

'I haven't seen him since the camp at Pindi in '87,* I said. 'He was goin' strong then—about seven feet high and four feet thick.'

'Adequate chap. Infernally adequate,' said Tertius, pulling his moustache and staring into the fire.

'Got dam' near court-martialled and broke* in Egypt in '84,' The Infant volunteered. 'I went out in the same trooper with him—as raw as he was. Only I showed it, and Stalky didn't.'

'What was the trouble?' said M'Turk, reaching forward absently to twitch my dress-tie into position.

'Oh, nothing. His colonel trusted him to take twenty Tommies out to wash, or groom camels, or something at the back of Suakin,* and Stalky got embroiled with Fuzzies* five miles in the interior. He conducted a masterly retreat and wiped up eight of 'em. He knew jolly well he'd no right to go out so far, so he took the initiative and pitched in a letter to his colonel, who was frothing at the mouth, complaining of the "paucity of support accorded to him in his operations". Gad, it might have been one fat brigadier slangin' another! Then he went into the Staff Corps.'

'That—is—entirely—Stalky,' said Abanazar from his armchair.

'You've come across him, too?' I said.

'Oh yes,' he replied in his softest tones. 'I was at the tail of that—that epic. Don't you chaps know?'

We did not—Infant, M'Turk, and I; and we called for information very politely.

''Twasn't anything,' said Tertius. 'We got into a mess up in the Khye-Kheen Hills a couple o' years ago, and Stalky pulled us through. That's all.'

M'Turk gazed at Tertius with all an Irishman's contempt for the tongue-tied Saxon.

'Heavens!' he said. 'And it's you and your likes govern Ireland. Tertius, aren't you ashamed?'

'Well, I can't tell a yarn. I can chip in when the other fellow starts *bukhing*.* Ask him.' He pointed to Dick Four, whose nose gleamed scornfully over the rug.

'I knew you wouldn't,' said Dick Four. 'Give me a whisky and soda. I've been drinking lemon-squash and ammoniated quinine while you chaps were bathin' in champagne, and my head's singin' like a top.'

He wiped his ragged moustache above the drink; and, his teeth chattering in his head, began:

'You know the Khye-Kheen-Malôt expedition when we scared the souls out of 'em with a field force they daren't fight against? Well, both tribes—there was a coalition against us—came in without firing a shot: and a lot of hairy villains, who had no more power over their men than I had, promised and vowed all sorts of things. On that very slender evidence, Pussy dear——'

'I was at Simla,' said Abanazar hastily.

'Never mind, you're tarred with the same brush. On the strength of those tuppenny-ha'penny treaties, your asses of Politicals reported the country as pacified, and the Government, being a fool, as usual, began road-makin'—dependin' on local supply for labour. 'Member *that*, Pussy? 'Rest of our chaps who'd had no look-in during the campaign didn't think there'd be any more of it, and were anxious to get back to India. But I'd been in two of these little rows before, and I had my suspicions. I engineered myself, *summo ingenio*,* into command of a road-patrol—no shovellin', only marching up and down genteelly with a guard. They'd withdrawn all the troops they could, but I nucleused about forty Pathans, recruits chiefly, of my regiment, and sat tight at the base-camp while the road-parties went to work, as per Political survey.'

'Had some rippin' sing-songs in camp, too,' said Tertius.

'My pup'—thus did Dick Four refer to his subaltern—'was a pious little beast. He didn't like the sing-songs, and so went down with pneumonia. I rootled round the camp, and found Tertius gassing about as a D.A.Q.M.G.,* which, God knows, he isn't cut out for. There were six or eight of the old Coll. at base-camp (we're always in force for a Frontier row), but I'd heard of Tertius as a steady old hack, and I told him he had to shake off his D.A.Q.M.G. breeches and help *me*. Tertius volunteered like a shot, and we settled it with the authorities, and out we went—forty Pathans, Tertius, and me, looking up the road-parties. Macnamara's—'member old Mac, the Sapper, who played the fiddle so damnably at Umballa?— Mac's party was the last but one. The last was Stalky's. He was at the head of the road with some of his pet Sikhs. Mac said he believed he was all right.'

'Stalky *is* a Sikh,' said Tertius. 'He takes his men to pray at the Durbar Sahib* at Amritzar, regularly as clockwork, when he can.'

'Don't interrupt, Tertius. It was about forty miles beyond Mac's before I found him; and my men pointed out gently, but firmly, that the country was risin'. What kind o' country, Beetle? Well, *I'm* no word-painter, thank goodness, but *you* might call it a hellish country! When we weren't up to our necks in snow, we were rolling down the khud.* The well-disposed inhabitants, who were to supply labour for the road-making (don't forget that, Pussy dear), sat behind rocks and took pot-shots at us. Old, old story! We all legged it in search of Stalky. I had a feeling that he'd be in good cover, and about dusk we found him and his road-party, as snug as a bug in a rug, in an old Malôt stone fort, with a watch-tower at one corner. It overhung the road they had blasted out of the cliff fifty feet below; and under the road things went down pretty sheer, for five or six hundred feet, into a gorge about half a mile wide and two or three miles long. There were chaps on the other side of the gorge scientifically gettin' our range. So I hammered on the gate and nipped in, and tripped over Stalky in a greasy, bloody old poshteen,* squatting on the ground, eating with his men. I'd only seen him for half a minute about three months before, but I might have met him yesterday. He waved his hand all sereno.

' "Hullo, Aladdin! Hullo, Emperor!"* he said. "You're just in time for the performance."

'I saw his Sikhs looked a bit battered. "Where's your command? Where's your subaltern?" I said.

' "Here—all there is of it," said Stalky. "If you want young Everett, he's dead, and his body's in the watch-tower. They rushed our road-party last week, and got him and seven men. We've been besieged for five days. I suppose they let you through to make sure of you. The whole country's up. Strikes me you walked into a first-class trap." He grinned, but neither Tertius nor I could see where the deuce the fun was. We hadn't any grub for our men, and Stalky had only four days' whack for his. That came of dependin' upon your asinine Politicals, Pussy dear, who told us that the inhabitants were friendly.

'To make us quite comfy, Stalky took us up to the watch-tower to see poor Everett's body, lyin' in a foot o' drifted snow. It looked like a girl of fifteen—not a hair on the little fellow's face. He'd been shot through the temple, but the Malôts had left their mark on him. Stalky unbuttoned the tunic, and showed it to us—a rummy sickle-shaped cut on the chest. 'Member the snow all white on his eyebrows, Tertius? 'Member when Stalky moved the lamp and it looked as if he was alive?'

'Ye—es,' said Tertius, with a shudder. "Member the beastly look on Stalky's face, though, with his nostrils all blown out, same as he used to look when he was bullyin' a fag? That was a lovely evening.'

'We held a council of war up there over Everett's body.

Stalky said the Malôts and Khye-Kheens were up together; havin' sunk their blood-feuds to settle us. The chaps we'd seen across the gorge were Khye-Kheens. It was about half a mile from them to us as a bullet flies, and they'd made a line of sungars* under the brow of the hill to sleep in and starve us out. The Malôts, he said, were in front of us promiscuous. There wasn't good cover behind the fort, or they'd have been there too. Stalky didn't mind the Malôts half as much as he did the Khye-Kheens. He said the Malôts were treacherous curs. What I couldn't understand was, why in the world the two gangs didn't join in and rush us. There must have been at least five hundred of 'em. Stalky said they didn't trust each other very well, because they were ancestral enemies when they were at home; and the only time they'd tried a rush he'd hove a couple of blasting-charges among 'em, and that had sickened 'em a bit.

'It was dark by the time we finished, and Stalky, always sereno, said: "You command now. I don't suppose you mind my taking any action I may consider necessary to reprovision the fort?" I said "Of course not," and then the lamp blew out. So Tertius and I had to climb down the tower steps (we didn't want to stay with Everett) and got back to our men. Stalky had gone off—to count the stores, I supposed. Anyhow, Tertius and I sat up in case of a rush (they were plugging at us pretty generally, you know), relieving each other till the mornin'.

'Mornin' came. No Stalky. Not a sign of him. I took counsel with his senior native officer—a grand, white-whiskered old chap—Rutton Singh, from Jullundur way. He only grinned, and said it was all right. Stalky had been out of the fort twice before, somewhere or other, accordin' to him. He said Stalky 'ud come back unchipped, and gave me to understand that Stalky was an invulnerable *Guru* of sorts. All the same, I put the whole command on half rations, and set 'em to pickin' out loop-holes.

'About noon there was no end of a snowstorm, and the enemy stopped firing. We replied gingerly, because we were awfully short of ammunition. Don't suppose we fired five shots an hour, but we generally got our man. Well, while I was talking with Rutton Singh I saw Stalky coming down from the watch-tower, rather puffy about the eyes, his poshteen coated with claret-coloured ice.

'"No trustin' these snowstorms," he said. "Nip out quick and snaffle what you can get. There's a certain amount of friction between the Khye-Kheens and the Malôts just now."

'I turned Tertius out with twenty Pathans, and they bucked about in the snow for a bit till they came on to a sort of camp about eight hundred yards away, with only a few men in charge and half-a-dozen sheep by the fire. They finished off the men, and snaffled the sheep and as much grain as they could carry, and came back. No one fired a shot at 'em. There didn't seem to be anybody about, but the snow was falling pretty thick.

'"That's good enough," said Stalky when we got dinner ready and he was chewin' mutton-kababs off a cleanin'-rod. "There's no sense riskin' men. They're holding a pow-wow between the Khye-Kheens and the Malôts at the head of the gorge. I don't think these so-called coalitions are much good."

'Do you know what that maniac had done? Tertius and I shook it out of him by instalments. There was an underground granary cellar-room below the watch-tower, and in blasting the road Stalky had blown a hole into one side of it. Being no one else *but* Stalky, he'd kept the hole open for his own ends; and laid poor Everett's body slap over the well of the stairs that led down to it from the watch-tower. He'd had to remove and replace the corpse every time he used the passage. The Sikhs wouldn't go near the place, of course. Well, he'd got out of this hole, and dropped on to the road. Then, in the night *and* a howling snowstorm, he'd dropped over the edge of the khud, made his way down to the bottom of the gorge, forded the nullah,* which was half frozen, climbed up on the other side along a track he'd discovered, and come out on the right flank of the Khye-Kheens. He had then—listen to this!—crossed over a ridge that paralleled their rear, walked half a mile behind that, and come out on the left of their line where the gorge gets shallow and where there was a regular track between the Malôt and the Khye-Kheen camps. That was about two in the morning, and, as it turned out, a man spotted him—a Khye-Kheen. So Stalky abolished him quietly, and left him—*with* the Malôt mark on his chest, same as Everett had.

' "I was just as economical as I could be," Stalky said to us. "If he'd shouted I should have been slain. I'd never had to do that kind of thing but once before, and that was the first time I tried that path. It's perfectly practicable for infantry, you know."

' "What about your first man?" I said.

' "Oh, that was the night after they killed Everett, and I went out lookin' for a line of retreat for my men. A man found me. I abolished him—*privatim**—scragged him. But on thinkin' it over it occurred to me that if I could find the body (I'd hove it down some rocks) I might decorate it with the Malôt mark and leave it to the Khye-Kheens to draw inferences. So I went out again the next night and did. The Khye-Kheens are shocked at the Malôts perpetratin' these two dastardly outrages after they'd sworn to sink all blood-feuds. I lay up behind their sungars early this morning and watched 'em. They all went to confer about it at the head of the gorge. Awf'ly annoyed they are. Don't wonder." You know the way Stalky drops out his words, one by one.'

'My God!' said The Infant explosively, as the full depth of the strategy dawned on him.

'Dear-r man!' said M'Turk, purring rapturously.

'Stalky stalked,' said Tertius. 'That's all there is to it.'

'No, he didn't,' said Dick Four. 'Don't you remember how he insisted that he had only applied his luck? Don't you remember how Rutton Singh grabbed his boots and grovelled in the snow, and how our men shouted?'

'None of our Pathans believed that was luck,' said Tertius. 'They swore Stalky ought to have been born a Pathan, and —'member we nearly had a row in the fort when Rutton Singh said Stalky was a Sikh? Gad, how furious the old chap was with my Pathan Jemadar!* But Stalky just waggled his finger and they shut up.

'Old Rutton Singh's sword was half out, though, and he swore he'd cremate every Khye-Kheen and Malôt he killed. That made the Jemadar pretty wild, because he didn't mind fighting against his own creed, but he wasn't going to crab a fellow-Mussulman's chances of Paradise. Then Stalky jabbered

Pushtu* and Punjabi in alternate streaks. Where the deuce did he pick up his Pushtu from, Beetle?'

'Never mind his language, Dick,' said I. 'Give us the gist of it.'

'I flatter myself I can address the wily Pathan on occasion, but, hang it all, I can't make puns in Pushtu, or top off my arguments with a smutty story, as he did. He played on those two old dogs o' war like a—like a concertina. Stalky said—and the other two backed up his knowledge of Oriental nature— that the Khye-Kheens and the Malôts between 'em would organize a combined attack on us that night, as a proof of good faith. They wouldn't drive it home, though, because neither side would trust the other, on account, as Rutton Singh put it, of the little accidents. Stalky's notion was to crawl out at dusk with his Sikhs, manœuvre 'em along this ungodly goat-track that he'd found, to the back of the Khye-Kheen position, and then lob in a few long shots at the Malôts when the attack was well on. "That'll divert their minds and help to agitate 'em," he said. "Then you chaps can come out and sweep up the pieces, and we'll rendezvous at the head of the gorge. After that, I move we get back to Mac's camp and have something to eat." '

'*You* were commandin'?' The Infant suggested.

'I was about three months senior to Stalky, and two months Tertius's senior,' Dick Four replied. '*But* we were all from the same old Coll. I should say ours was the only little affair on record where some one wasn't jealous of some one else.'

'We weren't,' Tertius broke in, 'but there was another row between Gul Sher Khan and Rutton Singh. Our Jemadar said—he was quite right—that no Sikh living could stalk worth a damn; and that Koran Sahib* had better take out the Pathans, who understood that kind of mountain work. Rutton Singh said that Koran Sahib jolly well knew every Pathan was a born deserter, and every Sikh was a gentleman, even if he couldn't crawl on his belly. Stalky struck in with some woman's proverb or other, that had the effect of doublin' both men up with a grin. He said the Sikhs and the Pathans could settle their claims on the Khye-Kheens and Malôts later on, but he was going to take his Sikhs along for this mountain-climbing job, because Sikhs could shoot. They can too. Give 'em a mule-load of ammunition apiece, and they're perfectly happy.'

'And out he gat,' said Dick Four. 'As soon as it was dark, and he'd had a bit of a snooze, him and thirty Sikhs went down through the staircase in the tower, every mother's son of 'em salutin' little Everett where It stood propped up against the wall. The last I heard him say was, "Kubbadar! tumbleinga!"* and they tumbleingaed over the black edge of nothing. Close upon 9 P.M. the combined attack developed; Khye-Kheens across the valley, and Malôts in front of us, pluggin' at long range and yellin' to each other to come along and cut our infidel throats. Then they skirmished up to the gate, and began the old game of calling our Pathans renegades, and invitin' 'em to join the holy war. One of our men, a young fellow from Dera Ismail, jumped on the wall to slang 'em back, and jumped down, blubbing like a child. He'd been hit smack in the middle of the hand. Never saw a man yet who could stand a hit in the hand without weepin' bitterly. It tickles up all the nerves. So Tertius took his rifle and smote the others on the head to keep them quiet at the loopholes. The dear children wanted to open the gate and go in at 'em generally, but that didn't suit our book.

'At last, near midnight, I heard the wop, wop, wop, of Stalky's Martinis* across the valley, and some general cursing among the Malôts, whose main body was hid from us by a fold in the hillside. Stalky was brownin' 'em* at a great rate, and very naturally they turned half right and began to blaze at their faithless allies, the Khye-Kheens—regular volley firin'. In less than ten minutes after Stalky opened the diversion they were going it hammer and tongs, both sides the valley. When we could see, the valley was rather a mixed-up affair. The Khye-Kheens had streamed out of their sungars above the gorge to chastise the Malôts, and Stalky—I was watching him through my glasses—had slipped in behind 'em. Very good. The Khye-Kheens had to leg it along the hillside up to where the gorge got shallow and they could cross over to the Malôts, who were awfully cheered to see the Khye-Kheens taken in the rear.

'Then it occurred to me to comfort the Khye-Kheens. So I

turned out the whole command, and we advanced *à la pas de charge*,* doublin' up what, for the sake of argument, we'll call the Malôts' left flank. Even then, if they'd sunk their differences, they could have eaten us alive; but they'd been firin' at each other half the night, and they went on firin'. Queerest thing you ever saw in your born days! As soon as our men doubled up to the Malôts, they'd blaze at the Khye-Kheens more zealously than ever, to show they were on our side, run up the valley a few hundred yards, and halt to fire again. The moment Stalky saw our game he duplicated it his side the gorge; and, by Jove! the Khye-Kheens did just the same thing.'

'Yes, but,' said Tertius, 'you've forgot him playin' "Arrah, Patsy, mind the baby"* on the bugle to hurry us up.'

'Did he?' roared M'Turk. Somehow we all began to sing it, and there was an interruption.

'Rather,' said Tertius, when we were quiet. No one of the Aladdin company could forget that tune. 'Yes, he played "Patsy." Go on, Dick.'

'Finally,' said Dick Four, 'we drove both mobs into each other's arms on a bit of level ground at the head of the valley, and saw the whole crew whirl off, fightin' and stabbin' and swearin' in a blinding snowstorm. They were a heavy, hairy lot, and we didn't follow 'em.

'Stalky had captured one prisoner—an old pensioned Sepoy of twenty-five years' service, who produced his discharge—an awf'ly sportin' old card. He had been tryin' to make his men rush us early in the day. He was sulky—angry with his own side for their cowardice, and Rutton Singh wanted to bayonet him—Sikhs don't understand fightin' against the Government after you've served it honestly—but Stalky rescued him, and froze on to him tight—with ulterior motives, I believe. When we got back to the fort, we buried young Everett—Stalky wouldn't hear of blowin' up the place—and bunked. We'd only lost ten men, all told.'

'Only ten, out of seventy. How did you lose 'em?' I asked.

'Oh, there was a rush on the fort early in the night, and a few Malôts got over the gate. It was rather a tight thing for a minute or two, but the recruits took it beautifully. Lucky job we hadn't any badly wounded men to carry, because we had forty miles to Macnamara's camp. By Jove, how we legged it! Half way in, old Rutton Singh collapsed, so we slung him across four rifles and Stalky's overcoat; and Stalky, his prisoner, and a couple of Sikhs were his bearers. After that I went to sleep. You can, you know, on the march, when your legs get properly numbed. Mac swears we all marched into his camp snoring, and dropped where we halted. His men lugged us into the tents like gram-bags.* I remember wakin' up and seeing Stalky asleep with his head on old Rutton Singh's chest. *He* slept twenty-four hours. I only slept seventeen, but then I was coming down with dysentery.'

'Coming down! What rot! He had it on him before we joined Stalky in the fort,' said Tertius.

'Well, *you* needn't talk! You hove your sword at Macnamara and demanded a drumhead court-martial every time you saw him. The only thing that soothed you was putting you under arrest every half-hour. You were off your head for three days.'

'Don't remember a word of it,' said Tertius placidly. 'I remember my orderly giving me milk, though.'

'How did Stalky come out?' M'Turk demanded, puffing hard over his pipe.

'Stalky? Like a serene Brahmini bull.* Poor old Mac was at his Royal Engineer's wits' end to know what to do. You see I was putrid with dysentery, Tertius was ravin', half the men had frost-bite, and Macnamara's orders were to break camp and come in before winter. So Stalky, who hadn't turned a hair, took half his supplies to save him the bother o' luggin' 'em back to the Plains, and all the ammunition he could get at, and, *consilio et auxilio* Rutton Singhi,* tramped back to his fort with all his Sikhs and his precious prisoners, *and* a lot of dissolute hangers-on that he and the prisoner had seduced into service. He had sixty men of sorts—and his brazen cheek. Mac nearly wept with joy when he went. You see, there weren't any explicit orders to Stalky to come in before the passes were blocked: Mac is a great man for orders, and Stalky's a great man for orders—when they suit his book.'

'He told me he was goin' to the Engadine,'* said Tertius. 'Sat on my cot smokin' a cigarette, and makin' me laugh till I cried. Macnamara bundled the whole lot of us down to the plains next day. We were a walkin' hospital.'

'Stalky told me that Macnamara was a simple godsend to him,' said Dick Four. 'I used to see him in Mac's tent listenin' to Mac playin' the fiddle, and, between the pieces, wheedlin' Mac out of picks and shovels and dynamite cartridges hand-over-fist. Well, that was the last we saw of Stalky. A week or so later the passes were shut with snow, and I don't think Stalky wanted to be found particularly just then.'

'He didn't,' said the fair and fat Abanazar. 'He didn't. Ho, ho!'

Dick Four threw up his thin, dry hand with the blue veins at the back of it. 'Hold on a minute, Pussy. I'll let you in at the proper time. I went down to my regiment, and that spring, five months later, I got off with a couple of companies on detachment: nominally to look after some friends of ours across the Border; actually, of course, to recruit. It was a bit unfortunate, because an ass of a young Naik* carried a frivolous blood-feud he'd inherited from his aunt into those hills, and the local gentry wouldn't volunteer into my corps. Of course, the Naik had taken short leave to manage the business; that was all regular enough; *but* he'd stalked my pet orderly's uncle. It was an infernal shame, because I knew Harris of the Ghuznees would be covering that ground three months later, and he'd snaffle all the chaps I had my eyes on. Everybody was down on the Naik, because they felt he ought to have had the decency to postpone his—his disgustful amours* till our companies were full strength.

'Still, the beast had a certain amount of professional feeling left. He sent one of his aunt's clan by night to tell me that, if I'd take safeguard,* he'd put me on to a batch of beauties. I nipped over the Border like a shot, and about ten miles the other side, in a nullah, my rapparee*-in-charge showed me about seventy men variously armed, but standing up like a Queen's Company. Then one of 'em stepped out and lugged round an old bugle, just like—who's the man?—Bancroft,* ain't it?—feeling for his eyeglass in a farce, and played "Arrah, Patsy, mind the baby. Arrah, Patsy, mind" '—that was as far as he could get.

That also was as far as Dick Four could get, because we had

to sing the old song through twice, again and once more, and subsequently, in order to repeat it.

'He explained that if I knew the rest of the song he had a note for me from the man the song belonged to. Whereupon, my children, I finished that old tune on that bugle, and *this* is what I got. I knew you'd like to look at it. Don't grab.' (We were all struggling for a sight of the well-known unformed handwriting.) 'I'll read it aloud:

> "Fort Everett, *February* 19.
>
> "Dear Dick, or Tertius: The bearer of this is in charge of seventy-five recruits, all pukka* devils, but desirous of leading new lives. They have been slightly polished, and after being boiled may shape well. I want you to give thirty of them to my Adjutant, who, though God's Own ass, will need men this spring. The rest you can keep. You will be interested to learn that I have extended my road to the end of the Malôt country. All headmen and priests concerned in last September's affair worked one month each, supplying road-metal from their own houses. Everett's grave is covered by a forty-foot mound, which should serve well as a base for future triangulations. Rutton Singh sends his best salaams. I am making some treaties, and have given my prisoner—who also sends his salaams—local rank of Khan Bahadur.*
>
> "A. L. Corkran." '

'Well, that was all,' said Dick Four, when the roaring, the shouting, the laughter, and, I think, the tears, had subsided. 'I chaperoned the gang across the Border as quick as I could. They were rather homesick, but they cheered up when they recognized some of my chaps, who had been in the Khye-Kheen row, and they made a rippin' good lot. It's rather more than three hundred miles from Fort Everett to where I picked 'em up. Now, Pussy, tell 'em the latter end o' Stalky as you saw it.'

Abanazar laughed a little nervous, misleading, official laugh.

'Oh, it wasn't much. I was at Simla in the spring when our Stalky, out of his snows, began corresponding direct with the Government.'

'After the manner of a king,' suggested Dick Four.

'My turn now, Dick. He'd done a whole lot of things he shouldn't have done, and constructively pledged the Government to all sorts of action.'

'Pledged the State's ticker,* eh?' said M'Turk, with a nod to me.

'About that; but the embarrassin' part was that it was all so thunderin' convenient, so well reasoned, don't you know. Came in as pat as if he'd had access to all sorts of information —which he couldn't, of course.'

'Pooh!' said Tertius, 'I back Stalky against the Foreign Office any day.'

'He'd done pretty nearly everything he could think of, except strikin' coins in his own image and superscription, all under cover of buildin' this infernal road and bein' blocked by the snow. His report was simply amazin'. Von Lennaert tore his hair over it at first, and then he gasped, "Who the dooce is this unknown Warren Hastings?* He must be slain. He must be slain officially! The Viceroy'll never stand it. It's unheard of. He must be slain by His Excellency in person. Order him up here and pitch in a stinger." Well, I sent him no end of an official stinger, and I pitched in an unofficial telegram at the same time.'

'You!' This with amazement from The Infant, for Abanazar resembled nothing so much as a fluffy Persian cat.

'Yes—me,' said Abanazar. ''Twasn't much, but after what you've said, Dicky, it was rather a coincidence, because I wired:

> "Aladdin now has won his wife,
>   Your Emperor is appeased.
> I think you'd better come to life:
>   We hope you've all been pleased."

Funny how that old song came up in my head. That was fairly non-committal and encouragin'. The only flaw was that his Emperor wasn't appeased by very long chalks. Stalky extricated himself from his mountain fastnesses and loafed up to Simla at his leisure, to be offered up on the horns of the altar.'

'But,' I began, 'surely the Commander-in-Chief is the proper——'*

'His Excellency had an idea that if he blew up one single junior captain—same as King used to blow us up—he was holdin' the reins of empire, and, of course, as long as he had that idea, Von Lennaert encouraged him. I'm not sure Von Lennaert didn't put that notion into his head.'

'They've changed the breed, then, since my time,' I said.

'P'r'aps. Stalky was sent up for his wiggin' like a bad little boy. I've reason to believe that His Excellency's hair stood on end. He walked into Stalky for one hour—Stalky at attention in the middle of the floor, and (so he vowed) Von Lennaert pretending to soothe down His Excellency's top-knot in dumb show in the background. Stalky didn't dare to look up, or he'd have laughed.'

'Now, wherefore was Stalky not broken publicly?' said The Infant, with a large and luminous leer.

'Ah, wherefore?' said Abanazar. 'To give him a chance to retrieve his blasted career, and not to break his father's heart. Stalky hadn't a father, but that didn't matter. He behaved like a—like the Sanawar Orphan Asylum,* and His Excellency graciously spared him. Then he came round to my office and sat opposite me for ten minutes, puffing out his nostrils. Then he said, "Pussy, if I thought that basket-hanger——" '

'Hah! He remembered *that*,' said M'Turk.

' "That two-anna* basket-hanger* governed India, I swear I'd become a naturalized Muscovite tomorrow. I'm a *femme incomprise.** This thing's broken my heart. It'll take six months' shootin'-leave in India to mend it. Do you think I can get it, Pussy?" '

'He got it in about three minutes and a half, and seventeen days later he was back in the arms of Rutton Singh—horrid disgraced—with orders to hand over his command, etc., to Cathcart MacMonnie.'

'Observe!' said Dick Four. 'One colonel of the Political Department in charge of thirty Sikhs on a hilltop. Observe, my children!'

'Naturally, Cathcart not being a fool, even if he *is* a Political, let Stalky do his shooting within fifteen miles of Fort Everett for the next six months; and I always understood they and Rutton Singh *and* the prisoner were as thick as thieves. Then Stalky loafed back to his regiment, I believe. I've never seen him since.'

'I have, though,' said M'Turk, swelling with pride.

We all turned as one man.

'It was at the beginning of this hot weather. I was in camp in the Jullundur doab* and stumbled slap on Stalky in a Sikh village; sitting on the one chair of state, with half the population grovellin' before him, a dozen Sikh babies on his knees, an old harridan clappin' him on the shoulder, and a garland o' flowers round his neck. Told me he was recruitin'. We dined together that night, but he never said a word of the business of the Fort. 'Told me, though, that if I wanted any supplies I'd better say I was Koran Sahib's *bhai*;* and I did, and the Sikhs wouldn't take my money.'

'Ah! That must have been one of Rutton Singh's villages,' said Dick Four; and we smoked for some time in silence.

'I say,' said M'Turk, casting back through the years. 'Did Stalky ever tell you *how* Rabbits-Eggs came to rock King that night?'

'No,' said Dick Four.

Then M'Turk told.

'I see,' said Dick Four, nodding. 'Practically he duplicated that trick over again. There's nobody like Stalky.'

'That's just where you make the mistake,' I said. 'India's full of Stalkies—Cheltenham and Haileybury and Marlborough chaps—that we don't know anything about, and the surprises will begin when there is really a big row on.'

'Who will be surprised?' said Dick Four.

'The other side. The gentlemen who go to the front in first-class carriages. Just imagine Stalky let loose on the south side of Europe with a sufficiency of Sikhs and a reasonable prospect of loot. Consider it quietly.'

'There's something in that, but you're too much of an optimist, Beetle,' said The Infant.

'Well, I've a right to be. Ain't I responsible for the whole thing? You needn't laugh. Who wrote "Aladdin now has won his wife"—eh?'

'What's that got to do with it?' said Tertius.

'Everything,' said I.

'Prove it,' said The Infant.

And I have.

PART TWO

The Boer War

Rimmon*

(After Boer War)

DULY with knees that feign to quake—
  Bent head and shaded brow,—
Yet once again, for my father's sake,
  In Rimmon's House I bow.

The curtains part, the trumpet blares,
  And the eunuchs howl aloud;
And the gilt, swag-bellied idol glares
  Insolent over the crowd.

'This is Rimmon, Lord of the Earth—
  Fear Him and bow the knee!'
And I watch my comrades hide their mirth
  That rode to the wars with me.

For we remember the sun and the sand
  And the rocks whereon we trod,
Ere we came to a scorched and a scornful land
  That did not know our God;

As we remember the sacrifice,
  Dead men an hundred laid—
Slain while they served His mysteries,
  And that He would not aid—

Not though we gashed ourselves and wept,
  For the high-priest bade us wait;
Saying He went on a journey or slept,
  Or was drunk or had taken a mate.*

(Praise ye Rimmon, King of Kings,
  Who ruleth Earth and Sky!
And again I bow as the censer swings
  And the God Enthroned goes by.)

Ay, we remember His sacred ark
    And the virtuous men that knelt
To the dark and the hush behind the dark
    Wherein we dreamed He dwelt;

Until we entered to hale Him out,
    And found no more than an old
Uncleanly image girded about
    The loins with scarlet and gold.

Him we o'erset with the butts of our spears—
    Him and his vast designs—
To be the scorn of our muleteers
    And the jest of our halted lines.

By the picket-pins that the dogs defile,
    In the dung and the dust He lay,
Till the priests ran and chattered awhile
    And wiped Him and took Him away.

Hushing the matter before it was known,
    They returned to our fathers afar,
And hastily set Him afresh on His throne
    Because he had won us the war.

Wherefore with knees that feign to quake—
    Bent head and shaded brow—
To this dead dog, for my father's sake,
    In Rimmon's House I bow!

The Way That He Took*

Almost every word of this story is based on fact. The Boer War of 1899–1902 was a very small one as wars were reckoned, and was fought without any particular malice, but it taught our men the practical value of scouting in the field. They were slow to learn at the outset, and it cost them many unnecessary losses, as is always the case when men think they can do their work without taking trouble beforehand.*

THE guns of the Field-Battery were ambushed behind white-thorned mimosas, scarcely taller than their wheels, that marked the line of a dry nullah;* and the camp pretended to find shade under a clump of gums planted as an experiment by some Minister of Agriculture. One small hut, reddish stone with a tin roof, stood where the single track of the railway split into a siding. A rolling plain of red earth, speckled with loose stones and sugar-bush, ran northward to the scarps and spurs of a range of little hills—all barren and exaggerated in the heat-haze. Southward, the level lost itself in a tangle of scrub-furred hillocks, upheaved without purpose or order, seared and black-ened by the strokes of the careless lightning, seamed down their sides with spent watercourses, and peppered from base to summit with stones—riven, piled, scattered stones. Far away, to the eastward, a line of blue-grey mountains, peaked and horned, lifted itself over the huddle of the tortured earth. It was the only thing that held steady through the liquid mirage. The nearer hills detached themselves from the plain, and swam forward like islands in a milky ocean. While the Major stared through puckered eyelids, Leviathan* himself waded through the far shallows of it—a black and formless beast.

'That,' said the Major, 'must be the guns coming back.' He had sent out two guns, nominally for exercise—actually to show the loyal Dutch* that there was artillery near the railway if any patriot thought fit to tamper with it. Chocolate smears, looking as though they had been swept with a besom through the raffle of stones, wandered across the earth—unbridged, ungraded, unmetalled. They were the roads to the brown mud huts, one in each valley, that were officially styled farm-houses. At very long intervals a dusty Cape-cart or a tilted wagon would move along them, and men, dirtier than the dirt, would come to sell fruit or scraggy sheep. At night the farm-houses were lighted up in a style out of all keeping with Dutch economy; the scrub would light itself on some far headland, and the house-lights twinkled in reply. Three or four days later the Major would read bad news in the Cape Town papers thrown to him from the passing troop trains.

The guns and their escort changed from Leviathan to the likeness of wrecked boats, their crews struggling beside them. Presently they took on their true shape, and lurched into camp amid clouds of dust.

The Mounted Infantry* escort set about its evening meal; the hot air filled with the scent of burning wood; sweating men rough-dried sweating horses with wisps of precious forage; the sun dipped behind the hills, and they heard the whistle of a train from the south.

'What's that?' said the Major, slipping into his coat. The decencies had not yet left him.

'Ambulance train,' said the Captain of Mounted Infantry, raising his glasses. 'I'd like to talk to a woman again, but it won't stop here. . . . It *is* stopping, though, and making a beastly noise. Let's look.'

The engine had sprung a leaky tube, and ran lamely into the siding. It would be two or three hours at least before she could be patched up.

Two doctors and a couple of Nursing Sisters stood on the rear platform of a carriage. The Major explained the situation, and invited them to tea.

'We were just going to ask *you*,' said the medical Major of the ambulance train.

'No, come to our camp. Let the men see a woman again!' he pleaded.

Sister Dorothy, old in the needs of war, for all her twenty-four years, gathered up a tin of biscuits and some bread and butter new cut by the orderlies. Sister Margaret picked up the teapot, the spirit-lamp, and a water-bottle.

'Cape Town water,' she said with a nod. 'Filtered too. *I* know Karroo* water.' She jumped down lightly on to the ballast.

'What do you know about the Karroo, Sister?' said the Captain of Mounted Infantry, indulgently, as a veteran of a month's standing. He understood that all that desert as it seemed to him was called by that name.

She laughed. 'This is my home. I was born out they-ah—just behind that big range of hills—out Oudtshorn* way. It's only sixty miles from here. Oh, how good it is!'

She slipped the Nurses' cap from her head, tossed it through the open car-window, and drew a breath of deep content. With the sinking of the sun the dry hills had taken life and glowed against the green of the horizon. They rose up like jewels in the utterly lucid air, while the valleys between flooded with purple shadow. A mile away, stark-clear, withered rocks showed as though one could touch them with the hand, and the voice of a native herd-boy in charge of a flock of sheep came in clear and sharp over twice that distance. Sister Margaret devoured the huge spaces with eyes unused to shorter ranges, snuffed again the air that has no equal under God's skies, and, turning to her companion, said: 'What do *you* think of it?'

'I am afraid I'm rather singular,' he replied. 'Most of us hate the Karroo. I used to, but it grows on one somehow. I suppose it's the lack of fences and roads that's so fascinating. And when one gets back from the railway——'

'You're quite right,' she said, with an emphatic stamp of her foot. 'People come to Matjesfontein*—ugh!—with their lungs, and they live opposite the railway station and that new hotel, and they think *that's* the Karroo. They say there isn't anything in it. It's *full* of life when you really get into it. You see that? I'm *so* glad. D'you know, you're the first English officer I've heard who has spoken a good word for my country.'

'I'm glad I pleased you,' said the Captain, looking into Sister Margaret's black-lashed grey eyes under the heavy brown hair shot with grey where it rolled back from the tanned forehead. This kind of nurse was new in his experience. The average Sister did not lightly stride over rolling stones, and—was it possible that her easy pace up-hill was beginning to pump him?* As she walked, she hummed joyously to herself, a queer catchy tune of one line several times repeated:

> Vat jou goed en trek, Ferreira,
> Vat jou goed en trek.

It ran off with a little trill that sounded like:

> Swaar draa, alle en die ein kant;
> Jannie met die hoepelbeen!*

'Listen!' she said, suddenly. 'What was that?'

'It must be a wagon on the road. I heard the whip, I think.'

'Yes, but you didn't hear the wheels, did you? It's a little bird that makes just that noise, "Whe-ew"!' she duplicated it perfectly. 'We call it'—she gave the Dutch name, which did not, of course, abide with the Captain. 'We must have given him a scare! You hear him in the early mornings when you are sleeping in the wagons. It's just like the noise of a whiplash, isn't it?'

They entered the Major's tent a little behind the others, who were discussing the scanty news of the campaign.

'Oh no,' said Sister Margaret coolly, bending over the spirit-lamp, 'the Transvaalers will stay round Kimberley and try to put Rhodes in a cage.* But, of course, if a commando gets through to De Aar they will all rise*——'

'You think so, Sister?' said the medical Major deferentially.

'I know so. They will rise anywhere in the Colony if a commando comes actually to them. Presently they will rise in Prieska*—if it is only to steal the forage at Van Wyk's Vlei.* Why not?'

'We get most of our opinions of the war from Sister Margaret,' said the civilian doctor of the train. 'It's all new to me, but, so far, all her prophecies have come true.'

A few months ago that doctor had retired from practice to a country house in rainy England, his fortune made and, as he tried to believe, his life-work done. Then the bugles blew; and, rejoicing at the change, he found himself, his experience, and his fine bedside manner, buttoned up in a black-tabbed khaki coat, on a hospital train that covered eleven hundred miles a week, carried a hundred wounded each trip and dealt him more experience in a month than he had ever gained in a year of Home practice.

Sister Margaret and the Captain of Mounted Infantry took their cups outside the tent. The Captain wished to know something more about her. Till that day he had believed South Africa to be populated by sullen Dutchmen and slack-waisted women; and in some clumsy fashion betrayed the belief.

'Of course, you don't see any others where you are,' said Sister Margaret, leniently, from her camp-chair. 'They are all at the war. I have two brothers, and a nephew, my sister's son, and—oh, I can't count my cousins.' She flung her hands outward with a curiously un-English gesture. 'And then, too, you have never been off the railway. You have only seen Cape Town? All the schel*—all the useless people are there. You should see *our* country beyond the ranges—out Oudtshorn way. We grow fruit and vines. It is much prettier, *I* think, than Paarl.'*

'I'd like to very much. I may be stationed in Africa after the war is over.'

'Ah, but we know the English officers. They say that this is a "beastly country", and they do not know how to.—to be nice to people. Shall I tell you? There was an aide-de-camp at Government House three years ago. He sent out invitations to dinner to Piet—to Mr Van der Hooven's wife. *And* she had been dead eight years, and Van der Hooven—he has the big farms round Craddock—just then was thinking of changing his politics, you see—he was against the Government,—and taking a house in Cape Town, because of the Army meat contracts. That was why, you see?'

'I see,' said the Captain, to whom this was all Greek.

'Piet was a little angry—not much—but he went to Cape Town, and that aide-de-camp had made a joke about it—about inviting the dead woman—in the Civil Service Club. You see? So of *course* the opposition there told Van der Hooven that the aide-de-camp had said he could not remember all the old Dutch vrouws* that had died, and so Piet van der Hooven went away angry, and now he is more hot than ever against the Government. If you stay with us you must not be like *that*. You see?'

'I won't,' said the Captain seriously. 'What a night it is, Sister!' He dwelt lovingly on the last word, as men did in South Africa.

The soft darkness had shut upon them unawares and the world had vanished. There was not so much breeze as a slow motion of the whole dry air under the vault of the immeasurably deep heavens. 'Look up,' said the Captain. 'Doesn't it make you feel as if we were tumbling down into the stars—all upside down?'

'Yes,' said Sister Margaret, tilting her head back. 'It is always like that. I know. And those are *our* stars.'

They burned with a great glory, large as the eyes of cattle by lamp-light; planet after planet of the mild Southern sky. As the Captain said, one seemed to be falling from out the hidden earth sheer through space, between them.

'Now, when I was little,' Sister Margaret began very softly, 'there was one day in the week at home that was all our own. We could get up as soon as we liked after midnight, and there was the basket in the kitchen—our food. We used to go out at three o'clock sometimes, my two brothers, my sisters, and the two little ones—out into the Karroo for all the day. All —the— long—day. First we built a fire, and then we made a kraal* for the two little ones—a kraal of thorn bushes so that they should not be bitten by anything. You see? Often we made the kraal before morning—when those'—she jerked her firm chin at the stars—'were just going out. Then we old ones went hunting lizards—and snakes and birds and centipedes, and all that sort of nice thing. Our father collected them. He gave us half-a-crown for a spuugh-slange—a kind of snake. You see?'

'How old were you?' Snake-hunting did not strike the Captain as a safe amusement for the young.

'I was eleven then—or ten, perhaps, and the little ones were two and three. Why? Then we came back to eat, and we sat under a rock all afternoon. It was hot, you see, and we played—we played with the stones and the flowers. You should see our Karroo in spring! All flowers! All our flowers! Then we came home, carrying the little ones on our backs asleep—came home through the dark—just like this night. That was our own day! Oh, the good days! We used to watch the meer-cats* playing, too, and the little buck. When I was at Guy's,* learning to nurse, how home-sick that made me!'

'But what a splendid open-air life!' said the Captain.

'Where else *is* there to live except the open air?' said Sister Margaret, looking off into twenty thousand square miles of it with eyes that burned.

'You're quite right.'

'I'm sorry to interrupt you two,' said Sister Dorothy, who had been talking to the Gunner Major; 'but the guard says we shall be ready to go in a few minutes. Major Devine and Dr Johnson have gone down already.'

'Very good, Sister. We'll follow.' The Captain rose unwillingly and made for the worn path from the camp to the rail.

'Isn't there another way?' said Sister Margaret. Her grey nursing gown glimmered like some big moth's wing.

'No. I'll bring a lantern. It's quite safe.'

'I did not think of *that*,' she said with a laugh; 'only *we* never come home by the way we left it when we live in the Karroo. If any one—suppose you had dismissed a Kaffir, or got him sjamboked,* and he saw you go out? He would wait for you to come back on a tired horse, and then. . . . You see? But, of course, in England where the road is all walled, it is different. How funny! Even when we were little we learned never to come home by the way we went out.'

'Very good,' said the Captain obediently. It made the walk longer, and he approved of that.

'That's a curious sort of woman,' said the Captain to the Major, as they smoked a lonely pipe together when the train had gone.

'*You* seemed to think so.'

'Well—I couldn't monopolize Sister Dorothy in the presence of my senior officer. What was she like?'

'Oh, it came out that she knew a lot of my people in London. She's the daughter of a chap in the next county to us, too.'

* * *

The General's flag still flew before his unstruck tent to amuse Boer binoculars, and loyal lying correspondents still telegraphed accounts of his daily work. But the General himself had gone to join an army a hundred miles away*; drawing off, from time to time, every squadron, gun and company that he dared. His last words to the few troops he left behind covered the entire situation.

'If you can bluff 'em till we get round 'em up North to tread on their tails, it's all right. If you can't, they'll probably eat you up. Hold 'em as long as you can.'

So the skeleton remnant of the brigade lay close among the kopjes* till the Boers, not seeing them in force on the sky-line, feared that they might have learned the rudiments of war. They rarely disclosed a gun, for the reason that they had so few; they scouted by fours and fives instead of clattering troops and chattering companies, and where they saw a too obvious way opened to attack, they, lacking force to drive it home, looked elsewhere. Great was the anger in the Boer commando across the river—the anger and unease.

'The reason is they have so few men,' the loyal farmers reported, all fresh from selling melons to the camp, and drinking Queen Victoria's health in good whisky. 'They have no horses—only what they call Mounted Infantry. They are afraid of us. They try to make us friends by giving us brandy. Come on and shoot them. Then you will see us rise and cut the line.'

'Yes, we know how you rise, you Colonials,'* said the Boer commandant above his pipe. 'We know what has come to all your promises from Beaufort West,* and even from De Aar. *We* do the work—all the work,—and you kneel down with your parsons and pray for our success. What good is that? The President* has told you a hundred times God is on our side. Why do you worry *Him*? We did not send you Mausers* and ammunition for *that*.'

'We kept our commando-horses ready for six months—and forage is very dear. We sent all our young men,' said an honoured member of local society.

'A few here and a few servants there. What is that? You should have risen down to the sea all together.'

'But you were so quick. Why did not you wait the year? We were not ready, Jan.'

'That is a lie. All you Cape people lie. You want to save your cattle and your farms. Wait till *our* flag flies from here to Port

Elizabeth, and you shall see what you will save when the President learns how you have risen—you clever Cape people.'

The saddle-coloured sons of the soil looked down their noses. 'Yes—it is true. Some of our farms are close to the line. They say at Worcester* and in the Paarl* that many soldiers are always coming in from the sea. One must think of that—at least till they are shot. But we know there are very few in front of you here. Give them what you gave the fools at Stormberg,* and you will see how we can shoot rooineks.'*

'Yes. I know that cow. She is always going to calve. Get away. I am answerable to the President—not to the Cape.'

But the information stayed in his mind, and, not being a student of military works, he made a plan to suit. The tall kopje on which the English had planted their helio-station* commanded the more or less open plain to the northward, but did not command the five-mile belt of broken country between that and the outmost English pickets, some three miles from camp. The Boers had established themselves very comfortably among these rock-ridges and scrub-patches, and the 'great war' drizzled down to long shots and longer stalking. The young bloods wanted rooineks to shoot, and said so.

'See here,' quoth the experienced Jan van Staden that evening to as many of his commando as cared to listen. 'You youngsters from the Colony talk a lot. Go and turn the rooineks out of their kopjes to-night. Eh? Go and take their bayonets from them and stick them into them. Eh? You don't go!' He laughed at the silence round the fire.

'Jan—Jan,' said one young man appealingly, 'don't make a mock of us.'

'I thought that was what you wanted so badly. No? Then listen to me. Behind us the grazing is bad. We have too many cattle here.' (They had been stolen from farmers who had been heard to express fears of defeat.) 'To-morrow, by the sky's look, it will blow a good wind. So, to-morrow early I shall send all our cattle north to the new grazing. That will make a great dust for the English to see from their helio yonder.' He pointed to a winking night-lamp stabbing the darkness with orders to an outlying picket. 'With the cattle we will send all our women. Yes, all the women and the wagons we can spare, and the lame ponies and the broken carts we took from Andersen's farm. That will make a big dust—the dust of our retreat. Do you see?'

They saw and approved, and said so.

'Good. There are many men here who want to go home to their wives. I shall let thirty of them away for a week. Men who wish to do this will speak to me to-night.' (This meant that Jan needed money, and furlough would be granted on strictly business lines.) 'These men will look after the cattle and see that they make a great dust for a long way. They will run about behind the cattle showing their guns, too. So *that*, if the wind blows well, will be our retreat. The cattle will feed beyond Koopman's Kop.'

'No good water there,' growled a farmer who knew that section. 'Better go on to Zwartpan. It is always sweet at Zwartpan.'

The commando discussed the point for twenty minutes. It was much more serious than shooting rooineks. Then Jan went on:

'When the rooineks see our retreat they may all come into our kopjes together. If so, good. But it is tempting God to expect such a favour. *I* think they will first send some men to scout.' He grinned broadly, twisting the English word. 'Almighty! To scoot! They have none of that new sort of rooinek that they used at Sunnyside.' (Jan meant an incomprehensible animal from a place called Australia across the Southern seas who played what they knew of the war-game to kill.) 'They have only some Mounted Infantry,'—again he used the English words. 'They were once a Red-jacket regiment, so their scoots will stand up bravely to be shot at.'

'Good—good, we will shoot them,' said a youngster from Stellenbosch,* who had come up on free pass as a Cape Town excursionist just before the war to a farm on the border, where his aunt was taking care of his horse and rifle.

'But if you shoot their scoots I will sjambok you myself,' said Jan, amid roars of laughter. 'We must let them *all* come into the kopjes to look for us; and I pray God will not allow any of us to be tempted to shoot them. They will cross the ford in front of their camp. They will come along the road—so!' He imitated with ponderous arms the Army style of riding. 'They will trot up the road this way and that way'—here he snaked his hard finger in the dust—'between kopjes, till they come here, where they can see the plain and all our cattle going away. Then they will *all* come in close together. Perhaps they will even fix their bayonets. *We* shall be up here behind the rock —there and there.' He pointed to two flat-topped kopjes, one on either side of the road, some eight hundred yards away. 'That is our place. We will go there before sunrise. Remember we must be careful to let the very last of the rooineks pass before we begin shooting. They will come along a little careful at first. But we do not shoot. Then they will see our fires and the fresh horse-dung, so they will know we have gone on. They will run together and talk and point and shout in this nice open place. Then we begin shooting them from above.'

'Yes, uncle, but if the scoots see nothing and there are no shots and we let them go back quite quiet, they will think it was a trick. Perhaps the main body may never come here at all. Even rooineks learn in time—and so we may lose even the scoots.'

'I have thought of that too,' said Jan, with slow contempt, as the Stellenbosch boy delivered his shot. 'If you had been *my* son I should have sjamboked you more when you were a youngster. I shall put *you* and four or five more on the Nek (the pass), where the road comes from their camp into these kopjes. You go there before it is light. Let the scoots pass in or I will sjambok you myself. When the scoots come back after seeing nothing here, then you may shoot them, but *not* till they have passed the Nek and are on the straight road back to their camp again. Do you understand? Repeat what I have said, so that I shall know.'

The youth obediently repeated his orders.

'Kill their officers if you can. If not, no great matter, because the scoots will run to camp with the news that our kopjes are empty. Their helio-station will see your party trying to hold the Nek so hard—and all the time they will see our dust out yonder, and they will think you are the rear-guard, and they will think *we* are escaping. They will be angry.'

'Yes—yes, uncle, we see,' from a dozen elderly voices.

'But this calf does not. Be silent! They will shoot at you, Niclaus, on the Nek, because they will think you are to cover our getting away. They will shell the Nek. They will miss. You will then ride away. All the rooineks will come after you, hot and in a hurry—perhaps, even, with their cannon. They will pass our fires and our fresh horse-dung. They will come here as their scoots came. They will see the plain so full of our dust. They will say, "The scoots spoke truth. It is a full retreat." *Then* we up there on the rocks will shoot, and it will be like the fight at Stormberg in daytime. Do you understand *now*?'

Those of the commando directly interested lit new pipes and discussed the matter in detail till midnight.

Next morning the operations began with—if one may borrow the language of some official despatches—'the precision of well-oiled machinery'.

The helio-station reported the dust of the wagons and the movements of armed men in full flight across the plain beyond the kopjes. A Colonel, newly appointed from England, by reason of his seniority, sent forth a dozen Mounted Infantry under command of a Captain. Till a month ago they had been drilled by a cavalry instructor, who taught them 'shock' tactics to the music of trumpets. They knew how to advance in echelon of squadrons, by cat's-cradle of troops, in quarter column of stable-litter,* how to trot, to gallop, and above all to charge. They knew how to sit their horses unremittingly, so that at the day's end they might boast how many hours they had been in the saddle without relief, and they learned to rejoice in the clatter and stamp of a troop moving as such, and therefore audible five miles away.

They trotted out two and two along the farm road, that trailed lazily through the wind-driven dust; across the half-dried ford to a nek between low stony hills leading into the debatable land. (Vrooman of Emmaus from his neatly bushed hole noted that one man carried a sporting Lee-Enfield rifle with a short fore-end. Vrooman of Emmaus argued that the owner of it was the officer to be killed on his return, and went to sleep.) They saw nothing except a small flock of sheep and a Kaffir herdsman who spoke broken English with curious fluency. He had heard that the Boers had decided to retreat on account of their sick and wounded. The Captain in charge of the detachment turned to look at the helio-station four miles away. 'Hurry up,' said the dazzling flash. 'Retreat apparently continues, but suggest you make sure. Quick.'

'Ye-es,' said the Captain, a shade bitterly, as he wiped the sweat from a sun-skinned nose. 'You want me to come back and report all clear. If anything happens it will be my fault. If they get away it will be my fault for disregarding the signal. I love officers who suggest and advise, and want to make their reputations in twenty minutes.'

'Don't see much 'ere, sir,' said the sergeant, scanning the bare cup of the hollow where a dust-devil danced alone.

'No? We'll go on.'

'If we get among these steep 'ills we lose touch of the 'elio.'

'Very likely. Trot.'

The rounded mounds grew to spiked kopjes, heart-breaking to climb under a hot sun at four thousand feet above sea level. This is where the scouts found their spurs peculiarly useful.

Jan van Staden had thoughtfully allowed the invading force a front of two rifle-shots or four thousand yards, and they kept a thousand yards within his estimate. Ten men strung over two miles feel that they have explored all the round earth.

They saw stony slopes combing over in scrub, narrow valleys clothed with stone, low ridges of splintered stone, and tufts of brittle-stemmed bush. An irritating wind, split up by many rocky barriers, cuffed them over the ears and slapped them in the face at every turn. They came upon an abandoned camp-fire, a little fresh horse-dung, and an empty ammunition-box splintered up for firewood, an old boot, and a stale bandage.

A few hundred yards farther along the road a battered Mauser had been thrown into a bush. The glimmer of its barrel drew the scouts from the hillside, and here the road after passing between two flat-topped kopjes entered a valley nearly half a mile wide, rose slightly, and over the nek of a ridge gave clear view across the windy plain northward.

'They're on the dead run, for sure,' said a trooper. 'Here's their fires and their litter and their guns, and that's where they're bolting to.' He pointed over the ridge to the bellying dust-cloud a mile long. A vulture high overhead flickered down, steadied herself, and hung motionless.

'See!' said Jan van Staden from the rocks above the road, to his waiting commando. 'It turns like a well-oiled wheel. They look where they need not look, but *here*, where they should look on both sides, they look at our retreat—straight before them. It is tempting our people too much. I pray God no one will shoot them.'

'That's about the size of it,' said the Captain, rubbing the dust from his binoculars. 'Boers on the run. I expect they find their main line of retreat to the north is threatened. We'll get back and tell the camp.' He wheeled his pony, and his eye traversed the flat-topped kopje commanding the road. The stones at its edge seemed to be piled with less than Nature's carelessness.

'That 'ud be a dashed ugly place if it were occupied—and that other one, too. Those rocks aren't five hundred yards from the road, either of 'em. Hold on, sergeant, I'll light a pipe.' He bent over the bowl, and above his lighted match squinted at the kopje. A stone, a small roundish brown boulder on the lip of another one, seemed to move very slightly. The short hairs of his neck grated his collar. 'I'll have another squint at their retreat,' he cried to the sergeant, astonished at the steadiness of his own voice. He swept the plain, and, wheeling, let the glass rest for a moment on the kopje's top. One cranny between the rocks was pinkish, where blue sky should have shown. His men, dotted down the valley, sat heavily on their horses—it never occurred to them to dismount.* He could hear the squeak of the leather as a man shifted. An impatient gust blew through the valley and rattled the bushes. On all sides the expectant hills stood still under the pale blue.

'And we passed within a quarter of a mile of 'em! We're done!' The thumping heart slowed down, and the Captain began to think clearly—so clearly that the thoughts seemed solid things. 'It's Pretoria gaol* for us all. Perhaps that man's only a look-out, though. We'll have to bolt! And I led 'em into it . . . You fool!' said his other self, above the beat of the blood in his eardrums. 'If they could snipe you all from up there, why haven't they begun already? Because you're the bait for the rest of the attack. They don't want you *now*. You're to go back and bring up the others to be killed. Go back! Don't detach a man or they'll suspect. Go back all together. Tell the sergeant you're going. Some of them up there will understand English. Tell it aloud! Then back you go with the news—the real news.'

'The country's all clear, sergeant,' he shouted. 'We'll go back and tell the Colonel.' With an idiotic giggle he added, 'It's a good road for guns, don't you think?'

'Hear you that?' said Jan van Staden, gripping a burgher's arm. 'God is on our side to-day. They *will* bring their little cannons after all!'

'Go easy. No good bucketing the horses to pieces. We'll need 'em for the pursuit later,' said the Captain. 'Hullo, there's a vulture! How far would you make him?'

'Can't tell, sir, in this dry air.'

The bird swooped towards the second flat-topped kopje, but suddenly shivered sideways, and wheeled off again, followed intently by the Captain's glance.

'And that kopje's simply full of 'em, too,' he said, flushing. 'Perfectly confident they are, that we'll take this road—and then they'll scupper the whole boiling of us! They'll let us through to fetch up the others. But I mustn't let 'em know we know. By Jove, they do *not* think much of us! Don't blame 'em.'

The cunning of the trap did not impress him until later.

Down the track jolted a dozen well-equipped men, laughing and talking—a mark to make a pious burgher's mouth water. Thrice had their Captain explicitly said that they were to march easy, so a trooper began to hum a tune that he had picked up in Cape Town streets:

> Vat jou goed en trek, Ferreira,
> Vat jou goed en trek;
> Jannie met die hoepelbeen, Ferreira,
> Jannie met die hoepelbeen!

Then with a whistle:

> Swaar draa—alle en die ein kant—

The Captain, thinking furiously, found his mind turn to a camp in the Karroo, months before; an engine that had halted in that waste, and a woman with brown hair, early grizzled—an extraordinary woman. . . . Yes, but as soon as they had dropped the flat-topped kopje behind its neighbour he must hurry back and report. . . . A woman with grey eyes and black eyelashes. . . . The Boers would probably be massed on those two kopjes. How soon dare he break into a canter? . . . A woman with a queer cadence in her speech. . . . It was not more than five miles home by the straight road—

'Even when we were children we learned not to go back by the way we had come.'

The sentence came back to him, self-shouted, so clearly that he almost turned to see if the scouts had heard. The two flat-topped kopjes behind him were covered by a long ridge. The camp lay due south. He had only to follow the road to the Nek—a notch, unscouted as he recalled now, between the two hills.

He wheeled his men up a long valley.

'Excuse me, sir, that ain't our road!' said the sergeant. 'Once we get over this rise, straight on, we come into direct touch with the 'elio, on that flat bit o' road where they 'elioed us goin' out.'

'But we aren't going to get in touch with them just now. Come along, and come quick.'

'What's the meaning of this?' said a private in the rear. 'What's 'e doin' this detour for? We sha'n't get in for hours an' hours.'

'Come on, men. Flog a canter out of your brutes, somehow,' the Captain called back.

For two throat-parched hours he held west by south, away from the Nek, puzzling over a compass already demented by the ironstone in the hills, and then turned south-east through an eruption of low hills that ran far into the re-entering bend of the river that circled the left bank of the camp.

Eight miles to eastward that student from Stellenbosch had wriggled out on the rocks above the Nek to have a word with Vrooman of Emmaus. The bottom seemed to have dropped out of at least one portion of their programme; for the scouting party were not to be seen.

'Jan is a clever man,' he said to his companion, 'but he does

not think that even rooineks may learn. Perhaps those scouts
will have seen Jan's commando, and perhaps they will come
back to warn the rooineks. That is why I think he should have
shot them *before* they came to the Nek, and made quite sure
that only one or two got away. It would have made the English
angry, and they would have come out across the open in hun-
dreds to be shot. Then when we ran away they would have
come after us without thinking. If you can make the English
hurry, they never think. Jan is wrong this time.'

'Lie down, and pray you have not shown yourself to their
helio-station,' growled Vrooman of Emmaus. 'You throw with
your arms and kick with your legs like a rooinek. When we get
back I will tell Jan and he will sjambok you. All will yet come
right. They will go and warn the rest, and the rest will hurry
out by this very Nek. Then we can shoot. Now you lie still and
wait.'

' 'Ere's a rummy picnic. We left camp, as it were, by the
front door, an' now we're comin' in by the back door. 'E 'as
given us a giddy-go-round, an' no mistake,' said a dripping
private as he dismounted behind the infantry lines.

'Did you see our helio?' This was the Colonel, hot from
racing down from the helio-station. 'There were a lot of Boers
waiting for you on the Nek. We saw 'em. We tried to get at you
with the helio, and tell you we were coming out to help you.
Then we saw you didn't come over that flat bit of road where
we had signalled you going out, and we wondered why. We
didn't hear any shots.'

'I turned off, sir, and came in by another road,' said the
Captain.

'By another road!' The Colonel lifted his eyebrows. 'Perhaps
you're not aware, sir, that the Boers have been in full retreat for
the last three hours, and that those men on the Nek were
simply a rear-guard put out to delay us for a little. We could see
that much from here. Your duty, sir, was to have taken them in
the rear, and then we could have brushed them aside. The Boer
retreat has been going on all morning, sir—all morning. You
were despatched to see the front clear and to return at once.
The whole camp has been under arms for three hours; and
instead of doing your work you wander all about Africa with

your scouts to avoid a handful of skulking Boers! You should have sent a man back at once—you should have—'

The Captain got off his horse stiffly.

'As a matter of fact,' said he, 'I didn't know for sure that there were any Boers on the Nek, but I went round it in case it was so. But I *do* know that the kopjes beyond the Nek are simply crawling with Boers.'

'Nonsense. We can see the whole lot of 'em retreating out yonder.'

'Of course you can. That's part of their game, sir. I saw 'em lying on the top of a couple of kopjes commanding the road, where it goes into the plain on the far side. They let us come in to see, and they let us go out to report the country clear and bring you up. Now they are waiting for *you*. The whole thing is a trap.'

'D'you expect any officer of my experience to believe that?'

'As you please, sir,' said the Captain hopelessly. 'My responsibility ends with my report.'

The Outsider*

From Stormberg's midnight mountain*
  From Sanna's captured Post,*
Where Afric's Magersfontein*
  Rails down her wounded host.
Three days and nights to s'uth'ard
  'Twixt Durban Road and Paarl—
In dust and horse-dung smothered—
  There lies a cursèd kraal.*
               Stellenbosch Hymn

ABOUT the time that Gentleman Cadet Walter Setton was posted to the 2nd Battalion of Her Majesty's Royal Rutlandshire Regiment, the Vicar, his father, read a telegram that the Pretoria Government was searching the mines of the Rand* for hidden arms. The Vicar and his wife were on their way to the Army and Navy Stores to buy Walter's many uniforms; and the Vicar doubted that he would escape for less than two hundred pounds.

'But we cannot repine,' said his wife. 'Walter's position demands——' She ceased for a breath. 'And as an officer—you see, William? We have much to be thankful for.'

The Vicar lowered the paper, remembering how the accident of a legacy had saved Walter from other fates. He and his wife had agreed to forget a terrible afternoon when Walter, aged sixteen, had been examined *viva voce* by a person, sent down by a friend, with a view to getting him a 'position in the City' at something under eighteen shillings a week. He had forgotten, too, how he and his wife were grateful for this chance. A week later, when the Vicar's aunt was gathered to her mothers and the money was sure, they wrote a stately letter declining that post for Walter, which letter remains for a curiosity in a business man's desk to this day.

'Yes,' said the Vicar, 'we have much to be thankful for. As an officer——' He turned down the paper.

Had he read ten lines further he would have learned that

'much amusement has been caused in mining circles owing to the activity of the police, who are searching Thumper's Deep, on information supplied by Mr J. Thrupp, who asserts that two thousand stand of arms are buried at the bottom of the shaft.'

At the hour the Vicar was speculating in 'tunics, richly laced, lined silk, £6:14:6'; 'undress trousers, blue doe or twill, £1:16:0'; forage caps (badge extra), £1:0:6', and all the other grim realities of war, Jerry Thrupp, in charge of the thirty-odd thousand pounds of modern machinery on Thumper's Deep, was cheering a batch of perspiring Johannesburg* police to break out the bottom of South Africa. Business was slack in Johannesburg by reason of a Raid,* and Jerry's ten years on the Rand had taught him that the police were least dangerous when most busy. Two thousand rifles in a concrete vault, ten feet below the solid foot of the shaft, would be a great haul for the Government. That they worked in the living rock was to them a detail. The Devil had given these Uitlanders powers denied to sons of the soil; and no community in their senses would start a revolution on less than twenty thousand rifles. A scant fifteen hundred only had, so far, come to light anywhere.

'Where you think we shall find them?' a panting Hollander* asked.

'About the Marquesas Islands* if you hold your line straight,' said Jerry, and shot up in the cage. Three minutes later he telephoned that the winding-gear was out of order and would take half a day to repair.

'They had a very nice time,' he explained to his professional friends. 'They dug four feet into the bottom of the shaft before they sickened, and Patsy Gee burned a hundredweight of his precious Revolutionary Committee's papers in my boiler fires while they were doing it. But as a revolution, if you ask me, it's bumble-puppy.* After this we shall have war.'

'Not a bit of it,' said Hagan of the consolidated Ophir and Bonanza. 'We shall be passed over to Oom Paul* to play with.'

'Never mind,' said Jerry. 'It's war. Soon or late, it's war.'

Time, Circumstance, and Necessity continued in charge of this world, of Jerry Thrupp, and Second-Lieutenant Walter Setton. To the former they brought from eight to twelve hours' work a day—shifting, varying, but insistent. Sometimes a batch of the three hundred and twenty-four stamps in the Thumper's Deep crushing-mills would go wrong; and Jerry must doctor them ere the output suffered. Sometimes a sick friend in charge of the cyanide process would call Jerry in to watch the health of the big vats that win the last of the gold; or a furlong or two of tram-lines would need re-laying. His winding-engines, his boilers, his crushing-tables, his dynamos, and the hundred things that men needed below the surface were always with him. For recreation Jerry consorted with fellow-engineers of the Rand, their wives, and their children; and, being energetic, found opportunities for what he called 'over-time'. When Hagan's ankle was crushed, thanks to a Kaffir's carelessness, Jerry carried him home; and, because Hagan's ten-year-old son was in hospital with typhoid, Jerry, as a matter of course, visited and reported on the boy daily. He lent the Vincents the money that took them home in the terrible year '98, when Johannesburg lost heart and business shut down, and Vincent was turned out into Commissioner Street with Mrs Vincent seven months gone. It is even said that by bribes and threats he kept the conservancy people up to their work in his street when the typhoid that comes from neglected filth struck down three heads of families in two hundred yards of the street.

'After the war,' Jerry would say as excusing himself, 'it will be all right. We've got to do what we can till after the war.'

The life of Second-Lieutenant Walter Setton followed its appointed channel. His battalion, nominally efficient, was actually a training school for recruits; and to this lie, written, acted, and spoken many times a day, he adjusted himself. When he could by any means escape from the limited amount of toil expected by the Government, he did so; employing the same shameless excuses that he had used at school or Sandhurst. He knew his drills: he honestly believed that they covered the whole art of war. He knew the 'internal economy of his regiment'. That is to say, he could answer leading questions about coal and wood allowances, cubic-footage of barrack accommodation, canteen-routine, and the men's messing arrangements. For the rest, he devoted himself with no thought of wrong to getting as much as possible out of the richest and easiest life the world has yet made; and to despising the 'outsider'—the man beyond his circle. His training to this end was as complete as that of his brethren. He did it blindly, politely, unconsciously, with perfect sincerity. As a child he had learned early to despise his nurse, for she was a servant and a woman; his sisters he had looked down upon, and his governess, for much the same reasons. His home atmosphere had taught him to despise the terrible thing called 'Dissent'. At his private school his seniors showed him how to despise the junior master who was poor, and here his home training served again. At his public school he despised the new boy—the boy who boated when Setton played cricket, or who wore a coloured tie when the order of the day was for black. They were all avatars of the outsider. If you got mixed up with an outsider, you ended by being 'compromised'. He had no clear idea what that meant, but suspected the worst. His religion he took from his parents, and it had some very sound dogmas about outsiders behaving decently. Science to him was a name connected with examination papers. He could not work up any interest in foreign armies, because, after all, a foreigner was a foreigner, and the rankest form of outsider. Meals came when you rang for them. You were carried over the world, which is the Home Counties, in vehicles for which you paid. You were moved about London by the same means; and if you crossed the Channel you took a steamer. But how, or why, or when, these things were made, or worked, or begotten, or what they felt, or thought, or said, who belonged to them, he had not, nor ever wished to have, the shadow of an idea. It was sufficient for him and for high Heaven (this in his heart of hearts, well learned at his mother's knee) that he was an officer and a gentleman incapable of a lie or a mean action. For the rest his code was simple. Money bought you half the things in this world; and your position secured you the others. If you had money, you took care to get your money's worth. If you had a position, you did not compromise yourself by mixing with outsiders.

And, in the fullness of time, one old gentleman who knew his own mind* knocked the bottom out of Lieutenant Setton's and Jerry Thrupp's world. Jerry came first, unwillingly, with a few thousand others, by way of Komati Poort.* He helped the women and children out of Johannesburg, the few that remained; and left his house barricaded in charge of a Hollander official.

'Remember,' said Jerry, 'I advise you to look after this house. If anything happens to it you won't be happy when I come back.'

'We shall chase you into the sea!' said the Hollander.

'Shouldn't wonder—seeing how behind-hand we are, but then we'll chase you back again. I hope you won't blow yourselves up before you're shot. S'long, you four-coloured* impostor.'

He climbed into a cattle-truck, where his valise was stolen, and arrived at Delagoa Bay, his shirt torn to the waist in a scuffle to get water for a sick man. His home, his business, and all his belongings were gone, but the war that men had doubted was upon them at last, and Jerry was happy. He went round to Cape Town on the deck of a crowded steamer, and disappeared into thronged and panic-stricken Adderley Street.* Here he met Phil Tenbroek, ex-mine-manager, also ruined for the time being, and conferred with him about raising a corps of Railway Volunteers* in event of future trouble.

Lieutenant Setton, seven thousand miles away, was scornful when he heard that some General* would not undertake the war with less than seventy thousand troops. Thirty thousand, he held, was more than enough; for the Rutlandshires' Mess would remember that the Army was not what it had been in '81.* He wished very much to see how the Boers would look after a Cavalry Brigade had boxed their ears across ten miles of open country. Except twice, near Salisbury,* he had never seen anything that remotely resembled ten miles of open country in all his life. He had never seen a Cavalry Brigade, nor, indeed, a target at any greater distance than 900 yards. Having spoken, he went up to Town to see a play, pending the absorption of the Transvaal.

The Rutlandshires landed at Cape Town fairly late in the war, and, serene as hundreds before him, Lieutenant Setton, dining at the Mount Nelson,* gave, in the fine clear voice he had inherited from his mother, his opinion that 'those Colonials* looked a most awful set of outsiders'. He hoped, aloud, that it would not be his fate 'to have to work with the bounders'.

In another place, at another time, an informal after-dinner court of inquiry, with unlimited powers, sat on his irreproachable Regiment after this fashion:—

'Are those Rutlandshires any use?' The questioner had good right to ask.

'Mark Two, I think. It's the same old brand—Badajoz, Talavera, Inkerman, Toulouse, Tel-el-Kebir——'*

'Same tactics as those which were so brilliantly successful at Tel-el-Kebir,' a bearded officer whispered as though he were quoting Scripture.

'Ye-es. Same old catchwords—same old training. "Shoulder to shoulder"—"up, boys, and at 'em!" Southsea, Chichester, Canterbury; with the Long Valley* for a campaign. Colonel past his work; Second-in-Command devoutly hoping never to see a soldier again when he's got his pension; a jewel of an Adjutant, who's mothered his men till they can't button their own breeches; Sergeant-Major great on eyewash, and a bit of a lawyer. The rest, the regular type—all in a blue funk of funking. They want a chance "to get in with the bayonet", of course.'

'That's the last refuge of the lazy man,' said a quiet-faced civilian, who had not yet spoken.

'Oh, they'll learn in time,' the spade-bearded officer grunted.

'When half the men are in Pretoria* and half the rest are wounded—if that's what you mean! I'm *so* sick of that "in time". The Colonel will die—I wish he was dead now—"fighting heroically" in some dam'-fool trap he's walked into with his eyes open!'

'Well, I'm going to split 'em up. They were promised they should go in—ah—shoulder to shoulder, but the hospitals are quite full enough.'

To their immense rage the Rutlandshires were rent into four or five pieces, and distributed where they could not do much harm. The Colonel, as was prophesied, died heroically, shot through the stomach in sight of four companies to whom he was explaining the cowardice of advancing in open order when the enemy were yet a mile distant. This fixed in the Second's mind the fact that a Mauser* can carry two thousand yards—wisdom which he did not live long to profit by. He went down at eleven hundred before an insignificant crack in the veldt, which happened to be lined with Boers. Thus his successor discovered that a donga* is better flanked than fronted. Truly they learned.

To Lieutenant Setton, through the death of a Captain, fell the charge of two companies, which operated with an Australian contingent on a disturbed and dusty border. The men clung to him for a week expecting miracles; but he could not smite water from rocks, nor vary the daily beef-tin and dry biscuit. They learned a little rude well-sinking from their allies, and a little stealing on their own account. After this, to his relief, they abandoned him as nurse and midwife. Had he played the game with an eye to the rules, he might have profited as much as his more open-minded fellows, but his demon tempted him one clear twilight to capture a solitary horseman in difficulties with a spent horse. It was not 'sporting' to pot him at eight hundred yards, so Setton took horse and rode a somewhat uncertain wallop directly at the man, who naturally retreated between two steep hills, where, for just this end, he had posted four confederates. They, being children of nature and buck-hunters to boot, allowed their quarry to pass, and after twenty rounds at four hundred yards—the Boer in a hurry is not a good shot—dropped him with a broken arm. Setton was not pleased; but the five Australians who, without orders, so soon as they saw what he would be at, had galloped parallel with him behind the kopjes, were immensely gratified. They dismounted, lay down, and slew the Boer on the tired horse as he returned to join his fellow-plunderers, of whom they shot two and wounded one. They reached camp with Setton and—much more valuable—three efficient Boer ponies.

'If you'd only told us you were goin' to commit suicide this way,' said a Queensland trooper, 'we'd have rounded up the whole mob—usin' you for bait.'

The shattered arm ended Setton's career as a combatant officer, but in the great scarcity of sounder material they made

him Station Commandant of the entirely desolate siding of
Pipkameelepompfontein, which, as everyone knows,

> Is on the road to Bloemfontein:*
> And there the Mausers
> Tear your trousers
> And make your horses jompfontein.

But the tide of war had rolled on, leaving only a mass of
worrying work for the Railway Pioneer Corps which Phil Ten-
broek had organized from the wreck of the mine personnel
months before. Three short low bridges, little larger than
culverts, but two of them built on a curve, crossed three dry
shallow watercourses, and, of course, the Boers blew them up
on departure.* Phil, Commandant of the Railway Pioneers,
busy on a bridge elsewhere, could only spare thirty men on the
job, but he gave Lieutenant Hagan, late in charge of the
machinery of the Consolidated Ophir and Bonanza, his choice,
and Hagan took the cream. They lumbered into Pip-
kameelepompfontein in open trucks—thirty men, each anxious
to return to the Rand; each holding more or less of property
there; most of them skilled mechanicians in their own depart-
ment, and all exalted, body, soul, and spirit, by a rancorous,
razor-edged, personal hatred of the State* that had shamed,
tricked, and ruined them. They found there a Station Com-
mandant, moved by none of their springs—a being from
another planet, fenced about with neatly piled boxes of rivets
and a mass of crated ironwork that was pouring up from the
South, who proposed to camp them a mile from the broken
bridges.

'What, no good water?' said Hagan.

'Oh, no. But I expect a detachment of Regulars shortly.
They must have the nearest camp.'

'Good Lord, man! Your blessed Regulars can't get forward
till we've mended the bridges. We must be close to our work.'

'I'm afraid your knowledge of the British Army is a little
limited,' said the Station Commandant.

'I *was* fool enough to cross a ridge after some Regulars had
reported it cleared,' said Hagan sweetly. ''Twasn't any fault of
theirs my knowledge didn't last till the Day of Judgment. But,

look here, this isn't a question of precedence. We don't want to *live* here. We want to mend the bridges and get up to the Rand again.'

After a while, but ungraciously, Setton gave way, and the Railway Pioneers went to work like beavers. The Regulars arrived 'to protect the bridge-head', two companies of them, fresh from home, and Setton, with unspeakable delight, found himself once more among men who talked his chosen tongue, and thought his lofty thoughts. As he wrote to his mother: 'You can get as good hunting-talk here as you can at home.' The Pioneers were not a seemly corps. They unstacked the accurately piled rivet-boxes, and dumped them where they could be easiest handled; they dismantled an abandoned farm-house to get at the roof-beams, because they were short of poles; they stuck a home-made furnace at the far end of the platform where it made itself a black, unlovely bed of cinders; they worked at all hours of the day and night, ate when they had leisure, and called their officers by their lesser names. Hagan asked Setton—once only—what arrangements he had made for Kaffir labour. Setton had made none, for he had no instructions. Whereupon Hagan, talking unknown tongues, made his own arrangements, and strange niggers crept out of the Karroo* by scores. Setton wished to know something about them. 'It's all right,' said Hagan, over his shoulder. 'I'm responsible. It's cheaper for us' (he meant the Consolidated Ophir and Bonanza) 'to pay out of our pocket than to wait for the Government to fiddle through it. *I* want to get back to the Rand.'

The last sentence always annoyed Setton. These voluble Johannesburg gipsies made it their dawn-song, their noon chorus, and their midnight chant. It swung girders into place, sent home rivets, and spiked nails. It echoed among the hills at twilight, when the startlingly visible night-picket of the Regulars went out to relieve its fellows, cut in black paper against the green skyline, on the tallest kopje. It greeted every truck of new material, this drawling, nasal '*I* want to get back to the Rand'.

It helped to build the bridges, though that Setton did not notice. He did not know a spike from a chair, a girder from an artesian well, a thirty-foot rail from a tie-rod. The things lumbered up the siding which he wished to keep neat. Men took them out of the trucks and did things to or with them, and the things, somehow or other, spanned the watercourses. But Lieutenant Setton would no more have dreamed of taking an interest in the manner of their fitment than at school he would have read five lines beyond the day's appointed construe.*

When the last of the three bridges was nearly finished, Hagan dashed into his office with a wire from Phil, who wanted him back at once. The big centre girder of Folly Bridge was going up, and only Hagan could take charge of that end of it which was not under Phil's comprehending eye.

'But the men here know exactly what's to be done. If anything goes wrong, ask Jerry—I mean Private Thrupp. He ought to begin riveting up to-morrow, and after that they've only to lay the track. It's as easy as falling off a log.'

Setton did not approve of this unbuttoned man with the rampant voice—had, indeed, withdrawn markedly from his society. Nor did Setton comprehend how a private could be in charge of anything—least of all when a Regular officer—not to mention a Station Commandant—was on the horizon. He assumed that Hagan would have told the senior non-com. of the Pioneers to come to him for orders for the day; but Hagan, eating, sleeping, and thinking bridges only, had not communicated with Sergeant Rayne—late accountant of Thumper's Deep, and promoted because Government had insisted that the Corps must keep books. Hagan had spent his last hours at an informal committee-meeting with Jerry and another private— Fulsom, ex-head of the Little North Bear's machinery—and, under the lee of a karroo-bush, drawing diagrams in the dirt, had settled every last detail of the bridge that was to help the Corps back to their own Rand.

Brightly and briskly, then, in the diamond-clear dawn uprose Lieutenant Walter Setton to command the station of Pipkameelepompfontein. But early as it was, the Pioneers were before him. The situation when he arrived at the bank of the third watercourse was briefly this. They were lowering, with hand-made derricks, two fourteen-foot girders, one from either bank, to meet in the middle, where Jerry and Fulsom stood ready to join them. The twenty-eight-foot girder, which should have covered the span, had been sent round by Naauwpoort* by mistake, and Jerry believed devoutly that the Cape Minister of Railways,* whom he habitually alluded to as 'the worst rebel but one of the lot', had caused the delay on purpose. The mischief of it was that, expecting the twenty-eight iron, they had used up the last of their wood sleepers to lay a sharp curve just before the bridge, where iron sleepers were difficult to bend and adjust. Consequently, they had no temporary crib of sleepers in the middle of the watercourse to take the weight of the two fourteen-foot irons when these were lowered. So Jerry had extemporized a stage of rivet-boxes and laths sufficient to bear his weight and Fulsom's, and knowing his men, trusted to rivet up the butt-strap, temporarily, at any rate, while the men on the derricks held the girders, lowering them or raising them fractionally at his signal. It was unorthodox engineering, but it would carry the line. By four in the morning the heels of the girders were neatly butted against their permanent resting-places, and their noses began to dip towards the meeting in the centre.

'North girder!' Jerry raised his hand and lowered it slowly.

The obedient gang at the derrick slacked away with immense care. They were not watching Private Thrupp, but Jerry of Thumper's Deep, and Fulsom of the Little North Bear—both mighty men.

'Ready with the rivets, now! Here she comes! Hold her! Hold her! As you are! Not another hairbreadth. South girder —lift a shade. A fraction of a hair!' He laid a spirit-level across the half-inch gap between the two girders, and cocked his head to one side. Nobody breathed except Lieutenant Setton, who had walked some distance in a hurry. He observed that a bucket of blazing coals—stolen, of course—was slung under the belly of either 'iron thing'. He always thought of concrete objects beyond his experience as 'things'. Four men passed up two flat iron things—the specially designed butt-straps—one to Jerry and one to Fulsom, who faced Jerry on the other side of the girder. So close was the adjustment that the weight of the straps as they were slid between the flanges of the girder made the south girder—held by ropes—not chains—dip a fraction, and Jerry swore as only a Rand mechanician on twelve hundred a year and a bonus has a right to swear—emphatically and authoritatively.

'What are you doing there, men?' The voice passed Jerry like the summer wind. One hand was on the spirit-level, the other held a riveting hammer; one eye squinted at the bubble in the glass, the other, red with emotion, glared through the holes in the butt-strap, waiting till the expansion of the heated girders should bring the rivet-holes in line. Astronomers watching for an eclipse gaze not so earnestly as did Jerry and Fulsom.

'I say, what are you men doing there without orders?' cried Lieutenant Setton for the second time.

'Hah!' said Jerry, wagging the hammer to command silence. He was half aware now of some disturbing presence. The rivet-holes covered each other absolutely.

'Rivets to me! Quick, McGinnies. Meet me, Fulsom.' A man passed up the pincers with the red-hot rivet, and Jerry hammered like an artist. 'That'll make old——' (he mentioned the Cape Minister of Railways by name) 'pretty sick! Thought he'd hang us up by sending our stuff round by Naauwpoort, did he? Hold on! Rivet, rivet, McGinnies! What's the use of you? Derricks, there! Hold on! What are you men doing? Oh, good Lord!'

If Jerry on the rivet-boxes was losing his temper, Lieutenant Setton by the south girder had lost his altogether.

'You thought!' he shouted to the amazed gang at the derrick. 'You thought! Who in the world told you to think? D'you suppose you're here to do what you please? *I* gave no orders for the work to go on. Your orders, if you'd thought to come to my office to get them, are to clean up some of the filthy mess you've made round the Station.'

Then to Sergeant Rayne: 'Fall in your men at once, and march them up to the station. You'll get your orders there.'

'But half a mo', sir. Half a minute, sir. We can't let go——'

'Do you refuse duty, then? I warn you it'll be the worse for you. You can't do this—you can't do that? Let go that rope-thing at once. It's mutiny, by God!'

They let go at the south end. They fell back, not knowing the limits of Imperial power. The unsupported girder bit heavily on the single rivet that Jerry and Fulsom had put in—bit and shore through. The north gang let go an instant later. A howl of rage came out of the ravine as both girders dropped into a dolorous, open-sided V, knocked over the light staging, and twisting as they fell, scattered the fire in the coal-bucket among the dry scrub and fragments of timbering in the bed of the watercourse. They lit at once and blazed merrily. A man with a hammer erupted.

'Who slacked away without orders?' he demanded in a voice no private should use. One or two men had heard it before—at the time of the big dynamite explosion in Johannesburg—and straightened up.

'Fall in with your company there, and don't talk,' said Lieutenant Setton. He was willing to concede much to a mere Volunteer—even in time of war.

'It was him, Jerry,' whispered Sergeant Rayne.

Jerry turned a full mulberry-colour as he strove to control himself—he was quivering all over. Then he grew pale and rigid.

'Ha-half a minute, please. I want to explain to you exactly how the work stands. The girders were just in position, and I was riveting them up—my name is Thrupp.'

It carried some weight on the Rand, but Lieutenant Setton almost laughed aloud.

'If you wouldn't mind listening to me, please. It was an absolutely vital matter—absolutely vital. We were actually riveting the butt-strap when you meddled with the derrick. Let me show you!'—he laid one shaking hand on the Lieutenant's cuff—to lead him to the wreck.

'Meddle with the derrick! What the devil do you mean by your insolence? Do you know who I am?'

'In half an hour—in five minutes—we could have put in enough rivets to hold her. We shall have to go to work again. It means half a day's delay, though, even if the girders aren't twisted by the fall. . . . You can see it hung on only one rivet.'

'Fall in with your company—for the last time.'

'But you don't understand—you don't understand. Let me explain a minute, and come here'—again the hand on the cuff. 'Of course, you don't realize what you've done. It was only a question of minutes—minutes—do you see?—before we should have had those two girders—those short irons down there—riveted up. Good Lord! That scrub's burning like tinder! We must shovel earth on it, or it will twist the girders out of shape; and'—the voice rose almost to a shriek—'we shall have to send down the line for duplicates. I—you—tell the men to chuck earth on that blaze, for God's sake. The girders will buckle! They'll be ruined.'

'March this man to the guard-tent,' said Lieutenant Setton, who had endured enough. It was the insolence and insubordination of the man that galled him. 'Another time, perhaps, you'll take the trouble to obey orders.'

'What for? What have I done? My dear chap, this isn't the time to fiddle about with guard-tents. The whole donga's alight, and we shall have those girders buckling in ten minutes. You can't be going to leave the mess as it is—you *can't*!'

'Oh, I've stood enough of this. Silence. Understand you're a prisoner.'

'Me? Oh, yes. I'm anything you please if you'll only let me put out that fire. Where the deuce d'you think I'd want to run to? I'll come up to the guard-tent the minute it's out. I give you my word of honour!'

By this time the Railway Pioneer Corps was in two minds—some laughing and others looking very black. Only Sergeant Rayne, busy with a pocket-book, seemed to take no interest in the affair.

'March me off? With that fire burning? We'll be delayed a week at least. Why—why—why—' again Jerry turned plum-colour. Fulsom and McGinnies, who knew his habits, closed in on him at once.

'Come on, Jerry,' whispered Fulsom. 'You've done all you can. Come on.'

'All that I can? What do *I* matter? I'm thinking about the bridge.' He walked in a sort of stupor, looking back from time to time to watch the smoke in the donga. The Railway Pioneer Corps followed slowly to sweep up the platform of Pipkameelepòmpfontein.

'Rayne has got down every word you said in shorthand,' said Fulsom, when the prisoner reached the guard-tent. 'And he's going to wire Hagan now. For God's sake, don't open your mouth, Jerry, and we'll get that young ass Stellenbosched in a day or two.'

'Hung up for a week—hung up for a week!' moaned Jerry. 'Am I mad or is he? Tell Rayne to wire for spare girders. God knows where they are to come from! Perhaps Phil may have a couple at Folly Bridge. Better wire there as well. Those two will have buckled by now.'

* * *

'And you say he refused your orders?' This was Hagan, dirty and drawn after a journey in a draughty cattle-truck, standing at the foot of Setton's cot by dawnlight.

'He was extremely insolent, if that's what you mean. He deliberately questioned my authority before all the men several times. He kept pawing me all over, too. I don't suppose he really meant half he said.'

'Didn't he?' Hagan gulped, but curbed himself.

'The trouble with you Volunteers,' said Setton, rising on one arm, 'is that you've absolutely no notion of military discipline; and on active service one can't allow that sort of thing. However, I think forty-eight hours in the guard-tent will teach him a little sense. I've no intention of carrying the matter any further, so we needn't discuss it.'

Hagan stared at him with a horror that carried something of admiration, and a little—not much—pity. He had come up with Colonel Palling, R.E.,* and had shown him the third bridge.

'Is this his tent?' one cried without, and there entered a Colonel of Her Majesty's Royal Engineers, not in a common regimental rage, but such cold fury as an overworked man responsible for a few miles of track in war-time may justly wear. He chewed his three-months' beard, and looked at Lieutenant Setton, who stood to attention.

'You will go,' he whispered at last. 'You will go back to the base by the train this morning. You will give this note to the General there.'

'Yes, sir.'

'Do you know why you go?'

'No, sir.'

The Colonel's neck-veins swelled. 'I—I wish to speak to this officer,' he said.

It is the first maxim of internal economy that one should never reprimand a superior in the presence of his equal or his subordinate. Hagan withdrew. A sentry a few yards away stood fast. He was a Reservist of some experience.

'Gawd 'as been 'eavenly good to me,' he said later to fifteen comrades. 'I've 'eard quite a few things in my time. I've 'eard the Dook 'imself* pass the time o' day with an 'Orse battery that turned up on the wrong flank in the Long Valley. I 'eard "Smutty" Chambers lyin' be'ind an ant-'ill at Modder* getting sunstroke. I 'eard wot General Mike said when the cavalry was too late at Stinkersdrift. But all that was "Let me kiss 'im for 'is mother" '* to wot I 'eard this mornin'. There wasn't any common damn-your-eyes routine to it. Palling, 'e just felt about with 'is fingers till 'e'd found that little beggar's immortal soul—'e did. An' then 'e pulled it fair out of 'im like a bloomin' pull-through,* an' then 'e blew 'is nose on it like a bloomin' 'andkerchief, an' then 'e threw it away. Swore at 'im? No. You chaps don't take me. It was chronic. That's what it was—just chronic!'

*   *   *

In the peaceful and loyal district of Stellenbosch, there was a subaltern, temporarily attached as supernumerary on the Accounts side of the Numdah* and Boot-lace Issue Department, who knew exactly how the Army ought to be reorganized. And he said: 'It's all very well to talk about makin' the Army a business, like those newspaper chaps do, but they don't understand the spirit of the Service. How can they? Well, don't you see, if they bring in all those so-called reforms that they're always talkin' about, they simply fill up the Service with a lot of bounders and outsiders. They simply won't get the class of men to join that the Army really wants. No one will take up the Service as a profession then. I know *I* shan't for one.'

Stellenbosch*

(*Composite Columns*)*

THE General 'eard the firin' on the flank,
   An' 'e sent a mounted man to bring 'im back
The silly, pushin' person's name an' rank
   'Oo'd dared to answer Brother Boer's attack:
For there might 'ave been a serious engagement,
   An' 'e might 'ave wasted 'alf a dozen men;
So 'e ordered 'im to stop 'is operations round the kopjes,
   An' 'e told 'im off before the Staff at ten!

     And it all goes into the laundry,
     But it never comes out in the wash,
     'Ow we're sugared* about by the old men
     ('Eavy-sterned amateur old men!)
     That 'amper an' 'inder an' scold men
     For fear o' Stellenbosch!

The General 'ad 'produced a great effect,'
   The General 'ad the country cleared—almost;
The General ' 'ad no reason to expect,'
   And the Boers 'ad us bloomin' well on toast!
For we might 'ave crossed the drift* before the twilight,
   Instead o' sitting down an' takin' root;
But we was not allowed, so the Boojers scooped the crowd,
   To the last survivin' bandolier an' boot.

The General saw the farm'ouse in 'is rear,
   With its stoep* so nicely shaded from the sun;
Sez 'e, 'I'll pitch my tabernacle 'ere,'
   An' 'e kept us muckin' round till 'e 'ad done.
For 'e might 'ave caught the confluent pneumonia
   From sleepin' in his gaiters in the dew;
So 'e took a book an' dozed while the other columns
    closed,
   And De Wet's* commando out an' trickled through!

The General saw the mountain-range ahead,
  With their 'elios showin' saucy on the 'eight,
So 'e 'eld us to the level ground instead,
  An' telegraphed the Boojers wouldn't fight.
For 'e might 'ave gone an' sprayed 'em with a pompom,*
  Or 'e might 'ave slung a squadron out to see—
But 'e wasn't takin' chances in them 'igh an' 'ostile
    kranzes—*
  He was markin' time to earn a K.C.B.*

The General got 'is decorations thick
  (The men that backed 'is lies could not complain),
The Staff 'ad D.S.O.'s* till we was sick,
  An' the soldier—'ad the work to do again!
For 'e might 'ave known the District was an 'otbed,
  Instead of 'andin' over, upside-down,
To a man 'oo 'ad to fight 'alf a year to put it right,
  While the General sat an' slandered 'im in town!

      An' it all went into the laundry,
      But it never came out in the wash.
      We were sugared about by the old men
      (Panicky, perishin' old men)
      That 'amper an' 'inder an' scold men
      For fear o' Stellenbosch!

A Sahibs' War*

PASS?* Pass? Pass? I have one pass already, allowing me to go by the *rêl* from Kroonstadt* to Eshtellenbosch, where the horses are, where I am to be paid off, and whence I return to India. I am a—trooper of the Gurgaon Rissala (cavalry regiment), the One Hundred and Forty-first Punjab Cavalry. Do not herd me with these black Kaffirs. I am a Sikh—a trooper of the State. The Lieutenant-Sahib does not understand my talk? Is there *any* Sahib on this train who will interpret for a trooper of the Gurgaon Rissala going about his business in this devil's devising of a country, where there is no flour, no oil, no spice, no red pepper, and no respect paid to a Sikh? Is there no help? . . . God be thanked, here is such a Sahib! Protector of the Poor! Heaven-born! Tell the young Lieutenant-Sahib that my name is Umr Singh; I am—I *was*—servant to Kurban Sahib, now dead; and I have a pass to go to Eshtellenbosch, where the horses are. Do not let him herd me with these black Kaffirs! . . . Yes, I will sit by this truck till the Heaven-born has explained the matter to the young Lieutenant-Sahib who does not understand our tongue.

* * *

What orders? The young Lieutenant-Sahib will not detain me? Good! I go down to Eshtellenbosch by the next *terain*? Good! I go with the Heaven-born? Good! Then for this day I am the Heaven-born's servant. Will the Heaven-born bring the honour of his presence to a seat? Here is an empty truck; I will spread my blanket over one corner thus—for the sun is hot, though not so hot as our Punjab in May. I will prop it up thus, and I will arrange this hay thus, so the Presence can sit at ease till God sends us a *terain* for Eshtellenbosch. . . .

The Presence knows the Punjab? Lahore? Amritzar? Attaree, belike? My village is north over the fields three miles from Attaree, near the big white house which was copied from a certain place of the Great Queen's by—by—I have forgotten

the name. Can the Presence recall it? Sirdar Dyal Singh*
Attareewalla! Yes, that is the very man; but how does the
Presence know? Born and bred in Hind, was he? O-o-oh! This
is quite a different matter. The Sahib's nurse was a Surtee*
woman from the Bombay side? That was a pity. She should
have been an up-country wench; for those make stout nurses.
There is no land like the Punjab. There are no people like the
Sikhs. Umr Singh is my name, yes. An old man? Yes. A
trooper only after all these years? Ye-es. Look at my uniform,
if the Sahib doubts. Nay—nay; the Sahib looks too closely. All
marks of rank were picked off it long ago, but—but it is true—
mine is not a common cloth such as troopers use for their coats,
and—the Sahib has sharp eyes—that black mark is such a mark
as a silver chain leaves when long worn on the breast. The
Sahib says that troopers do not wear silver chains? No-o.
Troopers do not wear the Arder of Beritish India? No. The
Sahib should have been in the Police of the Punjab. I am not a
trooper, but I have been a Sahib's servant for nearly a year
—bearer, butler, sweeper, any and all three. The Sahib says
that Sikhs do not take menial service? True; but it was for
Kurban Sahib—my Kurban Sahib—dead these three months!

*   *   *

Young—of a reddish face—with blue eyes, and he lilted a
little on his feet when he was pleased, and cracked his finger-
joints. So did his father before him, who was Deputy-Commis-
sioner of Jullundur in my father's time when I rode with the
Gurgaon Rissala. *My* father? Jwala Singh. A Sikh of Sikhs—he
fought against the English at Sobraon* and carried the mark to
his death. So we were knit as it were by a blood-tie, I and my
Kurban Sahib. Yes, I was a trooper first—nay, I had risen to
a Lance-Duffadar,* I remember—and my father gave me a
dun stallion of his own breeding on that day; and *he* was a
little baba, sitting upon a wall by the parade-ground with his
ayah*—all in white, Sahib—laughing at the end of our
drill. And his father and mine talked together, and mine
beckoned to me, and I dismounted, and the baba put his hand
into mine—eighteen—twenty-five—twenty-seven years gone
now—Kurban Sahib—my Kurban Sahib! Oh, we were great

friends after that! He cut his teeth on my sword-hilt, as the saying is. He called me Big Umr Singh—Buwwa* Umwa Singh, for he could not speak plain. He stood only this high, Sahib, from the bottom of this truck, but he knew all our troopers by name—every one. . . . And he went to England, and he became a young man, and back he came, lilting a little in his walk, and cracking his finger-joints—back to his own Regiment and to me. He had not forgotten either our speech or our customs. He was a Sikh at heart, Sahib. He was rich, open-handed, just, a friend of poor troopers, keen-eyed, jestful, and careless. *I* could tell tales about him in his first years. There was very little he hid from *me*. I was his Umr Singh, and when we were alone he called me Father, and I called him Son. Yes, that was how we spoke. We spoke freely together on every-thing—about war, and women, and money, and advancement, and such all.

We spoke about this war, too, long before it came. There were many box-wallahs, pedlars, with Pathans a few, in this country, notably at the city of Yunasbagh (Johannesburg), and they sent news in every week how the Sahibs* lay without weapons under the heel of the Boer-*log*;* and how big guns were hauled up and down the streets to keep Sahibs in order; and how a Sahib called Eger Sahib (Edgar) was killed for a jest by the Boer-*log*.* The Sahib knows how we of Hind hear all that passes over the earth? There was not a gun cocked in Yunasbagh that the echo did not come into Hind in a month. The Sahibs are very clever, but they forget their own cleverness has created the *dâk* (the post), and that for an anna or two all things become known. We of Hind listened and heard and wondered; and when it was a sure thing, as reported by the pedlars and the vegetable-sellers, that the Sahibs of Yunasbagh lay in bondage to the Boer-*log*, certain among us asked questions and waited for signs. Others of us mistook the meaning of those signs. *Wherefore, Sahib, came the long war in the Tirah!** This Kurban Sahib knew, and we talked together. He said, 'There is no haste. Presently we shall fight, and we shall fight for all Hind in that country round Yunasbagh.' Here he spoke the truth. Does the Sahib not agree? Quite so. It is for Hind that the Sahibs are fighting this war. Ye cannot in one place rule and in another bear service.

Either ye must everywhere rule or everywhere obey. God does not make the nations ringstraked. True—true—true!

So did matters ripen—a step at a time. It was nothing to me, except I think—and the Sahib sees this, too?—that it is foolish to make an army and break their hearts in idleness. Why have they not sent for the men of the Tochi—the men of the Tirah—the men of Buner?* Folly, a thousand times. *We* could have done it all so gently—so gently.

Then, upon a day, Kurban Sahib sent for me and said, 'Ho, Dada, I am sick, and the doctor gives me a certificate for many months.' And he winked, and I said, 'I will get leave and nurse thee, Child. Shall I bring my uniform?' He said, 'Yes, and a sword for a sick man to lean on. We go to Bombay, and thence by sea to the country of the Hubshis' (niggers). Mark his cleverness! He was first of all our men among the native regiments to get leave for sickness and to come here. Now they will not let our officers go away, sick or well, except they sign a bond not to take part in this war-game upon the road. But *he* was clever. There was no whisper of war when he took his sick-leave. I came also? Assuredly. I went to my Colonel, and sitting in the chair (I am—I was—of that rank for which a chair is placed when we speak with the Colonel) I said, 'My child goes sick. Give me leave, for I am old and sick also.'

And the Colonel, making the word double between English and our tongue, said, 'Yes, thou art truly *Sikh*'; and he called me an old devil—jestingly, as one soldier may jest with another; and he said my Kurban Sahib was a liar as to his health (that was true, too), and at long last he stood up and shook my hand, and bade me go and bring my Sahib safe again. My Sahib back again—aie me!

So I went to Bombay with Kurban Sahib, but there, at sight of the Black Water,* Wajib Ali, his bearer, checked, and said that his mother was dead. Then I said to Kurban Sahib, 'What is one Mussulman pig more or less? Give me the keys of the trunks, and I will lay out the white shirts for dinner.' Then I beat Wajib Ali at the back of Watson's Hotel,* and that night I prepared Kurban Sahib's razors. I say, Sahib, that I, a Sikh of the Khalsa,* an unshorn man, prepared the razors. But I did not put on my uniform while I did it. On the other hand,

Kurban Sahib took for me, upon the steamer, a room in all respects like to his own, and would have given me a servant. We spoke of many things on the way to this country; and Kurban Sahib told me what he perceived would be the conduct of the war. He said, 'They have taken men afoot to fight men ahorse, and they will foolishly show mercy to these Boer-*log* because it is believed that they are white.' He said, 'There is but one fault in this war, and that is that the Government have not employed *us*,* but have made it altogether a Sahibs' war. Very many men will thus be killed, and no vengeance will be taken.' True talk—true talk! It fell as Kurban Sahib foretold.

And we came to this country, even to Cape Town over yonder, and Kurban Sahib said, 'Bear the baggage to the big *dâk*-bungalow,* and I will look for employment fit for a sick man.' I put on the uniform of my rank and went to the big *dâk*-bungalow, called Maun Nihâl Seyn,* and I caused the heavy baggage to be bestowed in that dark lower place—is it known to the Sahib?—which was already full of the swords and baggage of officers. It is fuller now—dead men's kit all! I was careful to secure a receipt for all three pieces. I have it in my belt. They must go back to the Punjab.

Anon came Kurban Sahib, lilting a little in his step, which sign I knew, and he said, 'We are born in a fortunate hour. We go to Eshtellenbosch to oversee the despatch of horses.' Remember, Kurban Sahib was squadron-leader of the Gurgaon Rissala, and *I* was Umr Singh. So I said, speaking as we do— we did—when none was near, 'Thou art a groom and I am a grass-cutter,* but is this any promotion, Child?' At this he laughed, saying, 'It is the way to better things. Have patience, Father.' (Aye, he called me Father when none were by.) 'This war ends not to-morrow nor the next day. I have seen the new Sahibs,' he said, 'and they are fathers of owls—all—all—all!'

So we went to Eshtellenbosch, where the horses are; Kurban Sahib doing the service of servants in that business. And the whole business was managed without forethought by new Sahibs from God knows where, who had never seen a tent pitched or a peg driven. They were full of zeal, but empty of all knowledge. Then came little by little from Hind, those Pathans—they are just like those vultures up there, Sahib

—they always follow slaughter. And there came to Eshtel-
lenbosch some Sikhs—Muzbees,* though—and some Madras
monkey-men. They came with horses. Patiala sent horses.
Jhind and Nabha* sent horses. All the nations of the Khalsa
sent horses. All the ends of the earth sent horses. God knows
what the army did with them, unless they ate them raw.* They
used horses as a courtesan uses oil: with both hands. These
horses needed many men. Kurban Sahib appointed me to the
command (what a command for me!) of certain woolly ones—
Hubshis—whose touch and shadow are pollution. They were
enormous eaters; sleeping on their bellies; laughing without
cause; wholly like animals. Some were called Fingoes, and
some, I think, Red Kaffirs, but they were all Kaffirs—filth
unspeakable. I taught them to water and feed, and sweep and
rub down. Yes, I oversaw the work of sweepers—a *jemadar* of
mehters (headman of a refuse-gang) was I, and Kurban Sahib
little better, for five months. Evil months! The war went as
Kurban Sahib had said. Our new men were slain and no
vengeance was taken. It was a war of fools armed with the
weapons of magicians. Guns that slew at half a day's march,
and men who, being new, walked blind into high grass and
were driven off like cattle by the Boer-*log*! As to the city of
Eshtellenbosch, I am not a Sahib—only a Sikh. I would have
quartered one troop only of the Gurgaon Rissala in that city—
one little troop—and I would have schooled that city till its
men learned to kiss the shadow of a Government horse upon
the ground. There are many *mullahs* (priests) in Eshtel-
lenbosch. They preached the *Jehad** (Holy War) against us.
This is true—all the camp knew it. And most of the houses
were thatched!* A war of fools indeed!

At the end of five months my Kurban Sahib, who had grown
lean, said, 'The reward has come. We go up towards the front
with horses to-morrow, and, once away, I shall be too sick to
return. Make ready the baggage.' Thus we got away, with some
Kaffirs in charge of new horses for a certain new regiment that
had come in a ship. The second day by *terain*, when we were
watering at a desolate place without any sort of a bazar to it,
slipped out from the horse-boxes one Sikandar Khan, that had
been a *jemadar* of *saises* (head-groom) at Eshtellenbosch, and

was by service a trooper in a Border regiment. Kurban Sahib gave him big abuse for his desertion; but the Pathan put up his hands as excusing himself, and Kurban Sahib relented and added him to our service. So there were three of us—Kurban Sahib, I, and Sikandar Khan—Sahib, Sikh, and *Sag* (dog). But the man said truly, 'We be far from our homes and both servants of the Raj. Make truce till we see the Indus again.' I have eaten from the same dish as Sikandar Khan—beef, too, for aught I know! He said, on the night he stole some swine's flesh in a tin from a mess-tent, that in his Book, the Koran, it is written that whoso engages in a holy war is freed from ceremonial obligations. Wah! He had no more religion than the sword-point picks up of sugar and water at baptism. He stole himself a horse at a place where there lay a new and very raw regiment. I also procured myself a grey gelding there. They let their horses stray too much, those new regiments.

Some shameless regiments would indeed have made away with *our* horses on the road! They exhibited indents and requisitions for horses, and once or twice would have uncoupled the trucks; but Kurban Sahib was wise, and I am not altogether a fool. There is not much honesty at the front. Notably, there was one congregation of hard-bitten horse-thieves; tall, light Sahibs, who spoke through their noses for the most part, and upon all occasions they said, 'Oah Hell!' which, in our tongue, signifies *Jehannum ko jao*. They bore each man a vine-leaf* upon their uniforms, and they rode like Rajputs. Nay, they rode like Sikhs. They rode like the Ustrelyahs! The Ustrelyahs, whom we met later, also spoke through their noses not little, and they were tall, dark men, with grey, clear eyes, heavily eyelashed like camel's eyes—very proper men—a new brand of Sahib to me. They said on all occasions, 'No fee-ah,' which in our tongue means *Durro mut* (Do not be afraid), so we called them the *Durro Muts*. Dark, tall men, most excellent horsemen, hot and angry, waging war as war, and drinking tea as a sandhill drinks water. Thieves? A little, Sahib. Sikandar Khan swore to me—and he comes of a horse-stealing clan for ten generations—he swore a Pathan was a babe beside a *Durro Mut* in regard to horse-lifting. The *Durro Muts* cannot walk on their feet at all. They are like hens on the high road. Therefore they must have horses. Very proper men, with a just lust for the war. Aah—'No fee-ah!' say the *Durro Muts*. *They* saw the worth of Kurban Sahib. *They* did not ask him to sweep stables. They would by no means let him go. He did substitute for one of their troop-leaders who had a fever, one long day in a country full of little hills—like the mouth of the Khyber; and when they returned in the evening, the *Durro Muts* said, 'Wallah! This is a man. Steal him!' So they stole my Kurban Sahib as they would have stolen anything else that they needed, and they sent a sick officer back to Eshtellenbosch in his place. Thus Kurban Sahib came to his own again, and I was his bearer and Sikandar Khan was his cook. The law was strict that this was a Sahibs' war, but there was no order that a bearer and a cook should not ride with their Sahib—and we had naught to wear but our uniforms. We rode up and down this accursed country, where there is no bazar, no pulse, no flour, no oil, no spice, no red pepper, no firewood; nothing but raw corn and a little cattle. There were no great battles as I saw it, but a plenty of gun-firing. When we were many, the Boer-*log* came out with coffee to greet us, and to show us *purwanas* (permits) from foolish English Generals who had gone that way before, certifying they were peaceful and well-disposed. When we were few, they hid behind stones and shot us. Now the order was that they were Sahibs, and this was a Sahibs' war. Good! But, as I understand it, when a Sahib goes to war, he puts on the cloth of war, and only those who wear that cloth may take part in the war. Good! That also I understand. But these people were as they were in Burma,* or as the Afridis are. They shot at their pleasure, and when pressed hid the gun and exhibited *purwanas*, or lay in a house and said they were farmers. Even such farmers as cut up the Madras troops* at Hlinedatalone in Burma! Even such farmers as slew Cavagnari Sahib and the Guides at Kabul!* We schooled *those* men, to be sure—fifteen, aye, twenty of a morning pushed off the verandah in front of the Bala Hissar. I looked that the Jung-i-lat Sahib (the Commander-in-Chief) would have remembered the old days;* but—no. All the people shot at us everywhere, and he issued proclamations saying that he did not fight the people, but a certain army, which army, in truth, was all the

Boer-*log*, who, between them, did not wear enough of uniform
to make a loin-cloth. A fools' war from first to last; for it is
manifest that he who fights should be hung if he fights with a
gun in one hand and a *purwana* in the other, as did all these
people. Yet we, when they had had their bellyful for the time,
received them with honour, and gave them permits, and
refreshed them and fed their wives and their babes, and
severely punished our soldiers who took their fowls. So the
work was to be done not once with a few dead, but thrice and
four times over. I talked much with Kurban Sahib on this, and
he said, 'It is a Sahibs' war. That is the order'; and one night,
when Sikandar Khan would have lain out beyond the pickets
with his knife and shown them how it is worked on the Border,
he hit Sikandar Khan between the eyes and came near to break-
ing in his head. Then Sikandar Khan, a bandage over his eyes,
so that he looked like a sick camel, talked to him half one
march, and he was more bewildered than I, and vowed he
would return to Eshtellenbosch. But privately to me Kurban
Sahib said we should have loosed the Sikhs and the Gurkhas on
these people till they came in with their foreheads in the dust.
For the war was not of that sort which they comprehended.

They shot us? Assuredly they shot us from houses adorned
with a white flag; but when they came to know our custom,*
their widows sent word by Kaffir runners, and presently there
was not quite so much firing. *No fee-ah!* All the Boer-*log* with
whom we dealt had *purwanas* signed by mad Generals attesting
that they were well disposed to the State. They had also rifles
not a few, and cartridges, which they hid in the roof. The
women wept very greatly when we burned such houses, but
they did not approach too near after the flames had taken good
hold of the thatch, for fear of the bursting cartridges. The
women of the Boer-*log* are very clever. They are more clever
than the men. The Boer-*log* are clever? Never, never, no! It is
the Sahibs who are fools. For their own honour's sake the
Sahibs must say that the Boer-*log* are clever; but it is the
Sahibs' wonderful folly that has made the Boer-*log*. The Sahibs
should have sent *us* into the game.

But the *Durro Muts* did well. They dealt faithfully with all
that country thereabouts—not in any way as we of Hind should

have dealt, but they were not altogether fools. One night when we lay on the top of a ridge in the cold, I saw far away a light in a house that appeared for the sixth part of an hour and was obscured. Anon it appeared again thrice for the twelfth part of an hour. I showed this to Kurban Sahib, for it was a house that had been spared—the people having many permits and swearing fidelity at our stirrup-leathers. I said to Kurban Sahib, 'Send half a troop, Child, and finish that house. They signal to their brethren.' And he laughed where he lay and said, 'If I listened to my bearer Umr Singh, there would not be left ten houses in all this land.' I said, 'What need to leave one? This is as it was in Burma. They are farmers to-day and fighters to-morrow. Let us deal justly with them.' He laughed and curled himself up in his blanket, and I watched the far light in the house till day. I have been on the Border in eight wars, not counting Burma. The first Afghan War;* the second Afghan War; two Mahsud Waziri wars (that is four); two Black Mountain wars, if I remember right; the Malakand and Tirah. I do not count Burma, or some small things. *I* know when house signals to house!

I pushed Sikandar Khan with my foot, and he saw it too. He said, 'One of the Boer-*log* who brought pumpkins for the Mess, which I fried last night, lives in yonder house.' I said, 'How dost thou know?' He said, 'Because he rode out of the camp another way, but I marked how his horse fought with him at the turn of the road; and before the night fell I stole out of the camp for evening prayer with Kurban Sahib's glasses, and from a little hill I saw the pied horse of that pumpkin-seller hurrying to that house.' I said naught, but took Kurban Sahib's glasses from his greasy hands and cleaned them with a silk handkerchief and returned them to their case. Sikandar Khan told me that he had been the first man in the Zenab valley to use glasses—whereby he finished two blood-feuds cleanly in the course of three months' leave. But he was otherwise a liar.

That day Kurban Sahib, with some ten troopers, was sent on to spy the land for our camp. The *Durro Muts* moved slowly at that time. They were weighted with grain and forage and carts, and they greatly wished to leave these all in some

town and go on light to other business which pressed. So
Kurban Sahib sought a short cut for them, a little off the line of
march. We were twelve miles before the main body, and we
came to a house under a high bushed hill, with a nullah, which
they call a donga,* behind it, and an old sangar of piled stones,
which they call a kraal, before it. Two thorn bushes grew on
either side of the door, like babul bushes,* covered with a
golden-coloured bloom, and the roof was all of thatch. Before
the house was a valley of stones that rose to another bush-
covered hill. There was an old man in the verandah—an old
man with a white beard and a wart upon the left side of his
neck; and a fat woman with the eyes of a swine and the jowl of a
swine; and a tall young man deprived of understanding. His
head was hairless, no larger than an orange, and the pits of his
nostrils were eaten away by a disease. He laughed and slavered
and he sported sportively before Kurban Sahib. The man
brought coffee and the woman showed us *purwanas* from three
General-Sahibs, certifying that they were people of peace and
goodwill. Here are the *purwanas*, Sahib. Does the Sahib know
the Generals who signed them?

They swore the land was empty of Boer-*log*. They held up
their hands and swore it. That was about the time of the
evening meal. I stood near the verandah with Sikandar Khan,
who was nosing like a jackal on a lost scent. At last he took my
arm and said, 'See yonder! There is the sun on the window of
the house that signalled last night. This house can see that
house from here,' and he looked at the hill behind him all hairy
with bushes, and sucked in his breath. Then the idiot with the
shrivelled head danced by me and threw back that head, and
regarded the roof and laughed like a hyena, and the fat woman
talked loudly, as it were, to cover some noise. After this I
passed to the back of the house on pretence to get water for tea,
and I saw fresh horse-dung on the ground, and that the ground
was cut with the new marks of hoofs; and there had dropped in
the dirt one cartridge. Then Kurban Sahib called to me in our
tongue, saying, 'Is this a good place to make tea?' and I replied,
knowing what he meant, 'There are over many cooks in the
cook-house. Mount and go, Child.' Then I returned and he
said, smiling to the woman, 'Prepare food, and when we have

loosened our girths we will come in and eat'; but to his men he said in a whisper, 'Ride away!' No. He did not cover the old man or the fat woman with his rifle. That was not his custom. Some fool of the *Durro Muts*, being hungry, raised his voice to dispute the order to flee, and before we were in our saddles many shots came from the roof—from rifles thrust through the thatch. Upon this we rode across the valley of stones, and men fired at us from the nullah behind the house, and from the hill behind the nullah, as well as from the roof of the house—so many shots that it sounded like a drumming in the hills. Then Sikandar Khan, riding low, said, 'This play is not for us alone, but for the rest of the *Durro Muts*,' and I said, 'Be quiet. Keep place!' for his place was behind me, and I rode behind Kurban Sahib. But these new bullets will pass through five men a-row! We were not hit—not one of us—and we reached the hill of rocks and scattered among the stones, and Kurban Sahib turned in his saddle and said, 'Look at the old man!' He stood in the verandah firing swiftly with a gun, the woman beside him and the idiot also—both with guns. Kurban Sahib laughed, and I caught him by the wrist, but—his fate was written at that hour. The bullet passed under my arm-pit and struck him in the liver, and I pulled him backward between two great rocks a-tilt—Kurban Sahib, my Kurban Sahib! From the nullah behind the house and from the hills came out Boer-*log* in number more than a hundred, and Sikandar Khan said, '*Now* we see the meaning of last night's signal. Give me the rifle.' He took Kurban Sahib's rifle—in this war of fools only the doctors carry swords—and lay belly-flat to the work, but Kurban Sahib turned where he lay and said, 'Be still. It is a Sahibs' war,' and Kurban Sahib put up his hand—thus; and then his eyes rolled on me, and I gave him water that he might pass the more quickly. And at the drinking his Spirit received permission. . . .

Thus went our fight, Sahib. We *Durro Muts* were on a ridge working from the north to the south, where lay our main body, and the Boer-*log* lay in a valley working from east to west. There were more than a hundred, and our men were ten, but they held the Boer-*log* in the valley while they swiftly passed along the ridge to the south. I saw three Boers drop in the

open. Then they all hid again and fired heavily at the rocks that
hid our men; but our men were clever and did not show, but
moved away and away, always south; and the noise of the battle
withdrew itself southward, where we could hear the sound of
big guns. So it fell stark dark, and Sikandar Khan found a deep
old jackal's earth amid rocks, into which we slid the body of
Kurban Sahib upright. Sikandar Khan took his glasses, and I
took his handkerchief and some letters and a certain thing
which I knew hung round his neck, and Sikandar Khan is
witness that I wrapped them all in the handkerchief. Then we
took an oath together, and lay still and mourned for Kurban
Sahib. Sikandar Khan wept till daybreak—even he, a Pathan, a
Mohammedan! All that night we heard firing to the southward,
and when the dawn broke the valley was full of Boer-*log* in carts
and on horses. They gathered by the house, as we could see
through Kurban Sahib's glasses, and the old man, who, I take
it, was a priest, blessed them, and preached the holy war,
waving his arm; and the fat woman brought coffee, and the
idiot capered among them and kissed their horses. Presently
they went away in haste; they went over the hills and were not;
and a black slave came out and washed the door-sills with
bright water. Sikandar Khan saw through the glasses that the
stain was blood, and he laughed, saying, 'Wounded men lie
there. We shall yet get vengeance.'

About noon we saw a thin, high smoke to the southward,
such a smoke as a burning house will make in sunshine, and
Sikandar Khan, who knows how to take a bearing across a hill,
said, 'At last we have burned the house of the pumpkin-seller
whence they signalled.' And I said, 'What need now that they
have slain my child? Let me mourn.' It was a high smoke, and
the old man, as I saw, came out into the verandah to behold it,
and shook his clenched hands at it. So we lay till the twilight,
foodless and without water, for we had vowed a vow neither to
eat nor to drink till we had accomplished the matter. I had a
little opium left, of which I gave Sikandar Khan the half,
because he loved Kurban Sahib. When it was full dark we
sharpened our sabres upon a certain softish rock which, mixed
with water, sharpens steel well, and we took off our boots and
we went down to the house and looked through the windows

very softly. The old man sat reading in a book, and the woman sat by the hearth; and the idiot lay on the floor with his head against her knee, and he counted his fingers and laughed, and she laughed again. So I knew they were mother and son, and I laughed, too, for I had suspected this when I claimed her life and her body from Sikandar Khan, in our discussion of the spoil. Then we entered with bare swords. . . . Indeed, these Boer-*log* do not understand the steel, for the old man ran towards a rifle in the corner; but Sikandar Khan prevented him with a blow of the flat across the hands, and he sat down and held up his hands, and I put my fingers on my lips to signify they should be silent. But the woman cried, and one stirred in an inner room, and a door opened, and a man, bound about the head with rags, stood stupidly fumbling with a gun. His whole head fell inside the door, and none followed him. It was a very pretty stroke—for a Pathan. Then they were silent, staring at the head upon the floor, and I said to Sikandar Khan, 'Fetch ropes! Not even for Kurban Sahib's sake will I defile my sword.' So he went to seek and returned with three long leather ones, and said, 'Four wounded lie within, and doubtless each has a permit from a General,' and he stretched the ropes and laughed. Then I bound the old man's hands behind his back, and unwillingly—for he laughed in my face, and would have fingered my beard—the idiot's. At this the woman with the swine's eyes and the jowl of a swine ran forward, and Sikandar Khan said, 'Shall I strike or bind? She was thy property on the division.' And I said, 'Refrain! I have made a chain to hold her. Open the door.' I pushed out the two across the verandah into the darker shade of the thorn-trees, and she followed upon her knees and lay along the ground, and pawed at my boots and howled. Then Sikandar Khan bore out the lamp, saying that he was a butler and would light the table, and I looked for a branch that would bear fruit. But the woman hindered me not a little with her screechings and plungings, and spoke fast in her tongue, and I replied in my tongue, 'I am childless to-night because of thy perfidy, and *my* child was praised among men and loved among women. He would have begotten men—not animals. Thou hast more years to live than I, but my grief is the greater.'

I stooped to make sure the noose upon the idiot's neck, and flung the end over the branch, and Sikandar Khan held up the lamp that she might well see. Then appeared suddenly, a little beyond the light of the lamp, the spirit of Kurban Sahib. One hand he held to his side, even where the bullet had struck him, and the other he put forward thus, and said, 'No. It is a Sahibs' war.' And I said, 'Wait a while, Child, and thou shalt sleep.' But he came nearer, riding, as it were upon my eyes, and said, 'No. It is a Sahibs' war.' And Sikandar Khan said, 'Is it too heavy?' and set down the lamp and came to me; and as he turned to tally on the rope, the spirit of Kurban Sahib stood up within arm's reach of us, and his face was very angry, and a third time he said, 'No. It is a Sahibs' war.' And a little wind blew out the lamp, and I heard Sikandar Khan's teeth chatter in his head.

So we stayed side by side, the ropes in our hand, a very long while, for we could not shape any words. Then I heard Sikandar Khan open his water-bottle and drink; and when his mouth was slaked he passed to me and said, 'We are absolved from our vow.' So I drank, and together we waited for the dawn in that place where we stood—the ropes in our hand. A little after third cockcrow we heard the feet of horses and gun-wheels very far off, and so soon as the light came a shell burst on the threshold of the house, and the roof of the verandah that was thatched fell in and blazed before the windows. And I said, 'What of the wounded Boer-*log* within?' And Sikandar Khan said, 'We have heard the order. It is a Sahibs' war. Stand still.' Then came a second shell—good line, but short—and scattered dust upon us where we stood; and then came ten of the little quick shells from the gun that speaks like a stammerer—yes, pompom* the Sahibs call it—and the face of the house folded down like the nose and the chin of an old man mumbling, and the forefront of the house lay down. Then Sikandar Khan said, 'If it be the fate of the wounded to die in the fire, *I* shall not prevent it.' And he passed to the back of the house and presently came back, and four wounded Boer-*log* came after him, of whom two could not walk upright. And I said, 'What hast thou done?' And he said, 'I have neither spoken to them nor laid hand on them. They follow in hope of mercy.' And I said, 'It is a Sahibs' war. Let them wait the Sahibs' mercy.' So they lay still, the four men and the idiot, and the fat woman under the thorn-tree, and the house burned furiously. Then began the known sound of cartouches* in the roof—one or two at first; then a trill, and last of all one loud noise and the thatch blew here and there, and the captives would have crawled aside on account of the heat that was withering the thorn-trees, and on account of wood and bricks flying at random. But I said, 'Abide! Abide! Ye be Sahibs, and this is a Sahibs' war, O Sahibs. There is no order that ye should depart from this war.' They did not understand my words. Yet they abode and they lived.

Presently rode down five troopers of Kurban Sahib's command, and one I knew spoke my tongue, having sailed to Calcutta often with horses. So I told him all my tale, using bazar-talk, such as his kidney of Sahib would understand; and at the end I said, 'An order has reached us here from the dead that this is a Sahibs' war. I take the soul of my Kurban Sahib to witness that I give over to the justice of the Sahibs these Sahibs who have made me childless.' Then I gave him the ropes and fell down senseless, my heart being very full, but my belly was empty, except for the little opium.

They put me into a cart with one of their wounded, and after a while I understood that they had fought against the Boer-*log* for two days and two nights. It was all one big trap, Sahib, of which we, with Kurban Sahib, saw no more than the outer edge. They were very angry, the *Durro Muts*—very angry indeed. I have never seen Sahibs so angry. They buried my Kurban Sahib with the rites of his faith upon the top of the ridge overlooking the house, and I said the proper prayers of the faith, and Sikandar Khan prayed in his fashion and stole five signalling-candles, which have each three wicks, and lighted the grave as if it had been the grave of a saint on a Friday. He wept very bitterly all that night, and I wept with him, and he took hold of my feet and besought me to give him a remembrance from Kurban Sahib. So I divided equally with him one of Kurban Sahib's handkerchiefs—not the silk ones, for those were given him by a certain woman; and I also gave him a button from a coat, and a little steel ring of no value that

Kurban Sahib used for his keys, and he kissed them and put them into his bosom. The rest I have here in that little bundle, and I must get the baggage from the hotel in Cape Town— some four shirts we sent to be washed, for which we could not wait when we went up-country—and I must give them all to my Colonel-Sahib at Sialkot in the Punjab. For my child is dead—my baba is dead! . . .

I would have come away before; there was no need to stay, the child being dead; but we were far from the rail, and the *Durro Muts* were as brothers to me, and I had come to look upon Sikandar Khan as in some sort a friend, and he got me a horse and I rode up and down with them; but the life had departed. God knows what they called me—orderly, *chaprassi* (messenger), cook, sweeper, I did not know nor care. But once I had pleasure. We came back in a month after wide circles to that very valley. I knew it, every stone, and I went up to the grave, and a clever Sahib of the *Durro Muts* (we left a troop there for a week to school those people with *purwanas*) had cut an inscription upon a great rock; and they interpreted it to me, and it was a jest such as Kurban Sahib himself would have loved. Oh! I have the inscription well copied here. Read it aloud, Sahib, and I will explain the jests. There are two very good ones. Begin, Sahib:—

In Memory of
WALTER DECIES CORBYN
Late Captain 141st Punjab Cavalry

The Gurgaon Rissala, that is. Go on, Sahib.

Treacherously shot near this place by
The connivance of the late
HENDRIK DIRK UYS
A Minister of God
Who thrice took the oath of neutrality
And Piet his son,
This little work

Aha! This is the first jest. The Sahib should see this little work!

Was accomplished in partial
And inadequate recognition of their loss

By some men who loved him

*Si monumentum requiris circumspice**

That is the second jest. It signifies that those who would desire to behold a proper memorial to Kurban Sahib must look out at the house. And, Sahib, the house is not there, nor the well, nor the big tank which they call dams, nor the little fruit-trees, nor the cattle. There is nothing at all, Sahib, except the two trees withered by the fire. The rest is like the desert here—or my hand—or my heart. Empty, Sahib—all empty!

'Wilful-Missing'*

(Deserters of the Boer War)

THERE is a world outside the one you know,
  To which for curiousness 'Ell can't compare—
It is the place where 'wilful-missings' go,
  As we can testify, for we are there.

You may 'ave read a bullet laid us low,
  That we was gathered in 'with reverent care'
And buried proper. But it was not so,
  As we can testify,—for we are there!

They can't be certain—faces alter so
  After the old aasvogel's* 'ad 'is share.
The uniform's the mark by which they go—
  And—ain't it odd?—the one we best can spare.

We might 'ave seen our chance to cut the show—
  Name, number, record, an' begin elsewhere—
Leavin' some not too late-lamented foe
  One funeral—private—British—for 'is share.

We may 'ave took it yonder in the low
  Bush-veldt that sends men stragglin' unaware
Among the Kaffirs, till their columns go,
  An' they are left past call or count or care.

We might 'ave been your lovers long ago,
  'Usbands or children—comfort or despair.
Our death (an' burial) settles all we owe,
  An' why we done it is our own affair.

Marry again, and we will not say no,
  Nor come to barstardise the kids you bear.
Wait on in 'ope—you've all your life below
  Before you'll ever 'ear us on the stair.

There is no need to give our reasons, though
  Gawd knows we all 'ad reasons which were fair;
But other people might not judge 'em so—
  And now it doesn't matter what they were.

What man can weigh or size another's woe?
  There are some things too bitter 'ard to bear.
Suffice it we 'ave finished—Domino!*
  As we can testify, for we are there,
In the side-world where 'wilful-missings' go.

The Comprehension of Private Copper*

PRIVATE COPPER'S father was a Southdown shepherd; in early youth Copper had studied under him. Five years' Army service had somewhat blunted Private Copper's pastoral instincts, but it occurred to him as a memory of the Chalk that sheep, or in this case buck, do not move towards one across turf, or in this case, the Colesberg kopjes* unless a stranger, or in this case an enemy, is in the neighbourhood. Copper, helmet back-first,* advanced with caution, leaving his mates of the picket a full mile behind. The picket, concerned for its evening meal, did not protest. A year ago it would have been an officer's command, moving as such. To-day it paid casual allegiance to a Canadian, nominally a sergeant, actually a trooper of Irregular Horse, discovered convalescent in Naauwport Hospital, and forthwith employed on odd jobs. Private Copper crawled up the side of a bluish rock-strewn hill thinly fringed with brush atop, and remembering how he had peered at Sussex conies through the edge of furze-clumps, cautiously parted the dry stems before his face. At the foot of the long slope sat three farmers smoking. To his natural lust for tobacco was added personal wrath because spiky plants were pricking his belly, and Private Copper slid the backsight up to fifteen hundred yards. . . .

'Good evening, khaki. Please don't move,' said a voice on his left, and as he jerked his head round he saw entirely down the barrel of a well-kept Lee-Metford* protruding from an insignificant tuft of thorn. Very few graven images have moved less than did Private Copper through the next ten seconds.

'It's nearer seventeen hundred than fifteen,' said a young man in an obviously ready-made suit of grey tweed, possessing himself of Private Copper's rifle. 'Thank *you*. We've got a post of thirty-seven men out yonder. You've eleven—eh? We don't want to kill 'em. We have no quarrel with poor uneducated khakis, and we do not want prisoners we do not keep. It is demoralizing to both sides—eh?'

Private Copper did not feel called upon to lay down the conduct of guerrilla warfare. This dark-skinned, dark-haired, and dark-eyed stranger was his first intimate enemy. He spoke, allowing for a clipped cadence that recalled to Copper vague memories of Umballa,* in precisely the same offensive accent that the young Squire of Wilmington had used fifteen years ago when he caught and kicked Alf Copper, a rabbit in each pocket, out of the ditches of Cuckmere. The enemy looked Copper up and down, folded and repocketed a copy of an English weekly which he had been reading, and said: 'You seem an inarticulate sort of swine—like the rest of them—eh?'

'You,' said Copper, thinking, somehow, of the crushing answers he had never given to the young Squire, 'are a renegid. Why, you ain't Dutch. You're English, same as me.'

'No, khaki. If you cannot talk civilly to a gentleman I will blow your head off.'

Copper cringed, and the action overbalanced him so that he rolled some six or eight feet downhill, under the lee of a rough rock. His brain was working with a swiftness and clarity strange in all his experience of Alf Copper. While he rolled he spoke, and the voice from his own jaws amazed him: 'If you did, 'twouldn't make you any less of a renegid.' As a useful afterthought he added, 'I've sprained my ankle.'

The young man was at his side in a flash. Copper made no motion to rise, but, cross-legged under the rock, grunted, "Ow much did old Krujer* pay you for this? What was you wanted for at 'ome? Where did you desert from?'

'Khaki,' said the young man, sitting down in his turn, 'you are a shade better than your mates. You did not make much more noise than a yoke of oxen when you tried to come up this hill, but you are an ignorant diseased beast like the rest of your people—eh? When you were at the Ragged Schools* did they teach you any history, Tommy—'istory, I mean?'

'Don't need no schoolin' to know a renegid,' said Copper. He had made three yards down the hill—out of sight, unless they could see through rocks, of the enemy's smoking-party.

The young man laughed, and tossed the soldier a black sweating stick of 'True Affection'.* (Private Copper had not smoked a pipe for three weeks.)

'*You* don't get this—eh?' said the young man. '*We* do. We take it from the trains as we want it. You can keep the cake—you po-ah Tommee.' Copper rammed the good stuff into his long-cold pipe and puffed luxuriously. Two years ago the sister of gunner-guard De Souza, East India Railway, had, at a dance given by the sergeants to the Allahabad Railway Volunteers,* informed Copper that she could not think of waltzing with 'a poo-ah Tommee'. Private Copper wondered why that memory should have returned at this hour.

'I'm going to waste a little trouble on you before I send you back to your picket *quite* naked*—eh? Then you can say how you were overpowered by twenty of us and fired off your last round—like the men we picked up at the drift playing cards at Stryden's farm—eh? What's your name—eh?'

Private Copper thought for a moment of a faraway housemaid who might still, if the local postman had not gone too far, be interested in his fate. On the other hand, he was, by temperament, economical of the truth. 'Pennycuik,' he said, 'John Pennycuik.'

'Thank you. Well, Mr John Pennycuik, I'm going to teach you a little 'istory, as you'd call it—eh?'

'Ow!' said Copper, stuffing his left hand in his mouth. 'So long since I've smoked I've burned my 'and—an' the pipe's dropped too. No objection to my movin' down to fetch it, is there—Sir?'

'I've got you covered,' said the young man graciously, and Private Copper, hopping on one leg, because of his sprain, recovered the pipe yet another three yards downhill and squatted under another rock slightly larger than the first. A roundish boulder made a pleasant rest for his captor, who sat cross-legged once more, facing Copper, his rifle across his knee, his hand on the trigger-guard.

'Well, Mr Pennycuik, as I was going to tell you. A little after you were born in your English workhouse, your kind, honourable, brave country, England, sent an English gentleman, who could not tell a lie, to say that so long as the sun rose and the rivers ran in their courses the Transvaal would belong to England.* Did you ever hear that, khaki—eh?'

'Oh no, sir,' said Copper. This sentence about the sun and the rivers happened to be a very aged jest of McBride, the professional humorist of D Company, when they discussed the probable length of the war. Copper had thrown beef-tins at McBride in the grey dawn of many wet and dry camps for intoning it.

'*Of* course you would not. Now, mann, I tell you, listen.' He spat aside and cleared his throat. 'Because of that little promise, my father he moved into the Transvaal and bought a farm—a little place of twenty or thirty thousand acres, don't—you—know.'

The tone, in spite of the sing-song cadence fighting with the laboured parody of the English drawl, was unbearably like the young Wilmington Squire's, and Copper found himself saying, 'I ought to. I've 'elped burn some.'

'Yes, you'll pay for that later. *And* he opened a store.'

'Ho! Shopkeeper was he?'

'The kind you call "sir" and sweep the floor for, Pennycuik. . . . You see, in those days one used to believe in the British Government. My father did. *Then* the Transvaal wiped thee earth with the English. They beat them six times running. You know *thatt*—eh?'

'Isn't what we've come 'ere for.'

'*But* my father (he knows better now) kept on believing in the English. I suppose it was the pretty talk about rivers and suns that cheated him—eh? Anyhow, he believed in his own country. Inn his own country. *So*—you see—he was a little startled when he found himself handed over to the Transvaal as a prisoner of war. That's what it came to, Tommy—a prisoner of war. You know what that is—eh? England was too honourable and too gentlemanly to take trouble. There were no terms made for my father.'

'So 'e made 'em 'imself. Useful old bird.' Private Copper sliced up another pipeful and looked out across the wrinkled sea of kopjes, through which came the roar of the rushing Orange River, so unlike quiet Cuckmere.

The young man's face darkened. 'I think I shall sjambok* you myself when I've quite done with you. *No*, my father (he was a fool) made no terms for eight years—ninety-six months

—and for every day of them the Transvaal made his life hell for my father and—his people.'

'I'm glad to hear that,' said the impenitent Copper.

'Are you? You can think of it when I'm taking the skin off your back—eh? . . . My father, he lost everything—everything down to his self-respect. You don't know what *thatt* means—eh?'

'Why?' said Copper. 'I'm smokin' baccy stole by a renegid. Why wouldn't I know?'

If it came to a flogging on that hillside there might be a chance of reprisals. Of course, he might be marched to the Boer camp in the next valley and there operated upon; but Army life teaches no man to cross bridges unnecessarily.

'Yes, after eight years, my father, cheated by your bitch of a country, he found out who was the upper dog in South Africa.'

'That's me,' said Copper valiantly. 'If it takes another 'alf-century, it's me an' the likes of me.'

'You? Heaven help you! You'll be screaming at a wagon-wheel in an hour. . . . Then it struck my father that he'd like to shoot the people who'd betrayed him. You—you—*you*! He told his son all about it. He told him never to trust the English. He told him to do them all the harm he could. Mann, I tell you, I don't want much telling. I was born in the Transvaal— I'm a burgher.* If my father didn't love the English, by the Lord, mann, I tell you, I hate them from the bottom of my soul.'

The voice quavered and ran high. Once more, for no conceivable reason, Private Copper found his inward eye turned upon Umballa cantonments of a dry dusty afternoon, when the saddle-coloured son of a local hotel-keeper came to the barracks to complain of a theft of fowls. He saw the dark face, the plover's-egg-tinted eyeballs, and the thin excited hands. Above all, he remembered the passionate, queerly-strung words. Slowly he returned to South Africa, using the very sentence his sergeant had used to the poultry-man.

'Go on with your complaint. I'm listenin'.'

'Complaint! Complaint about *you*, you ox! We strip and kick your sort by thousands.'

The young man rocked to and fro above the rifle, whose

muzzle thus deflected itself from the pit of Private Copper's stomach. His face was dusky with rage.

'Yess, I'm a Transvaal burgher. It took us about twenty years to find out how rotten you were. *We* know and you know it now. Your Army—it is the laughing-stock of the Continent.' He tapped the newspaper in his pocket. 'You think you're going to win, you poor fools! Your people—your own people— your silly rotten fools of people will crawl out of it as they did after Majuba. They are beginning now. Look what your own working-classes, the diseased, lying, drinking white stuff that you come out of, are saying.' He thrust the English weekly, doubled at the leading article, on Copper's knee. 'See what dirty dogs your masters are. They do not even back you in your dirty work. *We* cleared the country down to Ladysmith—to Estcourt. *We* cleared the country down to Colesberg.'*

'Yes. We 'ad to clean up be'ind you. Messy, I call it.'

'You've had to stop farm-burning* because your people daren't do it. They were afraid. You daren't kill a spy. You daren't shoot a spy when you catch him in your own uniform. You daren't touch our loyall people in Cape Town! Your masters won't let you. You will feed our women and children till we are quite ready to take them back.* *You* can't put your cowardly noses out of the towns you say you've occupied. *You* daren't move a convoy twenty miles. You think you've done something? You've done nothing, and you've taken a quarter of a million of men to do it! There isn't a nigger in South Africa that doesn't obey us if we lift our finger. You pay the stuff four pounds a month and they lie to you. *We* flog 'em, as I shall flog you.'

He clasped his hands together and leaned forward his out-thrust chin within two feet of Copper's left or pipe hand.

'Yuss,' said Copper, 'it's a fair knock-out.' The fist landed to a hair on the chin-point, the neck snicked like a gun-lock, and the back of the head crashed on the boulder behind.

Copper grabbed up both rifles, unshipped the cross-bandoliers, drew forth the English weekly, and picking up the lax hands, looked long and intently at the finger-nails.

'No! Not a sign of it there,' he said. ''Is nails are as clean as mine*—but 'e talks just like one of 'em though. And 'e's a landlord too! A landed proprietor! Shockin', I call it.'

The arms began to flap with returning consciousness. Private Copper rose up and whispered: 'If you open your head, I'll bash it.' There was no suggestion of sprain in the flung-back left boot. 'Now walk in front of me, both arms perpendicularly elevated. I'm only a third-class shot, so, if you don't object, I'll rest the muzzle of my rifle lightly but firmly on your collar-button—coverin' the serviceable vertebree.* If your friends see us thus engaged, you pray—'ard.'

Private and prisoner staggered downhill. No shots broke the peace of the afternoon, but once the young man checked and was sick.

'There's a lot of things I could say to you,' Copper observed, at the close of the paroxysm, 'but it doesn't matter. Look 'ere, you call me "pore Tommy" again.'

The prisoner hesitated.

'Oh, I ain't goin' to do anythin' *to* you. I'm reconnoiterin' on my own. Say "pore Tommy" 'alf-a-dozen times.'

The prisoner obeyed.

'*That*'s what's been puzzlin' me since I 'ad the pleasure o' meetin' you,' said Copper. 'You ain't 'alf-caste, but you talk *chee-chee*—*pukka* bazar *chee-chee*. *Pro*ceed.'

'Hullo,' said the sergeant of the picket, twenty minutes later, 'where did you round him up?'

'On the top o' yonder craggy mounting. There's a mob of 'em sitting round their Bibles seventeen 'undred yards (you said it was seventeen 'undred?) t'other side—an' I want some coffee.' He sat down on the smoke-blackened stones by the fire.

''Ow did you get 'im?' said McBride, professional humorist, quietly filching the English weekly from under Copper's armpit.

'On the chin—while 'e was waggin' it at me.'

'What is 'e? 'Nother Colonial rebel to be 'orribly disenfranchised, or a Cape Minister, or only a loyal farmer with dynamite in both boots? Tell us all about it, Burjer!'

'You leave my prisoner alone,' said Private Copper. ''E's 'ad losses an' trouble; an' it's in the family too. 'E thought I never read the papers, so 'e kindly lent me his very own *Jerrold's Weekly**—an' 'e explained it to me as patronizin' as a—as a militia subaltern doin' Railway Staff Officer. 'E's a left-over from Majuba—one of the worst kind, an' 'earin' the evidence as I did, I don't exactly blame 'im. It was this way.'

To the picket Private Copper held forth for ten minutes on the life-history of his captive. Allowing for some purple patches, it was an absolutely fair rendering.

'But what I disliked was this baccy-priggin'* beggar, 'oo's people, on 'is own showin', couldn't 'ave been more than thirty or forty years in the coun—on this Gawd-forsaken dust-'eap, comin' the squire over me. They're all parsons—we know *that*, but parson *an'* squire is a bit too thick for Alf Copper. Why, I caught 'im in the shameful act of tryin' to start a aristocracy on a gun an' a wagon an' a shambuk! Yes; that's what it was: a bloomin' aristocracy.'

'No, it weren't,' said McBride, at length, on the dirt, above the purloined weekly. 'You're the aristocrat, Alf. Old *Jerrold's* givin' it you 'ot. You're the uneducated 'ireling of a cal-callous aristocracy which 'as sold itself to the 'Ebrew financeer.* Meantime, Ducky'—he ran his finger down a column of assorted paragraphs—'you're slakin' your brutal instincks in furious excesses. Shriekin' women an' desolated 'omesteads is what you enjoy, Alf. . . . Halloa! What's a smokin' 'ektacomb?'

''Ere! Let's look. 'Aven't seen a proper spicy paper for a year. Good old *Jerrold's*!' Pinewood and Moppet, reservists, flung themselves on McBride's shoulders, pinning him to the ground.

'Lie over your own bloomin' side of the bed, an' we can all look,' he protested.

'They're only po-ah Tommies,' said Copper, apologetically, to the prisoner. 'Po-ah unedicated khakis. *They* don't know what they're fightin' for. They're lookin' for what the diseased, lying, drinkin' white stuff that they come from is sayin' about 'em!'

The prisoner set down his tin of coffee and stared helplessly round the circle.

'I—I don't understand them.'

The Canadian sergeant, picking his teeth with a thorn, nodded sympathetically.

'If it comes to that, *we* don't in my country! . . . Say, boys, when you're through with your English mail you might's well provide an escort for your prisoner. He's waitin'.'

''Arf a mo', sergeant,' said McBride, still reading. ''Ere's Old Barbarity* on the ramp again with some of 'is lady friends, 'oo don't like concentration camps.* Wish they'd visit ours. Pinewood's a married man. 'E'd know how to be'ave!'

'Well, I ain't goin' to amuse my prisoner alone. 'E's gettin' 'omesick,' cried Copper. 'One of you thieves read out what's vexin' Old Barbarity an' 'is 'arem these days. You'd better listen, Burjer, because, afterwards, I'm goin' to fall out an' perpetrate those nameless barbarities all over you to keep up the reputation of the British Army.'

From that English weekly, to bar out which a large and perspiring staff of Press censors toiled seven days of the week at Cape Town, did Pinewood of the Reserve read unctuously excerpts of the speeches of the accredited leaders of His Majesty's Opposition. The night-picket arrived in the middle of it, but stayed entranced without paying any compliments, till Pinewood had entirely finished the leading article, and several occasional notes.

'Gentlemen of the jury,' said Alf Copper hitching up what war had left to him of trousers—'you've 'eard what 'e's been fed with. *Do* you blame the beggar? . . . 'Cause I don't! . . . Leave 'im alone, McBride. 'E's my first and only cap-ture, an' I'm goin' to walk 'ome with 'im, ain't I, Ducky! . . . Fall in, Burjer. It's Bermuda, or Umballa, or Ceylon* for you—and I'd give a month's pay to be in your little shoes.'

As not infrequently happens, the actual moving off the ground broke the prisoner's nerve. He stared at the tinted hills round him, gasped and began to struggle—kicking, swearing, weeping, and fluttering all together.

'Pore beggar—oh, pore, *pore* beggar!' said Alf, leaning in on one side of him, while Pinewood blocked him on the other.

'Let me go! Let me go! Mann, I tell you, let me go——'

''E screams like a woman!' said McBride. 'They'll 'ear 'im five miles off.'

'There's one or two ought to 'ear 'im—in England,' said Copper, putting aside a wildly waving arm.

'Married, ain't 'e?' said Pinewood. 'I've seen 'em go like this before—just at the last. '*Old* on, old man. No one's goin' to 'urt you.'

The last of the sun threw the enormous shadow of a kopje over the little, anxious, wriggling group.

'Quit that,' said the sergeant of a sudden. 'You're only making him worse. Hands *up*, prisoner! Now you get a holt of yourself, or this'll go off.'

And indeed the revolver-barrel square at the man's panting chest seemed to act like a tonic; he choked, recovered himself, and fell in between Copper and Pinewood.

As the picket neared the camp it broke into song that was heard among the officers' tents:—

> ''E sent us 'is blessin' from London town
>   (The beggar that kep' the cordite down)?*
> But what do we care if 'e smile or frown,
>   The beggar that kep' the cordite down?
> The mildly nefarious,
> Wildly barbarious
>   Beggar that kep' the cordite down!'

Said a captain a mile away: 'Why are they singing *that*? We haven't had a mail for a month, have we?'

An hour later the same captain said to his servant: 'Jenkins, I understand the picket have got a—got a newspaper off a prisoner to-day. I wish you could lay hands on it, Jenkins. Copy of the *Times*, I think.'

'Yes, sir. Copy of the *Times*, sir,' said Jenkins, without a quiver, and went forth to make his own arrangements.

'Copy of the *Times*?' said the blameless Alf, from beneath his blanket. 'I ain't a member of the Soldiers' Institoot. Go an' look in the Reg'mental Readin'-room—Veldt Row, Kopje Street, second turnin' to the left between 'ere an' Naauwport.'

Jenkins summarized briefly in a tense whisper the thing that Alf Cooper need not be.

'But my particular copy of the *Times* is specially pro'ibited by the censor from corruptin' the morals of the Army. Get a written order from K. o' K.,* properly countersigned, an' I'll think about it.'

'I've got all *you* want,' said Jenkins. ''Urry up. I want to 'ave a squint myself.'

Something gurgled in the darkness, and Private Copper fell back smacking his lips.

'Gawd bless my prisoner, and make me a good boy. Amen. 'Ere you are, Jenkins. It's dirt cheap at a tot.'

Half-Ballade of Waterval*

(*Non-commissioned Officers in Charge of Prisoners*)

WHEN by the labour of my 'ands
  I've 'elped to pack a transport tight
With prisoners for foreign lands,*
  I ain't transported with delight.
  I know it's only just an' right,
    But yet it somehow sickens me,
For I 'ave learned at Waterval
    The meanin' of captivity.

Be'ind the pegged barb-wire strands,
  Beneath the tall electric light,
We used to walk in bare-'ead bands,
  Explainin' 'ow we lost our fight;
  An' that is what they'll do to-night
    Upon the steamer out at sea,
If I 'ave learned at Waterval
    The meanin' of captivity.

They'll never know the shame that brands—
  Black shame no livin' down makes white—
The mockin' from the sentry-stands,
  The women's laugh, the gaoler's spite.
  We are too bloomin'-much polite,
    But that is 'ow I'd 'ave us be . . .
Since I 'ave learned at Waterval
    The meanin' of captivity.

They'll get those draggin' days all right,
  Spent as a foreigner commands,
An' 'orrors of the locked-up night,
  With 'Ell's own thinkin' on their 'ands.
  I'd give the gold o' twenty Rands*

(If it was mine) to set 'em free,
For I 'ave learned at Waterval
The meanin' of captivity!

The Captive*

'He that believeth shall not make haste.'

Isaiah 28: 16

THE guard-boat lay across the mouth of the bathing-pool, her crew idly spanking the water with the flat of their oars. A red-coated militia-man, rifle in hand, sat at the bows, and a petty officer at the stern. Between the snow-white cutter and the flat-topped, honey-coloured rocks on the beach the green water was troubled with shrimp-pink prisoners of war bathing. Behind their orderly tin camp and the electric-light poles rose those stone-dotted spurs that throw heat on Simonstown.* Beneath them the little *Barracouta* nodded to the big *Gibraltar*,* and the old *Penelope*,* that in ten years has been bachelors' club, natural history museum, kindergarten, and prison, rooted and dug at her fixed moorings. Far out, a three-funnelled Atlantic transport with turtle bow and stern waddled in from the deep sea.*

Said the sentry, assured of the visitor's good faith, 'Talk to 'em? You can, to any that speak English. You'll find a lot that do.'

Here and there earnest groups gathered round ministers of the Dutch Reformed Church, who doubtless preached concili-ation, but the majority preferred their bath. The God who Looks after Small Things had caused the visitor that day to receive two weeks' delayed mails in one from a casual postman, and the whole heavy bundle of newspapers, tied with a strap, he dangled as bait. At the edge of the beach, cross-legged, undressed to his sky-blue army shirt, sat a lean, ginger-haired man, on guard over a dozen heaps of clothing. His eyes fol-lowed the incoming Atlantic boat.

'Excuse me, Mister,' he said, without turning (and the speech betrayed his nationality), 'would you mind keeping away from these garments? I've been elected janitor—on the Dutch vote.'

The visitor moved over against the barbed-wire fence and sat down to his mail. At the rustle of the newspaper-wrappers the ginger-coloured man turned quickly, the hunger of a Press-ridden people in his close-set iron-grey eyes.

'Have you any use for papers?' said the visitor.

'Have I any use?' A quick, curved forefinger was already snicking off the outer covers. 'Why, that's the New York post-mark! Give me the ads. at the back of *Harper's* and *M'Clure's* and I'm in touch with God's Country again! Did you know how I was aching for papers?'

The visitor told the tale of the casual postman.

'Providential!' said the ginger-coloured man, keen as a terrier on his task; 'both in time and matter. Yes! . . . The *Scientific American* yet once more! Oh, it's good! it's good!' His voice broke as he pressed his hawk-like nose against the heavily-inked patent-specifications at the end. 'Can I keep it? I thank you—I thank you! Why—why!—Well—well! The *American Tyler** of all things created! Do you subscribe to that?'

'I'm on the free list,' said the visitor, nodding.

He extended his blue-tanned hand with that air of oriental spaciousness which distinguishes the native-born American, and met the visitor's grasp expertly. 'I can only say that you have treated me like a Brother (yes, I'll take every last one you can spare), and if ever——' He plucked at the bosom of his shirt. 'Psha! I forgot I'd no card on me; but my name's Zigler—Laughton O. Zigler. An American? If Ohio's still in the Union, I am, sir. But I'm no extreme States'-rights man. I've used all of my native country and a few others as I have found occasion, and now I am the captive of your bow and spear. I'm not kicking at that. I am not a coerced alien, nor a naturalized Texas mule-tender, nor an adventurer on the instalment plan. *I* don't tag after our Consul when he comes around, expecting the American Eagle to lift me out o' this by the slack of my pants. No, sir! If a Britisher went into Indian Territory and shot up his surroundings with a Colt automatic (not that *she*'s any sort of weapon, but I take her for an illustration), he'd be strung up quicker'n a snow-flake 'ud melt in hell. No ambassador of yours 'ud save him. I'm my neck ahead on this game, anyway. That's how I regard the proposition.

'Have I gone gunning against the British? To a certain extent. I presume you never heard tell of the Laughton-Zigler automatic two-inch field-gun, with self-feeding hopper, single oil-cylinder recoil, and ball-bearing gear throughout? Or Laughtite, the new explosive? Absolutely uniform in effect, and one-ninth the bulk of any present effete charge—flake, cannonite, cordite, troisdorf, cellulose, cocoa, cord, or prism— I don't care what it is. Laughtite's immense. So's the Zigler automatic. It's me. It's fifteen years of me. You are not a gun-sharp? I am sorry. I could have surprised you. Apart from my gun, my tale don't amount to much of anything. I thank you, but I don't use any tobacco you'd be likely to carry . . . Bull Durham?* *Bull Durham*! I take it all back—every last word. Bull Durham—here! If ever you strike Akron, Ohio, when this fool war's over, remember you've Laughton O. Zigler in your vest-pocket. Including the city of Akron. We've a little club there . . . Hell! What's the sense of talking Akron with no pants?

'My gun? . . . For two cents I'd have shipped her to our Filipeens.* Came mighty near it too; but from what I'd read in the papers, you can't trust Aguinaldo's crowd on scientific matters. Why don't I offer it to our Army? Well, you've an effete aristocracy running yours, and we've a crowd of politicians. The results are practically identical. I am not taking any U.S. Army in mine.

'I went to Amsterdam with her—to this Dutch junta that supposes it's bossing the war.* I wasn't brought up to love the British for one thing, and for another I knew that if she got in her fine work (my gun) I'd stand more chance of receiving an unbiased report from a crowd o' dam' fool British officers than from a hatful of politicians' nephews doing duty as commissaries and ordnance-sharps. As I said, I put the brown man out of the question. That's the way *I* regarded the proposition.

'The Dutch in Holland don't amount to a row of pins. Maybe I misjudge 'em. Maybe they've been swindled too often by self-seeking adventurers to know a enthusiast when they see him. Anyway, they're slower than the Wrath o' God. But on delusions—as to their winning out next Thursday week at 9 A.M.—they are—if I may say so—quite British.

'I'll tell you a curious thing, too. I fought 'em for ten days before I could get the financial side of my game fixed to my liking. I knew they didn't believe in the Zigler, but they'd no call to be crazy-mean. I fixed it—free passage and freight for me and the gun to Delagoa Bay,* and beyond by steam and rail. Then I went aboard to see her crated, and there I struck my fellow-passengers—all deadheads,* same as me. Well, sir, I turned in my tracks where I stood and besieged the ticket-office, and I said, "Look at here, Van Dunk. I'm paying for my passage and her room in the hold—every square and cubic foot." Guess he knocked down the fare to himself; but I paid. I paid. I wasn't going to deadhead along o' *that* crowd of Pente-costal* sweepings. 'Twould have hoodooed my gun for all time. That was the way I regarded the proposition. No, sir, they were not pretty company.

'When we struck Pretoria I had a hell-and-a-half of a time trying to interest the Dutch vote in my gun an' her potentiali-ties. The bottom was out of things rather much just about that time.* Kruger was praying some and stealing some, and the Hollander lot was singing, "If you haven't any money you needn't come round." Nobody was spending his dough on anything except tickets to Europe.* We were both grossly neglected. When I think how I used to give performances in the public streets with dummy cartridges, filling the hopper and turning the handle till the sweat dropped off me, I blush, sir. I've made her do her stunts before Kaffirs—naked sons of Ham*—in Commissioner Street, trying to get a holt somewhere.

'Did I talk? I despise exaggeration—'tain't American or scientific—but as true as I'm sitting here like a blue-ended baboon in a kloof,* Teddy Roosevelt's Western tour* was a maiden's sigh compared to my advertising work.

''Long in the spring I was rescued by a commandant called Van Zyl—a big, fleshy man with a lame leg. Take away his hair and his gun and he'd make a first-class Schenectady bar-keep. He found me and the Zigler on the veldt (Pretoria wasn't wholesome at that time), and he annexed me in a somnambu-listic sort o' way. He was dead against the war from the start, but, being a Dutchman, he fought a sight better than the rest of that "God and the Mauser"* outfit. Adrian Van Zyl. Slept a heap in the daytime—and didn't love niggers. I liked him. I was the only foreigner in his commando. The rest was Georgia Crackers and Pennsylvania Dutch*—with a dash o' Philadelphia lawyer. I could tell you things about them would surprise you. Religion for one thing. Women for another. But I don't know as their notions o' geography weren't the craziest. Guess that must be some sort of automatic compensation. There wasn't one blamed ant-hill in their district they didn't know *and* use; but the world was flat, they said, and England was a day's trek from Cape Town.

'They could fight in their own way, and don't you forget it. But I guess you will not. They fought to kill, and, by what I could make out, the British fought to be killed. So both parties were accommodated.

'I am the captive of your bow and spear,* sir. The position has its obligations—on both sides. You could not be offensive or partisan to me. I cannot, for the same reason, be offensive to you. Therefore I will not give you my opinions on the conduct of your war.

'Anyway, I didn't take the field as an offensive partisan, but as an inventor. It was a condition and not a theory that confronted me. (Yes, sir, I'm a Democrat by conviction, and that was one of the best things Grover Cleveland* ever got off.)

'After three months' trek, old man Van Zyl had his commando in good shape and refitted off the British, and he reckoned he'd wait on a British General of his acquaintance that did business on a circuit between Stompiesneuk, Jackhalputs, Vrelegen, and Odendaalstroom, year in and year out. He was a fixture in that section.

' "He's a dam' good man," says Van Zyl. "He's a friend of mine. He sent in a fine doctor when I was wounded and our Hollander doc. wanted to cut my leg off. Ya, I'll guess we'll stay with him." Up to date, me and my Zigler had lived in innocuous desuetood owing to little odds and ends riding out of gear. How in thunder was I to know there wasn't the ghost of any road in the country? But raw hide's cheap and lastin'. I guess I'll make my next gun a thousand pounds heavier, though.

'Well, sir, we struck the General on his beat—Vrelegen it was—and our crowd opened with the usual compliments at two thousand yards. Van Zyl shook himself into his greasy old saddle and says, "Now we shall be quite happy, Mr Zigler. No more trekking. Joost twelve miles a day till the apricots are ripe."

'Then we hitched on to his outposts, and vedettes,* and cossack-picquets, or whatever they was called, and we wandered around the veldt arm in arm like brothers.

'The way we worked Lodge* was this way. The General, he had his breakfast at 8.45 A.M. to the tick. He might have been a Long Island commuter. At 8.42 A.M. I'd go down to the Thirty-fourth Street ferry to meet him—I mean I'd see the Zigler into position at two thousand (I began at three thousand, but that was cold and distant)—and blow him off to two full hoppers—eighteen rounds—just as they were bringing in his coffee. If his crowd was busy celebrating the anniversary of Waterloo or the last royal kid's birthday, they'd open on me with two guns (I'll tell you about them later on), but if they were disengaged they'd all stand to their horses and pile on the ironmongery, and washers, and typewriters, and five weeks' grub, and in half an hour they'd sail out after me and the rest of Van Zyl's boys; lying down and firing till 11.45 A.M. or maybe high noon. Then we'd go from labour to refreshment,* resooming at 2 P.M. and battling till tea-time. Tuesday and Friday was the General's moving days. He'd trek ahead ten or twelve miles, and we'd loaf around his flankers and exercise the ponies a piece. Sometimes he'd get hung up in a drift—stalled crossin' a crick—and we'd make playful snatches at his wagons. First time that happened I turned the Zigler loose with high hopes, sir; but the old man was well posted on rearguards with a gun to 'em, and I had to haul her out with three mules instead o' six. I was pretty mad. I wasn't looking for any experts back of the Royal British Artillery. Otherwise, the game was mostly even. He'd lay out three or four of our commando, and we'd gather in four or five of his once a week or thereon. One time, I remember, 'long towards dusk we saw 'em burying five of their boys. They stood pretty thick around the graves. We wasn't more than fifteen hundred yards off, but old Van Zyl wouldn't fire. He just took off his hat at the proper time. He said if you stretched a man at his prayers you'd have to hump his bad luck before the Throne as well as your own. I am inclined to agree with him. So we browsed along week in and week out. A war-sharp might have judged it sort of docile, but for an inventor needing practice one day and peace the next for checking his theories, it suited Laughton O. Zigler.

'And friendly? Friendly was no word for it. We was brothers-in-arms.

'Why, I knew those two guns of the Royal British Artillery as well as I used to know the old Fifth Avenoo stages. *They* might have been brothers too.

'They'd jolt into action, and wiggle around and skid and spit and cough and prise 'emselves back again during our hours of bloody battle till I could have wept, sir, at the spectacle of modern white men chained up to those old hand-power, back-number, flint-and-steel reaping-machines. One of 'em—I called her Baldy—she'd a long white scar all along her barrel—I'd made sure of twenty times. I knew her crew by sight, but she'd come switching and teetering out of the dust of my shells like—like a hen from under a buggy—and she'd dip into a gully, and next thing I'd know 'ud be her old nose peeking over the ridge sniffin' for us. Her runnin' mate had two grey mules in the lead, and a natural wood wheel repainted, and a whole raft of rope-ends trailin' around. 'J'ever see Tom Reed* with his vest off, steerin' Congress through a heat-wave? I've been to Washington often—too often—filin' my patents. I called her Tom Reed. We three 'ud play pussy-wants-a-corner all round the outposts on off-days—cross-lots through the sage and along the mesas* till we was short-circuited by cañons. Oh, it was great for me and Baldy and Tom Reed! I don't know as we didn't neglect the legitimate interests of our respective commanders sometimes for this ball-play. I know *I* did.

''Long towards the fall the Royal British Artillery grew shy—hung back in their breeching, sort of—and their shooting was 'way—'way off. I observed they wasn't taking any chances, not though I acted kitten almost underneath 'em.

'I mentioned it to Van Zyl, because it struck me I had about knocked their Royal British morale endways.

' "No," says he, rocking as usual on his pony. "My Captain Mankeltow he is sick. That is all."

' "So's your Captain Mankeltow's guns," I said. "But I'm going to make 'em a heap sicker before he gets well."

' "No," says Van Zyl. "He has had the enteric a little. Now he is better, and he was let out from hospital at Jackhalputs. Ah, that Mankeltow! He always makes me laugh so. I told him—long back—at Colesberg, I had a little home for him at Nooitgedacht.* But he would not come—no! He has been sick, and I am sorry."

' "How d'you know that?" I says.

' "Why, only to-day he sends back his love by Johanna Van der Merwe, that goes to their doctor for her sick baby's eyes. He sends his love, that Mankeltow, and he tells her tell me he has a little garden of roses all ready for me in the Dutch Indies*—Umballa.* He is very funny, my Captain Mankeltow."

'The Dutch and the English ought to fraternize, sir. They've the same notions of humour, to my thinking.

' "When he gets well," says Van Zyl, "you look out, Mr Americaan. He comes back to his guns next Tuesday. Then they shoot better."

'I wasn't so well acquainted with the Royal British Artillery as old man Van Zyl. I knew this Captain Mankeltow by sight, of course, and, considering what sort of a man with the hoe* he was, I thought he'd done right well against my Zigler. But nothing epoch-making.

'Next morning at the usual hour I waited on the General, and old Van Zyl come along with some of the boys. Van Zyl didn't hang round the Zigler much as a rule, but this was his luck that day.

'He was peeking through his glasses at the camp, and I was helping pepper the General's sow-belly*—just as usual—when he turns to me quick and says, "Almighty! How all these Englishmen are liars! You cannot trust one," he says. "Captain Mankeltow tells our Johanna he comes not back till Tuesday, and to-day is Friday, and there he is! Almighty! The English are all Chamberlains!"*

'If the old man hadn't stopped to make political speeches

he'd have had his supper in laager that night, I guess. I was busy attending to Tom Reed at two thousand when Baldy got in her fine work on me. I saw one sheet of white flame wrapped round the hopper, and in the middle of it there was one o' my mules straight on end. Nothing out of the way in a mule on end, but this mule hadn't any head. I remember it struck me as incongruous at the time, and when I'd ciphered it out I was doing the Santos-Dumont* act without any balloon and my motor out of gear. Then I got to thinking about Santos-Dumont and how much better my new way was. Then I thought about Professor Langley and the Smithsonian,* and wished I hadn't lied so extravagantly in some of my specifications at Washington. Then I quit thinking for quite a while, and when I resumed my train of thought I was nude, sir, in a very stale stretcher, and my mouth was full of fine dirt all flavoured with Laughtite.

'I coughed up that dirt.

' "Hullo!" says a man walking beside me. "You've spoke almost in time. Have a drink?"

'I don't use rum as a rule, but I did then, because I needed it.

' "What hit us?" I said.

' "Me," he said. "I got you fair on the hopper as you pulled out of that donga;* but I'm sorry to say every last round in the hopper's exploded and your gun's in a shocking state. I'm real sorry," he says. "I admire your gun, sir."

' "Are you Captain Mankeltow?" I says.

' "Yes," he says. "I presoom you're Mister Zigler. Your commanding officer told me about you."

' "Have you gathered in old man Van Zyl?" I said.

' "Commandant Van Zyl," he says, very stiff, "was, most unfortunately, wounded, but I am glad to say it's not serious. We hope he'll be able to dine with us to-night; and I feel sure," he says, "the General would be delighted to see you too, though he didn't expect," he says, "and no one else either, by Jove!" he says, and blushed like the British do when they're embarrassed.

'I saw him slide an Episcopalian Prayer-book up his sleeve, and when I looked over the edge of the stretcher there was half-a-dozen enlisted men—privates—had just quit digging and was

standing to attention by their spades. I guess he was right on
the General not expecting me to dinner; but it was all of a piece
with their sloppy British way of doing business. Any God's
quantity of fuss and flubdub to bury a man, and not an ounce
of forehandedness in the whole outfit to find out whether he
was rightly dead. And I am a Congregationalist anyway!

'Well, sir, that was my introduction to the British Army. I'd
write a book about it if anyone would believe me. This Captain
Mankeltow, Royal British Artillery, turned the doctor on me (I
could write another book about *him*) and fixed me up with a
suit of his own clothes, and fed me canned beef and biscuits,
and give me a cigar—a Henry Clay* and a whisky-and-
sparklet. He was a white man.

' "Ye-es, by Jove," he said, dragging out his words like a
twist of molasses, "we've all admired your gun and the way
you've worked it. Some of us betted you was a British deserter.
I won a sovereign on that from a yeoman. And, by the way," he
says, "you've disappointed me groom pretty bad."

' "Where does your groom come in?" I said.

' "Oh, he was the yeoman. He's a dam' poor groom," says
my Captain, "but he's a 'way-up barrister when he's at home.
He's been running around the camp with his tongue out, wait-
ing for the chance of defending you at the court-martial."

' "What court-martial?" I says.

' "On you as a deserter from the Artillery. You'd have had a
good run for your money. Anyway, you'd never have been
hung after the way you worked your gun. Deserter ten times
over," he says, "I'd have stuck out for shooting you like a
gentleman."

'Well, sir, right there it struck me at the pit of my stomach
—sort of sickish, sweetish feeling—that my position needed
regularizing pretty bad. I ought to have been a naturalized
burgher of a year's standing; but Ohio's my State, and I
wouldn't have gone back on her for a desertful of Dutchmen.
That and my enthoosiasm as an inventor had led me to the
existing crisis; but I couldn't expect this Captain Mankeltow to
regard the proposition that way. There I sat, the rankest breed
of unreconstructed American citizen, caught red-handed
squirting hell at the British Army for months on end. I tell *you*,

sir, I wished I was in Cincinnatah that summer evening. I'd
have compromised on Brooklyn.

' "What d'you do about aliens?" I said, and the dirt I'd
coughed up seemed all back of my tongue again.

' "Oh," says he, "we don't do much of anything. They're
about all the society we get. I'm a bit of a pro-Boer myself," he
says, "but between you and me the average Boer ain't over and
above intellectual. You're the first American we've met up
with, but of course you're a burgher."*

'It was what I ought to have been if I'd had the sense of a
common tick, but the way he drawled it out made me mad.

' "Of course I am not," I says. "Would *you* be a naturalized
Boer?"

' "I'm fighting against 'em," he says, lighting a cigarette,
"but it's all a matter of opinion."

' "Well," I says, "you can hold any blame opinion you
choose, but I'm a white man, and my present intention is to die
in that colour."

'He laughed one of those big, thick-ended, British laughs
that don't lead anywhere, and whacked up some sort of compli-
ment about America that made me mad all through.

'I am the captive of your bow and spear, sir, but I do not
understand the alleged British joke. It is depressing.

'I was introodooced to five or six officers that evening, and
every blame one of 'em grinned and asked me why I wasn't in
the Filipeens suppressing our war!* And that was British
humour! They all had to get it off their chests before they'd
talk sense. But they was sound on the Zigler. They had all
admired her. I made out a fairy-story of me being wearied of
the war, and having pushed the gun at them these last three
months in the hope they'd capture it and let me go home. That
tickled 'em to death. They made me say it three times over, and
laughed like kids each time. But half the British *are* kids;
'specially the older men. My Captain Mankeltow was less of it
than the others. He talked about the Zigler like a lover, sir, and
I drew him diagrams of the hopper-feed and recoil-cyclinder in
his note-book. He asked the one British question I was waiting
for—hadn't I made my working-parts too light? The British
think weight's strength.

'At last—I'd been shy of opening the subject before—at last I said, "Gentlemen, you are the unprejudiced tribunal I've been hunting after. I guess you ain't interested in any other gun-factory, and politics don't weigh with you. How did it feel your end of the game? What's my gun done, anyway?"

'"I hate to disappoint you," says Captain Mankeltow, "because I know how you feel as an inventor." I wasn't feeling like an inventor just then. I felt friendly; but the British haven't more tact than you can pick up with a knife out of a plate of soup.

'"The honest truth," he says, "is that you've wounded about ten of us one way and another, killed two battery horses and four mules, and—oh, yes," he said, "you've bagged five Kaffirs. But, buck up," he says. "We've all had mighty close calls"—shaves, he called 'em, I remember. "Look at my pants."

'They was repaired right across the seat with Minneapolis flour-bagging. I could see the stencil.

'"I ain't bluffing," he says. "Get the hospital returns, Doc."

'The doctor gets 'em and reads 'em out under the proper dates. That doctor alone was worth the price of admission.

'I was pleased right through that I hadn't killed any of these cheerful kids; but, none the less, I couldn't help thinking that a few more Kaffirs would have served me just as well for advertising purposes as white men. No, sir. Anywhichway you regard the proposition, twenty-one casualties after months of close friendship like ours was—paltry.

'They gave me taffy* about the gun—the British use taffy where we use sugar. It's cheaper, and gets there just the same. They sat around and proved to me that my gun was too good, too uniform—shot as close as a Männlicher rifle.*

'Says one kid chewing a bit of grass: "I counted eight of your shells, sir, burst in a radius of ten feet. All of 'em would have gone through one wagon-tilt. It was beautiful," he says. "It was too good."

'I shouldn't wonder if the boys were right. My Laughtite is too mathematically uniform in propelling power. Yes; she was too good for this refractory fool of a country. The training-gear was broke, too, and we had to swivel her around by the trail.

But I'll build my next Zigler fifteen hundred pounds heavier. Might work in a gasoline motor under the axles. I must think that up.

'"Well, gentlemen," I said, "I'd hate to have been the death of any of you; and if a prisoner can deed away his property, I'd love to present the Captain here with what he's seen fit to leave of my Zigler."

'"Thanks awf'ly," says my Captain. "I'd like her very much. She'd look fine in the Mess at Woolwich.* That is, if you don't mind, Mr Zigler."

'"Go right ahead," I says. "I've come out of all the mess I've any use for; but she'll do to spread the light among the Royal British Artillery."

'I tell you, sir, there's not much of anything the matter with the Royal British Artillery. They're brainy men languishing under an effete system which, when you take good holt of it, is England—just all England. Times I'd feel I was talking with real live citizens, and times I'd feel I'd struck the Beefeaters in the Tower.

'How? Well, this way. I was telling my Captain Mankeltow what Van Zyl had said about the British being all Chamberlains when the old man saw him back from hospital four days ahead of time.

'"Oh, damn it all!" he says, as serious as the Supreme Court. "It's too bad," he says. "Johanna must have misunderstood me, or else I've got the wrong Dutch word for these blarsted days of the week. I told Johanna I'd be out on Friday. The woman's a fool. Oah, da-amn it all!" he says. "I wouldn't have sold old Van Zyl a pup like that," he says. "I'll hunt him up and apologize."

'He must have fixed it all right, for when we sailed over to the General's dinner my Captain had Van Zyl about half-full of sherry and bitters, as happy as a clam. The boys all called him Adrian, and treated him like their prodigal father. He'd been hit on the collar-bone by a wad of shrapnel, and his arm was tied up.

'But the General was the peach. I presoom you're acquainted with the average run of British generals, but this was my first. I sat on his left hand, and he talked like—like the *Ladies' Home*

Journal. J'ever read the paper? It's refined, sir—and innocuous, and full of nickel-plated sentiments guaranteed to improve the mind. He was it. He began by a Lydia Pinkham* heart-to-heart talk about my health, and hoped the boys had done me well, and that I was enjoying my stay in their midst. Then he thanked me for the interesting and valuable lessons that I'd given his crowd—'specially in the matter of placing artillery and rearguard attacks. He'd wipe his long thin moustache between drinks—lime-juice and water he used— and blat off into a long "a-aah," and ladle out more taffy for me or old man Van Zyl on his right. I told him how I'd had my first Pisgah-sight* of the principles of the Zigler when I was a fourth-class postmaster on a star-route in Arkansas. I told him how I'd worked it up by instalments when I was machinist in Waterbury, where the dollar watches come from. He had one on his wrist then. I told him how I'd met Zalinski* (he'd never heard of Zalinski!) when I was an extra clerk in the Naval Construction Bureau at Washington. I told him how my uncle, who was a truck-farmer in Noo Jersey (he loaned money on mortgage too, for ten acres ain't enough now in Noo Jersey), how he'd willed me a quarter of a million dollars, because I was the only one of our kin that called him down when he used to come home with a hard-cider jag on him and heave ox-bows at his nieces. I told him how I'd turned in every red cent on the Zigler, and I told him the whole circus of my coming out with her, and so on, and so following; and every forty seconds he'd wipe his moustache and blat, "How interesting! Really, now? How interesting!"

'It was like being in an old English book, sir. Like *Brace-bridge Hall*.* But an American wrote *that*! I kept peeking around for the Boar's Head and the Rosemary and Magna Carta and the Cricket on the Hearth,* and the rest of the outfit. Then Van Zyl whirled in. He was no ways jagged, but thawed —thawed, sir, and among friends. They began discussing previous scraps all along the old man's beat—about sixty of 'em—as well as side-shows with other generals and columns. Van Zyl told 'im of a big beat he'd worked on a column a week or so before I'd joined him. He demonstrated his strategy with forks on the table.

' "There!" said the General, when he'd finished. "That proves my contention to the hilt. Maybe I'm a bit of a pro-Boer, but I stick to it," he says, "that under proper officers, with due regard to his race prejudices, the Boer 'ud make the finest mounted infantry in the Empire. Adrian," he says, "you're simply squandered on a cattle-run. You ought to be at the Staff College with De Wet."*

' "You catch De Wet and I come to your Staff College—eh," says Adrian laughing. "But you are so slow, Generaal. Why are you so slow? For a month," he says, "you do so well and strong that we say we shall hands-up and come back to our farms. Then you send to England and make us a present of two—three—six hundred young men, with rifles and wagons and rum and tobacco, and such a great lot of cartridges, that our young men put up their tails and start all over again. If you hold an ox by the horn and hit him by the bottom he runs round and round. He never goes anywhere. So, too, this war goes round and round. You know that, Generaal!"

' "Quite right, Adrian," says the General; "but you must believe your Bible."

' "Hooh!" says Adrian, and reaches for the whisky. I've never known a Dutchman a professing Atheist, but some few have been rather active Agnostics since the British sat down in Pretoria. Old man Van Zyl—he told me—had soured on religion after Bloemfontein surrendered.* He was a Free Stater for one thing.

' "He that believeth," says the General, "shall not make haste." That's in Isaiah. We believe we're going to win, and so we don't make haste. As far as I'm concerned I'd like this war to last another five years. We'd have an Army then. It's just this way, Mr Zigler," he says. "Our people are brim-full of patriotism, but they've been born and brought up between houses, and England ain't big enough to train 'em—not if you expect to preserve."

' "Preserve what?" I says. "England?"

' "No. The game," he says; "and that reminds me, gentlemen, we haven't drunk the King and Fox-hunting."

'So they drank the King and Fox-hunting. I drank the King because there's something about Edward that tickles me (he's

so blame British); but I rather stood out on the Fox-hunting.
I've ridden wolves in the cattle-country, and needed a drink
pretty bad afterwards, but it never struck me as I ought to
drink about it—he-red-it-arily.

' "No, as I was saying, Mr Zigler," he goes on, "we have to
train our men in the field to shoot and ride. I allow six months
for it; but many column-commanders—not that I ought to say
a word against 'em, for they're the best fellows that ever step-
ped, and most of 'em are my dearest friends—seem to think
that if they have men and horses and guns they can take tea
with the Boers. It's generally the other way about, ain't it, Mr
Zigler?"

' "To some extent, sir," I said.

' "I'm *so* glad you agree with me," he says. "My command
here I regard as a training depôt, and you, if I may say so, have
been one of my most efficient instructors. I mature my men
slowly but thoroughly. First I put 'em in a town which is liable
to be attacked by night, where they can attend riding-school in
the day. Then I use 'em with a convoy, and last I put 'em into a
column.* It takes time," he says, "but I flatter myself that any
men who have worked under me are at least grounded in the
rudiments of their profession. Adrian," he says, "was there
anything wrong with the men who upset Van Besters' apple-
cart last month when he was trying to cross the line to join
Piper with those horses he'd stole from Gabbitas?"

' "No, Generaal," says Van Zyl. "Your men got the horses
back and eleven dead; and Van Besters he ran to Delarey* in
his shirt. They was very good, those men. They shoot hard."

' "*So* pleased to hear you say so. I laid 'em down at the
beginning of this century—a 1900 vintage. *You* remember 'em,
Mankletow?" he says. "The Central Middlesex Broncho Bus-
ters—clerks and floor-walkers mostly," and he wiped his
moustache. "It was just the same with the Liverpool Buck-
jumpers, but they were stevedores. Let's see—they were a last-
century draft, weren't they? They did well after nine months.
You know 'em, Van Zyl? You didn't get much change out of
'em at Pootfontein?"

' "No," says Van Zyl. "At Pootfontein I lost my son
Andries."

' "I beg your pardon, Commandant," says the General; and the rest of the crowd sort of cooed over Adrian.

' "Excoose," says Adrian. "It was all right. They were good men those, but it is just what I say. Some are so dam' good we want to hands-up, and some are so dam' bad, we say, 'Take the Vierkleur* into Cape Town.' It is not upright of you, Generaal. It is not upright of you at all. I do not think you ever wish this war to finish."

' "It's a first-class dress-parade for Armageddon," says the General. "With luck, we ought to run half a million men through the mill. Why, we might even be able to give our Native Army* a look in. Oh, not here, of course, Adrian, but down in the Colony—say a camp-of-exercise at Worcester. You mustn't be prejudiced, Adrian. I've commanded a District in India, and I give you my word the native troops are splendid men."

' "Oh, I should not mind them at Worcester," says Adrian. "I would sell you forage for them at Worcester—yes, and Paarl and Stellenbosch;* but Almighty!" he says, "must I stay with Cronje* till you have taught half a million of these stupid boys to ride? I shall be an old man."

'Well, sir, then and there they began arguing whether St Helena would suit Adrian's health as well as some other places they knew about, and fixing up letters of introduction to Dukes and Lords of their acquaintance, so's Van Zyl should be well looked after. We own a fair-sized block of real estate—America does—but it made me sickish to hear this crowd fluttering round the Atlas (oh yes, they had an Atlas), and choosing stray continents for Adrian to drink his coffee in. The old man allowed he didn't want to roost with Cronje, because one of Cronje's kin had jumped one of his farms after Paardeberg. I forget the rights of the case, but it was interesting. They decided on a place called Umballa in India, because there was a first-class doctor there.

'So Adrian was fixed to drink the King and Fox-hunting, and study up the Native Army in India (I'd like to see 'em myself), till the British General had taught the male white citizens of Great Britain how to ride. Don't misunderstand me, sir. I loved that General. After ten minutes I loved him, and I wanted to laugh at him; but at the same time, sitting there and hearing him talk about the centuries, I tell you, sir, it scared me. It scared me cold! He admitted everything—he acknowledged the corn* before you spoke—he was more pleased to hear that his men had been used to wipe the veldt with than I was when I knocked out Tom Reed's two lead-horses—and he sat back and blew smoke through his nose and matured his men like cigars and—he talked of the everlastin' centuries!

'I went to bed nearer nervous prostration than I'd come in a long time. Next morning me and Captain Mankeltow fixed up what his shrapnel had left of my Zigler for transport to the railroad. She went in on her own wheels, and I stencilled her "Royal Artillery Mess, Woolwich", on the muzzle, and he said he'd be grateful if I'd take charge of her to Cape Town, and hand her over to a man in the Ordnance there. "How are you fixed financially? You'll need some money on the way home," he says at last.

' "For one thing, Cap," I said, "I'm not a poor man, and for another I'm not going home. I am a captive of your bow and spear. I decline to resign office."

' "Skittles!"* he says (that was a great word of his), "you'll take parole, and go back to America and invent another Zigler, a trifle heavier in the working-parts—I would. We've got more prisoners than we know what to do with as it is," he says. "You'll only be an additional expense to me as a taxpayer. Think of Schedule D,"* he says, "and take parole."

' "I don't know anything about your tariffs," I said, "but when I get to Cape Town I write home for money, and I turn in every cent my board'll cost your country to any ten-century-old department that's been ordained to take it since William the Conqueror came along."

' "But, confound you for a thick-headed mule," he says, "this war ain't any more than just started! Do you mean to tell me you're going to play prisoner till it's over?"

' "That's about the size of it," I says, "if an Englishman and an American could ever understand each other."

' "But, in Heaven's Holy Name, why?" he says, sitting down of a heap on an ant-hill.

' "Well, Cap," I says, "I don't pretend to follow your ways

of thought, and I can't see why you abuse your position to persecute a poor prisoner o' war on *his*!"

' "My dear fellow," he began, throwing up his hands and blushing, "I'll apologize."

' "But if you insist," I says, "there are just one and a half things in this world I can't do. The odd half don't matter here; but taking parole, and going home, and being interviewed by the boys, and giving lectures on my single-handed campaign against the hereditary enemies of my beloved country happens to be the one. We'll let it go at that, Cap."

' "But it'll bore you to death," he says. The British are a heap more afraid of what they call being bored than of dying, I've noticed.

' "I'll survive," I says. "I ain't British. I can think," I says.

' "By God," he says, coming up to me, and extending the right hand of fellowship, "you ought to be English, Zigler!"

'It's no good getting mad at a compliment like that. The English all do it. They're a crazy breed. When they don't know you, they freeze up tighter'n the St Lawrence. When they *do*, they go out like an ice-jam in April. Up till we prisoners left —four days—my Captain Mankeltow told me pretty much all about himself there was;—his mother and sisters, and his bad brother that was a trooper in some Colonial corps, and how his father who was a Lord didn't get on with him, and—well, everything, as I've said. They're undomesticated, the British, compared with us. They talk about their own family affairs as if they belonged to someone else. 'Tain't as if they hadn't any shame, but it sounds like it. I guess they talk out loud what we think, and we talk out loud what they think.

'I liked my Captain Mankeltow. I liked him as well as any man I'd ever struck. He was white. He gave me his silver drinking-flask, and I gave him the formula of my Laughtite. That's a hundred and fifty thousand dollars in his vest-pocket, on the lowest count, if he has the knowledge to use it. No, I didn't tell him the money-value. He was English. He'd send his valet to find out.

'Well, me and Adrian and a crowd of dam' Dutchmen was sent down the road to Cape Town in first-class carriages under escort. (What did I think of your enlisted men? They are largely different from ours, sir: very largely.) As I was saying, we slid down south, with Adrian looking out of the car-window and crying. Dutchmen cry mighty easy for a breed that fights as they do; but I never understood how a Dutchman could curse till we crossed into the Orange Free State Colony, and he lifted up his hand and cursed Steyn* for a solid ten minutes. Then we got into the Colony, and the rebs—ministers mostly and school-masters—came round the cars with fruit and sympathy and texts. Van Zyl talked to 'em in Dutch, and one man, a big red-bearded minister, at Beaufort West, I remember, he jest wilted on the platform.

' "Keep your prayers for yourself," says Van Zyl, throwing back a bunch of grapes. "You'll need 'em, and you'll need the fruit too, when the war comes down here. *You* done it," he says. "You and your picayune* Church that's deader than Cronje's dead horses!* What sort of a God have you been unloading on us, you black *aasvogels*?* The British came, and we beat 'em," he says, "and you sat still and prayed. The British beat us, and you sat still," he says. "You told us to hang on, and we hung on, and our farms was burned, and you sat still—you and your God. See here," he says, "I shot my Bible full of bullets after Bloemfontein went, and you and God didn't say anything. Take it and pray over it before we Federals help the British to knock hell out of you rebels."

'Then I hauled him back into the car. I judged he'd had a fit. But life's curious—and sudden—and mixed. I hadn't any more use for a reb than Van Zyl, and I knew something of the lies they'd fed us up with from the Colony for a year and more. I told the minister to pull his freight out of that, and went on with my lunch, when another man come along and shook hands with Van Zyl. He'd known him at close range in the Kimberley siege and before. Van Zyl was well seen by his neighbours, I judge. As soon as this other man opened his mouth I said, "You're Kentucky, ain't you?" "I am," he says; "and what may you be?" I told him right off, for I was pleased to hear good United States in any man's mouth; but he whipped his hands behind him and said, "I'm not knowing any man that fights for a Tammany* Dutchman. But I presoom you've been well paid, you dam', gun-runnin' Yank."

'Well, sir, I wasn't looking for that, and it near knocked me over, while old man Van Zyl started in to explain.

' "Don't you waste your breath, Mister Van Zyl," the man says. "I know this breed. The South's full of 'em." Then he whirls round on me and says, "Look at here, you Yank. A little thing like a King's neither here nor there, but what *you*'ve done," he says, "is to go back on the White Man in six places at once—two hemispheres and four continents—America, England, Canada, Australia, New Zealand, and South Africa. Don't open your head," he says. "You know right well if you'd been caught at this game in our country you'd have been jiggling in the bight of a lariat before you could reach for your naturalization papers. Go on and prosper," he says, "and you'll fetch up by fighting for niggers, as the North did." And he threw me half-a-crown—English money.

'Sir, I do not regard the proposition in that light, but I guess I must have been somewhat shook by the explosion. They told me at Cape Town one rib was driven in on to my lungs. I am not adducing this as an excuse, but the cold God's truth of the matter is—the money on the floor did it. . . . I gave up and cried. Put my head down and cried.

'I dream about this still sometimes. He didn't know the circumstances, but I dream about it. And it's Hell!

'How do you regard the proposition—as a Brother? If you'd invented your own gun, and spent fifty-seven thousand dollars on her—and had paid your own expenses from the word "go"? An American citizen has a right to choose his own side in an unpleasantness, and Van Zyl wasn't any Krugerite . . . and I'd risked my hide at my own expense. I got that man's address from Van Zyl; he was a mining man at Kimberley, and I wrote him the facts. But he never answered. Guess he thought I lied. . . . Damned Southern rebel!

'Oh, say. Did I tell you my Captain gave me a letter to an English Lord in Cape Town, and he fixed things so's I could lie up a piece in his house? I was pretty sick, and threw up some blood from where the rib had gouged into the lung—here. This Lord was a crank on guns, and he took charge of the Zigler. He had his knife into the British system as much as any American. He said he wanted revolution, and not reform, in your Army. He said the British soldier had failed in every point except courage. He said England needed a Monroe Doctrine* worse than America—a new doctrine, barring out all the Continent, and strictly devoting herself to developing her own Colonies. He said he'd abolish half the Foreign Office, and take all the old hereditary families clean out of it, because, he said, they was expressly trained to fool around with Continental diplomats, and to despise the Colonies. His own family wasn't more than six hundred years old. He was a very brainy man, and a good citizen. We talked politics and inventions together when my lung let up on me.

'Did he know my General? Yes. He knew 'em all. Called 'em Teddie and Gussie and Willie. They was all of the very best, and all his dearest friends; but he told me confidentially they was none of 'em fit to command a column in the field. He said they were too fond of advertising. Generals don't seem very different from actors or doctors or—yes, sir—inventors.

'He fixed things lovelily for me at Simonstown. Had the biggest sort of pull—even for a Lord. At first they treated me as a harmless lunatic; but after a while I got 'em to let me keep some of their books. If I was left alone in the world with the British system of book-keeping, I'd reconstruct the whole British Empire—beginning with the Army. Yes, I'm one of their most trusted accountants, and I'm paid for it. As much as a dollar a day. I keep that. I've earned it, and I deduct it from the cost of my board. When the war's over I'm going to pay up the balance to the British Government. Yes, sir, that's how I regard the proposition.

'Adrian? Oh, he left for Umballa four months back. He told me he was going to apply to join the National Scouts* if the war didn't end in a year. 'Tisn't in nature for one Dutchman to shoot another, but if Adrian ever meets up with Steyn there'll be an exception to the rule. Ye-es, when the war's over it'll take some of the British Army to protect Steyn from his fellow-patriots. But the war won't be over yet awhile. He that believeth don't hurry, as Isaiah says. The ministers and the school-teachers and the rebs'll have a war all to themselves long after the North is quiet.

'I'm pleased with this country—it's big. Not so many folk on the ground as in America. There's a boom coming sure. I've talked it over with Adrian, and I guess I shall buy a farm somewhere near Bloemfontein and start in cattle-raising. It's big and peaceful—a ten-thousand-acre farm. I could go on inventing there, too. I'll sell my Zigler, I guess. I'll offer the patent rights to the British Government; and if they do the "reelly-now-how-interesting" act over her, I'll turn her over to Captain Mankeltow and his friend the Lord. They'll pretty quick find some Gussie, or Teddie, or Algie who can get her accepted in the proper quarters. I'm beginning to know my English.

'And now I'll go in swimming, and read the papers after lunch. I haven't had such a good time since Willie died.'*

He pulled the blue shirt over his head as the bathers returned to their piles of clothing, and, speaking through the folds, added:—

'But if you want to realize your assets, you should lease the whole proposition to America for ninety-nine years.'

Chant-Pagan*

(*English Irregular, discharged*)

ME THAT 'ave been what I've been—
    Me that 'ave gone where I've gone—
Me that 'ave seen what I've seen—
    'Ow can I ever take on
With awful old England again,
An' 'ouses both sides of the street,
And 'edges two sides of the lane,
And the parson an' gentry between,
An' touchin' my 'at when we meet—
    Me that 'ave been what I've been?

Me that 'ave watched 'arf a world
'Eave up all shiny with dew,
Kopje* on kop* to the sun,
An' as soon as the mist let 'em through
Our 'elios winkin' like fun—
Three sides of a ninety-mile square,
Over valleys as big as a shire—
'*Are ye there? Are ye there? Are ye there?*'
An' then the blind drum of our fire . . .
An' I'm rollin' 'is lawns for the Squire,
                                        Me!

Me that 'ave rode through the dark
Forty mile, often, on end,
Along the Ma'ollisberg Range,*
With only the stars for my mark
An' only the night for my friend,
An' things runnin' off as you pass,
An' things jumpin' up in the grass,
An' the silence, the shine an' the size
Of the 'igh, unexpressible skies—
I am takin' some letters almost

As much as a mile to the post,
An' 'mind you come back with the change!'

Me!

Me that saw Barberton* took
When we dropped through the clouds on their 'ead,
An' they 'ove the guns over and fled—
Me that was through Di'mond 'Ill,
An' Pieters an' Springs an' Belfast—
From Dundee to Vereeniging* all—
Me that stuck out to the last
(An' five bloomin' bars on my chest)—
I am doin' my Sunday-school best,
By the 'elp of the Squire an' is wife
(Not to mention the 'ousemaid an' cook),
To come in an' 'ands up an' be still,
An' honestly work for my bread,
My livin' in that state of life
To which it shall please God to call

Me!

Me that 'ave followed my trade
In the place where the Lightnin's are made;
'Twixt the Rains and the Sun and the Moon—
Me that lay down an' got up
Three years with the sky for my roof—
That 'ave ridden my 'unger an' thirst
Six thousand raw mile on the hoof,
With the Vaal and the Orange for cup,
An' the Brandwater Basin* for dish,—
Oh! it's 'ard to be'ave as they wish
(Too 'ard, an' a little too soon),
I'll 'ave to think over it first—

Me!

I will arise an' get 'ence—
I will trek South and make sure
If it's only my fancy or not
That the sunshine of England is pale,
And the breezes of England are stale,

An' there's somethin' gone small with the lot.
For *I* know of a sun an' a wind,
An' some plains and a mountain be'ind,
An' some graves by a barb-wire fence,
An' a Dutchman I've fought 'oo might give
Me a job were I ever inclined
To look in an' offsaddle an' live
Where there's neither a road nor a tree—
But only my Maker an' me,
And I think it will kill me or cure,
So I think I will go there an' see.

PART THREE

The Great War

Gethsemane*

1914–18

THE Garden called Gethsemane
    In Picardy it was,
And there the people came to see
    The English soldiers pass.
We used to pass—we used to pass
    Or halt, as it might be,
And ship our masks in case of gas
    Beyond Gethsemane.

The Garden called Gethsemane,
    It held a pretty lass,
But all the time she talked to me
    I prayed my cup might pass.
The officer sat on the chair,
    The men lay on the grass,
And all the time we halted there
    I prayed my cup might pass.

It didn't pass—it didn't pass—
    It didn't pass from me.
I drank it when we met the gas
    Beyond Gethsemane!

'Swept and Garnished'*

WHEN the first waves of feverish cold stole over Frau Ebermann she very wisely telephoned the doctor and went to bed. He diagnosed the attack as mild influenza, prescribed the appropriate remedies, and left her to the care of her one servant in her comfortable Berlin flat. Frau Ebermann, beneath the thick coverlet, curled up with what patience she could until the aspirin should begin to act, and Anna should come back from the chemist with the formamint, the ammoniated quinine, the eucalyptus, and the little tin steam-inhaler. Meantime, every bone in her body ached; her head throbbed; her hot, dry hands would not stay the same size for a minute together; and her body, tucked into the smallest possible compass, shrank from the chill of the well-warmed sheets.

Of a sudden she noticed that an imitation-lace cover which should have lain mathematically square with the imitation-marble top of the radiator behind the green plush sofa had slipped away so that one corner hung over the bronze-painted steam-pipes. She recalled that she must have rested her poor head against the radiator-top while she was taking off her boots. She tried to get up and set the thing straight, but the radiator at once receded toward the horizon, which, unlike true horizons, slanted diagonally, exactly parallel with the dropped lace edge of the cover. Frau Ebermann groaned through sticky lips and lay still.

'Certainly, I have a temperature,' she said. 'Certainly, I have a grave temperature. I should have been warned by that chill after dinner.'

She resolved to shut her hot-lidded eyes, but opened them in a little while to torture herself with the knowledge of that ungeometrical thing against the far wall. Then she saw a child—an untidy, thin-faced little girl of about ten, who must have strayed in from the adjoining flat. This proved—Frau Ebermann groaned again at the way the world falls to bits when one is sick—proved that Anna had forgotten to shut the outer

door of the flat when she went to the chemist. Frau Ebermann
had had children of her own, but they were all grown-up now,
and she had never been a child-lover in any sense. Yet the
intruder might be made to serve her scheme of things.

'Make—put,' she muttered thickly, 'that white thing
straight on the top of that yellow thing.'

The child paid no attention, but moved about the room,
investigating everything that came in her way—the yellow cut-
glass handles of the chest of drawers, the stamped bronze hook
to hold back the heavy puce curtains, and the mauve enamel,
New Art* finger-plates on the door. Frau Ebermann watched
indignantly.

'Aie! That is bad and rude. Go away!' she cried, though it
hurt her to raise her voice. 'Go away by the road you came!'
The child passed behind the bed-foot, where she could not see
her. 'Shut the door as you go. I will speak to Anna, but—first,
put that white thing straight.'

She closed her eyes in misery of body and soul. The outer
door clicked, and Anna entered, very penitent that she had
stayed so long at the chemist's. But it had been difficult to find
the proper type of inhaler, and——

'Where did the child go?' moaned Frau Ebermann—'the
child that was here?'

'There was no child,' said startled Anna. 'How should any
child come in when I shut the door behind me after I go out?
All the keys of the flats are different.'

'No, no! You forgot this time. But my back is aching, and up
my legs also. Besides, who knows what it may have fingered
and upset? Look and see.'

'Nothing is fingered, nothing is upset,' Anna replied, as she
took the inhaler from its paper box.

'Yes, there is. Now I remember all about it. Put—put that
white thing, with the open edge—the lace, I mean—quite
straight on that——' she pointed. Anna, accustomed to her
ways, understood and went to it.

'Now is it quite straight?' Frau Ebermann demanded.

'Perfectly,' said Anna. 'In fact, in the very centre of the
radiator.' Anna measured the equal margins with her knuckle,
as she had been told to do when she first took service.

'And my tortoise-shell hair-brushes?' Frau Ebermann could not command her dressing-table from where she lay.

'Perfectly straight, side by side in the big tray, and the comb laid across them. Your watch also in the coralline watch-holder. Everything'—she moved round the room to make sure—'everything is as you have it when you are well.' Frau Ebermann sighed with relief. It seemed to her that the room and her head had suddenly grown cooler.

'Good!' said she. 'Now warm my nightgown in the kitchen, so it will be ready when I have perspired. And the towels also. Make the inhaler steam, and put in the eucalyptus; that is good for the larynx. Then sit you in the kitchen, and come when I ring. But, first, my hot-water bottle.'

It was brought and scientifically tucked in.

'What news?' said Frau Ebermann drowsily. She had not been out that day.

'Another victory,' said Anna. 'Many more prisoners and guns.'

Frau Ebermann purred, one might almost say grunted, contentedly.

'That is good too,' she said; and Anna, after lighting the inhaler-lamp, went out.

Frau Ebermann reflected that in an hour or so the aspirin would begin to work, and all would be well. To-morrow—no, the day after—she would take up life with something to talk over with her friends at coffee. It was rare—every one knew it—that she should be overcome by any ailment. Yet in all her distresses she had not allowed the minutest deviation from daily routine and ritual. She would tell her friends—she ran over their names one by one—exactly what measures she had taken against the lace cover on the radiator-top and in regard to her two tortoise-shell hair-brushes and the comb at right angles. How she had set everything in order—everything in order. She roved further afield as she wriggled her toes lux-uriously on the hot-water bottle. If it pleased our dear God to take her to Himself, and she was not so young as she had been—there was that plate of the four lower ones in the blue tooth-glass, for instance—He should find all her belongings fit

to meet His eye. 'Swept and garnished' were the words that
shaped themselves in her intent brain. 'Swept and garnished
for——'

No, it was certainly not for the dear Lord that she had swept;
she would have her room swept out to-morrow or the day after,
and garnished. Her hands began to swell again into huge pil-
lows of nothingness. Then they shrank, and so did her head, to
minute dots. It occurred to her that she was waiting for some
event, some tremendously important event, to come to pass.
She lay with shut eyes for a long time till her head and hands
should return to their proper size.

She opened her eyes with a jerk.

'How stupid of me,' she said aloud, 'to set the room in order
for a parcel of dirty little children!'

They were there—five of them, two little boys and three
girls—headed by the anxious-eyed ten-year-old whom she had
seen before. They must have entered by the outer door, which
Anna had neglected to shut behind her when she returned with
the inhaler. She counted them backward and forward as one
counts scales—one, two, three, four, five.

They took no notice of her, but hung about, first on one foot
then on the other, like strayed chickens, the smaller ones hold-
ing by the larger. They had the air of utterly wearied passen-
gers in a railway waiting-room, and their clothes were
disgracefully dirty.

'Go away!' cried Frau Ebermann at last, after she had strug-
gled, it seemed to her, for years to shape the words.

'You called?' said Anna at the living-room door.

'No,' said her mistress. 'Did you shut the flat door when you
came in?'

'Assuredly,' said Anna. 'Besides, it is made to catch shut of
itself.'

'Then go away,' said she, very little above a whisper. If Anna
pretended not to see the children, she would speak to Anna
later on.

'And now,' she said, turning toward them as soon as the door
closed. The smallest of the crowd smiled at her, and shook his
head before he buried it in his sister's skirts.

'Why—don't—you—go—away?' she whispered earnestly.

Again they took no notice, but, guided by the elder girl, set themselves to climb, boots and all, on to the green plush sofa in front of the radiator. The little boys had to be pushed, as they could not compass the stretch unaided. They settled themselves in a row, with small gasps of relief, and pawed the plush approvingly.

'I ask you—I ask you why do you not go away—why do you not go away?' Frau Ebermann found herself repeating the question twenty times. It seemed to her that everything in the world hung on the answer. 'You know you should not come into houses and rooms unless you are invited. Not houses and bedrooms, you know.'

'No,' a solemn little six-year-old repeated, 'not houses nor bedrooms, nor dining-rooms, nor churches, nor all those places.* Shouldn't come in. It's rude.'

'Yes, he said so,' the younger girl put in proudly. 'He said it. He told them only pigs would do that.' The line nodded and dimpled one to another with little explosive giggles, such as children use when they tell deeds of great daring against their elders.

'If you know it is wrong, that makes it much worse,' said Frau Ebermann.

'Oh yes; much worse,' they assented cheerfully, till the smallest boy changed his smile to a baby wail of weariness.

'When will they come for us?' he asked, and the girl at the head of the row hauled him bodily into her square little capable lap.

'He's tired,' she explained. 'He is only four. He only had his first breeches this spring.' They came almost under his armpits, and were held up by broad linen braces, which, his sorrow diverted for the moment, he patted proudly.

'Yes, beautiful, dear,' said both girls.

'Go away!' said Frau Ebermann. 'Go home to your father and mother!'

Their faces grew grave at once.

'H'sh! We *can't*,' whispered the eldest. 'There isn't anything left.'

'All gone,' a boy echoed, and he puffed through pursed lips. 'Like *that*, uncle told me. Both cows too.'

'And my own three ducks,' the boy on the girl's lap said sleepily.

'So, you see, we came here.' The elder girl leaned forward a little, caressing the child she rocked.

'I—I don't understand,' said Frau Ebermann. 'Are you lost, then? You must tell our police.'

'Oh no; we are only waiting.'

'But what are you waiting *for*?'

'We are waiting for our people to come for us. They told us to come here and wait for them. So we are waiting till they come,' the eldest girl replied.

'Yes. We are waiting till our people come for us,' said all the others in chorus.

'But,' said Frau Ebermann very patiently—'but now tell me, for I tell you that I am not in the least angry, where do you come from? Where do you come from?'

The five gave the names of two villages of which she had read in the papers.

'That is silly,' said Frau Ebermann. 'The people fired on us, and they were punished.* Those places are wiped out, stamped flat.'

'Yes, yes, wiped out, stamped flat. That is why and—I have lost the ribbon off my pigtail,' said the younger girl. She looked behind her over the sofa-back.

'It is not here,' said the elder. 'It was lost before. Don't you remember?'

'Now, if you are lost, you must go and tell our police. They will take care of you and give you food,' said Frau Ebermann. 'Anna will show you the way there.'

'No,'—this was the six-year-old with the smile,—'we must wait here till our people come for us. Mustn't we, sister?'

'Of course. We wait here till our people come for us. All the world knows that,' said the eldest girl.

'Yes.' The boy in her lap had waked again. 'Little children, too—as little as Henri, and *he* doesn't wear trousers yet. As little as all that.'

'I don't understand,' said Frau Ebermann, shivering. In spite of the heat of the room and the damp breath of the steam-inhaler, the aspirin was not doing its duty.

The girl raised her blue eyes and looked at the woman for an instant.

'You see,' she said, emphasizing her statements with her fingers, '*they* told *us* to wait *here* till *our* people came for us. So we came. We wait till our people come for us.'

'That is silly again,' said Frau Ebermann. 'It is no good for you to wait here. Do you know what this place is? You have been to school? It is Berlin, the capital of Germany.'

'Yes, yes,' they all cried; 'Berlin, capital of Germany. We know that. That is why we came.'

'So, you see, it is no good,' she said triumphantly, 'because your people can never come for you here.'

'They told us to come here and wait till our people came for us.' They delivered this as if it were a lesson in school. Then they sat still, their hands orderly folded on their laps, smiling as sweetly as ever.

'Go away! Go away!' Frau Ebermann shrieked.

'You called?' said Anna, entering.

'No. Go away! Go away!'

'Very good, old cat,' said the maid under her breath. 'Next time you *may* call,' and she returned to her friend in the kitchen.

'I ask you—ask you, *please* to go away,' Frau Ebermann pleaded. 'Go to my Anna through that door, and she will give you cakes and sweeties. It is not kind of you to come into my room and behave so badly.'

'Where else shall we go now?' the elder girl demanded, turning to her little company. They fell into discussion. One preferred the broad street with trees, another the railway station; but when she suggested an Emperor's palace, they agreed with her.

'We will go then,' she said, and added half apologetically to Frau Ebermann, 'You see, they are so little they like to meet all the others.'

'What others?' said Frau Ebermann.

'The others—hundreds and hundreds and thousands and thousands of the others.'

'That is a lie. There cannot be a hundred even, much less a thousand,' cried Frau Ebermann.

'So?' said the girl politely.

'Yes. *I* tell you; and I have very good information. I know how it happened. You should have been more careful. You should not have run out to see the horses and guns passing. That is how it is done when our troops pass through. My son has written me so.'

They had clambered down from the sofa, and gathered round the bed with eager, interested eyes.

'Horses and guns going by—how fine!' some one whispered.

'Yes, yes; believe me, *that* is how the accidents to the children happen. You must know yourself that it is true. One runs out to look——'

'But I never saw any at all,' a boy said sorrowfully. 'Only one noise I heard. That was when Aunt Emmeline's house fell down.'

'But listen to me. *I* am telling you! One runs out to look, because one is little and cannot see well. So one peeps between the man's legs, and then—you know how close those big horses and guns turn the corners—then one's foot slips and one gets run over. That's how it happens. Several times it has happened, but not many times; certainly not a hundred, perhaps not twenty. So, you see, you *must* be all. Tell me now that you are all that there are, and Anna shall give you the cakes.'

'Thousands,' a boy repeated monotonously. 'Then we all come here to wait till our people come for us.'

'But now we will go away from here. The poor lady is tired,' said the elder girl, plucking his sleeve.

'Oh, you hurt, you hurt!' he cried, and burst into tears.

'What is that for?' said Frau Ebermann. 'To cry in a room where a poor lady is sick is very inconsiderate.'

'Oh, but look, lady!' said the elder girl.

Frau Ebermann looked and saw.

'*Au revoir*, lady.' They made their little smiling bows and curtseys undisturbed by her loud cries. '*Au revoir*, lady. We will wait till our people come for us.'

When Anna at last ran in, she found her mistress on her knees, busily cleaning the floor with the lace cover from the radiator, because, she explained, it was all spotted with the blood of five children—she was perfectly certain there could not be more than five in the whole world—who had gone away for the moment, but were now waiting round the corner, and Anna was to find them and give them cakes to stop the bleeding, while her mistress swept and garnished that Our dear Lord when He came might find everything as it should be.

Mary Postgate*

OF Miss Mary Postgate, Lady McCausland wrote that she was 'thoroughly conscientious, tidy, companionable, and ladylike. I am very sorry to part with her, and shall always be interested in her welfare'.

Miss Fowler engaged her on this recommendation, and to her surprise, for she had had experience of companions, found that it was true. Miss Fowler was nearer sixty than fifty at the time, but though she needed care she did not exhaust her attendant's vitality. On the contrary, she gave out, stimulatingly and with reminiscences. Her father had been a minor Court official in the days when the Great Exhibition of 1851 had just set its seal on Civilization made perfect. Some of Miss Fowler's tales, none the less, were not always for the young. Mary was not young, and though her speech was as colourless as her eyes or her hair, she was never shocked. She listened unflinchingly to every one; said at the end, 'How interesting!' or 'How shocking!' as the case might be, and never again referred to it, for she prided herself on a trained mind, which 'did not dwell on these things'. She was, too, a treasure at domestic accounts, for which the village tradesmen, with their weekly books, loved her not. Otherwise she had no enemies; provoked no jealousy even among the plainest; neither gossip nor slander had ever been traced to her; she supplied the odd place at the Rector's or the Doctor's table at half an hour's notice; she was a sort of public aunt to very many small children of the village street, whose parents, while accepting everything, would have been swift to resent what they called 'patronage'; she served on the Village Nursing Committee as Miss Fowler's nominee when Miss Fowler was crippled by rheumatoid arthritis, and came out of six months' fortnightly meetings equally respected by all the cliques.

And when Fate threw Miss Fowler's nephew, an unlovely orphan of eleven, on Miss Fowler's hands, Mary Postgate stood to her share of the business of education as practised in private and public schools. She checked printed clothes-lists, and unitemized bills of extras; wrote to Head and House masters, matrons, nurses and doctors, and grieved or rejoiced over half-term reports. Young Wyndham Fowler repaid her in his holidays by calling her 'Gatepost', 'Postey', or 'Packthread', by thumping her between her narrow shoulders, or by chasing her bleating, round the garden, her large mouth open, her large nose high in air, at a stiff-necked shamble very like a camel's. Later on he filled the house with clamour, argument, and harangues as to his personal needs, likes and dislikes, and the limitations of 'you women', reducing Mary to tears of physical fatigue, or, when he chose to be humorous, of helpless laughter. At crises, which multiplied as he grew older, she was his ambassadress and his interpretress to Miss Fowler, who had no large sympathy with the young; a vote in his interest at the councils on his future; his sewing-woman, strictly accountable for mislaid boots and garments; always his butt and his slave.

And when he decided to become a solicitor, and had entered an office in London; when his greeting had changed from 'Hullo, Postey, you old beast', to 'Mornin', Packthread', there came a war which, unlike all wars that Mary could remember, did not stay decently outside England and in the newspapers, but intruded on the lives of people whom she knew. As she said to Miss Fowler, it was 'most vexatious'. It took the Rector's son, who was going into business with his elder brother; it took the Colonel's nephew on the eve of fruit-farming in Canada; it took Mrs Grant's son who, his mother said, was devoted to the ministry; and, very early indeed, it took Wynn Fowler, who announced on a postcard that he had joined the Flying Corps and wanted a cardigan waistcoat.

'He must go, and he must have the waistcoat,' said Miss Fowler. So Mary got the proper-sized needles and wool, while Miss Fowler told the men of her establishment—two gardeners and an odd man, aged sixty—that those who could join the Army had better do so. The gardeners left. Cheape, the odd man, stayed on, and was promoted to the gardener's cottage. The cook, scorning to be limited in luxuries, also left, after a spirited scene with Miss Fowler, and took the housemaid with her. Miss Fowler gazetted Nellie, Cheape's seventeen-year-old daughter, to the vacant post; Mrs Cheape to the rank of cook, with occasional cleaning bouts; and the reduced establishment moved forward smoothly.

Wynn demanded an increase in his allowance. Miss Fowler, who always looked facts in the face, said, 'He must have it. The chances are he won't live long to draw it, and if three hundred makes him happy——'

Wynn was grateful, and came over, in his tight-buttoned uniform, to say so. His training centre was not thirty miles away, and his talk was so technical that it had to be explained by charts of the various types of machines. He gave Mary such a chart.

'And you'd better study it, Postey,' he said. 'You'll be seeing a lot of 'em soon.' So Mary studied the chart, but when Wynn next arrived to swell and exalt himself before his womenfolk, she failed badly in cross-examination, and he rated her as in the old days.

'You *look* more or less like a human being,' he said in his new Service voice. 'You *must* have had a brain at some time in your past. What have you done with it? Where d'you keep it? A sheep would know more than you do, Postey. You're lamentable. You are less use than an empty tin can, you dowey* old cassowary.'

'I suppose that's how your superior officer talks to *you*?' said Miss Fowler from her chair.

'But Postey doesn't mind,' Wynn replied. 'Do you, Packthread?'

'Why? Was Wynn saying anything? I shall get this right next time you come,' she muttered, and knitted her pale eyebrows again over the diagrams of Taubes, Farmans, and Zeppelins.*

In a few weeks the mere land and sea battles which she read to Miss Fowler after breakfast passed her like idle breath. Her heart and her interest were high in the air with Wynn, who had finished 'rolling' (whatever that might be) and had gone on from a 'taxi' to a machine more or less his own. One morning it circled over their very chimneys, alighted on Vegg's Heath, almost outside the garden gate, and Wynn came in, blue with cold, shouting for food. He and she drew Miss Fowler's bath-chair, as they had often done, along the Heath foot-path to look at the biplane. Mary observed that 'it smelt very badly'.

'Postey, I believe you think with your nose,' said Wynn. 'I know you don't with your mind. Now, what type's that?'

'I'll go and get the chart,' said Mary.

'You're hopeless! You haven't the mental capacity of a white mouse,' he cried, and explained the dials and the sockets for bomb-dropping till it was time to mount and ride the wet clouds once more.

'Ah!' said Mary, as the stinking thing flared upward. 'Wait till our Flying Corps gets to work! Wynn says it's much safer than in the trenches.'

'I wonder,' said Miss Fowler. 'Tell Cheape to come and tow me home again.'

'It's all downhill. I can do it,' said Mary, 'if you put the brake on.' She laid her lean self against the pushing-bar and home they trundled.

'Now, be careful you aren't heated and catch a chill,' said overdressed Miss Fowler.

'Nothing makes me perspire,' said Mary. As she bumped the chair under the porch she straightened her long back. The exertion had given her a colour, and the wind had loosened a wisp of hair across her forehead. Miss Fowler glanced at her.

'What do you ever think of, Mary?' she demanded suddenly.

'Oh, Wynn says he wants another three pairs of stockings—as thick as we can make them.'

'Yes. But I mean the things that women think about. Here you are, more than forty——'

'Forty-four,' said truthful Mary.

'Well?'

'Well?' Mary offered Miss Fowler her shoulder as usual.

'And you've been with me ten years now.'

'Let's see,' said Mary. 'Wynn was eleven when he came. He's twenty now, and I came two years before that. It must be eleven.'

'Eleven! And you've never told me anything that matters in all that while. Looking back, it seems to me that *I*'ve done all the talking.'

'I'm afraid I'm not much of a conversationalist. As Wynn says, I haven't the mind. Let me take your hat.'

Miss Fowler, moving stiffly from the hip, stamped her rubber-tipped stick on the tiled hall floor. 'Mary, aren't you *anything* except a companion? Would you *ever* have been anything except a companion?'

Mary hung up the garden hat on its proper peg. 'No,' she said after consideration. 'I don't imagine I ever should. But I've no imagination, I'm afraid.'

She fetched Miss Fowler her eleven-o'clock glass of Contrexéville.*

That was the wet December when it rained six inches to the month, and the women went abroad as little as might be. Wynn's flying chariot visited them several times, and for two mornings (he had warned her by postcard) Mary heard the thresh of his propellers at dawn. The second time she ran to the window, and stared at the whitening sky. A little blur passed overhead. She lifted her lean arms towards it.

That evening at six o'clock there came an announcement in an official envelope that Second-Lieutenant W. Fowler had been killed during a trial flight. Death was instantaneous. She read it and carried it to Miss Fowler.

'I never expected anything else,' said Miss Fowler; 'but I'm sorry it happened before he had done anything.'

The room was whirling round Mary Postgate, but she found herself quite steady in the midst of it.

'Yes,' she said. 'It's a great pity he didn't die in action after he had killed somebody.'

'He was killed instantly. That's one comfort,' Miss Fowler went on.

'But Wynn says the shock of a fall kills a man at once—whatever happens to the tanks,' quoted Mary.

The room was coming to rest now. She heard Miss Fowler say impatiently, 'But why can't we cry, Mary?' and herself replying, 'There's nothing to cry for. He has done his duty as much as Mrs Grant's son did.'

'And when he died, *she* came and cried all the morning,' said Miss Fowler. 'This only makes me feel tired—terribly tired.

Will you help me to bed, please, Mary?—And I think I'd like the hot-water bottle.'

So Mary helped her and sat beside, talking of Wynn in his riotous youth.

'I believe,' said Miss Fowler suddenly, 'that old people and young people slip from under a stroke like this. The middle-aged feel it most.'

'I expect that's true,' said Mary, rising. 'I'm going to put away the things in his room now. Shall we wear mourning?'

'Certainly not,' said Miss Fowler. 'Except, of course, at the funeral. I can't go. You will. I want you to arrange about his being buried here. What a blessing it didn't happen at Salisbury!'

Every one, from the Authorities of the Flying Corps to the Rector, was most kind and sympathetic. Mary found herself for the moment in a world where bodies were in the habit of being despatched by all sorts of conveyances to all sorts of places. And at the funeral two young men in buttoned-up uniforms stood beside the grave and spoke to her afterwards.

'You're Miss Postgate, aren't you?' said one. 'Fowler told me about you. He was a good chap—a first-class fellow—a great loss.'

'Great loss!' growled his companion. 'We're all awfully sorry.'

'How high did he fall from?' Mary whispered.

'Pretty nearly four thousand feet, I should think, didn't he? You were up that day, Monkey?'

'All of that,' the other child replied. 'My bar made three thousand, and I wasn't as high as him by a lot.'

'Then *that's* all right,' said Mary. 'Thank you very much.'

They moved away as Mrs Grant flung herself weeping on Mary's flat chest, under the lych-gate, and cried, '*I* know how it feels! *I* know how it feels!'

'But both his parents are dead,' Mary returned, as she fended her off. 'Perhaps they've all met by now,' she added vaguely as she escaped towards the coach.

'I've thought of that too,' wailed Mrs Grant; 'but then he'll be practically a stranger to them. Quite embarrassing!'

Mary faithfully reported every detail of the ceremony to Miss

Fowler, who, when she described Mrs Grant's outburst, laughed aloud.

'Oh, how Wynn would have enjoyed it! He was always utterly unreliable at funerals. D'you remember——' And they talked of him again, each piecing out the other's gaps. 'And now,' said Miss Fowler, 'we'll pull up the blinds and we'll have a general tidy. That always does us good. Have you seen to Wynn's things?'

'Everything—since he first came,' said Mary. 'He was never destructive—even with his toys.'

They faced that neat room.

'It can't be natural not to cry,' Mary said at last. 'I'm *so* afraid you'll have a reaction.'

'As I told you, we old people slip from under the stroke. It's you I'm afraid for. Have you cried yet?'

'I can't. It only makes me angry with the Germans.'

'That's sheer waste of vitality,' said Miss Fowler. 'We must live till the War's finished.' She opened a full wardrobe. 'Now, I've been thinking things over. This is my plan. All his civilian clothes can be given away—Belgian refugees, and so on.'

Mary nodded. 'Boots, collars, and gloves?'

'Yes. We don't need to keep anything except his cap and belt.'

'They came back yesterday with his Flying Corps clothes'— Mary pointed to a roll on the little iron bed.

'Ah, but keep his Service things. Some one may be glad of them later. Do you remember his sizes?'

'Five feet eight and a half; thirty-six inches round the chest. But he told me he's just put on an inch and a half. I'll mark it on a label and tie it on his sleeping-bag.'

'So that disposes of *that*,' said Miss Fowler, tapping the palm of one hand with the ringed third finger of the other. 'What waste it all is! We'll get his old school trunk to-morrow and pack his civilian clothes.'

'And the rest?' said Mary. 'His books and pictures and the games and the toys—and—and the rest?'

'My plan is to burn every single thing,' said Miss Fowler. 'Then we shall know where they are and no one can handle them afterwards. What do you think?'

'I think that would be much the best,' said Mary. 'But there's such a lot of them.'

'We'll burn them in the destructor,' said Miss Fowler.

This was an open-air furnace for the consumption of refuse; a little circular four-foot tower of pierced brick over an iron grating. Miss Fowler had noticed the design in a gardening journal years ago, and had had it built at the bottom of the garden. It suited her tidy soul, for it saved unsightly rubbish-heaps, and the ashes lightened the stiff clay soil.

Mary considered for a moment, saw her way clear, and nodded again. They spent the evening putting away well-remembered civilian suits, underclothes that Mary had marked, and the regiments of very gaudy socks and ties. A second trunk was needed, and, after that, a little packing-case, and it was late next day when Cheape and the local carrier lifted them to the cart. The Rector luckily knew of a friend's son, about five feet eight and a half inches high, to whom a complete Flying Corps outfit would be most acceptable, and sent his gardener's son down with a barrow to take delivery of it. The cap was hung up in Miss Fowler's bedroom, the belt in Miss Postgate's; for, as Miss Fowler said, they had no desire to make tea-party talk of them.

'That disposes of *that*,' said Miss Fowler. 'I'll leave the rest to you, Mary. *I* can't run up and down the garden. You'd better take the big clothes-basket and get Nellie to help you.'

'I shall take the wheel-barrow and do it myself,' said Mary, and for once in her life closed her mouth.

Miss Fowler, in moments of irritation, had called Mary deadly methodical. She put on her oldest waterproof and gardening-hat and her ever-slipping goloshes, for the weather was on the edge of more rain. She gathered fire-lighters from the kitchen, a half-scuttle of coals, and a faggot of brushwood. These she wheeled in the barrow down the mossed paths to the dank little laurel shrubbery where the destructor stood under the drip of three oaks. She climbed the wire fence into the Rector's glebe just behind, and from his tenant's rick pulled two large armfuls of good hay, which she spread neatly on the fire-bars. Next, journey by journey, passing Miss Fowler's white face at the morning-room window each time, she brought down in the towel-covered clothes-basket, on the wheelbarrow, thumbed and used Hentys, Marryats, Levers, Stevensons, Baroness Orczys, Garvices, school-books, and atlases, unrelated piles of the *Motor Cyclist*, the *Light Car*, and catalogues of Olympia Exhibitions; the remnants of a fleet of sailing-ships from ninepenny cutters to a three-guinea yacht; a prep-school dressing-gown; bats from three-and-sixpence to twenty-four shillings; cricket and tennis balls; disintegrated steam and clockwork locomotives with their twisted rails; a grey-and-red tin model of a submarine; a dumb gramophone and cracked records; golf-clubs that had to be broken across the knee, like his walking-sticks, and an assegai; photographs of private and public school cricket and football elevens, and his O.T.C.* on the line of march; kodaks and film-rolls; some pewters, and one real silver cup, for boxing competitions and Junior Hurdles; sheaves of school photographs; Miss Fowler's photograph; her own which he had borne off in fun and (good care she took not to ask!) had never returned; a playbox with a secret drawer; a load of flannels, belts, and jerseys, and a pair of spiked shoes unearthed in the attic; a packet of all the letters that Miss Fowler and she had ever written to him, kept for some absurd reason through all these years; a five-day attempt at a diary; framed pictures of racing motors in full Brooklands* career, and load upon load of undistinguishable wreckage of tool-boxes, rabbit-hutches, electric batteries, tin soldiers, fret-saw outfits, and jig-saw puzzles.

Miss Fowler at the window watched her come and go, and said to herself, 'Mary's an old woman. I never realized it before.'

After lunch she recommended her to rest.

'I'm not in the least tired,' said Mary. 'I've got it all arranged. I'm going to the village at two o'clock for some paraffin. Nellie hasn't enough, and the walk will do me good.'

She made one last quest round the house before she started, and found that she had overlooked nothing. It began to mist as soon as she had skirted Vegg's Heath, where Wynn used to descend—it seemed to her that she could almost hear the beat of his propellers overhead, but there was nothing to see. She hoisted her umbrella and lunged into the blind wet till she had reached the shelter of the empty village. As she came out of Mr Kidd's shop with a bottle of paraffin in her string shopping-bag, she met Nurse Eden, the village nurse, and fell into talk with her, as usual, about the village children. They were just parting opposite the 'Royal Oak', when a gun, they fancied, was fired immediately behind the house. It was followed by a child's shriek dying into a wail.

'Accident!' said Nurse Eden promptly, and dashed through the empty bar, followed by Mary. They found Mrs Gerritt, the publican's wife, who could only gasp and point to the yard, where a little cart-lodge was sliding sideways amid a clatter of tiles. Nurse Eden snatched up a sheet drying before the fire, ran out, lifted something from the ground, and flung the sheet round it. The sheet turned scarlet and half her uniform too, as she bore the load into the kitchen. It was little Edna Gerritt, aged nine, whom Mary had known since her perambulator days.

'Am I hurted bad?' Edna asked, and died between Nurse Eden's dripping hands. The sheet fell aside and for an instant, before she could shut her eyes, Mary saw the ripped and shred-ded body.

'It's a wonder she spoke at all,' said Nurse Eden. 'What in God's name was it?'

'A bomb,' said Mary.

'One o' the Zeppelins?'

'No. An aeroplane. I thought I heard it on the Heath, but I fancied it was one of ours. It must have shut off its engines as it came down. That's why we didn't notice it.'

'The filthy pigs!' said Nurse Eden, all white and shaken. 'See the pickle I'm in! Go and tell Dr Hennis, Miss Postgate.' Nurse looked at the mother, who had dropped face down on the floor. 'She's only in a fit. Turn her over.'

Mary heaved Mrs Gerritt right side up, and hurried off for the doctor. When she told her tale, he asked her to sit down in the surgery till he got her something.

'But I don't need it, I assure you,' said she. 'I don't think it would be wise to tell Miss Fowler about it, do you? Her heart is so irritable in this weather.'

Dr Hennis looked at her admiringly as he packed up his bag.
'No. Don't tell anybody till we're sure,' he said, and
hastened to the 'Royal Oak', while Mary went on with the
paraffin. The village behind her was as quiet as usual, for the
news had not yet spread. She frowned a little to herself, her
large nostrils expanded uglily, and from time to time she mut-
tered a phrase which Wynn, who never restrained himself
before his women-folk, had applied to the enemy. 'Bloody
pagans! They *are* bloody pagans. But,' she continued, falling
back on the teaching that had made her what she was, 'one
mustn't let one's mind dwell on these things.'

Before she reached the house Dr Hennis, who was also a
special constable, overtook her in his car.

'Oh, Miss Postgate,' he said, 'I wanted to tell you that that
accident at the "Royal Oak" was due to Gerritt's stable tum-
bling down. It's been dangerous for a long time. It ought to
have been condemned.'

'I thought I heard an explosion too,' said Mary.

'You might have been misled by the beams snapping. I've
been looking at 'em. They were dry-rotted through and
through. Of course, as they broke, they would make a noise
just like a gun.'

'Yes?' said Mary politely.

'Poor little Edna was playing underneath it,' he went on, still
holding her with his eyes, 'and that and the tiles cut her to
pieces, you see?'

'I saw it,' said Mary, shaking her head. 'I heard it too.'

'Well, we cannot be sure.' Dr Hennis changed his tone com-
pletely. 'I know both you and Nurse Eden (I've been speaking
to her) are perfectly trustworthy, and I can rely on you not to
say anything—yet, at least. It is no good to stir up people
unless——'

'Oh, I never do—anyhow,' said Mary, and Dr Hennis went
on to the county town.

After all, she told herself, it might, just possibly, have been
the collapse of the old stable that had done all those things to
poor little Edna. She was sorry she had even hinted at other
things, but Nurse Eden was discretion itself. By the time she

reached home the affair seemed increasingly remote by its very monstrosity. As she came in, Miss Fowler told her that a couple of aeroplanes had passed half an hour ago.

'I thought I heard them,' she replied, 'I'm going down to the garden now. I've got the paraffin.'

'Yes, but—what *have* you got on your boots? They're soaking wet. Change them at once.'

Not only did Mary obey but she wrapped the boots in newspaper, and put them into the string bag with the bottle. So, armed with the longest kitchen poker, she left.

'It's raining again,' was Miss Fowler's last word, 'but—I know you won't be happy till that's disposed of.'

'It won't take long. I've got everything down there, and I've put the lid on the destructor to keep the wet out.'

The shrubbery was filling with twilight by the time she had completed her arrangements and sprinkled the sacrificial oil. As she lit the match that would burn her heart to ashes, she head a groan or a grunt behind the dense Portugal laurels.

'Cheape?' she called impatiently, but Cheape, with his ancient lumbago, in his comfortable cottage would be the last man to profane the sanctuary. 'Sheep,' she concluded, and threw in the match. The pyre went up in a roar, and the immediate flames hastened night around her.

'How Wynn would have loved this!' she thought, stepping back from the blaze.

By its light she saw, half hidden behind a laurel not five paces away, a bareheaded man sitting very stiffly at the foot of one of the oaks. A broken branch lay across his lap—one booted leg protruding from beneath it. His head moved ceaselessly from side to side, but his body was as still as the tree's trunk. He was dressed—she moved sideways to look more closely—in a uniform something like Wynn's, with a flap buttoned across the chest. For an instant, she had some idea that it might be one of the young flying men she had met at the funeral. But their heads were dark and glossy. This man's was as pale as a baby's, and so closely cropped that she could see the disgusting pinky skin beneath. His lips moved.

'What do you say?' Mary moved towards him and stooped.

'Laty! Laty! Laty!'* he muttered, while his hands picked at

the dead wet leaves. There was no doubt as to his nationality. It made her so angry that she strode back to the destructor, though it was still too hot to use the poker there. Wynn's books seemed to be catching well. She looked up at the oak behind the man; several of the light upper and two or three rotten lower branches had broken and scattered their rubbish on the shrubbery path. On the lowest fork a helmet, with dependent strings, showed like a bird's-nest in the light of a long-tongued flame. Evidently this person had fallen through the tree. Wynn had told her that it was quite possible for people to fall out of aeroplanes. Wynn told her, too, that trees were useful things to break an aviator's fall, but in this case the aviator must have been broken or he would have moved from his queer position. He seemed helpless except for his horrible rolling head. On the other hand, she could see a pistol-case at his belt—and Mary loathed pistols. Months ago, after reading certain Belgian reports together, she and Miss Fowler had had dealings with one—a huge revolver with flat-nosed bullets, which latter, Wynn said, were forbidden by the rules of war to be used against civilized enemies. 'They're good enough for us,' Miss Fowler had replied. 'Show Mary how it works.' And Wynn, laughing at the mere possibility of any such need, had led the craven winking Mary into the Rector's disused quarry, and had shown her how to fire the terrible machine. It lay now in the top left-hand drawer of her toilet-table—a memento not included in the burning. Wynn would be pleased to see how she was not afraid.

She slipped up to the house to get it. When she came through the rain, the eyes in the head were alive with expectation. The mouth even tried to smile. But at sight of the revolver its corners went down just like Edna Gerritt's. A tear trickled from one eye, and the head rolled from shoulder to shoulder as though trying to point out something.

'Cassée. Tout cassée,'* it whimpered.

'What do you say?' said Mary disgustedly, keeping well to one side, though only the head moved.

'Cassée,' it repeated. 'Che me rends. Le médecin!* Toctor!'

'Nein!' said she, bringing all her small German to bear with the big pistol. 'Ich haben der todt Kinder gesehn.'*

The head was still. Mary's hand dropped. She had been careful to keep her finger off the trigger for fear of accidents. After a few moments' waiting, she returned to the destructor, where the flames were falling, and churned up Wynn's charring books with the poker. Again the head groaned for the doctor.

'Stop that!' said Mary, and stamped her foot. 'Stop that, you bloody pagan!'

The words came quite smoothly and naturally. They were Wynn's own words, and Wynn was a gentleman who for no consideration on earth would have torn little Edna into those vividly coloured strips and strings. But this thing hunched under the oak-tree had done that thing. It was no question of reading horrors out of newspapers to Miss Fowler. Mary had seen it with her own eyes on the 'Royal Oak' kitchen table. She must not allow her mind to dwell upon it. Now Wynn was dead, and everything connected with him was lumping and rustling and tinkling under her busy poker into red-black dust and grey leaves of ash. The thing beneath the oak would die too. Mary had seen death more than once. She came of a family that had a knack of dying under, as she told Miss Fowler, 'most distressing circumstances'. She would stay where she was till she was entirely satisfied that It was dead—dead as dear papa in the late 'eighties; aunt Mary in 'eighty-nine; mamma in 'ninety-one; cousin Dick in 'ninety-five; Lady McCausland's housemaid in 'ninety-nine; Lady McCausland's sister in nineteen hundred and one; Wynn buried five days ago; and Edna Gerritt still waiting for decent earth to hide her. As she thought—her underlip caught up by one faded canine, brows knit and nostrils wide—she wielded the poker with lunges that jarred the grating at the bottom, and careful scrapes round the brick-work above. She looked at her wrist-watch. It was getting on to half-past four, and the rain was coming down in earnest. Tea would be at five. If It did not die before that time, she would be soaked and would have to change. Meantime, and this occupied her, Wynn's things were burning well in spite of the hissing wet, though now and again a book-back with a quite distinguishable title would be heaved up out of the mass. The exercise of stoking had given her a glow which seemed to reach to the marrow of her bones. She hummed—Mary never had a voice—to herself. She had never believed in all those advanced views—though Miss Fowler herself leaned a little that way—of woman's work in the world; but now she saw there was much to be said for them. This, for instance, was *her* work—work which no man, least of all Dr Hennis, would ever have done. A man, at such a crisis, would be what Wynn called a 'sportsman'; would leave everything to fetch help, and would certainly bring It into the house. Now a woman's business was to make a happy home for—for a husband and children. Failing these—it was not a thing one should allow one's mind to dwell upon—but——

'Stop it!' Mary cried once more across the shadows. 'Nein, I tell you! Ich haben der todt Kinder gesehn.'

But it was a fact. A woman who had missed these things could still be useful—more useful than a man in certain respects. She thumped like a pavior* through the settling ashes at the secret thrill of it. The rain was damping the fire, but she could feel—it was too dark to see—that her work was done. There was a dull red glow at the bottom of the destructor, not enough to char the wooden lid if she slipped it half over against the driving wet. This arranged, she leaned on the poker and waited, while an increasing rapture laid hold on her. She ceased to think. She gave herself up to feel. Her long pleasure was broken by a sound that she had waited for in agony several times in her life. She leaned forward and listened, smiling. There could be no mistake. She closed her eyes and drank it in. Once it ceased abruptly.

'Go on,' she murmured, half aloud. 'That isn't the end.'

Then the end came very distinctly in a lull between two raingusts. Mary Postgate drew her breath short between her teeth and shivered from head to foot. '*That*'s all right,' said she contentedly, and went up to the house, where she scandalized the whole routine by taking a luxurious hot bath before tea, and came down looking, as Miss Fowler said when she saw her lying all relaxed on the sofa, 'quite handsome!'

The Changelings

(R.N.V.R.)*

OR EVER the battered liners sank
    With their passengers to the dark,
I was head of a Walworth Bank,
    And you were a grocer's clerk.

I was a dealer in stocks and shares,
    And you in butters and teas;
And we both abandoned our own affairs
    And took to the dreadful seas.

Wet and worry about our ways—
    Panic, onset, and flight—
Had us in charge for a thousand days
    And a thousand-year-long night.

We saw more than the nights could hide—
    More than the waves could keep—
And—certain faces over the side
    Which do not go from our sleep.

We were more tired than words can tell
    While the pied craft fled by,
And the swinging mounds of the Western swell
    Hoisted us heavens-high . . .

Now there is nothing—not even our rank—
    To witness what we have been;
And I am returned to my Walworth Bank,
    And you to your margarine!

Sea Constables*

A TALE OF '15

THE head-waiter of the Carvoitz* almost ran to meet Portson and his guests as they came up the steps from the palm-court where the string band plays.

'Not seen you since—oh, ever so long,' he began. 'So glad to get your wire. Quite well—eh?'

'Fair to middling, Henri.' Portson shook hands with him. 'You're looking all right, too. Have you got us our table?'

Henri nodded toward a pink alcove, kept for mixed doubles, which discreetly commanded the main dining-room's glitter and blaze.

'Good man!' said Portson. 'Now, this is serious, Henri. We put ourselves unreservedly in your hands. We're weather-beaten mariners—though we don't look it—and haven't eaten a Christian meal in months. Have you thought of all that, Henri, *mon ami*?'

'The menu, I have compose it myself,' Henri answered with the gravity of a high priest.

It was more than a year since Portson—of Portson, Peake and Ensell, Stock and Share Brokers—had drawn Henri's attention to an apparently extinct Oil Company, which, a little later, erupted profitably; and it may be that Henri prided himself on paying all debts in full.

The most recent foreign millionaire and the even more recent foreign actress at a table near the entrance clamoured for his attention while he convoyed the party to the pink alcove. With his own hands he turned out some befrilled electrics and lit four pale rose-candles.

'Bridal!' some one murmured. 'Quite bridal!'

'So glad you like. There is nothing too good.' Henri slid away, and the four men sat down. They had coarse-grained complexions as of men who habitually did themselves well, and an air, too, of recent, red-eyed dissipation. Maddingham, the eldest, was a thick-set, middle-aged presence, with crisped grizzled hair, of the type that one associates with Board Meetings. He limped slightly. Tegg, who followed him, blinking, was neat, small, and sandy, of unmistakable Navy cut, but sheepish aspect. Winchmore, the youngest, was more on the lines of the conventional pre-war 'nut',* but his eyes were sunk in his head and his hands black-nailed and roughened. Portson, their host, with Vandyke beard and a comfortable little stomach, beamed upon them as they settled to their oysters.

'*That*'s what I mean,' said the carrying voice of the foreign actress, whom Henri had just disabused of the idea that she had been promised the pink alcove. 'They ain't *alive* to the War yet. Now, what's the matter with those four dubs* yonder joining the British Army or—or *doing* something?'

'Who's your friend?' Maddingham asked.

'I've forgotten her name for the minute,' Portson replied, 'but she's the latest thing in imported patriotic piece-goods. She sings "Sons of the Empire, Go Forward!" at the Palemseum.* It makes the aunties weep.'

'That's Sidney Latter. She's not half bad.' Tegg reached for the vinegar. 'We ought to see her some night.'

'Yes. We've a lot of time for that sort of thing,' Maddingham grunted. 'I'll take your oysters, Portson, if you don't want 'em.'

'Cheer up, Papa Maddingham! Soon be dead!' Winchmore suggested.

Maddingham glared at him. 'If I'd had you with me for *one* week, Master Winchmore——'

'Not the least use,' the boy retorted. 'I've just been made a full-Lootenant. I have indeed. I couldn't reconcile it with my conscience to take *Etheldreda* out any more as a plain sub. She's too flat in the floor.'

'Did you get those new washboards of yours fixed?' Tegg cut in.

'Don't talk shop already,' Portson protested. 'This is Vesiga soup. I don't know what he's arranged in the way of drinks.'

'Pol Roger '04,' said the waiter.

'Sound man, Henri,' said Winchmore. 'But—' he eyed the

waiter doubtfully, 'I don't quite like . . . What's your alleged nationality?'

'Henri's nephew, monsieur,' the smiling waiter replied, and laid a gloved hand on the table. It creaked corkily at the wrist. 'Bethisy-sur-Oise,' he explained. 'My uncle he buy me *all* the hand for Christmas. It is good to hold plates only.'

'Oh! Sorry I spoke,' said Winchmore.

'Monsieur is right. But my uncle is very careful, even with neutrals.' He poured the champagne.

'Hold a minute,' Maddingham cried. 'First toast of obligation: For what we are going to receive, thank God and the British Navy.'

'Amen!' said the others with a nod toward Lieutenant Tegg, of the Royal Navy afloat, and, occasionally, of the Admiralty ashore.

'Next! "Damnation to all neutrals!" ' Maddingham went on.

'Amen! Amen!' they answered between gulps that heralded the sole Colbert. Maddingham picked up the menu. 'Suprême of chicken,' he read loudly. 'Filet Béarnaise, Woodcock and Richebourg '74, Pêches Melba, Croûtes Baron. I couldn't have improved on it myself; though one might,' he went on—'one *might* have substituted quail *en casserole* for the woodcock.'

'Then there would have been no reason for the Burgundy,' said Tegg with equal gravity.

'You're right,' Maddingham replied.

The foreign actress shrugged her shoulders. 'What *can* you do with people like that?' she said to her companion. 'And yet *I*'ve been singing to 'em for a fortnight.'

'I left it all to Henri,' said Portson.

'My Gord!' the eavesdropping woman whispered. 'Get on to that! Ain't it typical? They leave everything to Henri in this country.'

'By the way,' Tegg asked Winchmore after the fish, 'where did you mount that one-pounder of yours after all?'

'Midships. *Etheldreda* won't carry more weight forward. She's wet enough as it is.'

'Why don't you apply for another craft?' Portson put in. 'There's a chap at Southampton just now, down with pneumonia and——'

'No, thank you. I know *Etheldreda*. She's nothing to write home about, but when she feels well she can shift a bit.'

Maddingham leaned across the table. 'If she does more than eleven in a flat calm,' said he, 'I'll—I'll give you *Hilarity*.'

'Wouldn't be found dead in *Hilarity*,' was Winchmore's grateful reply. 'You don't mean to say you've taken her into real wet water, Papa? Where did it happen?'

The others laughed. Maddingham's red face turned brick colour, and the veins on the cheek-bones showed blue through a blur of short bristles.

'He's been convoying neutrals—in a tactful manner,' Tegg chuckled.

Maddingham filled his glass and scowled at Tegg. 'Yes,' he said, 'and here's special damnation to me Lords of the Admiralty. A more muddle-headed set of brass-bound apes——'

'My! My! My!' Winchmore chirruped soothingly. 'It don't seem to have done you any good, Papa. Who were you conveyancing?'

Maddingham snapped out a ship's name and some details of her build.

'Oh, but that chap's a friend of *mine*!' cried Winchmore. 'I ran across him—the—not so long ago, hugging the Scotch coast—out of his course, he said, owing to foul weather and a new type of engine—a Diesel. That's him, ain't it?—the complete neutral!' He mentioned an outstanding peculiarity of the ship's rig.

'Yes,' said Portson. 'Did you board him, Winchmore?'

'No. There'd been a bit of a blow the day before and old *Ethel*'s only dinghy had dropped off the hooks. But he signalled me all his symptoms. He was as communicative as—as a lady in the Promenade.* (Hold on, Nephew of my Uncle! I'm going to have some more of that Béarnaise fillet.) His smell* attracted me. I chaperoned him for a couple of days.'

'Only two days. *You* hadn't anything to complain of,' said Maddingham wrathfully.

'I didn't complain. If he chose to hug things, 'twasn't any of my business. I'm not a Purity League. Didn't care what he hugged, so long as I could lie behind him and give him first chop at any mines that were going. I steered in his wake (I really *can* steer a bit now, Portson) and let him stink up the whole of the North Sea. I thought he might come in useful for bait. No Burgundy, thanks, Nephew of my Uncle. I'm sticking to the Jolly Roger.'

'Go on, then—before you're speechless. Was he any use as bait?' Tegg demanded.

'We never got a fair chance. As I told you, he hugged the coast till dark, and then he scraped round Gilarra Head and went up the bay nearly to the beach.'

'Lights out?' Maddingham asked.

Winchmore nodded. 'But I didn't worry about that. I was under his stern. As luck 'ud have it, there was a fishing-party in the bay, and we walked slam into the middle of 'em—a most ungodly collection of local talent. First thing I knew a steam-launch fell aboard us, and a boy—a nasty little Navy boy, Tegg,—wanted to know what I was doing. I told him, and he cursed me for putting the fish down just as they were rising. Then the two of us (he was hanging on to my quarter with a boat-hook) drifted on to a steam trawler and our friend the Neutral and a ten-oared cutter full of the military, all mixed up. They were subs from the garrison out for a lark. Uncle Newt explained over the rail about the weather and his engine-troubles, but they were all so keen to carry on with their fishing, they didn't fuss. They told him to clear off.'

'Was there anything on the move round Gilarra at that time?' Tegg inquired.

'Oh, they spun me the usual yarns about the water being thick with 'em,* and asked me to help. But I couldn't stop. The cutter's stern-sheets were piled up with mines, like lobster-pots, and from the way the soldiers handled 'em *I* thought I'd better get out. So did Uncle Newt. *He* didn't like it a bit. There were a couple of shots fired at something just as we cleared the Head, and one dropped rather close to him. (These duck-shoots in the dark are dam' dangerous, y'know.) He lit up at once—tail-light, head-light, and side-lights. I had no more trouble with him the rest of the night.'

'But what about the report that you sawed off the steam-launch's boat-hook?' Tegg demanded suddenly.

'What! You don't mean to say that little beast of a snotty reported it? He was scratchin' poor old *Ethel*'s paint to pieces. I never reported what he said to *me*. And he called me a damned amateur, too! Well! Well! War's war. I missed all that fishing-party that time. My orders were to follow Uncle Newt. So I followed—and poor *Ethel* without a dry rag on her.'

Winchmore refilled his glass.

'Well, don't get poetical,' said Portson. 'Let's have the rest of your trip.'

'There wasn't any rest,' Winchmore insisted pathetically. 'There was just good old *Ethel* with her engines missing like sin, and Uncle Newt thumping and stinking half a mile ahead of us, and me eating bread and Worcester sauce. I do when I feel that way. Besides, I wanted to go back and join the fishing-party. Just before dark I made out *Cordelia*—that South-ampton ketch that old Jarrott fitted with oil auxiliaries for a family cruiser last summer. She's a beamy bus, but she *can* roll, and she was doing an honest thirty degrees each way when I overhauled her. I asked Jarrott if he was busy. He said he wasn't. But he was. He's like me and Nelson* when there's any sea on.'

'But Jarrott's a Quaker. Has been for generations. Why does he go to war?' said Maddingham.

'If it comes to that,' Portson said, 'why do any of us?'

'Jarrott's a mine-sweeper,' Winchmore replied with deep feeling. 'The Quaker religion (I'm not a Quaker, but I'm *much* more religious than any of you chaps give me credit for) has decided that mine-sweeping is life-saving. Consequently'—he dwelt a little on the word—'the profession is crowded with Quakers—specially off Scarborough. See? Owin' to the purity of their lives, they "*all* go to Heaven when they die—Roll, Jordan, Roll!"'

'Disgustin',' said the actress audibly as she drew on her gloves. Winchmore looked at her with delight. 'That's a peach-Melba, too,' he said.

'And David Jarrott's a mine-sweeper,' Maddingham mused aloud. 'So you turned our Neutral over to him, Winchmore, did you?'

'Yes, I did. It was the end of my beat—I wish I didn't feel so sleepy—and I explained the whole situation to Jarrott, over the rail. Gave him all my silly instructions—those latest ones, y'know. I told him to do nothing to imperil existing political relations. I told him to exercise tact. I—I told him that in my capac'ty as Actin' Lootenant, you see. Jarrott's only a Lootenant-Commander—at fifty-four, too! Yes, I handed my Uncle Newt over to Jarrott to chaperone, and I went back to my—I can say it perfectly—pis-ca-to-rial party in the bay. Now I'm going to have a nap. In ten minutes I shall be on deck again. This is my first civilized dinner in nine weeks, so I don't apologize.'

He pushed his plate away, dropped his chin on his palm and closed his eyes.

'Lyndnoch and Jarrott's Bank, established 1793,' said Maddingham half to himself. 'I've seen old Jarrott in Cowes week bullied by his skipper and steward till he had to sneak ashore to sleep. And now he's out mine-sweeping with *Cordelia*! What's happened to his—I shall forget my own name next—Belfast-built two-hundred-tonner?'

'*Goneril*,' said Portson. 'He turned her over to the Service in October. She's—she was *Culana*.'

'*She* was *Culana*, was she? My God! I never knew that. Where did it happen?'

'Off the same old Irish corner I was watching last month. My young cousin was in her; so was one of the Raikes boys. A whole nest of mines, laid between patrols.'

'I've heard there's some dirty work going on there now,' Maddingham half whispered.

'You needn't tell *me* that,' Portson returned. 'But one gets a little back now and again.'

'What are you two talking about?' said Tegg, who seemed to be dozing too.

'*Culana*,' Portson answered as he lit a cigarette.

'Yes, that was rather a pity. But . . . What about this Newt of ours?'

'*I* took her over from Jarrott next day—off Margate,' said Portson. 'Jarrott wanted to get back to his mine-sweeping.'

'Every man to his taste,' said Maddingham. 'That never appealed to me. Had they detailed you specially to look after the Newt?'

'Me among others,' Portson admitted. 'I was going down Channel when I got my orders, and so I went on with him. Jarrott had been tremendously interested in his course up to date—specially off the Wash. He'd charted it very carefully and he said he was going back to find out what some of the kinks and curves meant. Has he found out, Tegg?'

Tegg thought for a moment. 'Cordelia was all right up to six o'clock yesterday evening,' he said.

'Glad of that. Then I did what Winchmore did. I lay behind this stout fellow and saw him well into the open.'

'Did you say anything to him?' Tegg asked.

'Not a thing. He kept moving all the time.'

'See anything?' Tegg continued.

'No. He didn't seem to be in demand anywhere in the Channel, and, when I'd got him on the edge of soundings, I dropped him—as per your esteemed orders.'

Tegg nodded again and murmured some apology.

'Where did you pick him up, Maddingham?' Portson went on.

Maddingham snorted.

'Well north and west of where you left him heading up the Irish Channel and stinking like a taxi. I hadn't had my breakfast. My cook was seasick; so were four of my hands.'

'I can see that meeting. Did you give him a gun across the bows?' Tegg asked.

'No, no. Not that time. I signalled him to heave to. He had his papers ready before I came over the side. You see,' Maddingham said pleadingly, 'I'm new to this business. Perhaps I wasn't as polite to him as I should have been if I'd had my breakfast.'

'He deposed that Maddingham came alongside swearing like a bargee,' said Tegg.

'Not in the least. This is what happened.' Maddingham turned to Portson. 'I asked him where he was bound for and he told me—Antigua.'

'Hi! Wake up, Winchmore. You're missing something.'

Portson nudged Winchmore, who was slanting sideways in his chair.

'Right! All right! I'm awake,' said Winchmore stickily. 'I heard every word.'

Maddingham went on. 'I told him that this wasn't his way to Antigua——'

'Antigua. Antigua!' Winchmore finished rubbing his eyes. ' "There was a young bride of Antigua——" '

'Hsh! Hsh!' said Portson and Tegg warningly.

'Why? It's the proper one. "Who said to her spouse, 'What a pig you are!' " '

'Ass!' Maddingham growled and continued: 'He told me that he'd been knocked out of his reckoning by foul weather and engine-trouble, owing to experimenting with a new type of Diesel engine. He was perfectly frank about it.'

'So he was with me,' said Winchmore. 'Just like a real lady. I hope you were a real gentleman, Papa.'

'I asked him what he'd got. He didn't object. He had some fifty thousand gallon of oil for his new Diesel engine, and the rest was coal. He said he needed the oil to get to Antigua with; he was taking the coal as ballast; and he was coming back, so he told me, with coconuts. When he'd quite finished, I said: "What sort of damned idiot do you take me for?" He said: "I haven't decided yet!" Then I said he'd better come into port with me, and we'd arrive at a decision. He said that his papers were in perfect order and that my instructions—mine, please!—were not to imperil political relations. I hadn't received these asinine instructions, so I took the liberty of contradicting him—perfectly politely, as I told them at the Inquiry afterward. He was a small-boned man with a grey beard, in a glengarry, and he picked his teeth a lot. He said: "The last time I met you, Mister Maddingham, you were going to Carlsbad, and you told me all about your blood-pressures in the *wagon-lit** before we tossed for upper berth. Don't you think you are a little old to buccaneer about the sea this way?" I couldn't recall his face—he must have been some fellow that I'd travelled with some time or other. I told him I wasn't doing this for amusement—it was business. Then I ordered him into port. He said: "S'pose I don't go?" I said: "Then I'll sink you." Isn't it extraordinary how natural it all seems after a few weeks? If any one had told me when I commissioned *Hilarity* last summer what I'd be doing this spring I'd—I'd . . . God! It *is* mad, isn't it?'

'Quite,' said Portson. 'But not bad fun.'

'Not at all, but that's what makes it all the madder. Well, he didn't argue any more. He warned me I'd be hauled over the coals for what I'd done, and I warned him to keep two cables ahead of me and not to yaw.'*

'Jaw?' said Winchmore sleepily.

'No. Yaw,' Maddingham snarled. 'Not to look as if he even wanted to yaw. I warned him that, if he did, I'd loose off into him, end-on. But I was absolutely polite about it. Give you my word, Tegg.'

'I believe you. Oh, I believe you,' Tegg replied.

'Well, so I took him into port—and that was where I first ran across our Master Tegg. He represented the Admiralty on that beach.'

The small blinking man nodded. 'The Admiralty had that honour,' he said graciously.

Maddingham turned to the others angrily. 'I'd been rather patting myself on the back for what I'd done, you know. Instead of which, they held a court-martial——'

'*We* called it an Inquiry,' Tegg interjected.

'*You* weren't in the dock. They held a court-martial on me to find out how often I'd sworn at the poor injured Neutral, and whether I'd given him hot-water bottles and tucked him up at night. It's all very fine to laugh, but they treated me like a pickpocket. There were two fat-headed civilian judges and that blackguard Tegg in the conspiracy. A cursed lawyer defended my Neutral and he made fun of *me*. He dragged in everything the Neutral had told him about my blood-pressures on the Carlsbad trip. And that's what you get for trying to serve your country in your old age!' Maddingham emptied and refilled his glass.

'We *did* give you rather a grilling,' said Tegg placidly. 'It's our national sense of fair play.'

'I could have stood it all if it hadn't been for the Neutral. We dined at the same hotel while this court-martial was going on, and he used to come over to my table and sympathize with me!

He told me that I was fighting for his ideals and the uplift of democracy, but I must respect the Law of Nations!'

'And we respected 'em,' said Tegg. 'His papers were perfectly correct; the Court discharged him. We had to consider existing political relations. I *told* Maddingham so at the hotel and he——'

Again Maddingham turned to the others. 'I couldn't make up my mind about Tegg at the Inquiry,' he explained. 'He had the air of a decent sailor-man, but he talked like a poisonous politician.'

'I was,' Tegg returned. 'I had been ordered to change into that rig. So I changed.'

Maddingham ran one fat square hand through his crisped hair and looked up under his eyebrows like a shy child, while the others lay back and laughed.

'I suppose I ought to have been on to the joke,' he stammered, 'but I'd blacked myself all over* for the part of Lootenant-Commander R.N.V.R. in time of war, and I'd given up thinking as a banker. If it had been put before me as a business proposition I might have done better.'

'I thought you were playing up to me and the judges all the time,' said Tegg. 'I never dreamed you took it seriously.'

'Well, I've been trained to look on the law as serious. I've had to pay for some of it in my time, you know.'

'I'm sorry,' said Tegg. 'We were obliged to let that oily beggar go—for reasons. But, as I told Maddingham, the night the award was given, *his* duty was to see that he was properly directed to Antigua.'

'Naturally,' Portson observed. 'That being the Neutral's declared destination. And what did Maddingham do? Shut up, Maddingham!'

Said Tegg, with downcast eyes: 'Maddingham took my hand and squeezed it. He looked lovingly into my eyes (he *did*!). He turned plum-colour, and he said: "I will"—just like a bridegroom at the altar. It makes me feel shy to think of it even now. I didn't see him after that till the evening when *Hilarity* was pulling out of the Basin, and Maddingham was cursing the tug-master.'

'I was in a hurry,' said Maddingham. 'I wanted to get to the

Narrows and wait for my Neutral there. I dropped down to Biller and Grove's yard that tide (they've done all my work for years) and I jammed *Hilarity* into the creek behind their slip, so the Newt didn't spot me when he came down the river. Then I pulled out and followed him over the Bar. He stood nor'-west at once. I let him go till we were well out of sight of land. Then I overhauled him, gave him a gun across the bows and ran alongside. I'd just had my lunch, and I wasn't going to lose my temper *this* time. I said: "Excuse me, but I understand you are bound for Antigua?" He was, he said; and as he seemed a little nervous about my falling aboard him in that swell, I gave *Hilarity* another sheer in—she's as handy as a launch—and I said: "May I suggest that this is not the course for Antigua?" By that time he had his fenders overside, and all hands yelling at me to keep away. I snatched *Hilarity* out and began edging in again. He said: "I'm trying a sample of inferior oil that I have my doubts about. If it works all right I shall lay my course for Antigua, but it will take some time to test the stuff and adjust the engines to it." I said: "Very good, let me know if I can be of any service," and I offered him *Hilarity* again once or twice— he didn't want her—and then I dropped behind and let him go on. Wasn't that proper, Portson?'

Portson nodded. 'I know that game of yours with *Hilarity*,' he said. 'How the deuce do you do it? My nerve always goes at close quarters in any sea.'

'It's only a little trick of steering,' Maddingham replied with a simper of vanity. 'You can almost shave with her when she feels like it. I had to do it again that same evening, to establish a moral ascendancy. He wasn't showing any lights, and I nearly tripped over him. He was a scared Neutral for three minutes, but I got a little of my own back for that damned court-martial. *But* I was perfectly polite. I apologized profusely. I didn't even ask him to show his lights.'

'But did he?' said Winchmore.

'He did—every one; and a flare now and then,' Maddingham replied. 'He held north all that night, with a falling barometer and a rising wind and all the other filthy things. Gad, how I hated him! Next morning we got it, good and tight from the nor'-nor'-west out of the Atlantic, off Carso Head. He dodged into a squall, and then he went about. We weren't a mile behind, but it was as thick as a wall. When it cleared, and I couldn't see him ahead of me, I went about too, and followed the rain. I picked him up five miles down wind, legging it for all he was worth to the south'ard—nine knots, I should think. *Hilarity* doesn't like a following sea. We got pooped* a bit, too, but by noon we'd struggled back to where we ought to have been—two cables astern of him. Then he began to signal, but his flags being end-on to us, of course, we had to creep up on his beam—well abeam—to read 'em. *That* didn't restore his morale either. He made out he'd been compelled to put back by stress of weather before completing his oil tests. I made back I was sorry to hear it, but would be greatly interested in the results. Then I turned in (I'd been up all night) and my Lootenant took on. He was a widower (by the way) of the name of Sherrin, aged forty-seven. He'd run a girls school at Weston-super-Mare after he'd left the Service in 'Ninety-five, and he believed the English were the Lost Tribes.'

'What about the Germans?' said Portson.

'Oh, they'd been misled by Austria, who was the Beast with Horns* in Revelations. Otherwise he was rather a dull dog. He set the tops'ls in his watch. *Hilarity* won't steer under any canvas, so we rather sported round our friend that afternoon, I believe. When I came up after dinner, she was biting his behind, first one side, then the other. Let's see—that would be about thirty miles east-sou'-east of Harry Island. We were running as near as nothing south. The wind had dropped, and there was a useful cross-rip coming up from the south-east. I took the wheel and, the way I nursed him from starboard, he had to take the sea over his port bow. I had my sciatica on me— buccaneering's no game for a middle-aged man—but I gave that fellow sprudel!* By Jove; I washed him out! He stood it as long as he could, and then he made a bolt for Harry Island. I had to ride in his pocket most of the way there because I didn't know that coast. We had charts, but Sherrin never understood 'em, and I couldn't leave the wheel. So we rubbed along together, and about midnight this Newt dodged in over the tail of Harry Shoals and anchored, if you please, in the lee of the Double Ricks. It was dead calm there, except for the swell, but there wasn't much room to manœuvre in, and *I* wasn't going to anchor. It looked too like a submarine rendezvous. But first, I came alongside and asked him what his trouble was. He told me he had overheated his something-or-other bulb. I've never been shipmates with Diesel engines, but I took his word for it, and I said I'd stand by till it cooled. Then he told me to go to Hell.'

'If you were inside the Double Ricks in the dark, you were practically there,' said Portson.

'That's what *I* thought. I was on the bridge, rabid with sciatica, going round and round like a circus-horse in about three acres of water, and wondering when I'd hit something. Ridiculous position. Sherrin saw it. He saved me. He said it was an ideal place for submarine attacks, and we'd better begin to repel 'em at once. As I said, I couldn't leave the wheel, so Sherrin fought the ship—both quick-firers and the maxims. He tipped 'em well down into the sea or well up at the Ricks as we went round and round. We made rather a row. And the row the gulls made when we woke 'em was absolutely terrifying. Give you my word!'

'And then?' said Winchmore.

'I kept on running in circles through this ghastly din. I took one sheer over toward his stern—I thought I'd cut it too fine, but we missed it by inches. Then I heard his capstan busy, and in another three minutes his anchor was up. He didn't wait to stow. He hustled out as he was—bulb or no bulb. He passed within ten feet of us (I was waiting to fall in behind him) and he shouted over the rail: "You think you've got patriotism. All you've got is uric acid and rotten spite!" I expect he was a little bored. I waited till we had cleared Harry Shoals before I went below, and then I slept till 9 A.M. He was heading north this time, and after I'd had breakfast and a smoke I ran alongside and asked him where he was bound for now. He was wrapped in a comforter, evidently suffering from a bad cold. I couldn't quite catch what he said, but I let him croak for a few minutes and fell back. At 9 P.M. he turned round and headed south (I was getting to know the Irish Channel by then) and I followed.

There was no particular sea on. It was a little chilly, but as he didn't hug the coast I hadn't to take the wheel. I stayed below most of the night and let Sherrin suffer. Well, Mr Newt kept up this game all the next day, dodging up and down the Irish Channel. And it was infernally dull. He threw up the sponge off Cloone Harbour. That was on Friday morning. He signalled: "Developed defects in engine-room. Antigua trip abandoned." Then he ran into Cloone and tied up at Brady's Wharf. You know you can't repair a dinghy at Cloone! I followed, of course, and berthed behind him. After lunch I thought I'd pay him a call. I wanted to look at his engines. I don't understand Diesels, but Hyslop, my engineer, said they must have gone round 'em with a hammer, for they were pretty badly smashed up. Besides that, they had offered all their oil to the Admiralty agent there, and it was being shifted to a tug when I went aboard him. So I'd done my job. I was just going back to *Hilarity* when his steward said he'd like to see me. He was lying in his cabin breathing pretty loud—wrapped up in rugs and his eyes sticking out like rabbit's. He offered me drinks. I couldn't accept 'em, of course. Then he said: "Well, Mr Maddingham, I'm all in." I said I was glad to hear it. Then he told me he was seriously ill with a sudden attack of bronchial pneumonia, and he asked me to run him across to England to see his doctor in Town. I said, of course, that was out of the question, *Hilarity* being a man-of-war in commission. He couldn't see it. He asked what had that to do with it? He thought this War was some sort of joke, and I had to repeat it all over again. He seemed rather afraid of dying (it's no game for a middle-aged man, of course) and he hoisted himself up on one elbow and began calling me a murderer. I explained to him—perfectly politely—that I wasn't in this job for fun. It was business. My orders were to see that he went to Antigua and now that he wasn't going to Antigua, and had sold his oil to us, that finished it as far as I was concerned. (Wasn't that perfectly correct?) He said: "But that finishes me, too. I can't get any doctor in this God-forsaken hole. I made sure you'd treat me properly as soon as I surrendered." I said there wasn't any question of surrender. If he'd been a wounded belligerent, I might have taken him aboard, though I certainly shouldn't have gone a yard out of my course to land him anywhere; but as it was, he was a neutral—altogether outside the game. You see my point? I tried awfully hard to make him understand it. He went on about his affairs all being at loose ends. He was a rich man—a million and a quarter, he said—and he wanted to redraft his will before he died. I told him a good many people were in his position just now—only they weren't rich. He changed his tack then and appealed to me on the grounds of our common humanity. "Why, if you leave me now, Mr Maddingham," he said, "you condemn me to death, just as surely as if you hanged me."'

'This *is* interesting,' Portson murmured. 'I never imagined you in this light before, Maddingham.'

'I was surprised at myself—give you my word. But I was perfectly polite. I said to him: "Try to be reasonable, sir. If you had got rid of your oil where it was wanted, you'd have condemned lots of people to death just as surely as if you'd drowned 'em." "Ah, but I didn't," he said. "That ought to count in my favour." "That was no thanks to you," I said. "You weren't given the chance. This is war, sir. If you make up your mind to that, you'll see that the rest follows." "I didn't imagine you'd take it as seriously as all that," he said—and he said it quite seriously, too. "Show a little consideration. Your side's bound to win anyway." I said: "Look here! I'm a middle-aged man, and I don't suppose my conscience is any clearer than yours in many respects, but this is business. I can do nothing for you."'

'You got that a bit mixed, I think,' said Tegg critically.

'*He* saw what I was driving at,' Maddingham replied, 'and he was the only one that mattered for the moment. "Then I'm a dead man, Mr Maddingham," he said. "That's *your* business," I said. "Good afternoon." And I went out.'

'And?' said Winchmore, after some silence.

'He died. I saw his flag half-masted next morning.'

There was another silence. Henri looked in at the alcove and smiled. Maddingham beckoned to him.

'But why didn't you lend him a hand to settle his private affairs?' said Portson.

'Because I wasn't acting in my private capacity. I'd been on the bridge for three nights and——' Maddingham pulled out his watch—'this time to-morrow I shall be there again—confound it! Has my car come, Henri?'

'Yes, Sare Francis. I am sorry.' They all complimented Henri on the dinner, and when the compliments were paid he expressed himself still their debtor. So did the nephew.

'Are you coming with me, Portson?' said Maddingham as he rose heavily.

'No. I'm for Southampton, worse luck! My car ought to be here, too.'

'I'm for Euston and the frigid calculating North,' said Winchmore with a shudder. 'One common taxi, please, Henri.'

Tegg smiled. 'I'm supposed to sleep in just now, but if you don't mind, I'd like to come with you as far as Gravesend, Maddingham.'

'Delighted. There's a glass all round left still,' said Maddingham. 'Here's luck! The usual, I suppose? "Damnation to all neutrals!"'

The Vineyard*

At the eleventh hour he came,
But his wages were the same
As ours who all day long had trod
The wine-press of the Wrath of God.*

When he shouldered through the lines
Of our cropped and mangled vines,
His unjaded eye could scan
How each hour had marked its man.

(Children of the morning-tide
With the hosts of noon had died;
And our noon contingents lay
Dead with twilight's spent array.)

Since his back had felt no load,
Virtue still in him abode;
So he swiftly made his own
Those last spoils we had not won.

We went home, delivered thence,
Grudging him no recompense
Till he portioned praise or blame
To our works before he came.

Till he showed us for our good—
    Deaf to mirth, and blind to scorn—
How we might have best withstood
    Burdens that he had not borne!

Introduction to *The Irish Guards in The Great War**

These volumes try to give soberly and with what truth is possible, the experiences of both Battalions of the Irish Guards from 1914 to 1918. The point of view is the Battalions', and the facts mainly follow the Regimental Diaries, supplemented by the few private letters and documents which such a war made possible, and by some tales that have gathered round men and their actions.

As evidence is released, historians may be able to reconstruct what happened in or behind the battle-line; what motives and necessities swayed the actors; and who stood up or failed under his burden. But a battalion's field is bounded by its own vision. Even within these limits, there is large room for error. Witnesses to phases of fights die and are dispersed; the ground over which they fought is battered out of recognition in a few hours; survivors confuse dates, places and personalities, and in the trenches, the monotony of the waiting days and the repetition-work of repairs breed mistakes and false judgements. Men grow doubtful or oversure, and, in all good faith, give directly opposed versions. The clear sight of a comrade so mangled that he seems to have been long dead is burnt in on one brain to the exclusion of all else that happened that day. The shock of an exploded dump, shaking down a firmament upon the land-scape, dislocates memory throughout half a battalion; and so on in all matters till the end of laborious enquiry is too often the opening of fresh confusion. When to this are added the personal prejudices and misunderstandings of men under heavy strain, carrying clouded memories of orders half given or half heard, amid scenes that pass like nightmares, the only wonder to the compiler of these records has been that any sure fact whatever should be retrieved out of the whirlpools of war.

It seemed to him best, then, to abandon all idea of such

broad and balanced narratives as will be put forward by
experts, and to limit himself to matters which directly touched
the men's lives and fortunes. Nor has he been too careful to
correct the inferences of the time by the knowledge of later
events. From first to last, the Irish Guards, like the rest of our
Armies, knew little of what was going on round them. Prob-
ably they knew less at the close of the War than at the begin-
ning when our forces were so small that each man felt himself
somebody indeed, and so stood to be hunted through the heat
from Mons to Meaux, turned again to suffer beneath the
Soupir ridges, and endured the first hideous winter of The
Salient* where, wet, almost weaponless, but unbroken, he
helped in the long miracle of holding the line.

But the men of '14 and '15, and what meagre records of their
day were safe to keep, have long been lost; while the crowded
years between remove their battles across dead Belgian towns
and villages as far from us as the fights in Homer.

Doubtless, all will be reconstructed to the satisfaction of
future years when, if there be memory beyond the grave, the
ghosts may laugh at the neatly groomed histories. Meantime,
we can take it for granted that the old Regular Army of Eng-
land passed away in the mud of Flanders in less than a year. In
training, morale, endurance, courage and devotion the Earth
did not hold its like, but it possessed neither the numbers,
guns, nor equipment necessary for the type of war that over-
took it. The fact of its unpreparedness has been extolled as
proof of the purity of its country's ideals, which must be great
consolation to all concerned. But, how slowly that equipment
was furnished, how inadequate were our first attempts at
bombs, trench-mortars, duck-boards, wiring and the rest, may
be divined through the loyal and guarded allusions in the
Diaries. Nor do private communications give much hint of it,
for one of the marvels of that marvellous time was the silence of
those concerned on everything that might too much distress
their friends at home. The censorship had imposed this as a
matter of precaution, but only the spirit of the officers could
have backed the law so completely; and, as better days came,
their early makeshifts and contrivances passed out of remem-
brance with their early dead. But the sufferings of our Armies

were constant. They included wet and cold in due season, dirt always, occasional vermin, exposure, extreme fatigue, and the hourly incidence of death in every shape along the front line and, later, in the farthest back-areas where the enemy aeroplanes harried their camps. And when our Regular troops had been expended, these experiences were imposed upon officers and men compelled to cover, within a few months, the long years of training that should go to the making of a soldier —men unbroken even to the disturbing impact of crowds and like experiences, which the conscript accepts from his youth. Their short home-leaves gave them sudden changes to the tense home atmosphere where, under cover of a whirl of 'entertainment', they and their kin wearied themselves to forget and escape a little from that life, on the brink of the next world, whose guns they could hear summoning in the silences between their talk. Yet, some were glad to return—else why should youngsters of three years' experience have found themselves upon a frosty night, on an iron-bound French road, shouting aloud for joy as they heard the stammer of a machine-gun over the rise, and turned up the well-known trench that led to their own dug-out and their brethren from whom they had been separated by the vast interval of ninety-six hours? Many have confessed to the same delight in their work, as there were others to whom almost every hour was frankly detestable except for the companionship that revealed them one to another till the chances of war separated the companions. And there were, too, many, almost children, of whom no record remains. They came out from Warley with the constantly renewed drafts, lived the span of a Second Lieutenant's life and were spent.* Their intimates might preserve, perhaps, memories of a promise cut short, recollections of a phrase that stuck, a chance-seen act of bravery or of kindness. The Diaries give their names and fates with the conventional expressions of regret. In most instances, the compiler has let the mere fact suffice; since, to his mind, it did not seem fit to heap words on the doom.

For the same reason, he has not dealt with each instance of valour, leaving it to stand in the official language in which it was acknowledged. The rewards represent but a very small proportion of the skill, daring and heroism actually noted; for no volume could hold the full tale of all that was done, either in the way of duty, under constraint of necessity and desire to keep alive, or through joy and pleasure in achieving great deeds.

Here the Irish rank and file by temperament excelled. They had all their race's delight in the drama of things; and, whatever the pinch—whether ambushed warfare or hand-to-hand shock, or an insolently perfect parade after long divorce from the decencies—could be depended upon to advance the regimental honour. Their discipline, of course, was that of the Guards, which, based upon tradition, proven experience and knowledge of the human heart, adjusts itself to the spirit of each of its battalions. Though the material of that body might be expended twice in a twelvemonth, the leaven that remained worked on the new supplies at once and from the first. In the dingy out-of-date barracks at Warley the Regimental Reserves gathered and grew into a full-fledged Second Battalion with reserves of its own, and to these the wounded officers and men sent home to be repatched, explained the arts and needs of a war which, apparently always at a stand, changed character every month. After the utter inadequacy of its opening there was a period of hand-made bombs and of loaded sticks for close work; of nippers for the abundant wire left uncut by our few guns; of remedies for trench-feet; of medicaments against lock-jaw from the grossly manured Belgian dirt, and of fancy timberings to hold up sliding trenches. In due course, when a few set battles, which sometimes gained several hundred yards, had wasted their many thousand lives, infallible forms of attack and defence developed themselves, were tried and generally found wanting, while scientific raids, the evolution of specialists, and the mass of regulated detail that more and more surrounded the life of the trenches, occupied their leisure between actions. Our battalions played themselves into the game at the awful price that must be paid for improvisation, however cheery; enduring with a philosophy that may have saved the war, the deviations and delays made necessary by the demands of the various political and other organizations at home.

In the same spirit they accepted the inevitable break-downs

in the business of war-by-experiment; for it is safe to say that there was hardly an operation in which platoons, companies, regiments, brigades, or divisions were not left with one or both flanks in the air. Among themselves, officers and men discussing such matters, make it quite clear how and why such and such units broke, were misled, or delayed on their way into the line. But when a civilian presumes to assist, all ranks unite against his uninformed criticisms. He is warned that, once over the top, no plans hold, for the machine-gun and the lie of the ground dictate the situation to the platoon-commander on whom all things depend and who sees, perhaps, fifty yards about him. There are limits, too, of shock and exhaustion beyond which humanity cannot be pressed without paying toll later. For which cause it may happen that a Division that has borne long agony unflinching, and sincerely believes itself capable of yet more, will, for no reason then apparent (at almost the mere rumour of noises in the night), collapse ignominiously on the same ground where, a month later, with two-thirds of its strength casualties, it cuts coolly and cleanly to its goal. And its fellows, who have borne the same yoke, allow for this.

The compiler of these records, therefore, has made little attempt to put forward any theory of what might or should have happened if things had gone according to plan; and has been scrupulous to avoid debatable issues of bad staff-work or faulty generalship. They were not lacking in the War, but the broad sense of justice in all who suffered from them, recognizing that all were equally amateurs, saved the depression of repeated failures from turning into demoralization.

Here, again, the Irish were reported by those who knew them best, to have been lenient in their judgements, though their private speech was as unrestrained as that of any other body of bewildered and overmastered men. 'Wearing down' the enemy through a period of four years and three months, during most of which time that enemy dealt losses at least equal to those he received, tested human virtue upon a scale that the world had never dreamed of. The Irish Guards stood to the test without flaw.

They were in no sense any man's command. They needed minute comprehension, quick sympathy and inflexible justice, which they repaid by individual devotion and a collective good-will that showed best when things were at their utter worst. Their moods naturally varied with the weather and the burden of fatigues (actions merely kill, while fatigue breaks men's hearts), but their morale was constant because their unofficial life, on which morale hinges, made for contentment. The discipline of the Guards, demanding the utmost that can be exacted of the man, requires of the officer unresting care of his men under all conditions. This care can be a source of sorrow and friction in rigid or over-conscientious hands, till, with the best will in the world, a battalion may be reduced to the mental state of nurse-harried children. Or, conversely, an adored Company Commander, bold as a lion, may, for lack of it, turn his puzzled company into a bear-garden. But there is an elasticity in Celtic psychology that does not often let things reach breaking-point either way; and their sense of humour and social duty—it is a race more careful to regard each other's feelings than each other's lives—held them as easily as they were strictly associated. A jest; the grave hearing out of absurd complaints that might turn to tragedy were the hearing not accorded; a prompt soothing down of gloomy, injured pride; a piece of flagrant buffoonery sanctioned, even shared, but never taken advantage of, went far in dark days to build up that understanding and understood inner life of the two Battalions to which, now, men look back lovingly across their civilian years. It called for a devotion from all, little this side of idolatry; and was shown equally by officers, N.C.O.'s, and men, stretcher-bearers, cooks, orderlies, and not least by the hard-bit, fantastic old soldiers, used for odd duties, who faithfully hobbled about France alongside the rush of wonderful young blood.

Were instances given, the impression might be false, for the tone and temper of the time that set the pace has gone over. But while it lasted, the men made their officers and the officers their men by methods as old as war itself; and their Roman Catholic priests, fearless even in a community none too regardful of Nature's first law, formed a subtle and supple link between both. That the priest, ever in waiting upon Death or pain, should learn to magnify his office was as natural as that doctors and front-line commanders should find him somewhat under their feet when occasion called for the secular, not the spiritual, arm. That Commanding Officers, to keep peace and save important pillars of their little society, should first advise and finally order the Padre not to expose himself wantonly in forward posts or attacks, was equally of a piece with human nature; and that the priests, to the huge content of the men, should disregard the order ('What's a casualty compared to a soul?') was most natural of all. Then the question would come up for discussion in the trenches and dug-outs, when everything that any one had on his mind was thrashed out through the long, quiet hours, or dropped and picked up again with the rise and fall of shell-fire. They speculated on all things in Heaven and earth as they worked in piled filth among the carcasses of their fellows, lay out under the stars on the eves of open battle, or vegetated through a month's feeding and idleness between one sacrifice and the next.

But none has kept minutes of those incredible symposia that made for them a life apart from the mad world which was their portion; nor can any pen re-create that world's brilliance, squalor, unreason and heaped boredom. Recollection fades from men's minds as common life closes over them, till even now they wonder what part they can ever have had in the shrewd, man-hunting savages who answered to their names so few years ago.

It is for the sake of these initiated that the compiler has loaded his records with detail and seeming triviality, since in a life where Death ruled every hour, nothing was trivial, and bald references to villages, billets, camps, fatigues and sports, as well as hints of tales that can never now fully be told, carry each their separate significance to each survivor, intimate and incommunicable as family jests.

As regards other readers, the compiler dares no more than hope that some of those who have no care for old history, or that larger number who at present are putting away from themselves odious memories, may find a little to interest, or even comfort, in these very details and flatnesses that make up the unlovely, yet superb, life endured for their sakes.

A Recantation*

1917

(TO LYDE OF THE MUSIC HALLS)

WHAT boots it on the Gods to call?
    Since, answered or unheard,
We perish with the Gods and all
    Things made—except the Word.

Ere certain Fate had touched a heart
    By fifty years made cold,
I judged thee, Lyde, and thy art
    O'erblown and over-bold.

But he—but he, of whom bereft
    I suffer vacant days—
He on his shield not meanly left—
    He cherished all thy lays.

Witness the magic coffer stocked
    With convoluted runes
Wherein thy very voice was locked
    And linked to circling tunes.

Witness thy portrait, smoke-defiled,
    That decked his shelter-place.
Life seemed more present, wrote the child,
    Beneath thy well-known face.

And when the grudging days restored
    Him for a breath to home,
He, with fresh crowds of youth, adored
    Thee making mirth in Rome.

Therefore, I humble, join the hosts,
    Loyal and loud, who bow
To thee as Queen of Song—and ghosts,
    For I remember how

Never more rampant rose the Hall
  At thy audacious line
Than when the news came in from Gaul
  Thy son had—followed mine.

But thou didst hide it in thy breast
  And, capering, took the brunt
Of blaze and blare, and launched the jest
  That swept next week the Front.

Singer to children! Ours possessed
  Sleep before noon—but thee,
Wakeful each midnight for the rest,
  No holocaust shall free!

Yet they who use the Word assigned,
  To hearten and make whole,
Not less than Gods have served mankind,
  Though vultures rend their soul.

A Friend of the Family*

THERE had been rather a long sitting at Lodge 'Faith and Works', 5837 E.C.,* that warm April night. Three initiations and two raisings, each conducted with the spaciousness and particularity that our Lodge prides itself upon, made the Brethren a little silent, and the strains of certain music had not yet lifted from them.

'There are two pieces that ought to be barred for ever,' said a Brother as we were sitting down to the 'Banquet.' ' "Last Post"* is the other.'

'I can just stand "Last Post". It's "Tipperary" breaks me,' another replied. 'But I expect every one carries his own firing-irons inside him.'

I turned to look. It was a sponsor for one of our newly raised Brethren—a fat man with a fish-like and vacant face, but evidently prosperous. We introduced ourselves as we took our places. His name was Bevin, and he had a chicken farm near Chalfont St Giles, whence he supplied, on yearly contract, two or three high-class London hotels. He was also, he said, on the edge of launching out into herb-growing.

'There's a demand for herbs,' said he; 'but it all depends upon your connections with the wholesale dealers. We ain't systematic enough. The French do it much better, especially in those mountains on the Swiss an' Italian sides. They use more herb remedies than we do. Our patent-medicine business has killed that with us. But there's a demand still, if your connections are sound. I'm going in for it.'

A large, well-groomed Brother across the table (his name was Pole, and he seemed some sort of professional man) struck in with a detailed account of a hollow behind a destroyed village near Thiepval,* where, for no ascertainable reason, a certain rather scarce herb had sprung up by the acre, he said, out of the overturned earth.

'Only you've got to poke among the weeds to find it, and

there's any quantity of bombs an' stuff knockin' about there still. They haven't cleaned it up yet.'

'Last time *I* saw the place,' said Bevin, 'I thought it 'ud be that way till Judgement Day. You know how it lay in that dip under that beet-factory. I saw it bombed up level in two days—into brick-dust mainly. They were huntin' for St Firmin Dump.' He took a sandwich and munched slowly, wiping his face, for the night was close.

'Ye-es,' said Pole. 'The trouble is, there hasn't been any judgement taken or executed. That's why the world is where it is now. We didn't need anything but justice—afterwards. Not gettin' that, the bottom fell out of things, naturally.'

'That's how I look at it too,' Bevin replied. 'We didn't want all that talk afterwards—we only wanted justice. What *I* say is, there *must* be a right and a wrong to things. It can't all be kiss-an'-make-friends, no matter what you do.'

A thin, dark Brother on my left, who had been attending to a cold pork pie (there are no pork pies to equal ours, which are home-made), suddenly lifted his long head, in which a pale-blue glass eye swivelled insanely.

'Well,' he said slowly. '*My* motto is "Never again." Ne-ver again for me.'

'Same here—till next time,' said Pole, across the table. 'You're from Sydney, ain't you?'

'How d'you know?' was the short answer.

'You spoke.' The other smiled. So did Bevin, who added: '*I* know how your push talk, well enough. Have you started that Republic of yours down under yet?'

'No. But we're goin' to. *Then* you'll see.'

'Carry on. No one's hindering,' Bevin pursued.

The Australian scowled. 'No. We know they ain't. And—and—that's what makes us all so crazy angry at you.' He threw back his head and laughed the spleen out of him. 'What *can* you do with an Empire that—that don't care what you do?'

'I've heard that before,' Bevin laughed, and his fat sides shook. 'Oh, I know *your* push inside-out.'

'When did you come across us? My name's Orton—no relation to the Tichborne one.'*

'Gallip'li—dead mostly. My battalion began there. We only lost half.'

'Lucky! They gambled *us* away in two days. 'Member the hospital on the beach?' asked Orton.

'Yes. An' the man without a face—preaching,' said Bevin, sitting up a little.

'Till he died,' said the Australian, his voice lowered.

'*And* afterwards,' Bevin added, lower still.

'Christ! Were *you* there that night?'

Bevin nodded. The Australian choked off something he was going to say, as a Brother on his left claimed him. I heard them talk horses, while Bevin developed his herb-growing projects with the well-groomed Brother opposite.

At the end of the Banquet, when pipes were drawn, the Australian addressed himself to Bevin, across me, and as the company rearranged itself, we three came to anchor in the big ante-room where the best prints are hung. Here our Brother across the table joined us, and moored alongside.

The Australian was full of racial grievances, as must be in a young country; alternating between complaints that his people had not been appreciated enough in England, or too fulsomely complimented by an hysterical Press.

'No-o,' Pole drawled, after a while. 'You're altogether wrong. We hadn't time to notice anything—we were all too busy fightin' for our lives. What *your* crowd down under are suffering from is growing-pains. You'll get over 'em in three hundred years or so—if you're allowed to last so long.'

'Who's going to stoush* us?' Orton asked fiercely.

This turned the talk again to larger issues and possibilities— delivered on both sides straight from the shoulder without malice or heat, between bursts of song from round the piano at the far end. Bevin and I sat out, watching.

'Well, *I* don't understand these matters,' said Bevin at last. 'But I'd hate to have one of your crowd have it in for me for anything.'

'Would you? Why?' Orton pierced him with his pale, artificial eye.

'Well, you're a trifle—what's the word?—vindictive?—spiteful? At least, that's what *I*'ve found. I expect it comes from drinking stewed tea with your meat four times a day,' said Bevin. 'No! I'd hate to have an Australian after me for anything in particular.'

Out of this came his tale—somewhat in this shape:

It opened with an Australian of the name of Hickmot or Hickmer—Bevin called him both—who, finding his battalion completely expended at Gallipoli, had joined up with what stood of Bevin's battalion, and had there remained, unrebuked and unnoticed. The point that Bevin laboured was that his man had never seen a table-cloth, a china plate, or a dozen white people together till, in his thirtieth year, he had walked for two months to Brisbane to join up. Pole found this hard to believe.

'But it's true,' Bevin insisted. 'This chap was born an' bred among the black fellers, as they call 'em, two hundred miles from the nearest town, four hundred miles from a railway, an' ten thousand from the grace o' God—out in Queensland near some desert.'

'Why, of course. We come out of everywhere,' said Orton. 'What's wrong with that?'

'Yes—but—— Look here! From the time that this man Hickmot was twelve years old he'd ridden, driven—what's the word?—conducted sheep for his father for thousands of miles on end, an' months at a time, alone with these black fellers that you daren't show the back of your neck to—else they knock your head in. That was all that he'd ever done till he joined up. He—he—didn't *belong* to anything in the world, you understand. And he didn't strike other men as being a—a human being.'

'Why? He was a Queensland drover. They're all right,' Orton explained.

'I dare say; but—well, a man notices another man, don't he? You'd notice if there was a man standing or sitting or lyin' near you, wouldn't you? So'd any one. But you'd never notice Hickmot. His bein' anywhere about wouldn't stay in your mind. He just didn't draw attention any more than anything else that happened to be about. Have you got it?'

'Wasn't he any use at his job?' Pole inquired.

'I've nothing against him that way, an' I'm—I was his platoon sergeant. He wouldn't volunteer specially for any

doings, but he'd slip out with the party and he'd slip back with
what was left of 'em. No one noticed him, and he never opened
his mouth about any doings. You'd think a man who had lived
the way he'd lived among black fellers an' sheep would be
noticeable enough in an English battalion, wouldn't you?'

'It teaches 'em to lie close; but *you* seem to have noticed
him,' Orton interposed, with a little suspicion.

'Not at the time—but afterwards. If he was noticeable it was
on account of his *un*noticeability—same way you'd notice there
not being an extra step at the bottom of the staircase when you
thought there was.'

'Ye-es,' Pole said suddenly. 'It's the eternal mystery of per-
sonality. "God before Whom ever lie bare——"'* Some people
can occlude their personality like turning off a tap. I beg your
pardon. Carry on!'

'Granted,' said Bevin. 'I think I catch your drift. I used to
think I was a student of human nature before I joined up.'

'What was your job—before?' Orton asked.

'Oh, I was *the* young blood of the village. Goal-keeper in our
soccer team, secretary of the local cricket and rifle—oh, lor'!—
clubs. Yes, an' village theatricals. My father was the chemist in
the village. *How* I did talk! *What* I did know!' He beamed upon
us all.

'*I* don't mind hearing you talk,' said Orton, lying back in his
chair. 'You're a little different from some of 'em. What hap-
pened to this dam' drover of yours?'

'He was with our push for the rest of the War—an' I don't
think he ever sprung a dozen words at one time. With his
upbringing, you see, there wasn't any subject that any man
knew about he *could* open up on. He kept quiet, and mixed
with his backgrounds. If there was a lump of dirt, or a hole in
the ground, or what was—was left after anythin' had hap-
pened, it would be Hickmot. That was all he wanted to be.'

'A camouflager?' Orton suggested.

'You have it! He was the complete camouflager all through.
That's him to a dot. Look here! He hadn't even a nickname in
his platoon! And then a friend of mine from our village, of the
name of Vigors, came out with a draft. Bert Vigors. As a matter
of fact, I was engaged to his sister. And Bert hadn't been with

us a week before they called him "The Grief". His father was
an oldish man, a market-gardener—high-class vegetables, bit
o' glass, an'—an' all the rest of it. Do you know anything about
that particular business?'

'Not much, I'm afraid,' said Pole, 'except that glass is expen-
sive, and one's man always sells the cut flowers.'

'Then you *do* know something about it. It is. Bert was the
old man's only son, an'—*I* don't blame him—he'd done his
damnedest to get exempted—for the sake of the business, you
understand. But he caught it all right. The tribunal* wasn't
takin' any the day he went up. Bert was for it, with a few
remarks from the patriotic old was-sers* on the Bench. Our
county paper had 'em all.'

'That's the thing that made one really want the Hun in
England for a week or two,' said Pole.

'*Mwor osee!** The same tribunal, havin' copped Bert, gave
unconditional exemption to the opposition shop—a man called
Margetts, in the market-garden business, which he'd
established *since* the War, with his two sons who, every one in
the village knew, had been pushed into the business to save
their damned hides. But Margetts had a good lawyer to advise
him. The whole case was frank and above-board to a degree—
our county paper had it all in, too. Agricultural produce—vital
necessity; the plough mightier than the sword; an' those ducks
on the Bench, who had turned down Bert, noddin' and smilin'
at Margetts, all full of his cabbage and green peas. What hap-
pened? The usual. Vigors' business—he's sixty-eight, with
asthma—goes smash, and Margetts and Co. double theirs. So,
then, that was Bert's grievance, an' he joined us full of it.
That's why they called him "The Grief". Knowing the facts, I
was with him; but being his sergeant, I had to check him,
because grievances are catchin', and three or four men with 'em
make Companies—er—sticky. Luckily Bert wasn't handy with
his pen. He had to cork up his grievance mostly till he came
across Hickmot, an' God in heaven knows what brought those
two together. No! *As* y'were! I'm wrong about God! I always
am. It was Sheep. Bert knew's much about sheep as I do—an'
that's Canterbury lamb—but he'd let Hickmot talk about 'em
for hours, in return for Hickmot listenin' to his

grievance. Hickmot 'ud talk sheep—the one created thing he'd ever open up on—an' Bert 'ud talk his grievance while they was waiting to go over the top. I've heard 'em again an' again, and, of course, I encouraged 'em. Now, look here! Hickmot hadn't seen an English house or a field or a road or—or anything any civ'lized man is used to in all his life! Sheep an' blacks! Market-gardens an' glass an' exemption-tribunals! An' the men's teeth chatterin' behind their masks between rum-issue an' zero. Oh, there was fun in Hell those days, wasn't there, boys?'

'Sure! Oh, sure!' Orton chuckled, and Pole echoed him.

'Look here! When we were lying up somewhere among those forsaken chicken-camps back o' Doullens, I found Hickmot making mud-pies in a farmyard an' Bert lookin' on. He'd made a model of our village according to Bert's description of it. He'd preserved it in his head through all those weeks an' weeks o' Bert's yap; an' he'd coughed it all up—Margetts' house and gardens, old Mr Vigors' ditto; both pubs; my father's shop, everything that he'd been told by Bert done out to scale in mud, with bits o' brick and stick. Haig* ought to have seen it; but as his sergeant I had to check him for misusin' his winkle-pin* on dirt. Come to think of it, a man who runs about uninhabited countries, with sheep, for a livin' must have gifts for mappin' and scalin' things somehow or other, or he'd be dead. *I* never saw anything like it—*all* out o' what Bert had told him by word of mouth. An' the next time we went up the line Hickmot copped it in the leg just in front of me.'

'Finish?' I asked.

'Oh, no. Only beginnin'. That was in December somethin' or other, 'Sixteen. In Jan'ry Vigors copped it for keeps. I buried him—snowin' blind it was—an' before we'd got him under the whole show was crumped. I wanted to bury him again just to spite 'em (I'm a spiteful man by nature), but the party wasn't takin' any more—even if they could have found it. But, you see, we had buried him all right, which is what they want at home, and I wrote the usual trimmin's about the Chaplain an' the full service, an' what his Captain had said about Bert bein' recommended for a pip, an' the irreparable loss an' so on. That was in Jan'ry 'Seventeen. In Feb'ry some time or other I got saved. My speciality had come to be bombin's and night-doings. Very pleasant for a young free man, but—there's a limit to what you can stand. It takes all men differently. Noise was what started me, at last. I'd got just up to the edge—wonderin' when I'd crack an' how many of our men I'd do in if it came on me while we were busy. I had that nice taste in the mouth and the nice temperature they call trench-fever, an'—I had to feel inside my head for the meanin' of every order I gave or was responsible for executin'. *You* know!'

'We do. Go on!' said Pole in a tone that made Orton look at him.

'So, you see, the bettin' was even on my drawin' a V.C. or getting Number Umpty rest-camp or—a firing-party before breakfast. But Gord saved me. (I made friends with Him the last two years of the War. The others went off too quick.) They wanted a bombin'-instructor for the training-battalion at home, an' He put it into their silly hearts to indent for me. It took 'em five minutes to make me understand I was saved. Then I vomited, an' then I cried. *You* know!' The fat face of Bevin had changed and grown drawn, even as he spoke; and his hands tugged as though to tighten an imaginary belt.

'I was never keen on bombin' myself,' said Pole. 'But bombin'-instruction's murder!'

'I don't deny it's a shade risky, specially when they take the pin* out an' start shakin' it, same as the Chinks* used to do in the woods at Beauty, when they were cuttin' 'em down. But you live like a Home-Defence Brigadier, besides week-end leaf. As a matter o' fact, I married Bert's sister soon's I could after I got the billet, an' I used to lie in our bed thinkin' of the old crowd on the Somme an'—feelin' what a swine I was. Of course, I earned two V.C.'s a week behind the traverse in the exercise of my ord'nary duties, but that isn't the same thing. An' yet I'd only joined up because—because I couldn't dam' well help it.'

'An' what about your Queenslander?' the Australian asked.

'*Too de sweet!* *Pronto!* We got a letter in May from a Brighton hospital matron, sayin' that one of the name of Hickmer was anxious for news o' me, previous to proceedin' to Roehampton for initiation into his new leg. Of course, we

applied for him by return. Bert had written about him to his
sister—my missus—every time he wrote at all; an' any pal o'
Bert's—well, *you* know what the ladies are like. I warned her
about his peculiarities. She wouldn't believe till she saw him.
He was just the same. You'd ha' thought he'd show up in
England like a fresh stiff on snow—but you never noticed him.
You never heard him; and if he didn't want to be seen he
wasn't there. He just joined up with his background. I knew he
could do that with men; but how in Hell, seein' how curious
women are, he could camouflage with the ladies—my wife an'
my mother to wit—beats *me*! He'd feed the chickens for us;
he'd stand on his one leg—it was off above the knee—and saw
wood for us. He'd run—I mean he'd hop—errands for Mrs B.
or mother; our dog worshipped him from the start, though I
never saw him throw a word to him; and *yet*—he didn't take
any place anywhere. You've seen a rabbit—you've seen a
pheasant—hidin' in a ditch? 'Put your hand on it sometimes
before it moved, haven't you? Well, that was Hickmot—with
two women in the house crazy to find out—find out—anything
about him that made him human. *You* know what women are!
He stayed with us a fortnight. He left us on a Sat'day to go to
Roehampton to try his leg. On Friday he came over to the
bombin'-ground—not sayin' anything, *as* usual—to watch me
instruct my Suicide Club, which was only half an hour's run by
rail from our village. He had his overcoat on, an' as soon as he
reached the place it was *mafeesh** with him, as usual. Rabbit-
trick again! You never noticed him. He sat in the bomb-proof
behind the pit where the duds* accumulate till it's time to
explode 'em. Naturally, that's strictly forbidden to the public.
So he went there, an' no one noticed him. When he'd had
enough of watchin', he hopped off home to feed our chickens
for the last time.'

'Then how did *you* know all about it?' Orton said.

'Because I saw him come into the place just as I was goin'
down into the trench. Then he slipped my memory till my train
went back. But it would have made no difference what our
arrangements were. If Hickmer didn't choose to be noticed, he
wasn't noticed. Just for curiosity's sake I asked some o' the

Staff Sergeants whether they'd seen him on the ground. Not one—not one single one had—or could tell me what he was like. An', Sat'day noon, he went off to Roehampton. We saw him into the train ourselves, with the lunch Mrs B. had put up for him—a one-legged man an' his crutch, in regulation blue,* khaki warm* an' kit-bag. Takin' everything together, per'aps he'd spoken as many as twenty times in the thirteen days he'd been with us. I'm givin' it you straight as it happened. An' now—look here!—this is what *did* happen.

'Between two and three that Sunday morning—dark an' blowin' from the north—I was woke up by an explosion an' people shoutin' "Raid!" The first bang fetched 'em out like worms after rain. There was another some minutes afterwards, an' me an' a Sergeant in the Shropshires on leaf told 'em all to take cover. They did. There was a devil of a long wait an' there was a third pop. Everybody, includin' me, heard aeroplanes. I didn't notice till afterwards that——'

Bevin paused.

'What?' said Orton.

'Oh, I noticed a heap of things afterwards. What we noticed first—the Shropshire Sergeant an' me—was a rick well alight back o' Margetts' house, an', with that north wind, blowin' straight on to another rick o' Margetts'. It went up all of a whoosh. The next thing we saw by the light of it was Margetts' house with a bomb-hole in the roof and the rafters leanin' sideways like—like they always lean on such occasions. So we ran there, and the first thing we met was Margetts in his split-tailed nightie callin' on his mother an' damnin' his wife. (A man always does that when he's cross. Have you noticed?) Mrs Margetts was in her nightie too, remindin' Margetts that he hadn't completed his rick insurance. An' that's a woman's lovin' care all over. Behind them was their eldest son, in trousers an' slippers, nursin' his arm an' callin' for the doctor. They went through us howlin' like *flammenwerfer** casualties— right up the street to the surgery.

'Well, there wasn't anything to do except let the show burn out. We hadn't any means of extinguishing conflagrations. Some of 'em fiddled with buckets, an' some of 'em tried to get out some o' Margetts' sticks, but his younger son kept shoutin', "Don't! Don't! It'll be stole! It'll be stole!" So it burned instead, till the roof came down, top of all—a little, cheap, dirty villa. In *reel* life one whizzbang* would have shifted it; but in our civil village it looked that damned important and particular you wouldn't believe. We couldn't get round to Margetts' stable because of the two ricks alight, but we found some one had opened the door early an' the horses was in Margetts' new vegetable piece down the hill which he'd hired off old Vigors to extend his business with. I love the way a horse always looks after his own belly—same as a Gunner. They went to grazin' down the carrots and onions till young Margetts ran to turn 'em out, an' then they got in among the glass frames an' cut themselves. Oh, we had a regular Russian night of it,* everybody givin' advice an' fallin' over each other. When it got light we saw the damage. House, two ricks an' stable *mafeesh*; the big glasshouse with every pane smashed and the furnace-end of it blown clean out. All the horses an' about fifteen head o' cattle—butcher's stores from the next field— feeding in the new vegetable piece. It was a fair clean-up from end to end—house, furniture, fittin's, plant, an' all the early crops.'

'Was there any other damage in the village?' I asked.

'I'm coming to it—the curious part—but I wouldn't call it damage. I was renting a field then for my chickens off the Merecroft Estate. It's accommodation-land, an' there was a wet ditch at the bottom that I had wanted for ever so long to dam up to make a swim-hole for Mrs Bevin's ducks.'

'Ah!' said Orton, half turning in his chair, all in one piece.

'S'pose I was allowed? Not me. Their Agent came down on me for tamperin' with the Estate's drainage arrangements. An' all I wanted was to bring the bank down where the ditch narrows—a couple of cartloads of dirt would have held the water back for half-a-dozen yards—not more than that, an' I could have made a little spill-way over the top with three boards—same as in trenches. Well, the first bomb—the one that woke me up—had done my work for me better than I could. It had dropped just under the hollow of the bank an' brought it all down in a fair landslide. I'd got my swim-hole for

Mrs Bevin's ducks, an' I didn't see how the Estate could kick at the Act o' God, d'you?'

'And Hickmot?' said Orton, grinning.

'Hold on! There was a Parish Council meetin' to demand reprisals, of course, an' there was the policeman an' me pokin' about among the ruins till the Explosives Expert came down in his motor-car at three P.M. Monday, an' he meets all the Margetts off their rockers, howlin' in the surgery, an' he sees my swim-hole fillin' up to the brim.'

'What did he say?' Pole inquired.

'He sized it up at once. (He had to get back to dine in Town that evening.) He said all the evidence proved that it was a lucky shot on the part of one isolated Hun 'plane goin' home, an' we weren't to take it to heart. I don't know that anybody but the Margetts did. He said they must have used incendiary bombs of a new type—which he'd suspected for a long time. I don't think the man was any worse than God intended him to be. I don't *reelly*! But the Shropshire Sergeant said——'

'And what did *you* think?' I interrupted.

'I didn't think. I knew by then. I'm not a Sherlock Holmes; but havin' chucked 'em an' chucked 'em back and kicked 'em out of the light an' slept with 'em for two years, an' makin' my livin' out of them at that time, I could recognize the fuse of a Mills bomb when I found it. I found all three of 'em. Curious about that second in Margetts' glasshouse. Hickmot mus' have raked the ashes out of the furnace, popped it in, an' shut the furnace door. It operated all right. Not one livin' pane left in the putty, and all the brickwork spread round the yard in streaks. Just like that St Firmin village we were talkin' about.'

'But how d'you account for young what's-his-name gettin' his arm broken?' said Pole.

'Crutch!' said Bevin. 'If you or me had taken on that night's doin's, with one leg, we'd have hopped and sweated from one flank to another an' been caught half-way between. Hickmot didn't. I'm as sure as I'm sittin' here that he did his doings quiet and comfortable at his full height—he was over six feet—and no one noticed him. This is the way *I* see it. He fixed the swim-hole for Mrs Bevin's ducks first. We used to talk over our own affairs in front of him, of course, and he knew just what she wanted in the way of a pond. So he went and made it at his leisure. Then he prob'ly went over to Margetts' and lit the first rick, knowin' that the wind 'ud do the rest. When young Margetts saw the light of it an' came out to look, Hickmot would have taken post at the back-door an' dropped the young swine with his crutch, same as we used to drop Huns comin' out of a dug-out. *You* know how they blink at the light. Then he must have walked off an' opened Margetts' stable door to save the horses. They'd be more to him than any man's life. Then he prob'ly chucked one bomb on top o' Margetts' roof, havin' seen that the first rick had caught the second and that the whole house was bound to go. D'you get me?'

'Then why did he waste his bomb on the house?' said Orton. His glass eye seemed as triumphant as his real one.

'For camouflage, of course. He was camouflagin' an air-raid. When the Margetts piled out of their place into the street, he prob'ly attended to the glasshouse, because that would be Margetts' chief means o' business. After that—I think so, because otherwise I don't see where all those extra cattle came from that we found in the vegetable piece—he must have walked off an' rounded up all the butcher's beasts in the next medder, an' driven 'em there to help the horses. And when he'd finished everything he'd set out to do, I'll lay my life an' kit he curled up like a bloomin' wombat not fifty yards away from the whole flamin' show—an' let us run round him. An' when he'd had his sleep out, he went up to Roehampton Monday mornin' by some train that he'd decided upon in his own mind weeks an' weeks before.'

'Did he know all the trains then?' said Pole.

'Ask me another. I only know that if he wanted to get from any place to another without bein' noticed, he did it.'

'And the bombs? He got 'em from you, of course,' Pole went on.

'What do *you* think? He was an hour in the park watchin' me instruct, sittin', as I remember, in the bomb-proof by the dud-hole, in his overcoat. He got 'em all right. He took neither more nor less than he wanted; an' I've told you what he did with 'em—one—two—*an*' three.'

'Ever see him afterwards?' said Orton.

'Yes. Saw him at Brighton when I went down there with the missus, not a month after he'd been broken in to his Roe-hampton leg. You know how the boys used to sit all along Brighton front in their blues, an' jump every time the coal was bein' delivered to the hotels behind them? I barged into him opposite the Old Ship,* an' I told him about our air-raid. I told him how Margetts had gone off his rocker an' walked about starin' at the sky an' holdin' reprisal-meetin's all by himself; an' how old Mr Vigors had bought in what he'd left—tho' of course I said what *was* left—o' Margetts' business; an' how well my swim-hole for the ducks was doin'. It didn't interest him. He didn't want to come over to stay with us any more, either. We were a long, long way back in his past. You could see that. He wanted to get back with his new leg, to his own God-forsaken sheep-walk an' his black fellers in Queensland. I expect he's done it now, an' no one has noticed him. But, by Gord! He *did* leak a little at the end. He did that much! When we was waitin' for the tram to the station, I said how grateful I was to Fritz for moppin' up Margetts an' makin' our swim-hole all in one night. Mrs B. seconded the motion. We couldn't have done less. Well, then Hickmot said, speakin' in his queer way, as if English words were all new to him: "Ah; go on an' bail up* in Hell," he says. "Bert was my friend." That was all. I've given it you just as it happened, word for word. *I'*d hate to have an Australian have it in for *me* for anything I'd done to *his* friend. Mark *you*, I don't say there's anything *wrong* with you Australians, Brother Orton. I only say they ain't like us or any one else that I know.'

'Well, do you want us to be?' said Orton.

'No, no. It takes all sorts to make a world, as the sayin' is. And now'—Bevin pulled out his gold watch—'if I don't make a move of it I'll miss my last train.'

'Let her go,' said Orton serenely. 'You've done some lorry-hoppin' in your time, haven't you—Sergeant?'

'When I was two an' a half stone lighter, Digger,' Bevin smiled in reply.

'Well, I'll run you out home before sun-up. I'm a haulage-contractor now—London and Oxford. There's an empty of mine ordered to Oxford. We can go round by your place as easy as not. She's lyin' out Vauxhall-way.'

'My Gord! An' see the sun rise again! Haven't seen him since I can't remember when,' said Bevin, chuckling. 'Oh, there was fun sometimes in Hell, wasn't there, Australia?'; and again his hands went down to tighten the belt that was missing.

Mesopotamia*

1917

THEY shall not return to us, the resolute, the young,
  The eager and whole-hearted whom we gave:
But the men who left them thriftily to die in their own
      dung,
  Shall they come with years and honour to the grave?

They shall not return to us, the strong men coldly slain
  In sight of help denied from day to day:
But the men who edged their agonies and chid them in their
      pain,
  Are they too strong and wise to put away?

Our dead shall not return to us while Day and Night
      divide—
  Never while the bars of sunset hold.
But the idle-minded overlings who quibbled while they died,
  Shall they thrust for high employments as of old?

Shall we only threaten and be angry for an hour?
  When the storm is ended shall we find
How softly but how swiftly they have sidled back to power
  By the favour and contrivance of their kind?

Even while they soothe us, while they promise large
      amends,
  Even while they make a show of fear,
Do they call upon their debtors, and take counsel with their
      friends,
  To confirm and re-establish each career?

Their lives cannot repay us—their death could not undo—
  The shame that they have laid upon our race.
But the slothfulness that wasted and the arrogance that slew,
  Shall we leave it unabated in its place?

A Madonna of the Trenches*

'Whatever a man of the sons of men
    Shall say to his heart of the lords above,
They have shown man, verily, once and again,
    Marvellous mercies and infinite love.

.   .   .   .

'O sweet one love, O my life's delight,
    Dear, though the days have divided us,
Lost beyond hope, taken far out of sight,
    Not twice in the world shall the Gods do thus.'
                Swinburne, *Les Noyades*.

SEEING how many unstable ex-soldiers came to the Lodge of Instruction (attached to Faith and Works E.C. 5837*) in the years after the War, the wonder is there was not more trouble from Brethren whom sudden meetings with old comrades jerked back into their still raw past. But our round, torpedo-bearded local Doctor—Brother Keede, Senior Warden—always stood ready to deal with hysteria before it got out of hand; and when I examined Brethren unknown or imperfectly vouched for on the Masonic side, I passed on to him anything that seemed doubtful. He had had his experience as medical officer of a South London Battalion, during the last two years of the War; and, naturally, often found friends and acquaintances among the visitors.

Brother C. Strangwick, a young, tallish, new-made Brother, hailed from some South London Lodge. His papers and his answers were above suspicion, but his red-rimmed eyes had a puzzled glare that might mean nerves. So I introduced him particularly to Keede, who discovered in him a Headquarters Orderly of his old Battalion, congratulated him on his return to fitness—he had been discharged for some infirmity or other—and plunged at once into Somme memories.

'I hope I did right, Keede,' I said when we were robing before Lodge.

'Oh, quite. He reminded me that I had him under my hands at Sampoux in 'Eighteen, when he went to bits. He was a Runner.'

'Was it shock?' I asked.

'Of sorts—but not what he wanted me to think it was. No, he wasn't shamming. He had Jumps to the limit—but he played up to mislead me about the reason of 'em. . . . Well, if we could stop patients from lying, medicine would be too easy, I suppose.'

I noticed that, after Lodge-working, Keede gave him a seat a couple of rows in front of us, that he might enjoy a lecture on the Orientation of King Solomon's Temple, which an earnest Brother thought would be a nice interlude between Labour and the high tea that we called our 'Banquet'. Even helped by tobacco it was a dreary performance. About half-way through, Strangwick, who had been fidgeting and twitching for some minutes, rose, drove back his chair grinding across the tesselated floor, and yelped: 'Oh, My Aunt! I can't stand this any longer.' Under cover of a general laugh of assent he brushed past us and stumbled towards the door.

'I thought so!' Keede whispered to me. 'Come along!' We overtook him in the passage, crowing hysterically and wringing his hands. Keede led him into the Tyler's* Room, a small office where we stored odds and ends of regalia and furniture, and locked the door.

'I'm—I'm all right,' the boy began piteously.

'"Course you are.' Keede opened a small cupboard which I had seen called upon before, mixed sal volatile and water in a graduated glass, and, as Strangwick drank, pushed him gently on to an old sofa. 'There,' he went on. 'It's nothing to write home about. I've seen you ten times worse. I expect our talk has brought things back.'

He hooked up a chair behind him with one foot, held the patient's hands in his own, and sat down. The chair creaked.

'Don't!' Strangwick squealed. 'I can't stand it! There's nothing on earth creaks like they do! And—and when it thaws we—we've got to slap 'em back with a spa-ade! Remember those Frenchmen's little boots under the duckboards? . . . What'll I do? What'll I do about it?'

Some one knocked at the door, to know if all were well.

'Oh, quite, thanks!' said Keede over his shoulder. 'But I shall need this room awhile. Draw the curtains, please.'

We heard the rings of the hangings that drape the passage from Lodge to Banquet Room click along their poles, and what sound there had been, of feet and voices, was shut off.

Strangwick, retching impotently, complained of the frozen dead who creak in the frost.

'He's playing up still,' Keede whispered. '*That*'s not his real trouble—any more than 'twas last time.'

'But surely,' I replied, 'men get those things on the brain pretty badly. Remember in October——'

'This chap hasn't, though. I wonder what's really helling him. What are you thinking of?' said Keede peremptorily.

'French End an' Butcher's Row,' Strangwick muttered.

'Yes, there were a few there. But suppose we face Bogey instead of giving him best every time.' Keede turned towards me with a hint in his eye that I was to play up to his leads.

'What was the trouble with French End?' I opened at a venture.

'It was a bit by Sampoux, that we had taken over from the French. They're tough, but you wouldn't call 'em tidy as a nation. They had faced both sides of it with dead to keep the mud back. All those trenches were like gruel in a thaw. Our people had to do the same sort of thing—elsewhere; but Butcher's Row in French End was the—er—show-piece. Luckily, we pinched a salient from Jerry just then, an' straightened things out—so we didn't need to use the Row after November. You remember, Strangwick?'

'My God, yes! When the duckboard-slats were missin' you'd tread on 'em, an' they'd creak.'

'They're bound to. Like leather,' said Keede. 'It gets on one's nerves a bit, but——'

'Nerves? It's real! It's real!' Strangwick gulped.

'But at your time of life, it'll all fall behind you in a year or so. I'll give you another sip of—paregoric,* an' we'll face it quietly. Shall we?'

Keede opened his cupboard again and administered a carefully dropped dark dose of something that was not sal volatile. 'This'll settle you in a few minutes,' he explained. 'Lie still, an' don't talk unless you feel like it.'

He faced me, fingering his beard.

'Ye-es. Butcher's Row wasn't pretty,' he volunteered. 'Seeing Strangwick here has brought it all back to me again. Funny thing! We had a Platoon Sergeant of Number Two—what the deuce was his name?—an elderly bird who must have lied like a patriot to get out to the Front at his age; but he was a first-class Non-Com., and the last person, you'd think, to make mistakes. Well, he was due for a fortnight's home leave in January, 'Eighteen. You were at B.H.Q.* then, Strangwick, weren't you?'

'Yes. I was Orderly. It was January twenty-first'; Strangwick spoke with a thickish tongue, and his eyes burned. Whatever drug it was, had taken hold.

'About then,' Keede said. 'Well, this Sergeant, instead of coming down from the trenches the regular way an' joinin' Battalion Details after dark, an' takin' that funny little train for Arras, thinks he'll warm himself first. So he gets into a dugout, in Butcher's Row, that used to be an old French dressing-station, and fugs up between a couple of braziers of pure charcoal! As luck 'ud have it, that was the only dug-out with an inside door opening inwards—some French anti-gas fitting, I expect—and, by what we could make out, the door must have swung to while he was warming. Anyhow, he didn't turn up at the train. There was a search at once. We couldn't afford to waste Platoon Sergeants. We found him in the morning. He'd got his gas all right. A machine-gunner reported him, didn't he, Strangwick?'

'No, sir. Corporal Grant—o' the Trench Mortars.'

'So it was. Yes, Grant—the man with that little wen on his neck. Nothing wrong with your memory, at any rate. What was the Sergeant's name?'

'Godsoe—John Godsoe,' Strangwick answered.

'Yes, that was it. I had to see him next mornin'—frozen stiff between the two braziers—and not a scrap of private papers on him. *That* was the only thing that made me think it mightn't have been—quite an accident.'

Strangwick's relaxing face set, and he threw back at once to the Orderly Room manner.

'I give my evidence—at the time—to you, sir. He passed—overtook me, I should say—comin' down from supports, after I'd warned him for leaf. I thought he was goin' through Parrot Trench as usual; but 'e must 'ave turned off into French End where the old bombed barricade was.'

'Yes. I remember now. You were the last man to see him alive. That was on the twenty-first of January, you say? Now, *when* was it that Dearlove and Billings brought you to me—clean out of your head?' . . . Keede dropped his hand, in the style of magazine detectives, on Strangwick's shoulder. The boy looked at him with cloudy wonder, and muttered: 'I was took to you on the evenin' of the twenty-fourth of January. But you don't think I did him in, do you?'

I could not help smiling at Keede's discomfiture; but he recovered himself. 'Then what the dickens *was* on your mind that evening—before I gave you the hypodermic?'

'The—the things in Butcher's Row. They kept on comin' over me. You've seen me like this before, sir.'

'But I knew that it was a lie. You'd no more got stiffs on the brain then than you have now. You've got something, but you're hiding it.'

''Ow do *you* know, Doctor?' Strangwick whimpered.

'D'you remember what you said to me, when Dearlove and Billings were holding you down that evening?'

'About the things in Butcher's Row?'

'Oh, no! You spun me a lot of stuff about corpses creaking; but you let yourself go in the middle of it—when you pushed that telegram at me. What did you mean, f'r instance, by asking what advantage it was for you to fight beasts of officers if the dead didn't rise?'*

'Did I say "beasts of officers"?'

'You did. It's out of the Burial Service.'

'I suppose, then, I must have heard it. As a matter of fact, I 'ave.' Strangwick shuddered extravagantly.

'Probably. And there's another thing—that hymn you were shouting till I put you under. It was something about Mercy and Love. Remember it?'

'I'll try,' said the boy obediently, and began to paraphrase, as nearly as possible thus: ' "Whatever a man may say in his heart unto the Lord, yea, verily I say unto you—Gawd hath shown man, again and again, marvellous mercy an'—an' somethin' or other love." '* He screwed up his eyes and shook.

'Now where did you get *that* from?' Keede insisted.

'From Godsoe—on the twenty-first Jan. . . . 'Ow could *I* tell what 'e meant to do?' he burst out in a high, unnatural key— 'Any more than I knew *she* was dead.'

'Who was dead?' said Keede.

'Me Auntie Armine.'

'The one the telegram came to you about, at Sampoux, that you wanted me to explain—the one that you were talking of in the passage out here just now when you began: "O Auntie," and changed it to "O Gawd," when I collared you?'

'That's her! I haven't a chance with you, Doctor. *I* didn't know there was anything wrong with those braziers. How could I? We're always usin' 'em. Honest to God, I thought at first go-off he might wish to warm himself before the leaf-train. I—I didn't know Uncle John meant to start—'ouse-keepin'.' He laughed horribly, and then the dry tears came.

Keede waited for them to pass in sobs and hiccoughs before he continued: 'Why? Was Godsoe your uncle?'

'No,' said Strangwick, his head between his hands. 'Only we'd known him ever since we were born. Dad 'ad known him before that. He lived almost next street to us. Him an' Dad an' Ma an'—an' the rest had always been friends. So we called him Uncle—like children do.'

'What sort of a man was he?'

'One o' *the* best, sir. Pensioned Sergeant with a little money left him—quite independent—and very superior. They had a sittin'-room full o' Indian curios that him and his wife used to let Sister an' me see when we'd been good.'

'Wasn't he rather old to join up?'

'That made no odds to him. He joined up as Sergeant Instructor at the first go-off, an' when the Battalion was ready he got 'imself sent along. He wangled me into 'is platoon when I went out—early in 'Seventeen. Because Ma wanted it, I suppose.'

'I'd no notion you knew him that well,' was Keede's comment.

'Oh, it made no odds to him. He 'ad no pets in the platoon, but 'e'd write 'ome to Ma about me an' all the doin's. You see,'—Strangwick stirred uneasily on the sofa—'we'd known him all our lives—lived in the next street an' all. . . . . An' him well over fifty. Oh dear me! *Oh* dear me! What a bloody mix-up things are, when one's as young as me!' he wailed of a sudden.

But Keede held him to the point. 'He wrote to your mother about you?'

'Yes. Ma's eyes had gone bad followin' on air-raids. Blood-vessels broke behind 'em from sittin' in cellars an' bein' sick. She had to 'ave 'er letters read to her by Auntie. Now I think of it, that was the only thing that you might have called anything at all——'

'Was that the aunt that died, and that you got the wire about?' Keede drove on.

'Yes—Auntie Armine—Ma's younger sister, an' she nearer fifty than forty. What a mix-up! An' if I'd been asked any time about it, I'd 'ave sworn there wasn't a single sol'tary item concernin' her that everybody didn't know an' hadn't known all along. No more conceal to her doin's than—than so much shop-front. She'd looked after Sister an' me, when needful—whoopin' cough an' measles—just the same as Ma. We was in an' out of her house like rabbits. You see, Uncle Armine is a cabinet-maker, an' second-'and furniture, an' we liked playin' with the things. She 'ad no children, and when the War came, she said she was glad of it. But she never talked much of her feelin's. She kept herself to herself, you understand.' He stared most earnestly at us to help out our understandings.

'What was she like?' Keede inquired.

'A biggish woman, an' had been 'andsome, I believe, but, bein' used to her, we two didn't notice much—except, per'aps, for one thing. Ma called her 'er proper name, which was Bella; but Sis an' me always called 'er Auntie Armine. See?'

'What for?'

'We thought it sounded more like her—like somethin' movin' slow, in armour.'

'Oh! And she read your letters to your mother, did she?'

'Every time the post came in she'd slip across the road from opposite an' read 'em. An'—an' I'll go bail for it that that was all there was to it for as far back as *I* remember. Was I to swing to-morrow, I'd go bail for *that*! 'Tisn't fair of 'em to 'ave unloaded it all on me, because—because—if the dead *do* rise, why, what in 'ell becomes of me an' all I've believed all me life? I want to know *that*! I—I——'

But Keede would not be put off. 'Did the Sergeant give you away at all in his letters?' he demanded, very quietly.

'There was nothin' to give away—we was too busy—but his letters about me were a great comfort to Ma. I'm no good at writin'. I saved it all up for my leafs. I got me fourteen days every six months an' one over. . . . I was luckier than most, that way.'

'And when you came home, used you to bring 'em news about the Sergeant?' said Keede.

'I expect I must have; but I didn't think much of it at the time. I was took up with me own affairs—naturally. Uncle John always wrote to me once each leaf, tellin' me what was doin' an' what I was li'ble to expect on return, an' Ma 'ud 'ave that read to her. Then o' course I had to slip over to his wife an' pass her the news. An' then there was the young lady that I'd thought of marryin' if I came through. We'd got as far as pricin' things in the windows together.'

'And you didn't marry her—after all?'

Another tremor shook the boy. '*No!*' he cried. ''Fore it ended, I knew what reel things reelly mean! I—I never dreamed such things could be! . . . An' she nearer fifty than forty an' me own Aunt! . . . But there wasn't a sign nor a hint from first to last, so 'ow *could* I tell? Don't you *see* it? All she said to me after me Christmas leaf in 'Eighteen, when I come to say good-bye—all Auntie Armine said to me was: "You'll be seein' Mister Godsoe soon?" "Too soon for my likings," I says. "Well, then, tell 'im from me," she says, "that I expect to be through with my little trouble by the twenty-first of next month, an' I'm dyin' to see him as soon as possible after that date."'

'What sort of trouble was it?' Keede turned professional at once.

'She'd 'ad a bit of a gatherin' in 'er breast, I believe. But she never talked of 'er body much to any one.'

'*I* see,' said Keede. 'And she said to you?'

Strangwick repeated: ' "Tell Uncle John I hope to be finished of my drawback by the twenty-first, an' I'm dyin' to see 'im as soon as 'e can after that date." An' then she says, laughin': "But you've a head like a sieve. I'll write it down, an' you can give it to him when you see 'im." So she wrote it on a bit o' paper an' I kissed 'er good-bye—I was always her favourite, you see—an' I went back to Sampoux. The thing hardly stayed in my mind at all, d'ye see. But the next time I was up in the front line—I was a Runner, d'ye see—our platoon was in North Bay Trench an' I was up with a message to the Trench Mortar there that Corporal Grant was in charge of. Followin' on receipt of it, he borrowed a couple of men off the platoon, to slue* 'er round or somethin'. I give Uncle John Auntie Armine's paper, an' I give Grant a fag, an' we warmed up a bit over a brazier. Then Grant says to me: "I don't like it"; an' he jerks 'is thumb at Uncle John in the bay studyin' Auntie's message. Well, *you* know, sir, you had to speak to Grant about 'is way of prophesyin' things—after Rankine shot himself with the Very light.'*

'I did,' said Keede, and he explained to me: 'Grant had the Second Sight—confound him! It upset the men. I was glad when he got pipped. What happened after that, Strangwick?'

'Grant whispers to me: "Look, you damned Englishman. 'E's for it." Uncle John was leanin' up against the bay, an' hummin' that hymn I was tryin' to tell you just now. He looked different all of a sudden—as if 'e'd got shaved. *I* don't know anything of these things, but I cautioned Grant as to his style of speakin', if an officer 'ad 'eard him, an' I went on. Passin' Uncle John in the bay, 'e nods an' smiles, which he didn't often, an' he says, pocketin' the paper: "This suits *me*. I'm for leaf on the twenty-first, too." '

'He said that to you, did he?' said Keede.

'*Pre*cisely the same as passin' the time o' day. O' course I returned the agreeable about hopin' he'd get it, an' in due course I returned to 'Eadquarters. The thing 'ardly stayed in my mind a minute. That was the eleventh January—three days after I'd come back from leaf. You remember, sir, there wasn't anythin' doin' either side round Sampoux the first part o' the month. Jerry was gettin' ready for his March Push, an' as long as he kept quiet, we didn't want to poke 'im up.'

'I remember that,' said Keede. 'But what about the Sergeant?'

'I must have met him, on an' off, I expect, goin' up an' down, through the ensuin' days, but it didn't stay in me mind. Why needed it? And on the twenty-first Jan., his name was on the leaf-paper when I went up to warn the leaf-men. I noticed *that*, o' course. Now that very afternoon Jerry 'ad been tryin' a new trench-mortar, an' before our 'Eavies could out it, he'd got a stinker into a bay an' mopped up 'alf-a-dozen. They were bringin' 'em down when I went up to the supports, an' that blocked Little Parrot, same as it always did. *You* remember, sir?'

'Rather! And there was that big machine-gun behind the Half-House waiting for you if you got out,' said Keede.

'I remembered that too. But it was just on dark an' the fog was comin' off the Canal, so I hopped out of Little Parrot an' cut across the open to where those four dead Warwicks are heaped up. But the fog turned me round, an' the next thing I knew I was knee-over in that old 'alf-trench that runs west o' Little Parrot into French End. I dropped into it—almost atop o' the machine-gun platform by the side o' the old sugar-boiler an' the two Zoo-ave* skel'tons. That gave me my bearin's, an' so I went through French End, all up those missin' duck-boards, into Butcher's Row where the *poy-looz** was laid in six deep each side, an' stuffed under the duckboards. It had froze tight, an' the drippin's had stopped, an' the creakin's had begun.'

'Did that really worry you at the time?' Keede asked.

'No,' said the boy with professional scorn. 'If a Runner starts noticin' such things he'd better chuck. In the middle of the Row, just before the old dressin'-station you referred to, sir, it come over me that somethin' ahead on the duckboards was just like Auntie Armine, waitin' beside the door; an' I thought to meself 'ow truly comic it would be if she could be dumped where I was then. In 'alf a second I saw it was only the dark an'

some rags o' gas-screen, 'angin' on a bit o' board, 'ad played me
the trick. So I went on up to the supports an' warned the leaf-
men there, includin' Uncle John. Then I went up Rake Alley to
warn 'em in the front line. I didn't hurry because I didn't want
to get there till Jerry ad' quieted down a bit. Well, then a
Company Relief dropped in—an' the officer got the wind up
over some lights on the flank, an' tied 'em into knots, an' I 'ad
to hunt up me leaf-men all over the blinkin' shop. What with
one thing an' another, it must 'ave been 'alf-past eight before I
got back to the supports. There I run across Uncle John,
scrapin' mud off himself, havin' shaved—quite the dandy. He
asked about the Arras train, an' I said, if Jerry was quiet, it
might be ten o'clock. "Good!" says 'e. "I'll come with you." So
we started back down the old trench that used to run across
Halnaker, back of the support dug-outs. You know, sir.'

Keede nodded.

'Then Uncle John says something to me about seein' Ma an'
the rest of 'em in a few days, an' had I any messages for 'em?
Gawd knows what made me do it, but I told 'im to tell Auntie
Armine I never expected to see anything like her up in our part
of the world. And while I told him I laughed. That's the last
time I 'ave laughed. "Oh—you've seen 'er, 'ave you?" says he,
quite natural-like. Then I told 'im about the sand-bags an' rags
in the dark, playin' the trick. "Very likely," says he, brushin'
the mud off his puttees. By this time, we'd got to the corner
where the old barricade into French End was—before they
bombed it down, sir. He turns right an' climbs across it. "No,
thanks," says I. "I've been there once this evenin'." But he
wasn't attendin' to me. He felt behind the rubbish an' bones
just inside the barricade, an' when he straightened up, he had a
full brazier in each hand.

' "Come on, Clem," he says, an' he very rarely give me my
own name. "You aren't afraid, are you?" he says. "It's just as
short, an' if Jerry starts up again he won't waste stuff here. He
knows it's abandoned." "Who's afraid now?" I says. "Me for
one," says he. "I don't want my leaf spoiled at the last minute."
Then 'e wheels round an' speaks that bit you said come out o'
the Burial Service.'

For some reason Keede repeated it in full, slowly: 'If after the manner of men I have fought with beasts at Ephesus, what advantageth it me, if the dead rise not?'

'That's it,' said Strangwick. 'So we went down French End together—everything froze up an' quiet, except for their creakin's. I remember thinkin'——' His eyes began to flicker.

'Don't think. Tell what happened,' Keede ordered.

'Oh! Beg y' pardon! He went on with his braziers, hummin' his hymn, down Butcher's Row. Just before we got to the old dressin'-station he stops and sets 'em down an' says: "Where did you say she was, Clem? Me eyes ain't as good as they used to be."

' "In 'er bed at 'ome," I says. "Come on down. It's perishin' cold, an' *I'm* not due for leaf."

' "Well, I am," 'e says. "*I* am. . . ." An' then—'give you me word I didn't recognize the voice—he stretches out 'is neck a bit, in a way 'e 'ad, an' he says: "Why, Bella!" 'e says. "Oh, Bella!" 'e says. "Thank Gawd!" 'e says. Just like that! An' then I saw—I tell you I *saw*—Auntie Armine herself standin' by the old dressin'-station door where first I'd thought I'd seen her. He was lookin' at 'er an' she was lookin' at him. I saw it, an' me soul turned over inside me because—because it knocked out everything I'd believed in. I 'ad nothin' to lay 'old of, d'ye see? An' 'e was lookin' at 'er as though he could 'ave et 'er, an' she was lookin' at 'im the same way, out of 'er eyes. Then he says: "Why, Bella," 'e says, "this must be only the second time we've been alone together in all these years." An' I saw 'er half 'old out her arms to 'im in that perishin' cold. An' she nearer fifty than forty an' me own Aunt! You can shop me for a lunatic to-morrow, but I saw it—I *saw* 'er answerin' to his spoken word! . . . Then 'e made a snatch to unsling 'is rifle. Then 'e cuts 'is hand away saying: "No! Don't tempt me, Bella. We've all Eternity ahead of us. An hour or two won't make any odds." Then he picks up the braziers an' goes on to the dug-out door. He's finished with me. He pours petrol on 'em, an' lights it with a match, an' carries 'em inside, flarin'. All that time Auntie Armine stood with 'er arms out—an' a look in 'er face! *I* didn't know such things was or could be! Then he comes out an' says: "Come in, my dear"; an' she stoops an' goes into the dug-out with that look on her face—that look on her face! An' then 'e shuts the door from inside an' starts wedgin' it up. So 'elp me Gawd, I saw an' 'eard all these things with my own eyes an' ears!'

He repeated his oath several times. After a long pause Keede asked him if he recalled what happened next.

'It was a bit of a mix-up, for me, from then on. I must have carried on—they told me I did, but—but I was—I felt a—a long way inside of meself, like—if you've ever had that feelin'. I wasn't rightly on the spot at all. They woke me up sometime next mornin', because 'e 'adn't showed up at the train; an' some one had seen him with me. I wasn't 'alf cross-examined by all an' sundry till dinner-time.

'Then, I think, I volunteered for Dearlove, who 'ad a sore toe, for a front-line message. I 'ad to keep movin', you see, because I 'adn't anything to 'old *on* to. Whilst up there, Grant informed me how 'e'd found Uncle John with the door wedged an' sand-bags stuffed in the cracks. I hadn't waited for that. The knockin' when 'e wedged up was enough for me. Like Dad's coffin.'

'No one told *me* the door had been wedged.' Keede spoke severely.

'No need to black a dead man's name, sir.'

'What made Grant go to Butcher's Row?'

'Because he'd noticed Uncle John had been pinchin' charcoal for a week past an' layin' it up behind the old barricade there. So when the 'unt began, he went that way straight as a string, an' when he saw the door shut, he knew. He told me he picked the sand-bags out of the cracks an' shoved 'is 'and through and shifted the wedges before any one come along. It looked all right. You said yourself, sir, the door must 'ave blown to.'

'Grant knew what Godsoe meant, then?' Keede snapped.

'Grant knew Godsoe was for it, an' nothin' earthly could 'elp or 'inder. He told me so.'

'And then what did you do?'

'I expect I must 'ave kept on carryin' on, till 'Eadquarters give me that wire from Ma—about Auntie Armine dyin'.'

'When had your Aunt died?'

'On the mornin' of the twenty-first. The mornin' of the twenty-first! That tore it, d'ye see? As long as I could think, I

had kep' tellin' myself it was like those things you lectured
about at Arras when we was billeted in the cellars—the Angels
of Mons,* and so on. But that wire tore it.'

'Oh! Hallucinations! I remember. And that wire tore it?' said
Keede.

'Yes! You see'—he half lifted himself off the sofa—'there
wasn't a single gor-dam thing left abidin' for me to take hold
of, 'ere or 'ereafter. If the dead *do* rise—and I saw 'em—why—
why, *anything* can 'appen. Don't you understand?'

He was on his feet now, gesticulating stiffly.

'For I saw 'er,' he repeated. 'I saw 'im an' 'er—she dead
since mornin' time, an' he killin' 'imself before my livin' eyes
so's to carry on with 'er for all Eternity—an' she 'oldin' out 'er
arms for it! I want to know where I'm *at*! Look 'ere, you two—
why stand *we* in jeopardy every hour?'

'God knows,' said Keede to himself.

'Hadn't we better ring for some one?' I suggested. 'He'll go
off the handle in a second.'

'No, he won't. It's the last kick-up before it takes hold. I
know how the stuff works. Hul-lo!'

Strangwick, his hands behind his back and his eyes set, gave
tongue in the strained, cracked voice of a boy reciting. 'Not
twice in the world shall the Gods do thus,' he cried again and
again.

'And I'm damned if it's goin' to be even once for me!' he
went on with sudden insane fury. '*I* don't care whether we '*ave*
been pricin' things in the windows. . . . *Let* 'er sue if she likes!
She don't know what reel things mean. *I* do—I've 'ad occasion
to notice 'em. . . . *No*, I tell you! I'll 'ave 'em when I want 'em,
an' be done with 'em; but not till I see that look on a face . . .
that look. . . . I'm not takin' any. The reel thing's life an'
death. It *begins* at death, d'ye see? *She* can't understand. . . .
Oh, go on an' push off to Hell, you an' your lawyers. I'm fed
up with it—fed up!'

He stopped as abruptly as he had started, and the drawn face
broke back to its natural irresolute lines. Keede, holding both
his hands, led him back to the sofa, where he dropped like a
wet towel, took out some flamboyant robe from a press, and
drew it neatly over him.

'Ye-es. *That*'s the real thing at last,' said Keede. 'Now he's got it off his mind he'll sleep. By the way, who introduced him?'

'Shall I go and find out?' I suggested.

'Yes; and you might ask him to come here. There's no need for us to stand to all night.'

So I went to the Banquet, which was in full swing, and was seized by an elderly, precise Brother from a South London Lodge, who followed me, concerned and apologetic. Keede soon put him at ease.

'The boy's had trouble,' our visitor explained. 'I'm most mortified he should have performed his bad turn here. I thought he'd put it be'ind him.'

'I expect talking about old days with me brought it all back,' said Keede. 'It does sometimes.'

'Maybe! Maybe! But over and above that, Clem's had post-War trouble, too.'

'Can't he get a job? He oughtn't to let that weigh on him, at his time of life,' said Keede cheerily.

''Tisn't that—he's provided for—but'—he coughed confidentially behind his dry hand—'as a matter of fact, Worshipful Sir, he's—he's implicated for the present in a little breach of promise action.'

'Ah! That's a different thing,' said Keede.

'Yes. That's his reel trouble. No reason given, you understand. The young lady in every way suitable, an' she'd make him a good little wife too, if I'm any judge. But he says she ain't his ideel or something. No getting at what's in young people's minds these days, is there?'

'I'm afraid there isn't,' said Keede. 'But he's all right now. He'll sleep. You sit by him, and when he wakes, take him home quietly. . . . Oh, we're used to men getting a little upset here. You've nothing to thank us for, Brother—Brother——'

'Armine,' said the old gentleman. 'He's my nephew by marriage.'

'That's all that's wanted!' said Keede.

Brother Armine looked a little puzzled. Keede hastened to explain. 'As I was saying, all he wants now is to be kept quiet till he wakes.'

The Mother's Son*

I HAVE a dream—a dreadful dream—
    A dream that is never done.
I watch a man go out of his mind,
    And he is My Mother's Son.

They pushed him into a Mental Home,
    And that is like the grave:
For they do not let you sleep upstairs,
    And you're not allowed to shave.

And it was *not* disease or crime
    Which got him landed there,
But because They laid on My Mother's Son
    More than a man could bear.

What with noise, and fear of death,
    Waking, and wounds and cold,
They filled the Cup for My Mother's Son
    Fuller than it could hold.

They broke his body and his mind
    And yet They made him live,
And They asked more of My Mother's Son
    Than any man could give.

For, just because he had not died,
    Nor been discharged nor sick,
They dragged it out with My Mother's Son
    Longer than he could stick. . . .

And no one knows when he'll get well—
    So, there he'll have to be:
And, 'spite of the beard in the looking-glass,
    I know that man is me!

The Gardener*

One grave to me was given,
  One watch till Judgment Day;
And, God looked down from Heaven
  And rolled the stone away.

One day in all the years,
  One hour in that one day,
His Angel saw my tears,
  And rolled the stone away!

EVERY one in the village knew that Helen Turrell did her duty by all her world, and by none more honourably than by her only brother's unfortunate child. The village knew, too, that George Turrell had tried his family severely since early youth, and were not surprised to be told that, after many fresh starts given and thrown away, he, an Inspector of Indian Police, had entangled himself with the daughter of a retired non-commissioned officer, and had died of a fall from a horse a few weeks before his child was born. Mercifully, George's father and mother were both dead, and though Helen, thirty-five and independent, might well have washed her hands of the whole disgraceful affair, she most nobly took charge, though she was, at the time, under threat of lung trouble which had driven her to the South of France. She arranged for the passage of the child and a nurse from Bombay, met them at Marseilles, nursed the baby through an attack of infantile dysentery due to the carelessness of the nurse, whom she had had to dismiss, and at last, thin and worn but triumphant, brought the boy late in the autumn, wholly restored, to her Hampshire home.

All these details were public property, for Helen was as open as the day, and held that scandals are only increased by hushing them up. She admitted that George had always been rather a black sheep, but things might have been much worse if the mother had insisted on her right to keep the boy. Luckily, it seemed that people of that class would do almost anything for money, and, as George had always turned to her in his scrapes, she felt herself justified—her friends agreed with her—in cutting the whole non-commissioned officer connection, and giving the child every advantage. A christening, by the Rector, under the name of Michael, was the first step. So far as she knew herself, she was not, she said, a child-lover, but, for all his faults, she had been very fond of George, and she pointed out that little Michael had his father's mouth to a line; which made something to build upon.

As a matter of fact, it was the Turrell forehead, broad, low, and well-shaped, with the widely spaced eyes beneath it, that Michael had most faithfully reproduced. His mouth was somewhat better cut than the family type. But Helen, who would concede nothing good to his mother's side, vowed he was a Turrell all over, and, there being no one to contradict, the likeness was established.

In a few years Michael took his place, as accepted as Helen had always been—fearless, philosophical, and fairly good-looking. At six, he wished to know why he could not call her 'Mummy', as other boys called their mothers. She explained that she was only his auntie, and that aunties were not quite the same as mummies, but that, if it gave him pleasure, he might call her 'Mummy' at bedtime, for a pet-name between themselves.

Michael kept his secret most loyally, but Helen, as usual, explained the fact to her friends; which when Michael heard, he raged.

'Why did you tell? *Why* did you tell?' came at the end of the storm.

'Because it's always best to tell the truth,' Helen answered, her arm round him as he shook in his cot.

'All right, but when the troof's ugly I don't think it's nice.'

'Don't you, dear?'

'No, I don't, and'—she felt the small body stiffen—'now you've told, I won't call you "Mummy" any more—not even at bedtimes.'

'But isn't that rather unkind?' said Helen softly.

'I don't care! I don't care! You've hurted me in my insides and I'll hurt you back. I'll hurt you as long as I live!'

'Don't, oh, don't talk like that, dear! You don't know what——'

'I will! And when I'm dead I'll hurt you worse!'

'Thank goodness, I shall be dead long before you, darling.'

'Huh! Emma says, "Never know your luck." ' (Michael had been talking to Helen's elderly, flat-faced maid.) 'Lots of little boys die quite soon. So'll I. *Then* you'll see!'

Helen caught her breath and moved towards the door, but the wail of 'Mummy! Mummy!' drew her back again, and the two wept together.

At ten years old, after two terms at a prep. school, something or somebody gave him the idea that his civil status was not quite regular. He attacked Helen on the subject, breaking down her stammered defences with the family directness.

'Don't believe a word of it,' he said, cheerily, at the end. 'People wouldn't have talked like they did if my people had been married. But don't you bother, Auntie. I've found out all about my sort in English Hist'ry and the Shakespeare bits. There was William the Conqueror* to begin with, and—oh, heaps more, and they all got on first-rate. 'Twon't make any difference to you, my being *that*—will it?'

'As if anything could——', she began.

'All right. We won't talk about it any more if it makes you cry.' He never mentioned the thing again of his own will, but when, two years later, he skilfully managed to have measles in the holidays, as his temperature went up to the appointed one hundred and four he muttered of nothing else, till Helen's voice, piercing at last his delirium, reached him with assurance that nothing on earth or beyond could make any difference between them.

The terms at his public school and the wonderful Christmas, Easter, and Summer holidays followed each other, variegated and glorious as jewels on a string; and as jewels Helen treasured them. In due time Michael developed his own interests, which ran their courses and gave way to others; but his interest in Helen was constant and increasing throughout. She repaid it with all that she had of affection or could command of counsel and money; and since Michael was no fool, the War took him just before what was like to have been a most promising career.

He was to have gone up to Oxford, with a scholarship, in October. At the end of August he was on the edge of joining the first holocaust of public-school boys who threw themselves into the Line;* but the Captain of his O.T.C.,* where he had been sergeant for nearly a year, headed him off and steered him directly to a commission in a battalion so new that half of it still wore the old Army red, and the other half was breeding meningitis through living overcrowdedly in damp tents. Helen had been shocked at the idea of direct enlistment.

'But it's in the family,' Michael laughed.

'You don't mean to tell me that you believed that old story all this time?' said Helen. (Emma, her maid, had been dead now several years.) 'I gave you my word of honour—and I give it again—that—that it's all right. It is indeed.'

'Oh, *that* doesn't worry me. It never did,' he replied valiantly. 'What I meant was, I should have got into the show earlier if I'd enlisted—like my grandfather.'

'Don't talk like that! Are you afraid of its ending so soon, then?'

'No such luck. You know what K.* says.'

'Yes. But my banker told me last Monday it couldn't *possibly* last beyond Christmas—for financial reasons.'

'Hope he's right, but our Colonel—and he's a Regular—says it's going to be a long job.'

Michael's battalion was fortunate in that, by some chance which meant several 'leaves', it was used for coast-defence among shallow trenches on the Norfolk coast; thence sent north to watch the mouth of a Scotch estuary, and, lastly, held for weeks on a baseless rumour of distant service. But, the very day that Michael was to have met Helen for four whole hours at a railway-junction up the line, it was hurled out, to help make good the wastage of Loos*, and he had only just time to send her a wire of farewell.

In France luck again helped the battalion. It was put down near the Salient,* where it led a meritorious and unexacting life, while the Somme was being manufactured; and enjoyed the peace of the Armentières and Laventie sectors when that battle began. Finding that it had sound views on protecting its own flanks and could dig, a prudent Commander stole it out of its own Division, under pretence of helping to lay telegraphs, and used it round Ypres at large.

A month later, and just after Michael had written Helen that there was nothing special doing and therefore no need to worry, a shell-splinter dropping out of a wet dawn killed him at once. The next shell uprooted and laid down over the body what had been the foundation of a barn wall, so neatly that none but an expert would have guessed that anything unpleasant had happened.

By this time the village was old in experience of war, and, English fashion, had evolved a ritual to meet it. When the postmistress handed her seven-year-old daughter the official telegram to take to Miss Turrell, she observed to the Rector's gardener: 'It's Miss Helen's turn now.' He replied, thinking of his own son: 'Well, he's lasted longer than some.' The child herself came to the front-door weeping aloud, because Master Michael had often given her sweets. Helen, presently, found herself pulling down the house-blinds one after one with great care, and saying earnestly to each: 'Missing *always* means dead.' Then she took her place in the dreary procession that was impelled to go through an inevitable series of unprofitable emotions. The Rector, of course, preached hope and proph-esied word, very soon, from a prison camp. Several friends, too, told her perfectly truthful tales, but always about other women, to whom, after months and months of silence, their missing had been miraculously restored. Other people urged her to communicate with infallible Secretaries of organizations who could communicate with benevolent neutrals, who could extract accurate information from the most secretive of Hun prison commandants. Helen did and wrote and signed every-thing that was suggested or put before her.

Once, on one of Michael's leaves, he had taken her over a munition factory, where she saw the progress of a shell from blank-iron to the all but finished article. It struck her at the time that the wretched thing was never left alone for a single second; and 'I'm being manufactured into a bereaved next of kin,' she told herself, as she prepared her documents.

In due course, when all the organizations had deeply or sincerely regretted their inability to trace, etc., something gave way within her and all sensation—save of thankfulness for the release—came to an end in blessed passivity. Michael had died and her world had stood still and she had been one with the full shock of that arrest. Now she was standing still and the world was going forward, but it did not concern her—in no way or relation did it touch her. She knew this by the ease with which she could slip Michael's name into talk and incline her head to the proper angle, at the proper murmur of sympathy.

In the blessed realization of that relief, the Armistice with all its bells broke over her and passed unheeded. At the end of another year she had overcome her physical loathing of the living and returned young, so that she could take them by the hand and almost sincerely wish them well. She had no interest in any aftermath, national or personal, of the War, but, moving at an immense distance, she sat on various relief committees and held strong views—she heard herself delivering them—about the site of the proposed village War Memorial.

Then there came to her, as next of kin, an official intimation, backed by a page of a letter to her in indelible pencil, a silver identity-disc, and a watch, to the effect that the body of Lieutenant Michael Turrell had been found, identified, and re-interred* in Hagenzeele Third Military Cemetery—the letter of the row and the grave's number in that row duly given.

So Helen found herself moved on to another process of the manufacture—to a world full of exultant or broken relatives, now strong in the certainty that there was an altar upon earth where they might lay their love. These soon told her, and by means of time-tables made clear, how easy it was and how little it interfered with life's affairs to go and see one's grave.

'*So* different,' as the Rector's wife said, 'if he'd been killed in Mesopotamia, or even Gallipoli.'

The agony of being waked up to some sort of second life drove Helen across the Channel, where, in a new world of abbreviated titles, she learnt that Hagenzeele Third could be comfortably reached by an afternoon train which fitted in with the morning boat, and that there was a comfortable little hotel not three kilometres from Hagenzeele itself, where one could spend quite a comfortable night and see one's grave next morning. All this she had from a Central Authority who lived in a board and tar-paper shed on the skirts of a razed city full of whirling lime-dust and blown papers.

'By the way,' said he, 'you know your grave, of course?'

'Yes, thank you,' said Helen, and showed its row and number typed on Michael's own little typewriter. The officer would have checked it, out of one of his many books; but a large Lancashire woman thrust between them and bade him tell her where she might find her son, who had been corporal in the A.S.C.* His proper name, she sobbed, was Anderson, but, coming of respectable folk, he had of course enlisted under the name of Smith; and had been killed at Dickiebush, in early 'Fifteen. She had not his number nor did she know which of his two Christian names he might have used with his alias; but her Cook's tourist ticket expired at the end of Easter week, and if by then she could not find her child she should go mad. Whereupon she fell forward on Helen's breast; but the officer's wife came out quickly from a little bedroom behind the office, and the three of them lifted the woman on to the cot.

'They are often like this,' said the officer's wife, loosening the tight bonnet-strings. 'Yesterday she said he'd been killed at Hooge. Are you sure you know your grave? It makes such a difference.'

'Yes, thank you,' said Helen, and hurried out before the woman on the bed should begin to lament again.

Tea in a crowded mauve-and-blue striped wooden structure, with a false front, carried her still further into the nightmare. She paid her bill beside a stolid, plain-featured Englishwoman, who, hearing her inquire about the train to Hagenzeele, volunteered to come with her.

'I'm going to Hagenzeele myself,' she explained. 'Not to Hagenzeele Third; mine is Sugar Factory, but they call it La Rosière now. It's just south of Hagenzeele Three. Have you got your room at the hotel there?'

'Oh yes, thank you. I've wired.'

'That's better. Sometimes the place is quite full, and at others there's hardly a soul. But they've put bathrooms into the old Lion d'Or—that's the hotel on the west side of Sugar Factory—and it draws off a lot of people, luckily.'

'It's all new to me. This is the first time I've been over.'

'Indeed! This is my ninth time since the Armistice. Not on my own account. *I* haven't lost any one, thank God—but, like every one else, I've a lot of friends at home who have. Coming over as often as I do, I find it helps them to have some one just look at the —the place and tell them about it afterwards. And one can take photos for them, too. I get quite a list of commissions to execute.' She laughed nervously and tapped her slung kodak. 'There are two or three to see at Sugar Factory this time, and plenty of others in the cemeteries all about. My system is to save them up, and arrange them, you know. And when I've got enough commissions for one area to make it worth while, I pop over and execute them. It *does* comfort people.'

'I suppose so,' Helen answered, shivering as they entered the little train.

'Of course it does. (Isn't it lucky we've got window-seats?) It must do or they wouldn't ask one to do it, would they? I've a list of quite twelve or fifteen commissions here'—she tapped the kodak again—'I must sort them out to-night. Oh, I forgot to ask you. What's yours?'

'My nephew,' said Helen. 'But I was very fond of him.'

'Ah, yes! I sometimes wonder whether *they* know after death? What do you think?'

'Oh, I don't—I haven't dared to think much about that sort of thing,' said Helen, almost lifting her hands to keep her off.

'Perhaps that's better,' the woman answered. 'The sense of loss must be enough, I expect. Well, I won't worry you any more.'

Helen was grateful, but when they reached the hotel Mrs Scarsworth (they had exchanged names) insisted on dining at the same table with her, and after the meal, in the little, hideous salon full of low-voiced relatives, took Helen through her 'commissions' with biographies of the dead, where she happened to know them, and sketches of their next of kin. Helen endured till nearly half-past nine, ere she fled to her room.

Almost at once there was a knock at her door and Mrs Scarsworth entered; her hands, holding the dreadful list, clasped before her.

'Yes—yes—*I* know,' she began. 'You're sick of me, but I want to tell you something. You—you aren't married, are you? Then perhaps you won't . . . But it doesn't matter. I've *got* to tell some one. I can't go on any longer like this.'

'But please——' Mrs Scarsworth had backed against the shut door, and her mouth worked dryly.

'In a minute,' she said. 'You—you know about these graves of mine I was telling you about downstairs, just now? They really *are* commissions. At least several of them are.' Her eye wandered round the room. 'What extraordinary wall-papers they have in Belgium, don't you think? . . . Yes. I swear they are commissions. But there's *one*, d'you see, and—and he was more to me than anything else in the world. Do you understand?'

Helen nodded.

'More than any one else. And, of course, he oughtn't to have been. He ought to have been nothing to me. But he *was*. He *is*. That's why I do the commissions, you see. That's all.'

'But why do you tell me?' Helen asked desperately.

'Because I'm *so* tired of lying. Tired of lying—always lying—year in and year out. When I don't tell lies I've got to act 'em and I've got to think 'em, always. *You* don't know what that means. He was everything to me that he oughtn't to have been—the one real thing—the only thing—that ever happened to me in all my life; and I've had to pretend he wasn't. I've had to watch every word I said, and think out what lie I'd tell next, for years and years!'

'How many years?' Helen asked.

'Six years and four months before, and two and three-quarters after. I've gone to him eight times, since. To-morrow'll make the ninth, and—and I can't— I *can't* go to him again with nobody in the world knowing. I want to be honest with some one before I go. Do you understand? It doesn't matter about *me*. I was never truthful, even as a girl. But it isn't worthy of *him*. So—so I—I had to tell you. I can't keep it up any longer. Oh, I can't!'

She lifted her joined hands almost to the level of her mouth, and brought them down sharply, still joined, to full arms' length below her waist. Helen reached forward, caught them, bowed her head over them, and murmured: 'Oh, my dear! My dear!' Mrs Scarsworth stepped back, her face all mottled.

'My God!' said she. 'Is *that* how you take it?'

Helen could not speak, and the woman went out; but it was a long while before Helen was able to sleep.

Next morning Mrs Scarsworth left early on her round of commissions, and Helen walked alone to Hagenzeele Third. The place was still in the making, and stood some five or six feet above the metalled road, which it flanked for hundreds of yards. Culverts across a deep ditch served for entrances through the unfinished boundary wall. She climbed a few wooden-faced earthen steps and then met the entire crowded level of the thing in one held breath. She did not know that Hagenzeele Third counted twenty-one thousand dead already. All she saw was a merciless sea of black crosses, bearing little strips of stamped tin at all angles across their faces. She could distinguish no order or arrangement in their mass; nothing but a waist-high wilderness as of weeds stricken dead, rushing at her. She went forward, moved to the left and the right hopelessly, wondering by what guidance she should ever come to her own. A great distance away there was a line of whiteness. It proved to be a block of some two or three hundred graves whose headstones had already been set, whose flowers were planted out, and whose new-sown grass showed green. Here she could see clear-cut letters at the end of the rows, and, referring to her slip, realized that it was not here she must look.

A man knelt behind a line of headstones—evidently a gardener, for he was firming a young plant in the soft earth. She went towards him, her paper in her hand. He rose at her approach and without prelude or salutation asked: 'Who are you looking for?'

'Lieutenant Michael Turrell—my nephew,' said Helen slowly and word for word, as she had many thousands of times in her life.

The man lifted his eyes and looked at her with infinite compassion before he turned from the fresh-sown grass toward the naked black crosses.

'Come with me,' he said, 'and I will show you where your son lies.'

When Helen left the Cemetery she turned for a last look. In the distance she saw the man bending over his young plants; and she went away, supposing him to be the gardener.*

Epitaphs of the War* (Selection)
1914–18

A SERVANT

We were together since the War began.
He was my servant—and the better man.

A SON

My son was killed while laughing at some jest. I would I
 knew
What it was, and it might serve me in a time when jests
 are few.

AN ONLY SON

I have slain none except my Mother. She
(Blessing her slayer) died of grief for me.

EX-CLERK

Pity not! The Army gave
Freedom to a timid slave:
In which Freedom did he find
Strength of body, will, and mind:
By which strength he came to prove
Mirth, Companionship, and Love:
For which Love to Death he went:
In which Death he lies content.

THE WONDER

Body and Spirit I surrendered whole
To harsh Instructors—and received a soul . . .
If mortal man could change me through and through
From all I was—what may The God not do?

THE COWARD

I could not look on Death, which being known,
Men led me to him, blindfold and alone.

SHOCK

My name, my speech, my self I had forgot.
My wife and children came—I knew them not.
I died. My Mother followed. At her call
And on her bosom I remembered all.

PELICANS IN THE WILDERNESS

A Grave near Halfa*

The blown sand heaps on me, that none may learn
  Where I am laid for whom my children grieve. . . .
O wings that beat at dawning, ye return
  Out of the desert to your young at eve!

TWO CANADIAN MEMORIALS

I

We giving all gained all.
  Neither lament us nor praise.
Only in all things recall,
  It is Fear, not Death that slays.

II

From little towns in a far land we came,
  To save our honour and a world aflame.
By little towns in a far land we sleep;
  And trust that world we won to you to keep!*

THE FAVOUR

Death favoured me from the first, well knowing I could
    not endure
  To wait on him day by day. He quitted my betters and
    came
Whistling over the fields, and, when he had made all sure,
  'Thy line is at end,' he said, 'but at least I have saved its
    name.'

THE BEGINNER

On the first hour of my first day
  In the front trench I fell.

(Children in boxes at a play
  Stand up to watch it well.)

R.A.F. (AGED EIGHTEEN)

Laughing through clouds, his milk-teeth still unshed,
Cities and men he smote from overhead.
His deaths delivered, he returned to play
Childlike, with childish things now put away.

NATIVE WATER-CARRIER (M.E.F.)*

Prometheus* brought down fire to men.
  This brought up water.
The Gods are jealous—now, as then,
  Giving no quarter.

BOMBED IN LONDON

On land and sea I strove with anxious care
To escape conscription. It was in the air!

THE SLEEPY SENTINEL

Faithless the watch that I kept: now I have none to keep.
I was slain because I slept: now I am slain I sleep.
Let no man reproach me again, whatever watch is unkept—
I sleep because I am slain. They slew me because I slept.

A DRIFTER OFF TARENTUM

He from the wind-bitten North with ship and companions
    descended,
  Searching for eggs of death spawned by invisible hulls.
Many he found and drew forth. Of a sudden the fishery
    ended
  In flame and a clamorous breath known to the eye-pecking
    gulls.

CONVOY ESCORT

I was a shepherd to fools
Causelessly bold or afraid.

They would not abide by my rules.
Yet they escaped. For I stayed.

UNKNOWN FEMALE CORPSE

Headless, lacking foot and hand,
Horrible I come to land.
I beseech all women's sons
Know I was a mother once.

V.A.D.* (MEDITERRANEAN)

Ah, would swift ships had never been, for then we ne'er had
    found,
These harsh Ægean rocks between, this little virgin
    drowned,
Whom neither spouse nor child shall mourn, but men she
    nursed through pain
And—certain keels for whose return the heathen look in
    vain.

BATTERIES OUT OF AMMUNITION

If any mourn us in the workshops, say
We died because the shift kept holiday.

COMMON FORM

If any question why we died,
Tell them, because our fathers lied.

A DEAD STATESMAN

I could not dig: I dared not rob:
Therefore I lied to please the mob.
Now all my lies are proved untrue
And I must face the men I slew.
What tale shall serve me here among
Mine angry and defrauded young?

APPENDIX

Kipling under Fire: The Battle of Kari Siding*

MY Bloemfontein trip was on Lord Roberts' order to report and do what I was told. This was explained at the station by two strangers, who grew into my friends for life, H. A. Gwynne, then Head Correspondent of Reuter's, and Perceval Landon of *The Times*. 'You've got to help us edit a paper for the troops,' they said, and forthwith inducted me into the newly captured 'office', for Bloemfontein had fallen—Boer fashion—rather like an outraged Sunday School a few days before.

★   ★   ★

But the Transvaal Boer, not being a town-bird, was unimpressed by the 'fall' of the Free State capital, and ran loose on the veldt with his pony and Mauser.

So there had to be a battle, which was called the Battle of Kari Siding. All the staff of the *Bloemfontein Friend* attended. I was put in a Cape cart, with native driver, containing most of the drinks, and with me was a well-known war-correspondent. The enormous pale landscape swallowed up seven thousand troops without a sign, along a front of seven miles. On our way we passed a collection of neat, deep and empty trenches well undercut for shelter on the shrapnel-side. A young Guards officer, recently promoted to *Brevet*-Major*—and rather sore with the paper that we had printed it *Branch*—studied them interestedly. They were the first dim lines of the dug-out, but his and our eyes were held. The Hun had designed them *secundum artem*,* but the Boer had preferred the open within reach of his pony. At last we came to a lone farm-house in a vale adorned with no less than five white flags. Beyond the ridge was a sputter of musketry and now and then the whoop of a field-piece. 'Here,' said my guide and guardian, 'we get out and walk. Our driver will wait for us at the farm-house.' But the driver loudly objected. 'No, sar. They shoot. They shoot me.' 'But they are white-flagged all over,' we said. 'Yess, sar. That *why*,' was his answer, and he preferred to take his mules down into a decently remote donga and wait our return.

The farm-house . . . held two men and, I think, two women, who received us disinterestedly. We went on into a vacant world full of sunshine and distances, where now and again a single bullet sang to himself. What I most objected to was the sensation of being under

aimed fire—being, as it were, required as a head. 'What are they doing
this for?' I asked my friend. 'Because they think we are the Something
Light Horse. They ought to be just under this slope.' I prayed that the
particularly Something Light Horse would go elsewhere, which they
presently did, for the aimed fire slackened and a wandering Colonial,
bored to extinction, turned up with news from a far flank. 'No;
nothing doing and no one to see.' Then more cracklings and a most
cautious move forward to the lip of a large hollow where sheep were
grazing. Some of them began to drop and kick. 'That's both sides
trying sighting-shots,' said my companion. 'What range do you make
it?' I asked. 'Eight hundred at the nearest. That's close quarters
nowadays. You'll never see anything closer than this. Modern rifles
make it impossible. We're hung up till something cracks somewhere.'
There was a decent lull for meals on both sides, interrupted now and
again by sputters. Then one indubitable shell—ridiculously like a pip-
squeak in that vastness but throwing up much dirt. 'Krupp!* Four or
six pounder at extreme range,' said the expert. 'They still think we're
the—Light Horse. They'll come to be fairly regular from now on.'
Sure enough, every twenty minutes or so, one judgmatic shell pitched
on our slope. We waited, seeing nothing in the emptiness, and hearing
only a faint murmur as of wind along gas-jets, running in and out of
the unconcerned hills.

  Then pom-poms opened. These were nasty little one-pounders, ten
in a belt (which usually jammed about the sixth round). On soft
ground they merely thudded. On rock-face the shell breaks up and
yowls like a cat. My friend for the first time seemed interested. 'If
these are *their* pom-poms, it's Pretoria for us,'* was his diagnosis. I
looked behind me—the whole length of South Africa down to Cape
Town—and it seemed very far. I felt that I could have covered it in five
minutes under fair conditions, but—*not* with those aimed shots up my
back. The pom-poms opened again at a bare rock-reef that gave the
shells full value. For about two minutes a file of racing ponies, their
tails and their riders' heads well down, showed and vanished north-
ward. 'Our pom-poms,' said the correspondent. 'Le Gallais,* I expect.
Now we shan't be long.' All this time the absurd Krupp was faithfully
feeling for us, *vice*— Light Horse, and, given a few more hours,
might perhaps hit one of us. Then to the left, almost under us, a small
piece of hanging woodland filled and fumed with our shrapnel much as
a man's moustache fills with cigarette-smoke. It was most impressive
and lasted for quite twenty minutes. Then silence; then a movement of
men and horses from our side up the slope, and the hangar our guns
had been hammering spat steady fire at them. More Boer ponies on

more skylines; a last flurry of pom-poms on the right and a little frieze
of far-off meek-tailed ponies, already out of rifle range.

'*Maffeesh*,'* said the correspondent, and fell to writing on his knee.
'We've shifted 'em.'

Leaving our infantry to follow men on pony-back towards the Equ-
ator, we returned to the farm-house. In the donga where he was
waiting someone squibbed off a rifle just after we took our seats, and
our driver flogged out over the rocks to the danger of our sacred
bottles.

Then Bloemfontein, and Gwynne storming in late with his accounts
complete—one hundred and twenty-five casualties, and the general
opinion that 'French* was a bit of a butcher' and a tale of the General
commanding the cavalry who absolutely refused to break up his horses
by galloping them across raw rock—'not for any dam' Boer.'*

EXPLANATORY NOTES

5 THE WIDOW'S PARTY (*Barrack-Room Ballads*, 1892). *The Widow*: Queen Victoria.

7 THE DRUMS OF THE FORE AND AFT (*Wee Willie Winkie and Other Stories*): first published *Wee Willie Winkie and Other Child Stories*, 1889. The early editions had an epigraph, later omitted, from Isaiah 11:6 'And a little child shall lead them.'

No specific regiment is represented in Kipling's picture of 'The Fore and Aft', and no specific battle is the model for the one described, but it incorporates features of several engagements in the 2nd Afghan War of 1878–80, especially General Sir Donald Stewart's victory at Ahmed Khel in May 1880, in the face of a ferocious charge by several thousand Ghazis (see note to p. 29), and General G. R. S. Burrows's disastrous defeat at Maiwand in the following July. In the latter engagement Burrows's brigade, outmanœuvred, out-gunned, and outnumbered, disintegrated under a Ghazi attack, and the 66th Foot (the Berkshire Regiment) broke in panic as the front collapsed, although many of them subsequently rallied and sold their lives dearly. It was after visiting the Officers' and Sergeants' Messes of the Berkshires in Bermuda in 1894 that Kipling wrote 'That Day' (see above, pp. 39–40), in which a soldier tells of his own experience of such a débâcle. By then the regiment had been given the title 'Royal' for its exemplary steadiness in the battle of Tofrik in the Sudan in March 1885.

It has been suggested (by Charles Carrington in his biography of Kipling) that the story of the two drummer boys derives from an episode in Robert Orme's *History of the Military Transactions of the British Nation in Indostan* (London, 1763–78). In an account of the War of Coromandel in South-East India in 1759 Orme describes the storming by the British of the fortress of Masulipatam, in the course of which one part of the attacking force fled, leaving its commander, Captain Yorke, 'alone, with only two drummers, who were black boys, beating the grenadiers march, which they continued, but in vain, for none rejoined'. Captain Yorke went back, rallied the troops, and renewed the attack, in the course of which he was wounded in both thighs but carried to safety by his men, while 'each of the black drummers was killed dead at his side' (vol. 2, part 2, pp. 486–7).

Two words: see additional note on p. 364.

the Horse Guards: Army Headquarters, from the fact that the Commander-in-Chief and other senior personnel had their offices in the Horse Guards building in Whitehall.

8 *the Empress*: Queen Victoria had been proclaimed Empress of India on 1 January 1877.

in another two years: in accordance with the short-service system —basically six years with the Colours and six with the Reserve— introduced in 1870 by Edward Cardwell (1813–86) as Secretary of State for War, with a view to establishing effective reserve forces for use in the event of a major war.

9 *the Pocket-book*: *The Soldier's Pocket Book for Field Service* (London, 1869) by Sir Garnet Joseph Wolseley (1833–1913), later Field-Marshal Lord Wolseley, one of Britain's leading generals. He was an advocate of Army reform and somewhat given to self-advertisement, being indeed the original for 'the very model of a modern major-general' in *The Pirates of Penzance*. Kipling had a greater admiration for his main rival Sir Frederick Roberts, later Field-Marshal Lord Roberts of Kandahar (see note to p. 87).

10 *until that backing is re-introduced*: by the reintroduction of long-service enlistment as advocated by Roberts and others.

passed through Dr Barnardo's hands: been brought up in one of the homes for destitute children founded by the philanthropist Dr Thomas John Barnardo (1845–1905).

11 *Ishmaels*: it was prophesied of Ishmael (Genesis 16: 12) that his hand would be against every man's, and every man's hand against him.

12 *Bazar-Sergeant*: NCO responsible for Regimental Bazar in which Indian stall-keepers etc. provided goods and services for men of the battalion.

13 *jarnwar*: Hindustani *janwar* = beast, animal.

14 *hanty-room*: ante-room of Officers' Mess, used as sitting-room, as distinct from the dining-room.

15 *stories written in brief upon the Colours*: the regiment's battle-honours, embroidered on its Colours.

territorial idea: the policy which figured in the Army reforms of the early 1870s of associating each regiment with a particular geographical area for recruitment and other purposes.

batta: extra allowances for field service.

17 *. . . split on a pal*: Cockney saying, 'split' being slang for 'informing on', 'betraying confidence'.

Paythans: soldiers' pronunciation of 'Pathans' (general term for tribesmen of the North-West Frontier of India).

anna: coin of very small value, the sixteenth part of a rupee.

C.B. . . . K.C.B.: Commandership or Knight-Commandership of the Order of the Bath.

20 *housewife*: (pron. hussif) container for sewing materials.

21 *Babus*: English-speaking Indian clerks.

22 *Beni-Israel*: Children of Israel, with reference to a widely held theory that the Pathans were descendants of the Lost Tribes of Israel which disappeared after the Babylonian Captivity. Cf. p. 14 above: 'The War of the Lost Tribes.'

puckrowed: caught, laid hold of.

Kiswasti: why?

Pushtu: the language of Afghanistan.

Hya: Hindustani greeting.

Khana . . . peenikapanee: food, water to drink.

ke marfik: like.

bundobust: arrangement.

kushy: pleased.

E.P.: *sc.* E.P.I.P. = European Privates Indian Pattern.

23 *Scotch and Gurkha troops*: there was a special affinity, maintained for many decades, between certain Highland and Gurkha regiments such as the Seaforth Highlanders and 5th Gurkhas who were brigaded together throughout the 2nd Afghan War (see Field-Marshal Lord Roberts of Kandahar, *Forty-One Years in India*, London, 1897, vol. 2, p. 374 n.).

24 *the country*: i.e. Afghanistan.

25 *screw-guns*: light pieces of artillery designed for mountain warfare: they could be dismantled, loaded on mules, and then quickly reassembled by the component parts being screwed together.

26 *crowning the heights above*: standard practice in warfare on the North-West Frontier to avoid becoming targets for an enemy holding the higher ground.

27 *zymotic*: infectious.

Martini-Henry bullets: the Martini-Henry single-shot, breechloading rifle, with a calibre of ·45 inch, was then the standard issue for the British Army.

pickets: bullets.

28 . . . *impenetrable to the eye*: cordite, which was smokeless, was not adopted as a propellant until 1891.

29 *Ghazis*: fanatical Moslem warriors, dedicated to the slaughter of infidels.

right: all the texts have 'left', but Kipling's own description of the battle-plan on p. 26 shows that he meant the right! Cf. pp. 34–5.

30 . . . *Hallelujah*: source unidentified; probably a nigger-minstrel song.

. . . *in the morning*: from the negro spiritual 'Sweet Morning'.

kukris: curved Gurkha knives.

31 *Subadar-Major*: the senior Indian officer in an infantry regiment of the Indian Army at that date.

Jemadar: platoon commander.

cripple-stopper Snider bullets: 'cripple-stopper' was a small gun for killing wounded birds, but here it means bullets with stopping power enough to cripple where they do not kill. The Snider, recently superseded by the Martini-Henry, was the British Army's first breech-loading rifle. It remained the standard rifle for the Indian Army until late in the century.

32 '*stung by the splendour of a sudden thought*': a line from Robert Browning's poem 'A Death in the Desert'.

33 *the old tune of the Old Line*: 'The British Grenadiers' does not celebrate only the Grenadier Guards: grenades came into extensive use in the sieges of the late seventeenth century, and in the eighteenth all Line battalions had a Grenadier company specializing in their use.

36 *Rissaldar*: Indian officer equivalent to captain in an Indian cavalry regiment.

doolies: litters for the wounded.

37 *heliograph*: signalling device for flashing messages in Morse code by the use of mirrors reflecting the sun's rays.

39 THAT DAY (*The Seven Seas*): first published *Pall Mall Gazette*, 25 April 1895. For the occasion see note to p. 7.

sove-ki-poo: *sauve qui peut* (save himself who can; every man for himself).

41 A CONFERENCE OF THE POWERS (*Many Inventions*): first published *Pioneer*, 23 and 24 May 1890. The story deals with the later phases of the 3rd Burmese War. Hostilities broke out in

1885, organized resistance was quickly overcome, and the country was annexed on 1 January 1886; but members of the disbanded Burmese army carried on a mixture of guerrilla warfare and armed banditry for several years.

... *ocean foam*: from 'Philosophy', by James Thomson (1834–82). The first two lines are quoted ironically, to express thoughts Cleever in this story might have had before his eyes were opened: the third line is used here to stress the illusory nature of such convictions.

The Infant: nickname of a character who reappears in *Stalky and Co.* (see p. 105) and other stories. Boileau had figured in one of Kipling's earliest Indian stories, 'The Unlimited "Draw" of "Tick" Boileau', *Quartette*, 1885.

the Black Mountain Expedition: a punitive campaign carried out in October and November 1888 in an area of the North-West Frontier where two British officers and some Gurkha soldiers had been murdered by tribesmen.

the Horse Guards: see note to p. 7.

Fellaheen: Egyptian peasants. Egyptian regiments had proved incapable of standing up to Sudanese attacks in the campaigns of 1883–5 (see notes to pp. 58, 60), but they were now being retrained by British instructors, and were to play their part in the reconquest of the Sudan in 1896–8.

42 *Armageddon*: the last great battle between nations before the Day of Judgement (see Revelation 16: 16).

the Dragon of Wantley: a monster which figures in Percy's *Reliques of Ancient English Poetry* (London, 1765).

43 *the pundit caste*: Kipling adopts an attitude of anthropological detachment to the learned and literary worlds, which he had found uncongenial on his return from India.

45 *dacoits*: armed bandits, guerrillas.

bukh: talk.

daur: expedition.

46 *Pukka*: genuine, reliable, gentlemanly.

47 *Theebaw*: king of Burma 1878–85. His savagely despotic rule, tortures and massacres, intrigues with France, and attempted exploitation of British commercial interests led to increasing tensions with the Government of India, culminating in the war of 1885, which quickly resulted in his deposition.

49 *punchy*: short-backed and thickset (cf. 'Suffolk punch').

subchiz: outfit.

50 *Clive*: Robert Clive (1725–74), later Baron Clive, won fame as a
military commander in Britain's wars with France in the Carnatic,
and his victory at Plassey in 1757 established British supremacy in
Bengal (of which he subsequently became Governor).

Zazel: Azazel, a jinn or demon of Moslem legend: when God
commanded the angels to worship Adam Azazel refused, and was
cast down from Heaven.

53 *Andamans*: islands in the Bay of Bengal, where the Government of
India had established a penal settlement.

the Empire: well-known music-hall in Leicester Square.

54 *highly respectable gondoliers*: from the song 'I stole the Prince and I
brought him here' in Act 1 of Gilbert and Sullivan's *The
Gondoliers* (first performed in December 1889).

. . . as good as they: misquotation from 'The Ballad of Chevy
Chase' in Percy's *Reliques*.

a sufficiency of kissing: from James Thomson's poem 'Art' ('Singing is
sweet; but be sure of this, / Lips only sing when they cannot kiss').

55 THE YOUNG BRITISH SOLDIER (*Barrack-Room Ballads*): first
published *Scots Observer*, 28 June 1890.

rag-box: mouth (from 'rag' as slang for 'tongue').

on the shout: on a bout of drinking.

crack on nor blind: curse.

56 *Martini*: see note to p. 27.

limbers: the limber was a detachable part of gun-carriages, with
two wheels, axle, pole for horses, and frame containing ammuni-
tion chests.

58 THE LIGHT THAT FAILED, Chapter 2: the novel was first published,
with a rather factitious happy ending, in *Lippincott's Monthly
Magazine*, January 1891, but this version was quickly superseded by
the first English trade edition of the same year, with its declaration
that 'this is the story of *The Light that Failed* as it was originally
conceived by the Writer'. Chapter 1 describes Dick Heldar's boy-
hood love for Maisie, reminiscent of Kipling's for Florence Garrard,
and an episode in which they practise shooting with a revolver and
Dick's cheek is scorched by powder when she fires carelessly.
This is recalled at the end of Chapter 2. The historical context for
this chapter is Wolseley's expedition of 1884–5 to relieve General
Charles Gordon in Khartoum, where he was besieged by the

forces of the Mahdi—a Moslem fundamentalist Messiah who as religious and military leader had roused the Sudan to repudiate corrupt Egyptian rule. Gordon (1833–85) had previously been Governor-General of the Sudan, and had done much to suppress the slave-trade there: he was now expected to extricate the Egyptian garrisons, but once at Khartoum he refused to leave, since this would have meant abandoning large numbers who were dependent on Anglo–Egyptian protection. He was now trapped, and though his predicament was partly of his own making, public opinion had forced a reluctant government to mount a relief expedition. The battle described draws some of its features from that of Abu Klea, fought by the Desert, not the River, Column on 17 January 1885, in which the attacking dervishes succeeded in breaking into one side of the square.

All the way to Kandahar: a reference to Sir Frederick Roberts's march from Kabul to the relief of the forces in Kandahar in August 1880, in the 2nd Afghan War.

whale-boat: in his successful suppression of a rebellion in Canada in the Red River Expedition of 1870 Wolseley (see note to p. 9) had covered hundreds of miles by lake and river, using boats manned by Canadian *voyageurs* (boatmen). For his expedition up the Nile he could rely on Thomas Cook's steamers for transport on the lower reaches, up to the second Cataract at Wady Halfa, but for the higher reaches he had several hundred boats built of the kind he had used in Canada, and he employed *voyageurs* and West African Kroo Boys as boatmen.

59 *a camel-corps*: a Camel Corps was formed for this expedition with contingents from Guards, Line Infantry, and Heavy and Light Cavalry Regiments, to form the main part of the Desert Column. They fought their way to the river after the Battle of Abu Klea (see above).

Assiut and Assuan: posts on the Nile far to the north, between Cairo and Wady Halfa.

60 *from Suakin to the Sixth Cataract*: Suakin or Suakim was a British-held port on the Red Sea coast of the Sudan, NE of Khartoum; the Sixth Cataract was that nearest to the city. The land between was 'hopeless' because it consisted of hundreds of miles of barren desert controlled by the Mahdi's forces.

Arabi Pasha: Minister of War in Egypt in February 1882 and leader of a nationalist revolt. Britain intervened to restore order and protect European interests: Alexandria was bombarded by the Fleet on 11 July 1882, and Wolseley defeated Arabi's forces at Tel-el-Kebir on 13 September, from which point Britain became inextricably involved in Egyptian and Sudanese affairs.

first miserable work round Suakin: an Egyptian force under Valentine Baker Pasha marched inland from Suakin in February 1884 in an attempt to extricate Egyptian garrisons located near the coast, but it was destroyed by the dervishes. British troops had to be hastily deployed to restore the situation in the immediate hinterland, and they defeated the dervishes decisively at El Teb in February and Tamai in March (and again at Tofrik in March 1885); but the Hadendowah tribe under their leader Osman Digna remained a threat to Suakin.

61 *Hakodate*: Japanese port.

Berbera: port on Somaliland coast opposite Aden.

Tajurrah Bay: Golfe de Tadjoura in French Somaliland.

Fuzzies: the Sudanese warriors were nicknamed 'Fuzzy-Wuzzies' by the British because of their spectacularly long frizzed hair.

Verestchagin: Vasili Vasilievitch Vereschagin (1842–1904), Russian war artist.

62 *the Gate of the Two War-Ships*: Suakin was built on an island connected with the mainland by a causeway, at the end of a long deep inlet. Admiral Sir William Hewett, VC, who was in charge of the defence, anchored gunboats at appropriate points to increase the available fire-power if the town was attacked.

63 *Philae . . . Merawi and Huella*: Philae lies far to the north, near the First Cataract. Merawi and Huella lie to the south of the Nubian Desert, west and east respectively of the Fourth Cataract. (All editions read 'Herawi and Muella'.)

Euryalus: corvette in Admiral Hewett's Red Sea squadron.

64 *Pisan soldiery . . . bathing*: lost cartoon by Michelangelo for a wall-painting for the Council Chamber in Florence, preserved in an engraving by Marcantonio Raimondi (see Heinrich Wölfflin, *Classic Art*, trans. Peter and Linda Murray, London, 1953, pp. 48–9).

66–7 *a savage red disc . . . spoilt my aim . . . have to run home . . . aiming low and to the left*: echoes of Chapter 1.

67 *Gordon . . . was dead*: Khartoum was stormed and Gordon killed on 26 January 1885, two days before the advance party of the relieving force, under Sir Charles Wilson, sailed up the river only to find the town in the Mahdi's hands.

... *outside the city*: four Nile steamers had been sent downstream by Gordon to make contact with the relieving force. Wilson used two, the *Bordein* and the *Telahawieh*, for his reconnaissance to Khartoum but on the return journey both were wrecked. Those aboard were subsequently rescued from the island where they had taken refuge.

68 FUZZY-WUZZY (*Barrack-Room Ballads*): first published *Scots Observer*, 15 March 1890. On the title see note to p. 61.

Suakim: see notes to p. 60.

a Zulu impi dished us up in style: an *impi* was a Zulu regiment, and the reference is to the annihilation of a British force by the Zulus at Isandhlwana on 22 January 1879. The Khyber Hills are on the North-West Frontier of India; and the British experience of Boer marksmanship had been in the defeats of the 1st Boer War of 1880–1.

Martinis: see note to p. 27.

you broke the square: on two notable occasions, at the Battles of Tamai and Abu Klea (see notes to pp. 60 and 58).

70 THE MUTINY OF THE MAVERICKS (*Life's Handicap*): first published *Mine Own People*, 1891. *Mavericks*: unbranded cattle, strays; hence persons of roving, independent temperament. The fictional Irish regiment so nicknamed is that in which Kim's father served (*Kim*, Chapter 5). The notion that Irish troops in the British Army might make common cause with Indian nationalists had been canvassed by Maharajah Dhulip Singh (see below) in 1889: see 'The Irish Conspiracy' in *Early Verse by Rudyard Kipling*, pp. 452–5.

Sec. 7. (1) ... Navy: from the opening clause of a section of the Army Act prescribing the death penalty for any member of the armed forces inciting others to mutiny or sedition.

the I.A.A.: an invented abbreviation. Irish American Army?

Castle Garden: at tip of Manhattan, from 1885 a landing-depôt for immigrants.

a particular section of Scotland Yard: a Special Irish Branch was established at Scotland Yard (the headquarters of the Metropolitan Police) to counter Fenian terrorism in Britain in the early 1880s; this was then subsumed in the Special Branch.

Lucrezia Borgia: notorious daughter (1480–1519) of Pope Alexander VI, reputed to use murder as a regular instrument of policy.

71 ... *in clear daylight*: in June 1891 two officers and four ratings

were killed by the bursting of a gun on HMS *Cordelia* during gunnery practice in the Pacific; and in March 1889 HMS *Sultan* had run on a rock in the Comino Channel near Malta, the Captain being subsequently reprimanded for sailing too close to the shore.

bears: Stock Exchange slang for speculators selling in expectation of or to help produce a fall in prices.

P.D.Q.: pretty damned quick.

72 *Dhulip Singh*: the son, born 1837, of Maharajah Ranjit Singh, the last independent ruler of the Punjab. The Sikh Wars were fought during his minority; the Punjab was annexed by Britain; and he lived most of his life in England with great ostentation. After an official enquiry into his debts in 1880 he turned against Britain, and was prevented from revisiting India in 1886 when he issued an inflammatory proclamation to the Sikhs. He flirted with Russia as a potential ally, and died in Paris in 1893.

the Other Power: Russia, Britain's main rival and potential enemy in Asia.

Horse Guards: see note to p. 7.

73 *moonlighters*: persons committing outrages by night on tenants in Ireland who did not co-operate with the Land League in its anti-landlord campaign.

74 *rath*: enclosure made by strong earth wall, to serve as fort and residence for a chief; the remains could become associated with local superstitions.

75 *thirty years gone*: in the Indian Mutiny of 1857–8.

sugared: euphemism for 'buggered'.

76 *the Black Boneens*: nickname of a fictional regiment.

77 *Vittoria . . . Sebastopol*: regimental battle-honours embroidered on the Colours. Vittoria, Salamanca, and Toulouse were battles in the Peninsular War; Moodkee, Ferozshah, and Sobraon in the Sikh War; Inkerman, the Alma, and Sebastopol in the Crimean War.

79 *. . . waters o' the Oxus*: lines possibly by Kipling himself though he did not acknowledge them; singable, it has been pointed out, to the tune of 'Marching through Georgia'.

80 *. . . goin' to New Orleans*: source unidentified.

on his own hook: on his own account.

82 *hara-kiri*: suicide.

83 *pot-valiant*: rashly brave (lit. made brave by liquor).

84 *Sam Hall*: a music-hall song about an unrepentant murderer who 'damns the eyes' of all connected with him. ('The parson he did come— / He did come! / Yes the Parson he did come— / He did come! / The Parson he did come / And he looked so bloody glum / As he spoke of Kingdom Come— / Damn his eyes!').

. . . says the Shan-van Vogh: from an Irish revolutionary song of the Napoleonic period.

Belshazzar: see Daniel 5: 5–28 for the writing on the wall at Belshazzar's feast ('God hath numbered thy kingdom, and finished it. Thou art weighed in the balances, and art found wanting. Thy kingdom is divided, and given to the Medes and Persians').

85 *. . . a dream of the past*: source unidentified—the lines may be Kipling's own.

87 *the Commander-in-Chief*: Sir Frederick Sleigh Roberts, VC (1832–1914), later Field-Marshal Lord Roberts, the then Commander-in-Chief, India, nicknamed 'Bobs' because of his diminutive stature. He had won a VC in the Indian Mutiny, campaigned extensively on the North-West Frontier, and served in Abyssinia. He had won particular acclaim by his strategic and tactical successes in the 2nd Afghan War of 1878–80; and he was to play a crucial role as Commander-in-Chief in South Africa in 1900, reversing the early run of Boer successes. He did not, however, remain to grapple with the problems of the guerrilla war which then developed.

makin' us work on wather: in some campaigns—e.g. the Black Mountain Expedition—Roberts insisted that no 'wet canteen' should be provided. Cf. Kipling's poem 'The Way Av Ut' *Early Verse by Rudyard Kipling*, pp. 431–2.

Eblis: the Devil in Moslem mythology.

89 FORD O'KABUL RIVER (*Barrack-Room Ballads*): first published *National Observer*, 22 November 1890. The poem deals with an episode of the 2nd Afghan War in which forty-seven men of the 10th Hussars were drowned when crossing Kabul River near Jalalabad, some 75 miles from Kabul itself, on 31 March 1879. There is a full discussion of the circumstances in the *Kipling Journal* for March 1985.

91 THE LOST LEGION (*Many Inventions*): first published *Strand Magazine*, May 1892. The title recalls the lost legions of Quintilius Varus, whose army was annihilated in the Teutoburgian

Forest in AD 9, to the distress of the Emperor Augustus. The historical basis for the story is suggested by a passage in Lord Roberts's memoirs of *Forty-One years in India* (London, 1897, vol. I, pp. 111–12): 'On the 23rd May [1857], the day after the disarmament [of native regiments in Peshawur], news was received that the 55th Native Infantry had mutinied at Mardan, and that the 10th Irregular Cavalry, which was divided between Nowshera and Mardan, had turned against us. A force was at once despatched to restore order, and Nicholson [the formidable John Nicholson (1821–57), famous as a soldier and administrator] accompanied it as political officer. No sooner did the mutineers, on the morning of the 25th, catch sight of the approaching column than they broke out of the fort and fled towards the Swat Hills. Nicholson pursued with his levies and mounted police, and before night 120 fugitives were killed and as many more made prisoners. The remainder found no welcome among the hill tribes, and eventually became wanderers over the country until they died or were killed.'

John Lawrence: John Laird Mair Lawrence (1811–79), later Baron Lawrence of the Punjab and Grately, and Viceroy of India from 1863 to 1869, was Chief Commissioner of the Punjab when the Mutiny broke out. One of the giants of Indian administration, he had won the loyalty of the recently conquered Sikhs, and he kept the Punjab and Frontier calm while sending many of his troops, including Sikhs, to Delhi under Nicholson to besiege the mutineers.

93 *Mullah*: Moslem religious leader and teacher.

94 *a force*: the Punjab Frontier Force (nicknamed 'Piffers').

95 *the finest native cavalry in the world*: cavalry of the Queen's Own Corps of Guides, an élite unit which also included infantry, raised originally at Peshawur in the 1840s on the instructions of Henry Lawrence (John Lawrence's brother). It recruited from beyond as well as within the imperial frontier.

98 *breastplates*: not armour worn by riders—the Guides Cavalry wore khaki from their first foundation—but leather straps across the horses' chests.

100 *Rissala*: regiment (strictly a troop of cavalry or regiment of native horse).

101 *sag*: dog.

102 *cateran*: freebooter.

103 ARITHMETIC ON THE FRONTIER (*Departmental Ditties*, 1886).

'*All flesh is grass*': 1 Peter 1: 24 ('For all flesh is as grass').

'*villainous saltpetre*': gunpowder (see *1 Henry IV*, Act 1, Sc. 3).

Yusufzaies: members of Afghan tribe to NE of Peshawur.

jezail: long Afghan musket.

the Crammer's boast: prize pupil of private tutor preparing candidates for entry to the Royal Military College at Sandhurst.

tulwar: curved Indian sabre.

104 *captives of our bow and spear*: source unidentified, but cf. Jeremiah 6: 23.

105 SLAVES OF THE LAMP, Part 2 (*Stalky and Co.*): first published *Cosmopolis*, May 1897. The story forms the conclusion of *Stalky and Co.*, in which Kipling seeks to demonstrate how qualities developed at school were relevant to warfare on the North-West Frontier. The general historical context was the debate between advocates of a 'forward' policy in Afghanistan (by which Britain sought to control the tribes and hence help secure the mountain passes against the risk of Russian invasion) and those who believed that India's frontier was best defended on the Indus. The particular stimulus may have been his conversations with Sir George Scott Robertson (1852–1916) about the latter's defence of Chitral—one of Britain's most remote outposts—in March/April 1895, with a mixed garrison of Sikhs, Kashmir Rifles, and Chitralis.

That very Infant: see above pp. 41 f.

detrimentals: younger sons, ineligible suitors.

ex Tamar: from the troopship *Tamar*.

105–6 *Dickson . . . Abanazar*: Dickson ('Dick Four'), Tertius, and Abanazar are fictional versions of Kipling's schoolfellows at *Westward Ho!* 'Abanazar' was a character in the pantomime *Aladdin*, for which the boys were rehearsing in 'Slaves of the Lamp', Part 1.

106 *a lean Irishman*: M'Turk in *Stalky and Co.*, based on Kipling's school friend G. C. Beresford.

dâk-bungalow: rest-house provided for use of Government officials travelling on business; available to other travellers on payment of a fee.

provincial: relating to the provinces of India which they had served in.

107 *the night Rabbits-Eggs rocked King*: a reference to 'Slaves of the

Lamp', Part 1, in which Stalky, at feud with the unpopular Mr King, contrived an attack on him by a drunken carrier ('Rabbits-Eggs') who threw jagged stones through the house-master's study window in retaliation for being 'tweaked' by catapult by the unseen Stalky.

Stalky: based on Kipling's school friend L. C. Dunsterville (1865–1946).

the camp at Pindi in '87: a 'Camp of Exercise' for military training at Rawalpindi in the Punjab.

broke: cashiered.

at the back of Suakin: Dunsterville was stationed at Suakin in the summer of 1885 (see notes to p. 60).

Fuzzies: see note to p. 61.

108 *bukhing*: talking.

109 *summo ingenio*: with the greatest cleverness (Latin tag).

D.A.Q.M.G.: Deputy Assistant Quarter Master General.

Durbar Sahib: the Golden Temple of the Sikhs at Amritsar.

khud: precipitous hillside beside road.

110 *poshteen*: sheepskin coat of Afghan type.

Aladdin . . . Emperor: the roles played by Dick Four and Tertius in the pantomime.

111 *sungars*: stone breastworks.

Guru: religious teacher; hence an authority, a leader.

112 *nullah*: river-bed, usually a dry one.

113 *privatim*: privately.

Jemadar: see note to p. 31.

114 *Pushtu*: see note to p. 22.

Koran Sahib: Stalky's surname in *Stalky and Co.* is Corkran. Cf. p. 119.

115 *Kubbadar! tumbleinga!*: 'Look out; you'll fall' (Kipling).

Martinis: see note to p. 27.

brownin' 'em: firing into the group without selecting individual targets.

116 *à la pas de charge*: at the double.

Arrah, Patsy, mind the baby: popular song which had figured in the pantomime in 'Slaves of the Lamp', Part 1.

117 *gram-bags*: bags of pulse for feeding horses.

Brahmini bull: a bull dedicated to the god Siva and thus holy to Hindus—hence able to raid food-stalls, for example, with impunity.

consilio et auxilio Rutton Singhi: with the advice and help of Rutton Singh (Latin tag with pseudo-Latin genitive form of 'Singh').

Engadine: resort area in Switzerland.

118 *Naik*: corporal.

disgustful amours: an echo from an earlier episode in *Stalky and Co*.

take safeguard: accept guarantee of safe-conduct.

rapparee: freebooter.

Bancroft: Sir Squire Bancroft (1841–1926), well-known actor-manager.

119 *pukka*: genuine.

Khan Bahadur: honorific title awardable by Government of India.

120 *Pledged the State's ticker*: in 'Slaves of the Lamp', Part 1, Stalky had pawned the narrator's watch for the general good.

Warren Hastings: 1732–1818; the first Governor-General of India and one of the main architects of British power in the subcontinent.

. . . is the proper——: if an offence had been committed by an Army officer, the Commander-in-Chief would be the proper ultimate authority to take disciplinary action.

121 *Sanawar Orphan Asylum*: Military Orphanage in a hill-station.

two-anna: cheap.

basket-hanger: Mr King had had a decorative basket hanging in his window—a cause of aesthetic offence to M'Turk.

femme incomprise: woman misunderstood.

122 *Jullundur doab*: tongue of land between two rivers at Jullundur in the Punjab.

bhai: brother.

125 RIMMON (*The Five Nations*, 1903). *Rimmon*: a Babylonian deity. When Naaman, captain of the host of the King of Syria, was cured of leprosy by bathing in Jordan, he accepted the God of Israel as the only true god, but explained to the prophet Elisha that he would have to continue to bow down in the House (i.e.

temple) of Rimmon when the King his master worshipped there (2 Kings 5: 18). The poem is an attack on the re-establishment of the peace-time *status quo* by the military Old Guard, and its resistance to necessary Army reform.

Saying He went . . . a mate: in the prophet Elijah's challenge to the priests of Baal he mocked them for their god's failure to manifest his power, saying 'either he is talking, or he is pursuing, or he is in a journey, or peradventure he sleepeth, and must be awaked' (1 Kings 18: 27).

127 THE WAY THAT HE TOOK (*Land and Sea Tales for Scouts and Guides*): first published *Daily Express*, 12, 13, and 14 June, 1900.

Almost every word . . . beforehand: this headnote was added when the story was collected in *Land and Sea Tales* in 1923, in the aftermath of the Great War. When the story first appeared the Boer War was still in progress and was far from seeming 'a very small one as wars were reckoned' (cf. p. xvi above). On its original publication the story was headed by the verses

> Put forth to watch, unschooled, alone,
> 'Twixt hostile earth and sky;
> The mottled lizard 'neath the stone
> Is wiser here than I.

> What stir across the haze of heat?
> What omen down the wind?
> The buck that broke before my feet—
> They knew, but I am blind!

nullah: see note to p. 112.

Leviathan: a monstrous beast (biblical).

the loyal Dutch: the Afrikaners of Cape Colony, a self-governing British colony like Natal, as opposed to the burghers or citizens of the Transvaal and Orange Free State, the two independent Boer republics now at war with Britain. The 'loyalty' of the Cape Afrikaners was often suspect.

128 *Mounted Infantry*: the need for mobility in dealing with a highly mobile enemy led to the conversion of many units to Mounted Infantry, which travelled on horseback but fought on foot, like the original dragoons. Cf. Kipling's poem 'M.I.'.

129 *Karroo*: dry tableland in South Africa.

Oudtshorn: this reference, to a township some 200 miles east of Cape Town, locates this part of the story deep in Cape Colony.

Matjesfontein: health resort for lung complaints established in the Karroo in the 1880s.

129–30 *pump him*: leave him short of breath.

130 *Vat jou . . . hoepelbeen*:

'Pack your kit and trek, Ferreira
Pack your kit and trek.
A long pull, all on one side,
Johnnie with the lame leg.'   (Kipling's translation)

put Rhodes in a cage: on the outbreak of war in October 1899 the Boers besieged Mafeking, Ladysmith, and Kimberley (famous for its diamond mines). Cecil Rhodes (1853–1902), millionaire, former Premier of Cape Colony, and one of the main exponents of British hegemony in Africa, was among those trapped in Kimberley till the town was relieved in mid-February, 1900.

they will all rise: i.e. the Afrikaners of the Cape. De Aar was a railway junction over 400 miles NE of Cape Town but still well within the boundaries of Cape Colony.

Prieska: town about 10 miles NW of De Aar, on the Orange River. A short-lived Afrikaner rising did break out there early in 1900, on the arrival of a Boer raiding-party under General Steenkamp.

Vlei: hollow filled with water in rainy weather.

131 *schel—*: sc. skelms = rascals.

Paarl: town and fruit-growing area near Cape Town.

vrouws: housewives.

132 *kraal*: native settlement or cattle enclosure; here simply an enclosure made of thornbushes.

meer-cats: South African mongooses.

133 *Guy's*: Guy's Hospital, a famous teaching hospital in London, founded in 1724 by the bookseller Thomas Guy.

sjamboked: beaten (with a rhinoceros-hide whip).

133–4 *. . . a hundred miles away*: on 11 February 1900 Lord Roberts, the new Commander-in-Chief, with Kitchener of Khartoum (1850–1916), fresh from the reconquest of the Sudan, as his Chief of Staff, began a great flank-march to turn the main Boer positions on the Modder River. Major-General French (1852–1925), later Field Marshal Lord French, who commanded the Cavalry Division which led the advance, had moved much of his force from Colesberg in Cape Colony, where they had been stationed, weakening the remaining garrison there.

134 *kopjes*: small isolated hills, tactically significant features in the South African landscape.

Colonials: in this context, Boers of Cape Colony.

Beaufort West: town on railway between De Aar and Cape Town.

The President: Stephanus Johannes Paulus Kruger (1825–1904), President of the Transvaal Republic 1883–1900.

Mausers: modern German rifles, magazine, not single-shot, of which Kruger had purchased 37,000 in preparation for war. The British Army's single-shot Martini-Henry had been replaced by the Lee Metford magazine-rifle, and it in turn was superseded by the Lee-Enfield.

135 *Worcester . . . Paarl*: both towns on the railway line near Cape Town.

Stormberg: Stormberg Junction in Cape Colony had been the scene of a disastrous defeat for General Gatacre on 9/10 December 1899. An attempted night-attack on a Boer position with exhausted troops, incompetent guides, and inadequate communications and intelligence resulted in loss of direction, tactical disadvantage, significant casualties, demoralized flight, and the accidental abandonment of 600 men as prisoners.

rooineks: 'red-necks—English soldiers' (Kipling).

helio-station: see note to p. 37.

136 *Stellenbosch*: town near Cape Town. For the sinister significance its name was to acquire, see note to p. 145.

138 *echelon of squadrons . . . stable litter*: 'echelon of squadrons' is an authentic military term; 'cat's-cradle of troops' and 'quarter column of stable-litter' are derisive coinages to mock the irrelevance of formal cavalry manœuvres to the tactical realities of war.

140 *it never occurred to them to dismount*: an example of poor horse-care, as dismounting would have rested the horses.

Pretoria gaol: many British prisoners-of-war were held in Pretoria, the capital of the Transvaal.

145 THE OUTSIDER (*Uncollected Prose, Part II*, Sussex Edn.): first published *Daily Express*, 19, 20 and 21 June, 1900. The verse heading is a parody of the hymn 'From Greenland's icy mountains'.

Stormberg's midnight mountain: see note to p. 135.

Sanna's captured Post: in the course of Roberts's victorious march northwards (see note to pp. 133–4) the British Army occupied Bloemfontein, the capital of the Orange Free State, on 13 March 1900; but the new hazard of guerrilla warfare was signalled by

Christiaan De Wet's successful ambush, on 31 March, of a British column of artillery and mounted infantry at Sanna's Post, where Bloemfontein's waterworks were situated. Major-General Broadwood had sent no scouts ahead of his column, which walked straight into the trap. Kipling was at Bloemfontein at the time and saw something of the aftermath.

Magersfontein: scene of a British defeat on 11 December 1899, when Lieut.-General Lord Methuen attempted a night attack on Boer positions which he had not reconnoitred or indeed located. By marching the Highland Brigade in a close-packed column on to the Boers' killing-ground he guaranteed their humiliating defeat with heavy casualties.

a cursèd kraal: i.e. Stellenbosch. This town near Cape Town became the main base for the Army. More than usually incompetent officers were returned there, to tasks where they would do less harm than in the field; they were then said to have been 'Stellenbosched'. For 'kraal' see note on p. 132.

the Rand: the Witwatersrand, a ridge in the Transvaal where great deposits of gold had been discovered in 1886. The mines were worked by Uitlanders ('foreigners') or immigrants, many of whom were British. Their discontent at being excluded from the franchise led to fears that they might stage a rebellion: hence the Transvaal Government's search for arms.

146 *Johannesburg*: the industrial and commercial centre of the Rand.

a Raid: the ill-fated Jameson Raid, led by Dr Leander Starr Jameson, a close associate of Cecil Rhodes (see note to p. 130), in an attempt to topple the Transvaal Government and secure the position of the Uitlanders. The raiders were intercepted and humiliatingly captured by hastily mobilized Boer commandos on 2 January 1896.

Hollander: name given by the Boers to the Dutch of the Low Countries.

the Marquesas Islands: in the South Pacific (i.e. on the other side of the world).

bumble-puppy: whist played very inexpertly—a not unfair comparison for the Uitlanders' attempts at conspiracy. They most notably failed to rise to support Jameson's attempted coup.

Oom Paul: Uncle Paul—i.e. Paul Kruger (see note to p. 134).

148 *. . . knew his own mind*: Kruger, who declared war on 11 October 1899.

Komati Poort: town on railway route from Johannesburg and Pretoria to Lourenço Marques, the port in Delagoa Bay in Portuguese East Africa, which was the Boers' main link with the outside world.

149 *four-coloured*: a reference to the four colours of the Transvaal Republic's flag.

Adderley Street: main street in Cape Town.

a corps of Railway Volunteers: a Railway Pioneer Regiment was in fact raised in December 1899 from skilled men from the Rand mines, with two mining engineers playing a leading part.

some General: when Roberts took command after a series of disasters in late 1899, the strength of British forces in South Africa was approximately doubled.

in '81: the year of the British defeat at Majuba in the 1st Boer War of 1880–1.

near Salisbury: i.e. on manœuvres on Salisbury Plain.

the Mount Nelson: fashionable hotel in Cape Town.

those Colonials: the contingents of Australian, New Zealand, Canadian, and South African troops were among the most effective in this war.

150 *Badajoz . . . Tel-el-Kebir*: names which might figure in the regiment's list of battle-honours (cf. note on p. 77). Badajoz, Talavera, and Toulouse were fought in the Peninsular War, Inkerman in the Crimean War, and Tel-el-Kebir in Egypt in 1882. The tactics—now old-fashioned—which had been so successful at Tel-el-Kebir consisted of a night-march across the desert and a frontal attack on the enemy's zareba—much the same as those which went so disastrously wrong when attempted against the Boers at Magersfontein (see note to p. 145).

the Long Valley: part of the area used for manœuvres at Aldershot.

in Pretoria: i.e. prisoners-of-war. Cf. note to p. 140.

151 *Mauser*: see note to p. 134.

donga: a ravine or river-bed.

152 *Bloemfontein*: see note to pp. 133–4.

the Boers blew them up on departure: Roberts's armies depended on the railway for their supplies: hence the repair was a matter of urgency even if the front had moved on northwards.

the State: i.e. the Transvaal.

153 *the Karroo*: see note to p. 129.

154 *construe*: Latin translation.

155 *Naauwpoort*: railway junction in Cape Colony.

   the Cape Minister of Railways: probably Jacobus Wilhelmus Sauer
   (1850–1913), Commissioner of Public Works in Cape Colony
   from 1898 to 1900, who was known to disapprove of Britain's
   waging war on the Boer Republics.

159 *R.E.*: Royal Engineers.

160 *the Dook 'imself*: HRH the Duke of Cambridge (1819–1904), a
   cousin of the Queen's and Commander-in-Chief of the Army from
   1856 to 1895.

   Modder: the Modder River, scene on 28 November 1899 of
   another mismanaged battle, in which the British advance, against
   unlocated Boer positions, was pinned down for some ten hours by
   Mauser fire from entrenchments in the river-bed itself.

   Let me kiss 'im for 'is mother: a sentimental ballad very popular in
   England from the 1860s onward.

   pull-through: cord with weight at one end and loop at the other
   used to pull cleaning-rag through rifle-barrel.

   Numdah: saddle-cloth.

161 STELLENBOSCH (*The Five Nations*, 1903): see note to p. 145.

   Composite Columns: mobile forces of all arms to seek out and
   engage Boer forces.

   sugared: see note to p. 75.

   drift: ford. *stoep*: verandah.

   De Wet: see notes to pp. 145, 210.

162 *pompom*: light quick-firing gun.

   kranzes: cliffs flanking ravines.

   K.C.B.: see note to p. 17.

   D.S.O.'s: Distinguished Service Orders.

163 A SAHIBS' WAR (*Traffics and Discoveries*): first published *Windsor
   Magazine* and *Collier's Weekly*, December 1901. Both sides in the
   Boer War insisted that it was a white man's war and disclaimed
   any intention of using Africans as combatants. In practice Afri-
   cans were used by both sides as labourers, transport drivers,
   cattle-guards, scouts, and spies, and occasionally as combatants,
   e.g. in the defence of Mafeking where Colonel Baden-Powell
   called his native auxiliaries 'The Black Watch'. Cf. Thomas
   Pakenham, *The Boer War* (London, 1979), pp. 547–8. For a
   possible source episode, see additional note, p. 364 below.

Pass: African natives ('Kaffirs') were required to carry passes: Umr Singh has a military pass or travel-warrant and needs no other.

Kroonstadt: town on railway in Orange Free State, between Bloemfontein and Pretoria.

164 *Sirdar Dyal Singh*: Dyal Singh Majithia (1848–98), wealthy Punjabi philanthropist and public benefactor.

Surtee: from Surat north of Bombay.

Sobraon: British victory over the Sikhs in 1846 which ended the 1st Sikh War.

Lance-Duffadar: Indian cavalry equivalent of Lance-Corporal.

ayah: nursemaid.

165 *Buwwa*: sc. Burra = big.

the Sahibs: the British Uitlanders (see notes to pp. 145–6).

the Boer-log: the Boer-people.

... killed for a jest by the Boer-log: the shooting of a British Uitlander, Thomas Edgar, in December 1898, by a member of the Johannesburg Police, and the failure to bring the constable to justice, was a cause of outrage in the city and in Imperialist circles generally.

the long war in the Tirah: after the siege of Chitral (see note to p. 105) there was a widespread rebellion on the North-West Frontier of India, with risings in the Tochi valley, the Buner valley and the Malakand, and the Tirah valley, and expeditions to suppress these were mounted in 1897–8 and 1898–9.

166 *the men of the Tochi ... Buner*: the men of the Indian Army who had crushed the uprisings in Tochi, Tirah, and Buner.

the Black Water: the sea.

Watson's Hotel: fashionable hotel in Bombay.

the Khalsa: the Sikh faith and community (one tenet of which insisted on unshorn hair and beard).

167 *us*: i.e. the Indian Army.

dâk-bungalow: see note to p. 106.

Maun Nihâl Seyn: Mount Nelson Hotel (see note to p. 149), with a confusion between Nelson and Nicholson (see note to p. 91).

a grass-cutter: a low-caste occupation.

168 *Muzbees*: lower-caste Sikhs.

Patiala . . . Jhind and Nabha: areas of the Punjab.

. . . they ate them raw: a reference to the waste of horses consequent on poor horse-mastership throughout the war.

Jehad: a reference to the commitment of the Dutch Reformed Church of South Africa to the Boer cause.

thatched: and therefore easily burnt.

169 *vine-leaf*: the maple-leaf badge of the Canadian contingents.

170 *as they were in Burma*: i.e. dacoits or guerrillas.

the Madras troops: several regiments of Madras Infantry had been included in the Burma Field Force in 1885, and there were suggestions that they were not of the highest quality.

Cavagnari Sahib and the Guides at Kabul: after the earliest phase of the 2nd Afghan War Sir Louis Cavagnari was established in July 1879 as British Resident and head of the British Mission in Kabul. In September he and his companions were massacred by Afghan soldiery who rose in revolt. His escort of Guides (see note to p. 95) fought to the last man.

We schooled . . . old days: when Kabul was reoccupied by a British force under Sir Frederick Roberts 'a stern vengeance was meted out to all those whose complicity in the murder could be proved', to quote an older edition of *The Cambridge Modern History*. An eye-witness tells how members of the mutinous regiments were identified after being brought in from surrounding villages by cavalry patrols or small expeditions, and how those found guilty were hanged in batches of ten a day. (Howard Hensman, *The Afghan War of 1879–80*, London, 1881, pp. 82 ff., 132 ff.) The *Bala Hissar* was the citadel of Kabul. The Commander-in-Chief was of course Roberts.

171 *our custom*: i.e. that of the Australians, who had a reputation for executing summary justice in such circumstances.

172 *the first Afghan War*: i.e. the first phase of the 2nd Afghan War, prior to the murder of Cavagnari. The other wars mentioned were campaigns on the North-West Frontier.

173 *nullah . . . donga*: see notes to pp. 112 and 151.

babul bushes: thorny mimosa, common in India.

177 *pompom*: see note to p. 162.

178 *cartouches*: cartridge-boxes.

180 *Si monumentum requiris circumspice*: 'if you wish to see his monument, look about you' (Latin epitaph on Sir Christopher Wren in St Paul's Cathedral, of which he was the architect).

181 WILFUL-MISSING (*The Five Nations*, 1903).

aasvogel: 'vulture' (Kipling).

182 *Domino*: finished—it's all up!

183 THE COMPREHENSION OF PRIVATE COPPER (*Traffics and Discoveries*): first published *Strand* and *Everybody's Magazine*, October 1902.

Colesberg kopjes: Colesberg was a town and area in Cape Colony, near the border of the Orange Free State; for *kopjes* see note to p. 134.

helmet back-first: said to be an old soldier's trick to secure better shade and vision by turning the projecting rear-brim to the front (*Readers' Guide*, p. 1895).

Lee-Metford: see note to p. 31.

184 *Umballa*: city in the Punjab.

old Krujer: Kruger (see note to p. 134).

Ragged Schools: free elementary schools for children of the poorest classes.

True Affection: 'Men smoked pipes more than cigarettes at that epoch, and the popular brand was a cake—chewable also—called "Hignett's True Affection"' (Kipling, *Something of Myself*, 1937, pp. 150–1).

185 *Allahabad Railway Volunteers*: a kind of auxiliary force recruited from among the railway staff in India, many of whom, like the de Souza referred to, would be Eurasian.

send you back ... quite naked: a not uncommon practice of Boer commandos when they took prisoners with whom they did not wish to be encumbered.

an English gentleman ... belong to England: the Transvaal had been annexed in 1877, and during his period of service as High Commissioner for South-East Africa (1879–80) Sir Garnet Wolseley repeatedly asserted, sometimes in rhetorical language, that the Transvaal would remain British territory on a permanent basis. In fact the annexation was annulled after the 1st Boer War of 1880–1, in which the Boers inflicted a series of defeats on British forces, culminating in the Battle of Majuba.

186 *sjambok*: see note to p. 133.

187 *a burgher*: a citizen of the Transvaal.

188 *Ladysmith ... Estcourt ... Colesberg*: three towns in British territory, the first two in Natal, the third in Cape Colony.

farm-burning: part of the policy of denying the guerrillas sources of support.

. . . to take them back: Boer women and children were moved, for the same reason, to 'concentration' camps, a term which did not then have the horrific connotations it acquired under the Nazis. The commandos were initially relieved to be freed from obligations to defend or supply their dependents, but bad hygiene and defective medical attention soon led to an appallingly high mortality rate in the camps.

188–9 *'Is nails are as clean as mine*: Copper inspects the coloration of the Transvaaler's nails to check for signs there of his being a half-caste like the Eurasians whose speech his resembles. It is uncertain whether this comparison merely makes a point about the nature of the Transvaaler's accent or whether Kipling is implying that people treated as an inferior race, as the Uitlanders were in the Transvaal, might develop the characteristics of other 'inferior' races like the Eurasians in India (cf. C. A. Bodelsen, *Aspects of Kipling's Art*, London, 1964, pp. 155 ff.).

189 *serviceable vertebree*: cervical vertebrae.

chee-chee: the kind of English spoken by Eurasians.

pukka: genuine, proper.

190 *Jerrold's Weekly*: pseudonym for *Lloyd's Weekly News*, whose editor's name was Jerrold. It was banned by the military authorities in South Africa because of its pro-Boer sentiments.

baccy-priggin': tobacco-stealing.

the 'Ebrew financeer: a reference to the alleged role of Jewish magnates on the Rand—men like Rhodes's associate Alfred Beit—in initiating war with the Boer Republics.

191 *Old Barbarity*: Sir Henry Campbell-Bannerman (1836–1908), the leader of the Liberal Party, who became Prime Minister in 1906, and who, in a speech on 14 June 1901, condemned the burning of Boer farms and the enforced concentration of women and children in camps as 'methods of barbarism'.

some of 'is lady friends . . . camps: the scandal of conditions in the concentration camps had been exposed by Miss Emily Hobhouse, who briefed Campbell-Bannerman fully as part of her campaign to rouse the conscience of the nation. *She* was politically pro-Boer, but her charges were confirmed by an all-female committee of investigation chaired by Mrs Millicent Fawcett, all the members of which supported the war but condemned the conditions they found in the camps, making practical recommendations for their improvement.

Bermuda, or Umballa, or Ceylon: places where Boer prisoners-of-war were sent, safely remote from South Africa.

192 *the beggar that kep' the cordite down*: as Secretary of State for War in the previous Liberal government Campbell-Bannerman had been the subject of a vote of censure in the Commons in 1895 for not securing an adequate stock of cordite and ammunition for the Army. This defeat led to the fall of the government.

193 *K. o' K.*: Lord Kitchener of Khartoum. i.e. Horatio Herbert Kitchener (1850–1916), who had planned and carried out the reconquest of the Sudan. He served as Chief of Staff to Roberts in South Africa in 1900 and then, on Roberts's departure, as Commander-in-Chief from late 1900 to 1902.

194 HALF-BALLADE OF WATERVAL (*The Five Nations*, 1903). *Waterval*: village 15 miles from Pretoria 'where the majority of English prisoners were kept by the Boers' (Kipling). Over 4,000 were freed when the town fell. *Half-Ballade* refers to the poetic form used here.

for foreign lands: see note to p. 191.

Rands: see note to p. 145.

196 THE CAPTIVE (*Traffics and Discoveries*): first published *Collier's Weekly*, 6 December 1902.

Simonstown: naval base near Cape Town.

Barracouta . . . Gibraltar: a small and a large cruiser respectively.

Penelope: an older vessel, used latterly to provide floating accommodation and to house prisoners of war.

. . . deep sea: this paragraph is one of the few passages in Kipling's work the genesis of which he has described in detail: 'Again, in a South African, post-Boer War tale called "The Captive", which was built up round the phrase "a first-class dress parade for Armageddon", I could not get my lighting into key with the tone of the monologue. The background insisted too much. My Daemon [inspiration] said at last: "Paint the background first once and for all, as hard as a public-house sign, and leave it alone." This done, the rest fell into place with the American accent and outlook of the teller' (*Something of Myself*, 1937, pp. 209–10).

197 *American Tyler*: 'Tyler' is a Masonic title for the official who acts as doorkeeper when the Lodge is in session; the 'grasp' referred to

a few lines below is a Masonic sign of recognition; and 'Brother' means a Brother-Mason.

198 *Bull Durham*: American brand of tobacco.

our Filipeens: after America's war with Spain over Cuba in 1898, she acquired the Philippine Islands in the Pacific, but was soon faced with a rebellion led by General Aguinaldo. War broke out in 1899, and though the Filipinos were soon defeated in the field, guerrilla warfare continued until 1901.

bossing the war: there was considerable sympathy for the Boers throughout Europe, and some help was sent them from Holland in particular, but there was no controlling junta seeking to 'boss the war' from there.

199 *Delagoa Bay*: see note to p. 148.

deadheads: passengers who travel free of charge.

Pentecostal: speaking in all tongues, see Acts 2: 1–11.

just about that time: when Roberts's advance (see notes to pp. 133–4, 145) was overrunning the Orange Free State and threatening the Transvaal. Pretoria was taken on 5 June 1900.

tickets to Europe: Kruger (see note to p. 134) sailed for Europe in a Dutch warship in October 1900.

sons of Ham: see Genesis 9: 18–27. Black Africans were thought to be descendants of Ham, and Noah's curse—'a servant of servants shall he be unto his brethren'—was often cited by the Boers to justify their subjection.

kloof: cleft or gorge.

Teddy Roosevelt's Western tour: Theodore Roosevelt (1858–1919), a colourful politician and friend of Kipling's, President of the United States from 1901 to 1908, had campaigned nationwide for the Vice-Presidency in 1900.

200 *God and the Mauser*: Kruger had urged his people to put their trust in God and the Mauser (see note to p. 134).

Georgia Crackers and Pennsylvania Dutch: comparisons to help characterize the Boers. Georgia Crackers were poor-white hill-billies (with a reputation for marksmanship); Pennsylvania Dutch were German immigrants noted for their piety.

captive of your bow and spear: see note to p. 104.

Grover Cleveland: Stephen Grover Cleveland (1837–1908), Democratic President of the USA 1885–9 and 1893–7, used the phrase about being confronted by a condition, not a theory, in his address to Congress (on tariff reform) in 1887.

201 *vedettes*: mounted sentries.

   worked Lodge: ran affairs (Masonic phrase).

   from labour to refreshment: another Masonic phrase.

202 *Tom Reed*: Thomas Brackett Reed (1838–1902), American politician, Speaker of US House of Representatives 1889–91 and 1895–9.

   mesas: plateaux.

203 *Nooitgedacht*: site of Boer prisoner-of-war camp near Pretoria.

   Dutch Indies: East Indies, with reference to Dutch exploration and settlement there.

   Umballa: Umballa itself is in the Punjab.

   man with the hoe: the American Edwin Markham (1852–1940) published *The Man with the Hoe and Other Poems* in 1899; the allusion is to the primitive nature of the implement Mankeltow has been using.

   sow-belly: salted side of pork.

   Chamberlains: the Rt Hon. Joseph Chamberlain (1836–1914) was Secretary of State for the Colonies from 1895 to 1903 and played a significant part in the run-up to the Boer War. He was suspected of complicity in the Jameson Raid (see note to p. 146): hence this reference to his duplicity.

204 *Santos-Dumont*: Alberto Santos-Dumont (1873–1932), a Brazilian pioneer of aviation, and particularly of the use of airships.

   Professor Langley and the Smithsonian: Samuel Pierpoint Langley (1834–1906), American scientist who experimented with mechanical flight; Secretary of the Smithsonian Institution in Washington DC from 1887.

   donga: see note to p. 151.

205 *Henry Clay*: cigar, named after famous American politician (1777–1852).

206 *a burgher*: see note to p. 187.

   suppressing our war: see note to p. 198.

207 *taffy*: toffee, i.e. flattery.

   a Männlicher rifle: Austrian magazine-rifle.

208 *Woolwich*: Royal Artillery depôt at Woolwich in SE London.

209 *Lydia Pinkham* (1819–83): American feminist and manufacturer of a vastly successful patent medicine, Lydia E. Pinkham's Vegetable Compound.

Pisgah-sight: it was from Mount Pisgah that Moses saw the Promised Land (Deuteronomy 34: 1–4).

Zalinski: L. G. Zalinski (1849–1909), Polish-American soldier and scientist; inventor of the pneumatic dynamite torpedo gun.

Bracebridge Hall: a volume of tales and sketches, many set in England, by the American author Washington Irving (1783–1859); published 1822.

the Cricket on the Hearth: Christmas book by Charles Dickens, published 1846.

210 *De Wet*: General Christiaan Rudolf De Wet (1854–1922), Boer soldier and statesman, leader of Orange Free State commandos, and legendary for his exploits in guerrilla warfare.

after Bloemfontein surrendered: on 13 March 1900.

211 *a column*: a mobile fighting force to seek out and engage Boer forces.

Delarey: General Koom De la Rey (1847–1914), another notable guerrilla commander.

212 *Vierkleur*: Transvaal flag (of four colours; cf. Fr. 'tricoleur').

our Native Army: the Indian Army (cf. 'A Sahibs' War').

Worcester . . . Paarl and Stellenbosch: towns deep in Cape Colony.

Cronje: General Pieter Arnoldus (Piet) Cronje (1835–1911) had been forced to surrender with his army after his defeat at Paardeberg in February 1900.

213 *acknowledged the corn*: conceded the truth.

Skittles: nonsense.

Schedule D: for income tax assessment.

215 *Steyn*: Martinus Theunis Steyn (1857–1916), President of the Orange Free State, strongly committed to the war from first to last.

picayune: of little value or importance.

Cronje's dead horses: in the river-bed at Paardeberg, where British shelling inflicted many casualties.

aasvogels: vultures.

Tammany: politically corrupt (from Tammany Hall, the headquarters of the Democratic Party organization in New York, notorious for its corrupt practices).

217 *Monroe Doctrine*: doctrine formulated in 1823 by James Monroe,

President of the United States 1817–25, denying the right of nations of the Old World to intervene in the affairs of the New, and stipulating that America should not embroil herself with the affairs of Europe.

National Scouts: force of Boers, including Christiaan De Wet's brother Piet, who fought for the British.

218 *I haven't . . . Willie died*: catch-phrase of the day.

219 CHANT-PAGAN (*The Five Nations*, 1903).

kopje: small hill.

kop: mountain.

the Ma'ollisberg range: the Magaliesberg Mountains west of Pretoria.

220 *Barberton*: town in Transvaal captured by Major-General French (see note to pp. 133–4) after his forces had crossed the precipitous mountains which protected it.

Di'mond 'Ill . . . Vereeniging: *Diamond Hill*: battle fought 11–12 June 1900 near Pretoria; *Pieters*: the capture of the Pieters Plateau on 27 February 1900 was one of the stages in General Sir Redvers Buller's eventual victory at the Tugela River; *Springs*: village in Transvaal, scene of a clash early in 1901 during one of French's 'drives' to harry the commandos; *Belfast*: battle of 27 August 1900 in which Buller defeated the Boers under General Botha; *Dundee*: scene of first action of Boer War on 20 October 1899; *Vereeniging*: where the Boers accepted Britain's peace terms on 31 May 1902.

Brandwater Basin: valley in Drakensberg Mountains where a Boer force was trapped and forced to surrender in July 1900, though De Wet and Steyn escaped. (See notes to pp. 210 and 215.)

225 GETHSEMANE (*The Years Between*, 1919): Matthew 26: 36, 39: 'Then cometh Jesus . . . unto a place called Gethsemane . . . And he . . . fell on his face and prayed, saying, O my Father, if it be possible, let this cup pass from me: nevertheless, not as I will, but as thou wilt.'

226 'SWEPT AND GARNISHED' (*A Diversity of Creatures*): first published *Nash's and Pall Mall Magazine* and *Century Magazine*, January 1915. For the title, see Matthew 12: 43–5: 'When the unclean spirit is gone out of a man, he walketh through dry places, seeking rest, and findeth none. Then he saith, I will return into my house from whence I came out; and when he is come, he findeth it empty, swept, and garnished. Then goeth he, and

taketh with himself seven other spirits more wicked than himself, and they enter in and dwell there: and the last state of that man is worse than the first. Even so shall it be unto this wicked generation.' (Cf. Luke 11: 24–6.)

This story relates to atrocities, including the murder and mutilation of children, reported of the Germans invading neutral Belgium. In the Franco-Prussian War of 1870–1 large numbers of troops had been tied down guarding lines of communication against French civilians operating as *franc-tireurs* (sharp-shooters). In 1914 the Germans applied a deliberate policy of 'frightfulness' (*Schrecklichkeit*) 'designed to frighten the civilian population into absolute submission with the least possible diversion of German military strength' (John Terraine, *The Smoke and the Fire*, London, 1980, p. 26). After the War it became fashionable to disbelieve all atrocity stories since many were fabrications, but the application of this policy at Louvain, Dinant, Visé, Andenne, and other places is well-documented. Kipling wrote in horror about such events in a letter to his friend Frank Doubleday in September 1914.

227 *New Art*: i.e. Art Nouveau.

230 *all those places*: i.e. those entered, ravaged, and destroyed by German troops.

231 *The people fired on us, and they were punished*: the official German version when massacres of civilians had taken place or towns and villages been burnt down.

235 MARY POSTGATE (*A Diversity of Creatures*): first published *Nash's and Pall Mall Magazine* and *Century Magazine*, September 1915, with heading 'How does your garden grow?' (from the rhyme 'Mary, Mary, quite contrary').

237 *dowey*: dismal.

Taubes, Farmans, and Zeppelins: Taubes were German and Farmans French aeroplanes; Zeppelins were German airships.

239 *Contrexéville*: French mineral water.

243 *O.T.C.*: Officers' Training Corps at public school.

Brooklands: motor racing track.

246 *Laty*: Lady.

247 *Cassée. Tout cassée*: broken. All broken.

Che me rends. Le Médecin: I surrender. The doctor (French with German pronunciation of 'je').

Ich haben . . . gesehn: I have seen the dead child.

249 *pavior*: man who lays paving stones.

250 THE CHANGELINGS (*Debits and Credits*, 1926). *R.N.V.R.*: Royal Naval Volunteer Reserve.

251 SEA CONSTABLES (*Debits and Credits*): first published *Metropolitan*, September 1915. The story was written after the German announcement of a naval blockade of Britain in February 1915, and deals with the frustration of a neutral entrepreneur's attempt to supply fuel to German U-Boats. A similar theme is treated by Conrad in 'The Tale' (1917) in *Tales of Hearsay*.

Carvoitz: the *Readers' Guide* (p. 3120) ingeniously suggests that this is a composite name made up of portions of the titles of the Carlton, the Savoy, and the Ritz—all fashionable hotels.

252 *nut*: dandy, young man-about-town.

dubs: failures, duds.

Palemseum: another composite name, with elements of the titles of the Palladium, Empire, and Coliseum Music Halls.

254 *lady in the Promenade*: prostitute in the notorious Promenade at the Empire Music Hall in Leicester Square.

His smell: i.e. of oil, from his cargo of fuel for German submarines.

255 *thick with 'em*: i.e. with German submarines.

256 *like me and Nelson*: prone to sea-sickness.

259 *wagon-lit*: sleeping car.

260 *yaw*: deviate from course.

261 *blacked myself all over*: thrown myself completely into the part, like the actor said to have blacked himself all over in order to play Othello.

263 *pooped*: incommoded by a following sea coming over the stern.

Beast with Horns . . .: see Revelation 13: 1-18.

sprudel: mineral water (a variation on the colloquial phrase 'a dose of salts').

268 THE VINEYARD (*Debits and Credits*, 1926). Kipling often expressed in private his contempt for America's long delay in entering the War, and here he has been provoked by American suggestions on how Britain *should* have conducted it prior to her own belated participation.

At the eleventh hour . . . Wrath of God: see Matthew 20: 1–16 for the parable of the vineyard and the resentment of those who had toiled in it all day at receiving the same recompense as those who had worked only from the eleventh hour ('Saying, These last have wrought but one hour, and thou hast made them equal unto us, which have borne the burden and heat of the day').

269 *Introduction to* THE IRISH GUARDS IN THE GREAT WAR (1923).

270 *from Mons . . . The Salient*: in the retreat from Mons and subsequent advance to the Aisne in September 1914; *The Salient* was a projecting portion of the British line at Ypres.

271 *They came out . . . were spent*: the sentence summarizes the fate of Kipling's son John and of many others.

276 A RECANTATION (*The Years Between*, 1919). One of Kipling's imitations of Horace (hence the substitution of 'Rome' and 'Gaul' for 'London' and 'France'). The identity of the music-hall artiste referred to by the classical pseudonym of 'Lyde' has not been established; but in notes on *The Years Between* which Kipling wrote for Frank Doubleday he says that 'The incident of the music hall star going on with her work— "for the boys' sake"— on the very night she had received news of her own son's death is not fiction' (Kipling Papers, University of Sussex, 25/1. Quoted by permission of the University of Sussex Library and of A. P. Watt Ltd. on behalf of the National Trust).

278 A FRIEND OF THE FAMILY (*Debits and Credits*): first published *MacLean's Magazine*, 15 June 1924.

Lodge 'Faith and Works', 5837 E.C.: 'In the Interests of the Brethren' (*Debits and Credits*), first published in December 1918, describes the narrator's first introduction to this Masonic Lodge, which provided a haven for men on leave from the Front.

Last Post: British Army bugle call marking the end of the soldier's day; sounded also at military funerals and Remembrance Day parades.

Thiepval: on the Somme.

279 *the Tichborne one*: an Arthur Orton, from Australia, who falsely claimed to be the missing heir to the Tichborne baronetcy and estates, was convicted of perjury in a *cause célèbre* in 1872.

280 *stoush*: hit, strike.

282 *God before Whom ever lie bare*: cf. Collect for Church of England Communion Service: 'Almighty God, unto whom all hearts be

open, all desires known, and from whom no secrets are hid:
cleanse the thoughts of our hearts by the inspiration of thy Holy
Spirit . . .'

283 *The tribunal*: to consider pleas for exemption from military
service.

Mwor osee: soldiers' French for 'Moi aussi' (Me too).

284 *Haig*: Field-Marshal Sir Douglas Haig, later Earl Haig (1861–
1928), Commander-in-Chief of the British Armies on the Western
Front from December 1915 to the end of the War.

winkle-pin: bayonet.

285 *the pin*: the safety device which had to be withdrawn from a Mills
bomb (the standard grenade used by the British Army) to allow
the release of the striker lever which activated the detonating
mechanism.

the Chinks: Chinese labour corps, used behind the lines.

Too de sweet: soldiers' French for 'Tout de suite' (at once,
immediately).

286 *mafeesh*: finish, finished.

the duds: grenades which failed to explode (usually because of
faulty insertion of the percussion cap, fuse, and detonator). Such
'duds' would normally be detonated where they fell, not collected
up by hand and deposited in a storage pit—a near-suicidal
procedure!

287 *regulation blue*: bright blue hospital-issue uniform worn by
wounded servicemen when convalescing.

khaki warm: overcoat.

flammenwerfer: flame-thrower.

288 *whizzbang*: small calibre, high-velocity shell.

a regular Russian night of it: one of chaotic disorder?

291 *Old Ship*: the Old Ship Hotel in Brighton.

bail up: ask for payment.

MESOPOTAMIA (*The Years Between*): first published *Morning Post*
and *New York Times*, 11 July 1917. The Report of a Parliamen-
tary Commission on the earlier campaigns in Mesopotamia was
published on 27 June 1917, and was described by the *Times* as
'one of the most distressing documents ever submitted to Parlia-
ment'. It is an unsparing indictment of general mismanagement,
strategic blunders, and administrative failure, and particularly
damning are comments on the total inadequacy of the medical

arrangements, which led to a complete breakdown of provision after the Battle of Ctesiphon and the attempted relief of Kut, and which resulted in unnecessary agonies and degradation for the wounded. (There is, for example, an eye-witness account of wounded men suffering from dysentery left to lie helpless in pools of their own filth on the decks of river transports.) The case was all the more disgraceful by virtue of attempts by senior medical officers, named in the Report, to conceal the true facts, reporting officially that the arrangements had worked well and the wounded had been 'satisfactorily disposed of'.

294 A MADONNA OF THE TRENCHES (*Debits and Credits*): first published *MacLean's Magazine*, 15 August 1924.

Faith and Works E.C. 5837: see note to p. 278.

295 *the Tyler*: see note to p. 197.

296 *paregoric*: medicine with opium base.

297 *B.H.Q.*: Battalion Head-Quarters.

298 *. . . if the dead didn't rise*: a garbled version of 1 Corinthians 15: 32: 'If after the manner of men I have fought with beasts at Ephesus, what advantageth it me, if the dead rise not?'

299 *Gawd hath shown man . . . love*: see the Swinburne verses in the story heading.

302 *slue*: sc. slew, in the sense of 'swing round'.

Very light: illuminating flare fired from special pistol.

303 *Zoo-ave*: sc. Zouave (French Algerian infantryman).

poy-looz: sc. *poilus*, slang term for French private soldiers.

307 *the Angels of Mons*: a reference to the superstitious belief, widely current among civilians, that angels had appeared in the heavens during the Battle of Mons (August 1914), in support of the hard-pressed British Expeditionary Force.

309 THE MOTHER'S SON (*Limits and Renewals*, *1932*)

310 THE GARDENER (*Debits and Credits*): first published *McCall's Magazine*, April 1925.

312 *William the Conqueror*: William the Conqueror was the illegitimate son of the Duke of Normandy.

313 *threw themselves into the Line*: enlisted as privates so as to get to the Front as soon as possible.

O.T.C.: see note to p. 243.

K.: Kitchener (see note to p. 193), then Secretary of State for War. He had been quick to foresee a long war and the need to raise new armies.

Loos: the major attack by British troops in September–October 1915 (in which John Kipling was lost).

the Salient: a large projection of the British line at Ypres.

315 *found, identified, and reinterred*: Kipling became a member of the Imperial War Graves Commission in 1917 and served on it for the remainder of his life. His own son's body was never found after he was listed 'Missing' at Loos.

316 *A.S.C.*: Army Service Corps.

320 *supposing him to be the gardener*: Cf. John 20: 15: 'Jesus saith unto her, Woman, why weepest thou? Whom seekest thou? She, supposing him to be the gardener, saith unto him, Sir, if thou have borne him hence, tell me where thou hast laid him . . .'

321 EPITAPHS OF THE WAR (*The Years Between*, 1919; additional items in *Verse*).

322 *Halfa*: Al Halfaya in Mesopotamia.

From little towns . . .: written in response to a request from the citizens of Sault Ste. Marie, Ontario, who were planning a memorial to 350 men of their town who had died in the War.

323 *M.E.F.*: Mediterranean Expeditionary Force.

Prometheus: Titan of Greek legend, punished by the gods for stealing fire from heaven for the benefit of mankind.

324 *V.A.D.*: Voluntary Aid Detachment (nursing service, Territorial Force).

325 KIPLING UNDER FIRE: THE BATTLE OF KARI SIDING (*Something of Myself*, 1937). The Battle of Kari Siding was fought on 28 March 1900.

Brevet-Major: rank of major higher than his substantive rank in his own regiment.

secundum artem: according to art.

326 *Krupp*: famous German armaments firm.

Pretoria for us: i.e. as prisoners.

Le Gallais: Lieut.-Col. P. W. J. Le Gallais, in command of the Mounted Infantry.

vice: in place of.

327 *Maffeesh*—see note to p. 286.

French: Major-General John French (see note to pp. 133–4) who commanded the cavalry at Kari Siding, while Lieut.-General C. Tucker commanded the infantry. It is not clear who was in overall command.

the General commanding the cavalry . . . *Boer*: either French himself or possibly one of his brigade commanders—General Porter and General Gordon. The infantry attacked frontally, while the cavalry and mounted infantry were supposed to outflank the Boers and cut off their retreat; but both moved too slowly to achieve this.

ADDITIONAL NOTES

7 *Two words*: 'Threes About'—the command for cavalry to retire. The reference is to the flight of the 9th Lancers and 14th Light Dragoons together with two regiments of Bengal Native Cavalry at the Battle of Chilianwala (January 1849) in the 2nd Sikh War. The Brigade had been mishandled by an incompetent Brigadier, and it retired in disorder when some unidentified person shouted 'Threes About'. (See the Marquess of Anglesey, *A History of the British Cavalry 1816 to 1919*, vol. I, London, 1973, p. 281.)

163 *(continued from note on* A SAHIBS' WAR *on p. 348)*: It was decided not to use Indian troops in the Boer War, but the Marquess of Anglesey records that in a skirmish in the Orange River Colony on 1 August 1901 a sowar (trooper) of the 15th Bengal Lancers was killed while acting as orderly to a captain of that regiment 'who was in command of 300 South Australians' (*op. cit*, vol. IV, 1986, p. 214).

THE WORLD'S CLASSICS

A Select List

VIRGIL: The Aeneid
Translated by C. Day Lewis
Edited by Jasper Griffin

HORACE WALPOLE : The Castle of Otranto
Edited by W. S. Lewis

IZAAK WALTON and CHARLES COTTON:
The Compleat Angler
Edited by John Buxton
Introduction by John Buchan

OSCAR WILDE: Complete Shorter Fiction
Edited by Isobel Murray

The Picture of Dorian Gray
Edited by Isobel Murray

VIRGINIA WOOLF: Orlando
Edited by Rachel Bowlby

ÉMILE ZOLA:
The Attack on the Mill and other stories
Translated by Douglas Parmée

A complete list of Oxford Paperbacks, including The World's Classics, OPUS, Past Masters, Oxford Authors, Oxford Shakespeare, and Oxford Paperback Reference, is available in the UK from the Arts and Reference Publicity Department (BH), Oxford University Press, Walton Street, Oxford OX2 6DP.

In the USA, complete lists are available from the Paperbacks Marketing Manager, Oxford University Press, 200 Madison Avenue, New York, NY 10016.

Oxford Paperbacks are available from all good bookshops. In case of difficulty, customers in the UK can order direct from Oxford University Press Bookshop, Freepost, 116 High Street, Oxford, OX1 4BR, enclosing full payment. Please add 10 per cent of published price for postage and packing.